"No one writes historical romance better."

—Cathy Maxwell

FRIENDS TO LOVERS

"I am *not* your brother!" he repeated, his voice rough this time. And he leaned forward and kissed her.

As his lips covered hers with warm command, shock jolted through her. This was not the way things were supposed to be!

Her startled reaction was swiftly followed by sensations different from any she'd ever experienced. Heady, disturbing feelings curled through her from head to toes, bringing alive all parts in between.

For the first time she understood why women ruined themselves with men. She felt a promise of something wild and compelling in Richard's touch, and it terrified her. When he moved a warm hand to her waist, mere inches from her unbound breasts, she shoved herself away from him, ending up plastered against the wall beside the bed. "This is a really, really bad idea!" she said in a choked voice.

Books by Mary Jo Putney

The Lost Lords series
Loving a Lost Lord
Never Less Than a Lady
Nowhere Near Respectable
No Longer a Gentleman
Sometimes a Rogue
Not Quite a Wife
Not Always a Saint

Other titles
One Perfect Rose
The Bargain
The Rake
Mischief and Mistletoe
The Last Chance Christmas Ball
Once a Soldier

Once a
Rebel

MARY JO PUTNEY

ZEBRA BOOKS
KENSINGTON PUBLISHING CORP.
http://www.kensingtonbooks.com

ZEBRA BOOKS are published by

Kensington Publishing Corp.
119 West 40th Street
New York, NY 10018

First Kensington Books Hardcover Printing: June 2017
First Zebra Books Mass-Market Paperback Printing: September 2017
ISBN-13: 978-1-4201-4094-1
ISBN-10: 1-4201-4094-9

eISBN-13: 978-1-4201-4095-8
eISBN-10: 1-4201-4095-7

10 9 8 7 6 5 4 3 2 1

Printed in the United States of America

Acknowledgments

I had a wonderful time researching history that is literally right on my doorstep, and want to give special thanks to my Mayhem Consultant, a native Baltimorean who knows his local history, and where to find local historic cannons.

Over the years I've read numerous local articles whose authors I don't remember, but my thanks to all of my fellow Marylanders who share my passion for history.

My principal research books were Walter Lord's excellent *The Dawn's Early Light: The Climactic Shaping of "the Land of the Free" During the Hazardous Events of 1814 in Washington, Baltimore, and London.* Another fine book is Steve Vogel's *Through the Perilous Fight: From the Burning of Washington to the Star-Spangled Banner: The Six Weeks That Saved the Nation.* Out of print and hard to find but excellent is *The Rockets' Red Glare,* by Scott S. Sheads, a ranger-historian at the Fort McHenry National Monument for many years. This slim volume has many direct quotes from primary sources.

A very good PBS documentary is *The War of 1812,* by Lawrence Hott and Diane Garey. It describes the origins of the war and the fighting that took place on the Niagara Frontier, in the American West, and on the Great Lakes and the Chesapeake Bay.

Chapter 1

Kingston Court, Lancashire, 1799

"Richard! *Richard!*"

Lord George Gordon Richard Augustus Audley, third and most worthless son of the Marquess of Kingston, snapped awake at the hissing voice outside his open bedroom window. Callie? She wasn't supposed to be home from school for another week. He frowned; it had to be her. Only two people had ever called him Richard, and she was the only one who might be climbing up the thick vines below his window.

In the warm night he wore only his drawers. Though he and Callie had been best friends since they were in the nursery, they weren't on terms of seminudity, so he grabbed his robe and tied the sash as he swung from the bed.

He leaned out the casement and looked down into the rustling vines. In the light of a full moon, the heart-shaped face and shining red-blond hair were unmistakable. But what the devil was the Honorable Catherine Callista Brooke doing scrambling up to his room in the middle of the night?

"Callie, you're insane!" he said affectionately as he leaned out and extended a hand to help her up and over the sill. "If I'd known you were home from school, I could have called tomorrow in a perfectly civilized manner."

Her hand clamped onto his and she scrambled over the sill and into his room. She was dressed as a boy, which was sensible for climbing vine-covered walls.

He was about to say more when the moonlight revealed shining streaks on her face. Callie was *crying?* She never cried. She had nerves of Damascus steel. "What's wrong, Callie?" he asked sharply.

"Everything!" she replied in a raw voice.

She was shaking, so he instinctively wrapped comforting arms around her. He must have grown in the last months of school, because she seemed smaller as she buried her face against his shoulder. "Steady, Catkin," he said quietly as he patted her back. "We've been in and out of enough trouble to know how to fix problems."

"Not this kind of problem." She took a deep breath and stepped back, though she kept hold of his arms as if not trusting her balance.

Moonlight touched her face, revealing a dark mark on her left cheek. Swearing, he skimmed a gentle fingertip over the bruise. "Damnation, your father has been beating you again!"

Callie shrugged. "I'm used to that, being the most disobedient, rebellious, devil-touched daughter in England, as he informs me regularly. But this time . . ." Her voice broke before she continued. "It's much worse. He's going to marry me to some horrible old planter from the West Indies!"

"Good God, how has that come about?" Gordon steered her to a chair, then retrieved his hidden flask of forbidden brandy. He poured a small measure into a glass and added an equal amount of water before handing it over. "How would a planter from the Indies even know you exist?"

"He's some kind of distant connection of my father. A widower." She sipped at the watered brandy, coughed, sipped some more. "He called at Rush Hall to discuss business, saw me, and offered marriage because I'm so *beautiful*!" She almost spat the words out.

"Beautiful?" Gordon blinked at the thought. She was . . . *Callie*. Pretty enough with that sunset red-gold hair, and she was athletic and graceful as well. An old man might consider the hair and Callie's vibrant good spirits enough to be beauty. "You're only sixteen, so surely that means a long betrothal."

She shook her head violently. "He wants to marry immediately, before he returns to the Indies! He's staying at the Hall now. As soon as my father said he could have me and good riddance, the fellow sent to London for a special license. It came today. My father told me this evening that I'll be married the day after tomorrow."

"He can't force you to marry a stranger!" Gordon said, aghast. "Just keep saying no. It won't be easy, but you're practiced at disobedience."

She shook her head, shaking again. "If I don't obey, I'm afraid he'll take his anger out on my sisters."

Damnably, she was probably right. Callie's sisters were vulnerable, and her father was quite capable of bullying or hurting them to insure Callie's cooperation. Gordon wrapped an arm around her shoulders, murmuring soft, comforting words until she pulled away with a smile that almost worked. "You're talking to me like I'm one of your horses."

"It works with frightened fillies, so it seemed worth trying." He smiled when she rolled her eyes with elaborate disdain, but sobered swiftly. "What do you want me to do, Callie?"

"I'm going to run away and I need money," she said bluntly. "Can you lend me some?"

He frowned. "Run away to where?"

"My Aunt Beatrice. She's my godmother and has said I'm welcome to visit anytime. I'll be safe with her."

"But for how long? If your father comes to drag you off to get married, she won't be able to stand up to him."

Callie bit her lip. "Then I'll change my name and disappear into Manchester or Birmingham. I'll find some sort of work."

"Become a mill worker?" he asked incredulously. "This is not a good plan, Callie!"

"Not a mill worker! You know how good I am at sewing. I'm sure I can find a job as a seamstress," she said impatiently. "If you can lend me twenty or thirty pounds, it will be enough to get me away and support me until I'm established somewhere my father will never find me."

He bit his lip, thinking how many disastrous things might happen to a pretty, inexperienced girl, even one who was intelligent, ingenious, and brave.

He caught his breath as a thought struck. Yet it made sense. "I have a better idea, Callie. Marry me. We can be in Scotland in two days and we're old enough to marry there without permission."

She gasped, her hazel eyes widening. "And you think *I'm* insane! We're too young to get married, even if it is legal in Scotland. Marriage is forever." She bit her lip. "I've always wanted to marry for love."

"My parents did that and it didn't work out particularly well," he retorted. "I've always thought that in the unlikely event that I marry, it would be to a friend, and aren't we best friends?"

She frowned as she considered his proposal. "I suppose marrying you would be better than a fat old planter with damp hands."

He grinned. "I am *so* very flattered."

"You know I didn't mean it like that! It's just that marriage seems so . . . so extreme."

"It is, but so is being bullied into marriage to a man you can't stand." He shrugged. "If someday you meet someone you really want to marry, I won't stand in your way. It's easier to get a divorce in Scotland than in England. In the meantime, you'd be better off with me because I won't try to force you to do anything you don't want to."

"There is that," she admitted. "If we're married, we'll both be free of our fathers and able to look out for each other."

"It would be a grand adventure," he said, liking the idea more and more. "At twenty-one I'll have control of half the money my godfather left me. It's enough for us to live comfortably. Between now and then, we'll discover what life is like for average people. We'll find work with some decent country squire. You can be a lady's maid and I'll look after the horses."

Callie's face lit with laughter. "You're right, it would be an adventure! Far better than marrying a dreadful stranger. We'll make it work. We always do. No more adults telling us we're too rebellious and ill behaved!"

"Too wild and fated to come to a bad end!" Exhilarated, Gordon swept Callie into his arms and kissed her. He started the kiss as a friend, and ended it as . . . something else. She was sweet and warm and strong in his arms, and for the first time ever he thought of her as a girl. No, not a girl, but a young woman ripe for marriage.

She also reacted to the kiss, leaning into him, her lips parting. Heat kicked through him. He'd admired his share of pretty girls and stolen a few kisses, but this was different. More. She would be his wife and they would have physical and emotional intimacy beyond anything he could imagine. The prospect was alarming, but also exhilarating.

Callie drew back, her eyes shining. "The adventure of a lifetime," she breathed. "And the sooner we begin, Richard, the better!"

Within a quarter of an hour, they were on their way. Gordon had always been good at saving, and he had nearly a hundred pounds, a small fortune. He tucked it into a money belt around his waist, then dressed for the journey. He gave Callie a hat to stuff her hair under and a shapeless coat he'd outgrown. He grinned at the result. "You can pass as my little brother if no one looks too closely."

"That should make us harder to follow." She folded a light blanket into a canvas sack that could go into a saddlebag. "What route should we take?"

"There's only one decent road toward Scotland from here, but once we get beyond Lancaster, we can cut east on some less traveled roads. Slower, but we're less likely to be discovered."

"Do you think we'll be pursued?" She slung the canvas sack over one shoulder. "Even if they figure out that we've run off together, they might just think good riddance to both of us."

Gordon shook his head. "My father won't miss me. I'm just a third son and one he doesn't like. Since your father has an advantageous marriage for you, he won't shrug off your disappearance. But it will take them time to realize that we've eloped. If we travel fast, we should be in Scotland before they can catch us."

Silently they left his bedroom. He wondered if he'd ever see it again. Callie's father might not want to let her go, but his own father would be glad if he disappeared.

They left through the kitchen, adding bread and cheese to their bags. The wind was from the west and there was a faint, sulfurous smell of burning from the smoldering coal seam not far away. He wouldn't miss that smell.

In the stables, he saddled two horses that he knew had excellent endurance, and they headed out. They made good speed along the moonlit roads for several hours, but rain blew in from the Irish Sea as dawn approached.

Callie was drooping with fatigue, though she'd never admit it, so he suggested, "Let's stop for a few hours in that barn there. We and the horses need rest, and with the rain, it's hard to see the road."

Wordlessly Callie turned into the lane that led to the low barn. No farmhouse was near, so they should be safe for a few hours. In the barn, they tended to their horses, then curled up together in a pile of hay since the night was chilly. As Callie tucked the blanket around them, she murmured, "Thank you for saving me, Richard. We will do well together."

He brushed a kiss on the top of her head, feeling a tenderness and protectiveness that were new to him. "We will. Sleep well, Catkin."

He knew society would find their elopement outrageous, but they were both used to outraging people. It gave them so much in common. With a smile, he drifted off.

"They're in here!" a voice bellowed as the barn doors swung open.

Sunlight flooded into the barn as Gordon fought his way free from the blanket and hay. He knew this was disaster even before the looming figure of Callie's father, Lord Stanfield, appeared in the open doorway. Behind him—dear God, it was Gordon's father, Lord Kingston! And two Stanfield grooms.

"Lord George Audley. You filthy bastard, you've ruined my daughter!" Stanfield carried a driving whip in his right hand, and he slashed it viciously at Gordon.

The lash knocked Gordon off balance, and before he could regain his footing, the two grooms had grabbed his arms. Stanfield closed in and began pummeling Gordon with his huge fists, smashing into his face and gut. Gordon had learned some fighting skills at the Westerfield Academy, but he couldn't break free of the grooms.

Callie screamed and tried to wrench her father away. "Stop it! *Stop it!* You're going to kill him!"

"Good!" Her father jammed a knee into Gordon's genitals.

Gordon collapsed in agony as the world blackened. Callie dropped to her knees and covered him with her own body. "He hasn't ruined me! He was helping me to escape that vile marriage you're trying to force me into!"

Stanfield grabbed Callie's arm and wrenched her to her feet. "You're still a virgin?"

"Given the amount of ground they covered during the night, there hasn't been time to do much else," Gordon's father drawled. "I'm not sure the boy is capable of anything more. I've wondered if he's a molly boy. He certainly doesn't look like a son of mine. He's far too pretty. His mother was the worst mistake I ever made."

The insult pulled Gordon to consciousness and he tried to struggle to his feet. "Shut your evil mouth!"

Stanfield kicked him back into the hay, then kicked him again. "Mind if I beat him to death, Kingston?"

"Feel free to kill him," Gordon's father said with exquisite malice. "I have better sons." He turned and strolled from the barn.

Stanfield was winding up for another kick when Callie threw her full weight against him. "Stop this! You'll have to kill us both because I'll never let you get away with murdering him!"

When her father hesitated, Callie said frantically, "If you stop beating him, I promise that I'll marry your horrible friend and act like a good and obedient wife! I'm a virgin—he'll never know this happened. But you must promise to stop hurting Richard!"

Her father paused, frowning. "For all your wild behavior, you've never been a liar." His eyes narrowed. "You swear that you'll be a good, obedient daughter and go through with this marriage?"

"You have my word," she said bitterly. "But tell me, how did you find out so quickly that we'd eloped?"

"One of your sisters has a better sense of duty than you've ever had," her father replied. "She saw you sneaking out and guessed where you were going. After she woke me up, I drove over to Kingston Court. When Lord Kingston saw you were both gone, we set after you. Satisfied?"

Callie's lips thinned. "I can guess which sister it was. May she rot in hell!"

Her father shook her. "Don't forget your promise! You behave and I won't touch your filthy lover again."

She yanked free of his grip. "You can't order your servants to hurt him, either."

He frowned, then nodded. "But you'd better be a damned obedient bride!" He gestured to one of the grooms. "Take her outside."

As Callie was escorted roughly from the barn, Stanfield stood over Gordon's bleeding body, his hands on his hips. "I'm sorry that I can't finish the job, Lord George, but she's worth a pretty penny married off." His lips twisted in a vicious smile. "I won't kill you. But, by God, you'll wish I had!"

Chapter 2

❧

London, summer, 1814

Gordon was bored. Months had passed since anyone had tried to kill him. Luckily, this tedious spell of safety should end soon. Lord Kirkland had summoned him, and Kirkland was an excellent source of missions that required Gordon's varied and nefarious skills.

Gordon was bemused by the fact that he and Kirkland had become friends of a sort. They'd known each other since their school days at the Westerfield Academy, a small, elite school for boys of "good birth and bad behavior."

Gordon had hated all the schools his father had sent him to, of which the Westerfield Academy was the last. He actually enjoyed learning, but he picked up new material very quickly, and then was physically incapable of sitting still. When he was a boy at Kingston Court, he and his brothers had been tutored by a young curate who had allowed his most restless student to prowl around while his brothers struggled to master Latin or maths or the globes.

The marquess had never understood, so when Gordon reached an age to be sent off to school, he was placed in one of the most brutal academies in Britain so the masters would force him to sit still and behave properly. Despite the school's best efforts to beat him into submission, Gordon had become ever more difficult. At the end of the year, he was asked not to return. The same thing happened at the next school. And the next. Gordon was rather proud of that fact.

By the time he reached Westerfield, he was so angry and rebellious that even calm, caring Lady Agnes Westerfield, founder and headmistress of the school, had been unable to reach him. He'd hated the school, hated his classmates, and rejected all friendly overtures. He skipped classes whenever possible, and when he showed up, he acted conspicuously bored and uninterested. To amuse himself, he'd perform brilliantly on exams just to madden his teachers.

Gordon had particularly hated Kirkland. Despite his youth, Kirkland had a cool, ferociously intelligent composure that was damned unnerving. Gordon felt disapproval whenever the other boy looked his way.

His hatred had been sealed during one of the school's Kalarippayattu sessions. The ancient fighting technique had been introduced to the school by the half Hindu young Duke of Ashton, and learning it had become a school tradition. Gordon had enjoyed the fighting, which helped him work off his restlessness.

Despite his general anger with the forced captivity of school, he seldom truly lost his temper. But one day in a fighting session he succumbed to fury when matched against a sharp-tongued classmate. He might have killed the boy in a rage if Kirkland hadn't intervened, yanking Gordon out of the fight, slamming him to the ground, and pinning him there. "Control yourself!" he'd ordered with razor-edged menace.

Later, Gordon was grateful he'd been prevented from committing murder even though he despised the little bastard who'd provoked him. But the public humiliation made him hate Kirkland even more.

Yet here he was, whistling as he climbed the steps of Kirkland's handsome townhouse in Berkeley Square. He stopped whistling before wielding the knocker. It would be bad for his reputation to appear too cheerful.

Soames, the butler who admitted him, said, "His lordship is expecting you, Captain Gordon. He told me to send you to him immediately. He's in the music room." Soames gestured to the stairs.

"No need to take me up," Gordon said as he handed over his hat. As he climbed the steps, he heard piano music. Lady Kirkland, he presumed. She was said to play superbly.

The door to the music room was closed. As he quietly opened it, the full power of the performance swept over him. Gordon wasn't particularly knowledgeable about music, but he recognized skill when he heard it. He paused, drinking in the vibrant harmonies. No wonder young ladies were taught to create music. Though few would be this good.

He stepped into the room and saw that Kirkland and his lady were seated side by side on the piano bench and playing together. Their flying fingers perfectly coordinated as they produced that powerful, mesmerizing flood of sound.

Gordon caught his breath in surprise, and Kirkland looked up, startled. "Sorry, I lost track of time." He swiveled on the piano bench and rose to take Gordon's hand. "Thank you for coming on such short notice."

"My pleasure, Kirkland," Gordon replied. "I never know what interesting project you might have for me."

"I hope what he has for you isn't too lethal." Lady Kirkland also stood to greet him. She wasn't a classical beauty, but her deep warmth was a perfect complement to her husband's cool composure. "It's lovely to see you, Captain Gordon."

"I greatly enjoyed your playing," he said honestly. "I've heard of your talent, but it was still a surprise and a pleasure. Even more so in your case, Kirkland. Beautiful ladies are supposed to be musical. Such skills are less expected in spymasters."

Both Kirklands laughed. "Would you like to come to one of our informal musical evenings?" Lady Kirkland said. "Every month or so we invite a few friends over to make music."

"And talk. And eat," Kirkland said. "Several of life's greatest pleasures." His fond glance at his wife suggested what *the* greatest pleasure was.

"That's sounds enjoyable, but I have no musical ability whatsoever," Gordon said. "I know nothing of instruments and have an alarmingly bad singing voice."

Lady Kirkland smiled. "You don't have to perform. It's enough to enjoy. We performers need an audience, after all. I'll send you an invitation the next time we have such a gathering."

He inclined his head. "I will be pleased to attend if I can, Lady Kirkland."

"Call me Laurel. I owe you too much for formality."
She brushed a kiss on his cheek and glided from the
room.

Gordon touched his cheek as he gazed after her.
"You're a lucky man, Kirkland."

"A fact of which I am very aware." Kirkland gestured
toward a pair of chairs set by a front window. "We
might as well talk here. I'll ring for coffee."

After he'd done so, they settled in the chairs and
Kirkland said, "I believe you've lived among our young
cousins in the United States?"

Gordon frowned. "You know that I have. I'll tell you
now that I won't do any spying against the Americans
even though our countries are at war. I like them."

"I don't want you to spy against them. This particular war has been a damned fool waste of blood and resources and should never have happened," Kirkland
said forcefully. "There are reasons why our countries
came to blows, but Britain should have stayed focused
on France. Now that Napoleon has abdicated, Wellington's Peninsular army has been freed to turn elsewhere, which means the war in our former colonies
will become much fiercer."

"All sadly true," Gordon agreed. "What has that to
do with me?"

"I'm hoping to enlist you in a rescue mission," Kirkland replied. "No politics involved. There is an English-
born widow who lives in the American capital,
Washington. That whole area has become a war zone,
with the Royal Navy rampaging up and down the
Chesapeake Bay, burning towns and farms and bombarding American forts. Anything might happen. Her
family is concerned about the dangers and would like
her to be brought back to safety in England."

Gordon frowned. "Mounting a rescue across the Atlantic will take time and money. Anything could happen between now and when I'd reach America. Doesn't this woman have the sense to get out of the way of an invading army if one appears?"

"There's family estrangement, so they aren't sure of the woman's financial situation, but she's likely in reduced circumstances."

"Being poor always complicates life," Gordon agreed. "But what if she doesn't want to return to England?"

"Exercise your powers of persuasion," Kirkland said dryly.

"I have done many reprehensible things," Gordon said with equal dryness, "but I'm not in the business of kidnapping reluctant women."

"Nor am I. I told the government official who asked me to arrange this that I wouldn't countenance forcing a woman against her will." Kirkland smiled a little. "Which would be not only wrong, but difficult since females tend to have minds of their own. If she doesn't wish to return to the bosom of her estranged family, you're authorized to escort her to a safer place, at least until the fighting is over. If she is impoverished, provide her with what funds she needs. At the very least, discover her situation so her family will know how she is faring."

Family matters were the very devil. Warily Gordon asked, "Why is the widow estranged?"

"I don't know. The official who asked me, Sir Andrew Harding, wasn't forthcoming, but I believe the woman is a relation of Harding's wife."

Gordon had heard of Harding. He was extremely wealthy and had a great deal of political influence. A man who expected results.

He shook his head. "I don't think I should accept this commission. If the widow has been out of touch with her family, the address might be wrong. Even if I can find her quickly, she might not want to return to England if she's estranged. Sir Andrew should save his money. He and his wife are unlikely to achieve what they want."

"Quite possibly not," Kirkland said quietly. "But sometimes, people need to do *something* because it's unbearable to do nothing."

Gordon understood that impulse to action. His brow furrowed as he considered. Though he'd wanted some excitement, hurling himself headfirst into a war zone on what was likely a wild goose chase was rather more than he'd bargained for. But he'd been feeling restless, and there was some chance that he might be able to rescue the damsel in distress. Assuming a widow qualified as a damsel and she wanted to be rescued.

"I would need to go in prepared to be either British or American," he said, thinking out loud. "If I end up dealing with the Royal Navy or the British Army, it would help if I had letters of introduction from high level men in the government. You know the sort of thing. '*This is Lord George Audley, give him anything he asks for.*'"

Kirkland chuckled. "I can't produce anything quite so sweeping, but I can certainly give letters that will gain you some consideration. What about transportation?"

"If I do this, I'll need to charter a ship willing to go into a battle zone, and that will be expensive. Preferably a ship that has sailed the Chesapeake Bay."

"Understood. You'll have all the funds you need. I can provide a ship, but I'm not sure I have sailors experienced in those waters."

"This is going to be a very pricey exercise in futility," Gordon said wryly. "The ship will need to appear nondescript, but be fast, well armed, and willing to fly flags of different nations if required. I might know a vessel that would be suitable if the captain is available and willing. If he isn't, it will be up to you."

"It sounds like you've decided to accept this commission," Kirkland observed, his eyes glinting with amusement.

"Apparently I have," Gordon agreed. "What's the woman's name and address?"

Kirkland handed over a paper with a name and address written on it. "Interestingly, her married name is Audley, like yours. Do you have any American relatives named Matthias Audley?"

Gordon shrugged. "There may be a connection, but Audley isn't an uncommon name. I doubt if sharing the same name will weigh with the widow if she's reluctant to return to England." He got to his feet. "Now to see if the ship and captain I have in mind are in London, willing, and able."

"Do what you think best, Gordon." Kirkland also stood and drew a folded piece of paper from an inside pocket. "Here's a bank draft toward expenses. I'll collect the authorization letters and send them to your house. If you need anything else, just ask."

Gordon whistled at the size of the bank draft. "They really want her back safely!"

"Yes, and if she won't come, the family wants to insure that she has what she needs to live comfortably."

"If she's impoverished, she might be more willing to come with me. Here's hoping she's eager to return home and all goes smoothly."

"That seldom happens," Kirkland murmured. "Which is why I thought of you."

Gordon grinned. "I'll take that as a vote of confidence in my shifty skills."

"Exactly so." Kirkland offered his hand. "Let me know if you need anything. Good luck and Godspeed."

As Gordon shook the other man's hand, he felt a prickle at the base of his neck, and a conviction that he was going to need all the luck he could get.

The waterfront tavern was patronized by the better grade of local merchants, ship chandlers, and sailors. Gordon scanned the room, wondering if he'd recognize the man he was here to meet.

He'd first met Hawkins in a prison cellar in Portugal, where they were two of five men condemned to be executed in the morning. They'd worked together through a long night to escape, and the five had made a wry pact to keep in touch through Hatchards bookstore in London, sending letters to the notice of the "Rogues Redeemed."

Though occasional missives at the bookstore had given Gordon some idea of what Hawkins had been doing, they'd not met face to face since that night in Porto. Ah, there, in a booth built along the left-hand wall. The man sitting there raised his tankard in greeting, so Gordon wove his way across the room.

As he approached the table, Hawkins rose and offered a hand. Brown-haired and broadly built, he had the weathered complexion of a man who was much out of doors. "Gordon," he said in a deep voice. "Good to see you after all these years."

As they shook hands, Gordon said, "Full years for both of us, I imagine." He slid onto the bench opposite the other man. "Your voice is different than I remember."

Hawkins chuckled. "On the night we met, I was suffering from a slight case of being hanged. It took time for my voice to recover." He signaled a barmaid to bring over a drink for Gordon.

"You're lively for a hanged man," Gordon said. "There must be a story there."

"A tale for another day," Hawkins said with a dismissive gesture. "Have you any news of other members of our little brotherhood of Rogues Redeemed?"

"Will Masterson was with the army in Toulouse when Napoleon abdicated. I'm told he's resigning his commission and heading for home across the Peninsula." Gordon grinned. "I wonder if he intends to pay a visit to the cellar where we shared that deplorable brandy and discussed what we would do in the unlikely case we survived. Masterson is planning to settle down to a staid and boring life now."

"He may be staid, but I doubt he'll be boring." Hawkins took a thoughtful sip of ale. "I wonder if all five rogues are still alive. We live in dangerous times."

"You more than most, if I read your occasional letters properly. You've been keeping yourself busy as a blockade runner?"

"Yes, but with peace breaking out and fewer blockades to run, I may have to turn respectable," Hawkins said with wry humor.

"Did you run any blockades to ports in the United States? The Chesapeake Bay, by preference. If so, I might have some work for you."

Hawkins's eyes narrowed. "I've made runs up the bay as far as Baltimore. One of my men grew up near there and he knows the waters as well as any man living. What sort of job? With the Royal Navy bashing about the Chesapeake, sailing there now would be even more dangerous than regular blockade running."

"It's a rescue mission and needs to take place as

quickly as possible." Gordon briefly described what needed to be done.

Hawkins considered. "That sounds simpler than blockade running. My *Zephyr* can outrun anything in the Royal Navy. If the price is right, I can do this."

Gordon smiled. "Then let's talk about it."

Chapter 3

Washington, DC
August 20, 1814

Callie brushed a lock of damp hair from her eyes, then dried her fingers on a towel before she returned to pinning delicate silk. Like its namesake, the rebellious General Washington, this young capital city was fresh and exciting in comparison to her Lancashire home, but the hot and humid summer had her wishing wistfully for the soft, cool summers of her childhood. She tucked another pin into the gown she was altering for Mrs. Gerard, one of her best customers. The wife of a high official in President Madison's cabinet, Mrs. Gerard accepted a clean linen handkerchief from Sarah, Callie's housekeeper, cook, assistant, and friend.

After murmuring thanks, Mrs. Gerard said soberly, "We've decided to move to our country house for the rest of the summer. It will be safer there, and we'll get away from the heat and illness of this malaria-infested swamp."

Washington was famous for its unhealthy climate, but not everyone had a country house to escape the summer heat. Callie said, "The Royal Navy has been plundering the Chesapeake Bay for over a year. What does Mr. Gerard think will happen now?"

"Since Napoleon's abdication has released British Army troops to come here, the cities around the bay are in danger of land invasion. If troops are landed on the Patuxent River, they can march to Washington, Annapolis, or Baltimore."

Similar thoughts had been keeping Callie awake at night. Luckily, her customers kept her better informed than the news sheets. "Wouldn't Baltimore be the most likely target because of its shipping and privateers? They say the Royal Navy admirals call Baltimore 'that nest of pirates.'"

"Yes, and justly so," Mrs. Gerard agreed. "But I wish this war was over."

"So do I!" Callie accidentally stabbed her finger with a pin. "I've never seen the point of it."

Before Mrs. Gerard could reply, the door to the dress shop flew open. Callie's fourteen-year-old stepson, Trey, his black curls rioting around his face, burst into the salon. "The British have landed over on the Patuxent!"

Everyone in the parlor froze. "Speak of the devil," Mrs. Gerard muttered, turning pale. "And here they are."

Callie clamped down on her fear. Trey had an enthusiastic interest in the war, but he wasn't prone to spreading wild rumors. "Where did you hear this?"

"An army scout just brought the news to President Madison!" Trey said excitedly. "Now the scout is at a tavern telling everyone."

She had a chilling certainty that the British would

attack Washington. Baltimore was a more valuable target, but also much more difficult. Capturing the American capital would be easier, and it would crush and humiliate the fragile new republic.

The fitting session ended more quickly than usual so Mrs. Gerard could hasten home. Wanting to preserve normalcy for as long as possible, Callie said to Trey and his sister, Molly, "Shall we make a lemon ice for supper? We'll need lemons. Run down to the market, if you would. Molly, try to keep Trey out of trouble!"

Sixteen-year-old Molly laughed. "I don't think that's possible, but I'll do my best."

The ice house Callie had had dug behind her home had proved a godsend in this climate. There had been an ice house at her English home, but not the heat that made ices so particularly wonderful here.

Callie waited until the children were gone before turning to Sarah. A handsome woman in her fifties, Sarah Adams and her husband Joshua had been house slaves at the Jamaica plantation of Callie's husband, Matthew Newell. When Callie had fled the island with the children, she'd asked the couple if they wanted to come with her. When they said yes, she'd freed them immediately. Now Sarah and Joshua were as much family as her two stepchildren; a better family than the one she'd grown up with.

"What should we do, Miss Callista?" Sarah said. "Reckon Mrs. Gerard is right that the British soldiers will march on Baltimore?"

Callie worried her lip as she wondered how best to keep her family safe. "My instincts say they'll head for Washington."

"Your instincts have always been good. So what do we do now?"

Callie drew a deep breath. "Leave the city. Start

packing the necessities for the children and you and Joshua so that you can be off tomorrow morning."

"Where would we go? West into the countryside?" Sarah asked doubtfully.

"To Baltimore," Callie said. "The city is much larger than Washington and better defended. There's also a place for you to stay there. Mr. Newell owned a warehouse and he left it to me. The living quarters on the upper floor are rather primitive, but they'll do until you can come home."

Sarah frowned. "You talked about 'us' going. Won't you be with us?"

Callie shook her head. "All my worldly goods are here, and if the house is destroyed, we'll be in dire straits. Since I'm English born, I should be able to talk the British troops into sparing this house."

Sarah gasped. "It's too dangerous for you to stay here alone!"

"Other women will be staying in the city to protect their homes. British soldiers aren't monsters, Sarah. They have orders not to hurt unarmed civilians. Even the horrible Admiral Cockburn, who's been raiding up and down the bay since last year, only destroys property and militiamen, not women and children."

"Joshua should stay with you," Sarah said firmly.

"The children need you both." Callie smiled as if she wasn't half sick with fear. "Remember that Mr. Newell taught me how to use a gun, just in case. I can drive off looters if need be."

Since Sarah's frown didn't abate, Callie said, "Maybe my intuition is wrong and the British Army won't come close to Washington. Perhaps the fact that we're preparing to evacuate will guarantee that evacuation will be unnecessary."

Sarah snorted. "The world doesn't work that way! I'll start on the packing."

After her friend left the room, Callie drifted around the high-ceilinged drawing room that she'd transformed into a fashionable salon. Most of the furnishings were secondhand, but elegant. A handsome oriental screen in one corner provided privacy for ladies to change their garments. Joshua had built shelves along one wall to hold the tools of Callie's trade: pattern books and lengths of fabric and boxes of buttons and trimmings.

Callie skimmed her fingertips over laces and ribbons, scooped up a handful of buttons and let them trickle through her fingers. She'd worked hard to build this business and this life, and it might be swept away through no fault of her own. Life wasn't fair, a painful fact she'd learned as a girl.

She paused at a window and gazed out at the street in front of her home. One of the principal thoroughfares of the city, it ran all the way to the Capitol, a grand building designed to show the world that the United States was a nation to be reckoned with. If the British invaded the city, they might march down this very road.

Growing up as the daughter of a baron in England, she had never imagined this life she lived. Everything that happened had been her fault, of course. If she'd been better behaved, less rebellious, her father wouldn't have forced her into marriage with a stranger. She wouldn't have run off with her dearest friend, and he wouldn't have ended up dying on a prison ship on the long voyage to New South Wales.

Of all the mistakes she'd made, causing Richard's death was the one that weighed most heavily on her. He'd been as much a rebel as Callie, and they'd had enormous fun acting out different roles, like scenes from a play. Pirates and maidens. Greek and Amazon warriors. Athena and Mars—and sometimes they'd switched roles, with her being the lord and he the lady, and they'd end up rolling around in the grass laughing until their stomachs hurt. Ah, Richard . . .

She cut off the thought, knowing how futile her regrets were. If she hadn't run to him for help, or accepted his suggestion that they elope together, he'd be alive now. Or at least, he wouldn't have died as a direct result of her actions. Once he became old enough to escape his father's control, he would have found his way to a happier life. He had strength and wit and more kindness than he showed to the world.

He should have lived to become happy. Instead, his bones rested on a distant ocean floor.

Callie had been luckier. Though she would never have chosen to marry Matthew Newell, he'd been a better husband than she'd expected. Their marriage hadn't been a grand romance, but they had learned to be comfortable with each other. She'd mourned his death when his heart failed. Then she'd learned that she and her stepchildren were in danger, so she'd collected them and run for her life. For all of their lives.

That exhausting flight had brought her to this city, which she knew a little from her husband's business ventures, and where her family could be safe. She'd changed their names from Newell to Audley to honor her long lost friend, and indeed they had been safe here for the last three years.

But permanent safety wasn't guaranteed. Telling herself not to waste time on regrets, she sat down at her desk and began collecting the documents to give Sarah and Joshua when they traveled to Baltimore. She'd make duplicate copies of the papers that verified that

the children and the Adamses were free. She'd send
her remaining jewelry with them, so if the worst happened to her and this house, they'd have some resources with which to build a new life.

She would do anything to keep them safe—and she
could only pray that her efforts would be enough.

Chapter 4

❦

Hawkins's ship *Zephyr* was even faster than Gordon had expected, and they sailed into war with surprising quickness. As the schooner made its way up the broad Potomac River, Gordon leaned on the railing at the ship's bow and wished that this mission was taking place at a cooler season. He'd stripped off his coat, and his linen shirt clung to his shoulders despite the light breeze.

There must have been heavy rains upriver since the water was rough and muddy and occasionally tree trunks and other debris floated by. Luckily the *Zephyr* was nimble.

Gordon wondered what they would find when they reached Washington. Earlier in the afternoon, he'd heard the distant sound of cannon fire rolling between the verdant Maryland hills. Now the guns had fallen ominously silent, but small boats were crossing the wide river toward the Virginia shore. Fleeing advancing enemy troops, he guessed.

He was joined by Hawkins, who carried a spyglass in one hand. "If all goes well, which I don't expect," the captain said, "we could be on our way home later tonight."

Gordon shook his head. "Even if I locate the lady and persuade her to return to England, it will take time to pack up her life. A day or two at the least."

"If your widow has the sense God gave a sparrow, she'll have left Washington by now," Hawkins said pessimistically. "If that has happened, you'll never find her."

"True, but since I'm this close, I need to try, if only to justify all the money this mission is costing her family."

"I can't complain when I'm getting a good share of that money." Hawkins raised the spyglass to survey the horizon. His voice changed. "There's a boat in trouble up ahead. Looks like it hit a shoal or snag."

Even without the spyglass, Gordon could see that the small boat was in serious trouble. It was dead in the water, and as he watched, it tipped over on its side, sails flapping. Most of the passengers grabbed hold of the hull, but one small figure tumbled into the water and was seized by the current.

As the child was swept downstream toward the *Zephyr*, female screams slashed through the heavy air. "Lizzie! *Lizzie!*"

Gordon swore as he calculated the odds. It didn't look as if any of the child's family knew how to swim, and the speed of the current would take her past the *Zephyr* before a dinghy could be launched. No other boats were close enough to help.

He wrenched off his boots and tossed his hat behind him, then vaulted up onto the railing. "I'd take it kindly if you'd send a small boat after us."

"You swim well enough to do this?" Hawkins asked tersely.

"Yes." Gordon spent a moment marking the child's path because once he was in the water, he'd have trouble seeing her. Then he kicked off from the railing in a long, flat dive that carried him away from the ship and toward little Lizzie.

The water was pleasantly cool as he cleaved into it and set off with powerful strokes toward the child. He'd always loved swimming, and he and Callie had learned together in a Lancashire river. In later years, he'd swum in rougher seas, and once he'd swum for his life. He should be able to save one pocket-sized little girl.

The river looked very wide and dangerous now that he was in it, and the odds were about even whether or not he could reach Lizzie before her saturated clothing dragged her under forever. When he judged he was close to where the current would have brought her, he paused and kicked himself upward as hard as he could to get a better view. Where the devil was she?

There. Twenty feet or so to his right a pale, half-submerged face was on the verge of being swept past. The flailing child managed to raise her head enough to gulp air before she slipped below the surface again.

"Hold on!" he shouted, hoping a chance of rescue would encourage her to keep struggling. He threw himself through the water, knowing that if he couldn't reach her now, she was lost.

The small head surfaced a couple of yards away and great blue eyes stared at him blindly before she sank again. Kicking furiously, he jackknifed under the surface and lunged as far forward as he could.

The water was swift and murky, so it was pure chance that his stretching fingers touched fabric. He grabbed and managed to latch on to a solid handful of her floating skirts. Then he kicked upward.

They emerged into the sunshine and Lizzie clutched Gordon, coughing up water as she locked her arms around his neck in a stranglehold. He barely managed to keep both their heads above the surface.

He scissor-kicked and paddled sideways as he secured her against his right side. She was five or six, he estimated. Old enough to know the danger she'd been in. "Don't worry, Lizzie, you're safe now," he said soothingly. "Try not to choke me."

She began to cry but had the wit to loosen her grip. As she calmed down, Gordon scanned their surroundings. The *Zephyr* had come about and a dinghy was heading toward them. Another of the ship's rowboats had reached the sailboat and was taking passengers from the damaged vessel.

Hawkins himself was in the dinghy that pulled up alongside Gordon. He leaned down, arms outstretched. "Pass her to me!"

Gordon obeyed, and Lizzie was whisked out of the water, coughing and squeaking. Hawkins wrapped her in a large towel and handed her to a sailor behind him. Then he reached down and grabbed Gordon's hand, half lifting him from the water. "Well done," Hawkins said tersely as he hauled Gordon over the stern.

"It was a near thing." Gordon accepted a towel and used it to blot water from his dripping hair. Looking upriver, he added, "You're taking the sailboat in tow?"

"It might be repairable, and it goes against a sailor's grain to let any boat die," Hawkins explained. "Now to find out what news the passengers have of the war."

News would be a very good thing, Gordon silently agreed as he pulled off his shirt, wrung water out of it, and dragged it on again. In this heat, it would dry quickly.

The journey back to the *Zephyr* was slower because they were moving against the current. As they pulled up alongside the schooner, a boy of around twelve looked over the side of the railing and shouted, "Mama, Lizzie's all right!"

Hawkins effortlessly climbed a rope ladder to the main deck with the little girl tucked under his arm. Gordon followed and reached the deck in time to see Lizzie and her dark-haired mother reunited in a fierce hug.

The water-soaked party from the small sailboat included a grandmotherly female, a capable black woman who behaved like a nursemaid looking after her chicks, and a boy and a girl in age between Lizzie and her big brother. They were a weary and vulnerable collection of refugees.

After assuring herself that her daughter was well, the woman handed Lizzie off to the nursemaid and turned to Gordon. "I'm Abigail Green. This is my mother-in-law, Alice Green and"—she waved at the others—"the rest of the family. I'm told that you're Mr. Gordon. God bless and keep you for what you've done!"

"I'm just glad we were close enough to help," he said. "Were you fleeing British troops? We need any news of the war you can give us."

Mrs. Green hesitated. "You and your captain are English, aren't you?"

"By birth," Gordon agreed. "But we are no part of this war."

Hawkins added, "A goodly number of my crew is American. My pilot, Landers, was born and bred in St. Michael's, just across the bay."

Landers, a lanky redhead, nodded confirmation. "My pa builds privateers to fight the British, ma'am."

Reassured, Mrs. Green said, "This afternoon there was a battle a few miles east of Washington near a town called Bladensburg." She sighed and pushed wet hair from her forehead. "Hardly a battle. They say the American militia ran like frightened chickens. The road is clear for the blasted British to march right into the city! That's why we were heading to Virginia to stay with my family. My husband made me promise to go there if the British neared Washington."

"That's probably wise," Gordon agreed. "Does your family live near the river?"

"Yes, on one of the creeks, which is why I thought it would be quickest to sail over, but . . ." She shrugged helplessly. "Perhaps it would have been wiser to cross on the Long Bridge, but that's jammed with people and wagons fleeing the city, and going that way would take us closer to the British. If we'd lost Lizzie, though . . . !"

"But we didn't, Miz Abby." The nursemaid patted her mistress as if she were as small as Lizzie. "The Lord was on our side."

"I hope so!" Abigail bit her lip. "I . . . I don't even know if my husband is alive. He was with the militia."

"The British Army has sent some of the best troops in the world over here," Gordon said quietly. "Even Napoleon's army couldn't stand up to them. How far is that town—Bladensburg?—from Washington?"

"Only five or six miles," Abigail said starkly. "They could be in the city by nightfall."

"I'm here in hopes of rescuing a member of my family, a widow who hasn't the means to return to England," he said, simplifying the facts. "Her name is Mrs. Matthias Audley. Do you by any chance know her?"

"By reputation. She's the best dressmaker in Washington, they say," Mrs. Green replied. "But she might have left. Many people have, including most government officials. It's chaos."

The situation sounded unstable and dangerous. Gordon frowned. "Nonetheless, I must attempt to find her, or at least learn where she's gone. Riding would give me some flexibility to track her down. Do you think I'll be able to buy or hire a horse?"

The older Mrs. Green had been hugging the two middle children by her sides, but now she spoke up. "We can help. Our plantation, Tucker Hall, is on Tucker Creek, just north of here on the Maryland side. I think the water in the creek is deep enough for this ship to sail up a quarter mile or so." She pointed up the river. "There are several horses in the stable. My husband is there to protect our property. Tell him what happened with us and say I've given you permission to take a horse. Samson would be best. He's a large gray who's strong and steady."

Gordon sent a questioning glance at Hawkins. His friend said, "I'd just as soon not sail right up to the docks in Washington if there's going to be a battle for the city. I can drop you off at Tucker Creek, then take the Greens over to Virginia. After, I'll return and moor in the creek to wait for you."

Gordon nodded agreement, then excused himself and headed down to his cabin to prepare for the next stage of his journey. He looked forward to being back on land and having a horse between his legs again.

Up until now, he'd just been traveling. Now the real mission would begin.

When the *Zephyr* had gone as far up Tucker Creek as Hawkins deemed safe, Gordon was set down at a landing and the damaged sailboat was tied to the dock for future repairs. It was less than a half-mile walk along the creek to the Greens' plantation, which would have been considered a manor in England.

At Tucker Hall, he found Abigail's husband alive and well, though his blue militia uniform was filthy and the left shoulder had been scorched by a musket ball. He and his father, a vigorous man in his late fifties, were grateful to learn their womenfolk were safe, and even more grateful to learn that Gordon had fished little Lizzie from the river.

Abigail's husband planned to travel to Virginia to join his family, since it might not be safe for a militia officer to be found by the British. His father would stay and watch over their home if necessary.

Within half an hour, Gordon was heading into the war zone dressed as an English gentleman and riding Samson, the strong mount Alice Green had recommended.

What were the odds that the Widow Audley would be where she was supposed to be? Slim to none.

He'd always had good instincts for danger, and now those instincts were saying that the future would not be simple.

Chapter 5

❧

Washington, DC
August 24, 1814

Usually the capital of the young United States bustled with energy and ambition, but four days after the British Army had made its nearby landing, Washington was as deserted as a plague city. Callie had hardly slept at all the previous night. In the darkest hours, she saw the light of a fire to the northeast. A bridge burning, she guessed.

This morning she'd chosen her clothing carefully, deciding on a blue gown that was elegant but simple so that she would look like a modest lady deserving of respect. She also pulled her hair back into a prim knot since it was too colorful to be respectable.

Now it was late afternoon and the artillery that had boomed earlier had fallen menacingly silent. The nearby battle must be over, but what had happened? Callie moved restlessly around her house, oppressed by the silence and wishing desperately that there was something she could do.

She almost jumped out of her skin when her front door knocker was rapped, but it was a polite-sounding knock. With her loaded pistol in her left hand and concealed in the folds of her gown, she warily opened the door. A harried-looking man dressed as a clerk bowed slightly. "I'm Mr. Williams from the Treasury Department, ma'am. We're trying to move as many records as we can out of the city. Do you have a horse and wagon my department can borrow? I'll give you a receipt."

Grateful that her household had left for Baltimore the morning after Callie had received news of the British landing, she said, "I'm sorry, my horses and cart are in Baltimore with my family."

He sighed. "A wise decision, but I wish you had more horses and wagons!" He touched the brim of his hat. "You stay safe, ma'am."

"You also, Mr. Williams." She closed the door. He wasn't the first to come by foraging for transportation for vital documents, but he might be the last.

She'd told her two young seamstresses to stay home with their families. Many of the few people left in town were women like herself who were staying in the hope that they could save their homes. It wasn't a vain wish. Several women in towns around the Chesapeake had been able to persuade British officers not to torch their homes. It was worth the risk of her remaining here.

She was sewing trim on a gown when she heard shouting outside. Again she opened the door, and saw a battered militia officer trotting down the street. Seeing her, he called, "There's been a battle at Bladensburg and the British routed us! They could be here in a matter of hours, so lock your doors and pray!"

Now that the danger was imminent, she felt surprisingly calm. She'd never been good at waiting. After locking her front door, she left the house through the kitchen and walked quickly down the side street to bring the news to her friend Edith Turner, an older widow who had been the first to welcome Callie to the city. With invasion imminent, Edith had taken in several elderly friends who didn't have the strength to evacuate.

She answered the door at Callie's first knock, her face worried. "There's news?"

"Yes, a militiaman reported that the British routed our forces at Bladensburg."

Edith gasped. "That's only a few miles away!"

"The militiaman said to lock our doors and pray," Callie said grimly. She gave her friend a swift hug. "That's good advice. Stay safe, Edith!"

Her friend hugged her back. "You also, my dear."

As Callie returned to the safety of her own solid brick home, she heard a booming explosion to the east, in the direction of the battle. At a guess, American forces had blown up another bridge to slow the British advance. Wryly she wondered if Americans were doing more damage to their capital than the British would have done.

Half an hour or so later, she peered out her front curtains and saw retreating militiamen trickling past. One looked over and saw the movement of her curtain. He spoke to the young man next to him, and the two turned in to her front walk. More knocking. They looked more frightened than threatening, so she opened the door, though once more she kept her pistol handy.

"Ma'am." The taller of the two young men coughed, then started again. "Ma'am, could we have some water? Please? Me and my brother are like to keel over."

"Of course. Get in the shade of that tree and I'll bring you some," she replied.

Guessing there would be more men needing water, she brought two full buckets and a pair of ladles. "Help yourselves. There's more where this came from."

"The only Americans who knew how to fight were Commodore Barney's flotilla men," the taller brother said bitterly after he thirstily gulped down a ladleful of water. "They been fightin' the British Navy up and down the bay for months. *They* knew how to stand their ground! I heard some of 'em say they'd keep fighting all through the streets of Washington."

Seeing their humiliation, Callie said quietly, "If soldiers aren't experienced and the whole company collapses and retreats, there's no point in individual soldiers staying to fight. Your mother wouldn't like it if you got yourself killed for no good reason."

"The lady is right, Jem," the shorter brother said. "Ma would kill us again if she thought we was that stupid." He drank deeply, then poured a ladleful of water over his head to cool himself down. "We ran today, but by God, we'll fight again another day!"

"They'll not take Baltimore!" Jem used the ladle to fill his empty pewter canteen. "Thank you kindly, ma'am. We'll be on our way again. It's a long hike north."

Callie wished them well and refilled the water buckets, leaving them on the edge of her lawn with the ladles so other retreating soldiers could drink. Then she withdrew into her house again, pulled the curtains, and waited.

The summer days were long in August, and it wasn't yet full dark when she heard the sound of marching men. She took her pistol in hand again. A single shot wouldn't be of any use against an army, but she felt better for having a weapon to hand.

Needing to see, she pulled her curtains open a sliver and peered out. A group of several dozen soldiers were marching past her house with mounted officers in the lead. They were heading toward the capitol building and flying a white flag of truce.

She sighed with relief. Perhaps the British wanted to negotiate a ransom that would save the city from being destroyed.

Being female, Callie thought a ransom in return for sparing the capital was a fine idea, though she suspected that many men had too much pride to give money to the enemy even to save the city. But even if the government was willing to be reasonable, she wasn't sure there was anyone left in Washington with the authority to negotiate.

She studied the riders. That erect man in the lead wore the insignia of a major general and was surely Robert Ross, the commander of the army forces. One of Wellington's top generals in the Peninsular wars, he was said to be a just and honorable man who didn't wreak havoc on civilians. But the man riding next to him . . .

She frowned. An admiral of the Royal Navy rode beside Ross. That must be George Cockburn, who had been named the most hated man in America because of his months spent slashing and burning up and down the Chesapeake Bay. He'd destroyed whole towns as punishment for American destruction in Canada.

It was said that Cockburn's older brother had died fighting the rebels during the American Revolution, so the admiral had a very personal hatred for Americans. Callie hoped that since they were on land, General Ross had command over Cockburn.

The troops were moving in good order despite having fought and marched on a very long, hot day. The group was directly in front of her house when she heard noise from upstairs. Footsteps?

She went from nervous to near panic in the space of a heartbeat. The lock on the kitchen door at the back of the house was a simple one and wouldn't resist a determined housebreaker, and the servants' stairs ran up from the kitchen. The noise of marching troops must have drowned out any sounds until now.

Clutching her pistol, she headed for the stairs to investigate, but before she could start up, a ragged blast of rifle shots boomed from directly over her head. Hell and damnation! Some American soldiers weren't giving up, and they had chosen *her* house as a sniper post!

Her horror at the thought intensified when she ran to her front window and saw General Ross's horse crash to the ground, taking its rider with it. Several soldiers behind the officer also pitched over, wounded or dead.

Furious and disciplined, his troops immediately returned fire to the upper stories of Callie's house. Thunderous gunshots and shattering glass, followed by heavy feet pounding down the servants' stairs. She heard her back door slam as the shooters ran.

Out on the street, General Ross scrambled to his feet, apparently unhurt, praise God. But some of his men had not fared so well. From the reactions of the other troops, some soldiers had died or were seriously injured.

Ross called for another horse. After he remounted, he barked a command that caused the rider with the truce flag to hurl it to the ground.

Callie stood frozen, caught between an impulse to rush outside to see if she could aid the wounded and an equally strong desire to flee. She didn't want to abandon her home when she'd done nothing wrong. But would the British soldiers listen to her?

A mighty crash sounded against her front door and the glass panes at the top shattered as the wood splintered. Another two blows broke it down completely, and soldiers barreled into her drawing room.

"Find the bloody snipers!" one bellowed.

Instinctively Callie raised her pistol, gripping it with both hands. She was a good shot and could kill or wound one of the soldiers. But which one? She aimed at a slight youth in the lead, but he looked so *young*. They all looked so young!

Killing one man wouldn't save her. She lowered the pistol and said in her most English voice, "I don't know who fired those shots! I think some American soldiers came in the back of my house and fled after shooting at you."

"We'll get 'em!" Two soldiers shoved past her and ran toward the back of the house, but the others stayed.

A corporal wrenched the pistol from her hand and struck her on the side of the head with the barrel. "You shot my mate, you treasonous bitch! You'll pay for that!"

Dizzy and near collapse from the painful blow, she cried out, "I'm Catherine Audley, an English widow from Lancashire! I would never shoot a British soldier!"

The corporal snarled, "You carry a gun and your mates damn near killed General Ross!" He glanced at the pistol, then shoved it under his belt. To his men, he barked, "Break up that furniture and pile it here to start the fire."

On the verge of blacking out, Callie again said vehemently, "I'm *English*! I am not your enemy!"

"Too late to play the innocent!" As the corporal grabbed her arm and dragged her toward the door, the other soldiers began smashing furniture and tossing it into the center of the room. One soldier grabbed a chair and began battering the shelves that held fabrics and trims.

The glass-fronted cabinet that contained special buttons and delicate china cups for serving tea to her clients shattered when smashed with the butt of a musket. The soldier spotted a bowl of expensive silver buttons and poured them into his knapsack, then dragged the remnants of the cabinet to the center of the room. Another soldier found the silk gown she'd been carefully trimming and balled it up to add it to the pile.

She looked away, shuddering, unable to bear the sight of these vandals destroying the life she'd painstakingly built, the beautiful objects she'd cherished. Then her captor yanked her out the front door onto the lawn. She tried to fight back, but she was too dizzy and he was too strong. Down the side street she saw Edith Turner watching with her hands pressed over her mouth and her eyes wide with horror.

Ross and Cockburn and most of their troops had moved on, leaving this squad to wreak vengeance for the attack. The white flag of truce that had been thrown to the ground was now filthy with hoof and foot prints.

Swaying dizzily, Callie watched through the shattered front door as torches were thrust into the pile of broken furniture. Flames flickered, then caught hold and flared toward the ceiling. A soldier yelled, "Mick, fire in some of them Congreve rockets!"

Mick pulled two rockets from his knapsack and fired first one, then the other, into the house through the broken windows. The rockets exploded noisily and flames engulfed the drawing room and began racing through the rest of the structure. She stared numbly, hardly able to grasp how quickly her beloved home had become an inferno.

As the flames roared upward, her captor yanked her farther away, more likely for his safety than for hers. Even in the middle of the side street, she felt the searing heat.

There was worse to come. A soldier emerged from the back of the house swigging from a bottle of brandy he'd found in the pantry. It was swiftly emptied as he passed it around to his mates. The last man to drink hurled the empty bottle into the blaze, then turned to Callie with dangerously glittering eyes. "I say we string her up! She hurt my mate bad and coulda killed General Ross. Why should she be breathin' when so many of our lads died today?"

The man who held her arm retorted, "Mebbe later, but she's a fine-lookin', highborn lady and we shouldn't waste 'er. Let's show 'er what British soldiers are made of." He pulled her against him and clamped one hand over her breast.

Revolted, she began fighting frantically to free herself. She managed to knee her captor in the groin. He screeched and let her go, but two other men grabbed her, their expressions wolfish. She grabbed for one man's rifle and had managed to wrench it from his grasp when a ferociously aristocratic voice bellowed, "Be damned to you all!"

She and the soldiers all swung around, riveted, as an English gentleman galloped up on a white horse. He was garbed in clothing that cost more than a soldier's annual salary, and his eyes blazed as he commanded, "Unhand my wife!"

Chapter 6

❧

The young woman's bright hair had fallen around her shoulders, her elegant blue gown was streaked with soot, and her eyes were wide with shock, yet Gordon recognized her instantly. There was no one like Callie, *no one*, and he'd visited six continents. But what the devil was his childhood friend doing in the middle of a battle zone?

Explanations could wait. Heart pounding, he swung off his horse and cocked the pistol he held in one hand. "Release her or die, you villains!"

His fierce authority transformed the men from a mob to soldiers under discipline. Callie's captor released her and backed away, sputtering, "Your *wife?* But . . . but she said she's a widow!"

Keeping his pistol pointed at the corporal, who seemed to be the leader, Gordon stepped up to Callie and crushed her to him with his free arm as he murmured into her hair, "Play along with me, Catkin!"

As he'd hoped, using his private nickname convinced

her it really was her old friend. Her rigid figure soft-ened and she wrapped her arms around him as she cried, "Dear God in heaven, my love, I thought you were dead!"

She dissolved into wrenching sobs. He was pleased to see that her embrace didn't interfere with his grip on the pistol. Callie had always had the quickest wits in Lancashire. Her silky hair was scented with smoke and lavender.

One arm circling her waist, he gazed over her head—they used to be close to the same height—and gave the soldiers his most furiously intimidating gaze. "I'm Lord George Audley and I have been separated from my wife because I was risking my life on the king's busi-ness. It's an utter *outrage* to find her being mauled by British soldiers! I might have expected that of Ameri-cans, but royal soldiers? You're a disgrace to the uni-form you wear!"

The corporal stammered, "Sorry, sir, but there was an attack from her house. Killed General Ross's horse, wounded several men. When we broke in to find the shooters, she was holding a pistol and looked like she knew what to do with it."

"The pistol I gave you to defend yourself, sweet-heart?" he asked, keeping his gaze and his weapon fixed on the corporal.

Callie nodded and pulled away a little. "Yes," she said in a trembling voice, "but I didn't fire it. One shot wouldn't save me, and I couldn't bear to think of how the poor lad's mother would feel to learn her son was dead."

Gordon bared his teeth at the soldiers. "*This* is the woman you wanted to rape and murder! You should bloody well be ashamed of yourselves!"

Her voice a little stronger, she pointed at the corporal.

"He has my pistol, and I want it back." Her voice quavered. "It's the only thing I have left that you gave me. That, and my wedding ring." She raised her left hand and torchlight glinted from the gold band on her third finger. His Callie had always had a great sense of theater.

The shamefaced corporal stepped forward and offered the pistol, butt first. "Sorry, ma'am, but you looked guilty as sin."

"Well, she isn't!" Gordon brushed a kiss on her hair. "I'm sorry that you've had to endure this, love, but now I'll take you home to England where you'll be safe. We can set sail tonight."

"Not without the children!" she exclaimed.

He blinked. Children? Considering that she'd been married at sixteen, the existence of children shouldn't be a surprise, but it was a reminder of how many years had passed since they'd last seen each other. "Of course not. I assumed you sent them to safety. Where are they?"

"Baltimore."

Wonderful, her children were in a city that would soon have half the Royal Navy laying siege to it while Ross's army invaded by land. But even an old bachelor knew that children were nonnegotiable.

He gave her a reassuring squeeze. She was extremely squeezable. "Then we shall go to Baltimore and bring them home with us so we can be a family again."

Raising his gaze to the soldiers, he said coolly, "I understand that you were angry because General Ross could have been killed, but he wasn't, and it's time you rejoined his troops and helped burn that great government building at the end of this road. Now *go*!"

Happy that Gordon wasn't intending to tell Ross about their bad behavior, the soldiers jogged off after the other troops as quickly as exhausted men could manage.

Gordon kept his arm around Callie as the soldiers disappeared from sight. She was shaking a little, and no wonder. He felt shaky himself, both from shock at finding her and horror at the danger she'd been in. Rape was one of the oldest and ugliest parts of war, and he shuddered at what might have happened if he'd been a few minutes later.

She raised her head to speak, but before she could, an older woman appeared from the side street, her worried face illuminated by the light from the burning house. "Oh, my dear Catherine, your beautiful home! I'm so sorry! Are you all right?"

Callie stepped from his embrace to accept the woman's comforting hug. "Richard, this is my friend Mrs. Turner. She's been a very good neighbor to me." Callie turned bleak eyes on the inferno of her house. "I'm much better than I might have been, Edith, but . . . I'd hoped to prevent this sort of destruction."

"I saw the shooters running out of your kitchen. Flotilla men, I think. Brave fighters, but I'm so sorry they chose your house for their attack!" Mrs. Turner switched her interested gaze to Gordon. "This is really your husband whom you'd thought dead?"

"Yes, ma'am." Gordon gave the older woman a half bow. "Lord George Gordon Richard Augustus Audley at your service."

"Goodness!" Mrs. Turner blinked at the string of names. "Doesn't that make you Lady George Audley, my dear?"

Callie gave a lopsided smile. "This is America, so using a British courtesy title seemed out of place. Not to mention a bit pretentious for a dressmaker."

Shouts and shots were heard in the distance. Mrs. Turner frowned. "We need to get inside. Heaven only knows what kind of men are blustering around Washington now! Come to my house. You need food and a safe place to spend the night. You'll have to share a room, but I don't expect you'll mind that."

"No, ma'am. You're right that we need to go to ground for the night." Gordon gave Callie a fond glance. "We have much to talk about, my dear."

"How long has it been since you saw each other?" Mrs. Turner asked.

Callie sighed. "It seems like forever. Thank you for the offer, Edith, but you already have a full house. We can spend the night in the guesthouse at the back of my property."

Edith frowned. "Are you sure, dear? It's not much more than a shack."

"Yes, but it's a familiar, comfortable shack." And Callie yearned for it now. "However, I'd appreciate some food and drink if you can spare some. Bread and cheese and perhaps some of your lovely lemonade would be wonderful."

"I'll send a basket over right away." Edith hugged her again. "As dreadful as this night has been, at least your children and servants are safe and your husband is alive! Try to sleep, child. You look exhausted."

"I am, but with my husband here, I know all will be well." As Edith returned to her home, Callie said, "This way, Richard."

She guided him into a thicket of shrubbery behind her gardens, lit by the flames of her burning house. "The guesthouse was originally slave quarters, but there are no slaves in my household. It's private and surrounded by trees so it's far cooler than Edith's attic. There's also a stable for your horse. It's empty now because my horses

took the family to Baltimore, but there's water and
fodder available."

"You have more land than I guessed from seeing the
front of the house," Gordon observed as he collected
the reins of his very patient horse and followed Callie
onto a garden path that led back into the trees. The
brick pathway was well illuminated by the light of the
fire, though the flames were beginning to die down.
"I'm glad we'll have the privacy since we have so much
to talk about."

He couldn't wait to find out how Callie had come to
be here. After that, he and his alleged wife needed to
coordinate their lies.

While Richard stabled and tended his horse, Callie
retrieved the key to the guesthouse from under one of
the flowerpots that flanked the front door. It was a relief
to go inside. The cottage was small, with a sitting room
holding a battered sofa and chairs, and a cramped bedroom with a washstand, cupboard, and a double bed
pushed against one wall. A tiny alcove off the sitting
room was set up as a kitchen.

The furnishings were simple and the kitchenware
was mismatched pieces from the main house, but the
whitewashed walls, polished pine floors, and pleasantly faded rag rugs were soothing. A water pump was
mounted on the counter and basic items like tea and
sugar were kept in the kitchen. There was even wood
laid in the small fireplace, not that anyone would want
a fire on an August night in Washington.

As she lit a lamp, she tried to steady her churning
nerves. Losing her home and business was shattering,
but her children and closest friends were safe, at least
for now, which was a blessing beyond price.

Wonderful but most disorienting of all was the discovery that the dearest friend of her childhood was not dead but alive, shockingly handsome, and once more playing the role of her rescuer. But how the devil had he appeared in such a timely fashion?

As Callie was opening windows to let in fresh air, one of Edith's maids and a male escort arrived with a generous basket of food and drink. Callie was investigating the contents when Richard entered carrying his saddlebags.

In his beautifully tailored blue coat, buckskins, fine white linen, and polished boots, he looked ready to ride with a lady through Hyde Park at the fashionable hour. He set the saddlebags by the door, then peeled off his coat, cravat, and boots. Now he looked like a gentleman in a lady's boudoir: broad shouldered and beautiful and intensely masculine. She found herself staring and forced her gaze back to the food basket.

"Very pleasant and indeed fairly cool," he said as he scanned the room. "Lucky this cottage was tucked out of sight back here. Do you have guests often?"

"Almost never, but I like the sound of 'guest cottage' much better than 'old slave quarters.' This is more a retreat for privacy. Sometimes I'd work here when I wanted quiet or just to be alone. My servants, Sarah and Joshua, are married, and occasionally they'd stay here for a private night." She sliced bread and cheese and ham and laid the food out on a chipped platter so they could help themselves.

Lastly, she produced a bottle of red wine. "Edith is generous. Can you open this? There are various utensils in the drawer in the kitchen and glasses in the cabinet below."

"Wine seems like a very good idea now." He followed her instructions and opened the wine, then poured it into two mismatched glass tumblers. He handed her one, then clinked his glass to hers. "To survival!"

"To survival," she echoed before swallowing. Despite being half dressed, Richard was every inch the English gentleman, yet unnervingly . . . physical. Hard to ignore.

And in true gentlemanly fashion, he pulled out a battered wooden chair for her at the kitchen table. "Will my lady have a seat?"

She laughed as she settled with a flounce of blue skirts. "Those manners that were drilled into us as children never go away, do they?"

"We can ignore those lessons when we choose, but we never forget them," he agreed as he sat opposite her and began to assemble a cheese and ham sandwich. When he was done, he handed it to her. "And very useful manners can be in convincing other people that one is well bred even if battered and wearing rags."

"You've had to do that?" she asked curiously.

"Oh, yes," he said with a grin that was pure boyish mischief as he made a second sandwich for himself.

Callie had hardly eaten for the last few days, and she found now that she was ravenous. After two sandwiches and a second glass of wine, she felt ready to face whatever came next. She rose, saying, "Please excuse me a moment while I become as cool as is practical."

"Of course." Richard politely got to his feet, once more demonstrating his excellent manners. "Brutal heat you have here. It's a strong argument for returning to England."

She made a face. "Washington is as hot as Jamaica without the sea breeze. But it all balances out because winter can be seriously cold, snowy, and icy." She stepped into the bedroom and closed the door, then took off her gown and stays. She heard a crunch from the direction of her house and guessed it was the collapse of a charred beam. Strange that the fire still burned so close while she was in a very different world.

She wouldn't think about the house. Her life had changed with shattering suddenness twice before, and she'd learned that there was no point in looking back. Looking forward was the way to survive.

That morning, she'd chosen garments that fastened in the front so she could manage on her own. It was a relief to strip off the layers of clothing and her shoes and stockings. Her cool, muslin chemise would make a good nightgown.

She kept a hairbrush and comb in the bedroom cupboard, so she took them into the sitting room and sank into a chair. Though she couldn't bathe, brushing the tangles from her hair would make her feel more civilized.

Richard was gazing out a window, but he turned when she came back. "From what I can see on the skyline, there are several large fires burning in other parts of the city. Probably government buildings, but despite the attack from your house, General Ross is apparently leaving most private homes untouched."

She sighed. "Why was I so lucky as to be chosen by the American attackers when there are so many houses empty?"

"If I was a sniper, I'd look for a house that is solid, right on the route where my enemy will be marching, and preferably unoccupied. They might have thought the house was empty if you were lying low, so you were just very unlucky," he said sympathetically.

It was a day of both bad and good luck, actually. She

studied Richard as he stood with his back to the window. He was achingly familiar, but at the same time a stranger. The lantern light sketched his height, the breadth of his shoulders, his lean powerful build. His hair had darkened a little, but he was still strikingly blond, and the softer features of youth had become refined to sculpted male beauty.

Like her, Richard had stripped down as far as he could, which meant drawers and a loosened shirt falling over his hips, and bare feet. Barely decent. She tried not to stare at the triangle of bare skin at his throat. Blond hairs glinted golden in the lamplight.

Now that they'd settled into the cottage and eaten, she was uneasily aware of his unnerving masculinity. Though her friend Richard would never have hurt her, she wasn't as sure about Lord George Audley, who had been busy with the king's business and had cowed a mob of angry soldiers by sheer force of personality.

Deciding it was best to tackle the issue head on, she said, "It's odd. On the one hand, I feel that I know you as well as myself, yet at the same time, you are a stranger. It's easy to understand how you terrified those soldiers with just a few words."

He shrugged. "It's a knack one acquires when commanding men, which I've done as needed." He leaned against the frame of the window and crossed his arms across his chest. "I feel the same. Here is the person who was once my best friend, whom I haven't seen in half a lifetime. Which of us shall speak first about all the years since we last saw each other?"

"We'll take turns because there is so much ground to cover. First and most important, I'm really curious about how you came to be alive. I still don't quite believe it." Callie started brushing the ends of her hair, working her way up carefully in case she hit more tangles.

"What did you hear that made you believe I was dead?" he asked curiously.

"Not long after I reached Jamaica, my father wrote that you'd died of some horrid disease on the prison ship carrying you to Botany Bay." She'd wept bitter tears of grief and guilt. Those feelings had subsided in time, but never disappeared.

"Such a charming man, your father." Richard unbuttoned his cuffs and rolled the sleeves up. His forearms were powerful and also lightly dusted with gold.

Wishing she wasn't so aware of his physicality, she resumed brushing her hair, which gave her an excuse to drop her gaze. "He took great pleasure in telling me that lie."

"He might have thought he was telling the truth. Transportation ships are only a cut above slavers," he said dispassionately. "Disease swept through the vessel I was on and many sailors were casualties. Because I stayed healthy and had some sailing experience, the captain drafted me as a seaman. I proved useful and he developed a certain fondness for me." He grinned. "My good manners, you know."

Her brows arched. "So you convinced him you were an innocent young gentleman who had been tragically transported by an enemy?"

"I told him the truth, which wasn't far from that," Richard replied. "I don't know if you ever heard, but I was convicted of kidnapping you and stealing my own horse, which technically belonged to my father. So the charges were trumped up to get rid of me, but not entirely wrong."

"I can see my father taking pleasure in concocting the charges," she said, feeling sickened. "Your father didn't object?"

"I don't know how fond my father was of any of his

five sons, but he considered an heir necessary and didn't mind having a few spares. But me he hated," Richard said bluntly. "I look just like my mother, whom he first loved, then detested. As long as I was around, I was a reminder of her unfaithfulness. He wanted me dead."

"How dreadful!" Callie closed her eyes, feeling the pain that he wouldn't allow into his voice. "Back then, I didn't realize how complicated your situation was."

"I couldn't talk about it then, not even to you," he said calmly. "But it was a lifetime ago. I knew Lord Kingston hated me, so his behavior was no great shock. I decided I had to stay alive just to spite him. When the transportation ship reached Sydney Harbor, the captain looked the other way while I dived overboard and swam to shore. He must have listed my name among the casualties with burial at sea. No further explanations were needed."

She tried to imagine all he wasn't saying. The voyage must have been appalling. "How did you survive and make your way back to England?"

"That's a long and complicated story that can wait for another day. Suffice it to say that I worked my way around the globe, which took much time and many detours. And here I am." He smiled wryly. "Could either of us have imagined such a scene fifteen years ago?"

"My imagination is good, but not that good!" She hadn't fully registered the improbability of his timely appearance because amazement that he was alive had filled her mind. But the timing was equally amazing. "By what miracle did you gallop up on a white horse here and now?"

"I was hired to rescue the widowed Mrs. Audley and bring her back to England."

"Hired?" She dropped her brush and stared at him.

"By whom? When I left Jamaica, I cut off communication with everyone back in Britain."

"Maybe that's why someone wanted you to be found and rescued if necessary," he explained. "A fellow called Sir Andrew Harding made the request of a gentleman who is good at getting things done, and that gentleman asked me if I'd undertake the task."

"So you agreed to cross an ocean and enter a war zone to rescue a complete stranger? You've become a bold and dangerous adventurer, I see." Certainly he looked dangerous in a quietly lethal way.

"Not really," he said peaceably. "I consider myself more of a problem solver willing to do what's needed. This was an extreme request, but the money was good."

She frowned. "You had my address. I wonder how that happened. I did my best to vanish when I came here."

"You've never heard of Sir Andrew Harding? I was told Mrs. Audley was a connection of Sir Andrew's wife, so perhaps he's married to one of your sisters."

She was about to deny knowing the man, then paused when a vague memory surfaced. "I think the fellow visited Washington not long after I moved here, before this war broke out. He must have been on an official trade or diplomatic mission, because he was given a reception at the President's House. I made gowns for several women who attended, and they talked about the reception on their next visits. It was quite the grand affair, apparently. He brought his wife with him. How strange to think she might have been one of my sisters and she recognized me somewhere about town!"

"If so, why didn't she talk to you?"

Callie considered. "Maybe it was the sister who betrayed me to my father when I ran away with you. Perhaps she feared my reaction. And justly so! If she hadn't done that, you wouldn't have been beaten half to death and transported to the other side of the world."

"Strange to think that if not for her, we might have made it to Scotland and married," he said pensively. "But we were very, very young. Too young for marriage."

She'd believed that, too, but despite their youth, she thought they'd have made it work. "I ended up married anyway, but to a man more than three times my age."

"How did you come up with the name Mrs. Matthias Audley? Your husband wasn't an Audley, was he? You'd have mentioned that to me when you were trying to escape the marriage."

"His name was Matthew Newell. I chose Matthias as being similar but different from his real name." She smiled ruefully. "And I chose Audley in memory of my long dead childhood friend."

"I'm flattered, I think. Was he a horrid husband? I hope not. I often wondered." He smiled without humor. "If I'd been the praying sort, I would have prayed that he treated you well."

She hesitated, wondering how to explain Matthew. "He treated me kindly. I could have done much worse. But his situation in Jamaica was complicated, and he preferred to avoid conflict, which produced more complications."

"At least he treated you well." Richard smiled a little. "I want to know how many children we have. Do any of them look like me?"

"There are two, and neither looks at all like you." Wondering how he would react, Cassie continued, "They're quadroons."

Chapter 7

Much of Gordon's attention was focused on what a very beautiful woman Callie had become, how translucent her chemise was, and on the effort required to prevent his interest from showing. He'd never thought about her appearance when they were children—she'd been the indomitable Callie with the red-gold hair and freckles. He'd been startled when she'd said the planter from the Indies wanted to marry her because she was so beautiful.

At that age, to the extent he'd thought about Callie's appearance, he would have classified her as pretty enough, but nothing special. Familiarity had blinded him to the classical perfection of her features and the smooth grace of her movements. Her figure was a little fuller now, in the best possible way.

He forced his thoughts away from admiring her to thinking about the comment she'd just made. "A quadroon means being one quarter African and three quarters European, doesn't it? Your husband was half African?"

"No, he was as English as you or I."

"So your husband's first wife was half African?"

"No, she wasn't, either." Callie sighed, some of her tension fading at his mild acceptance. "It's a complicated story. They're my stepchildren. I have no child of my body, but they are *mine* even though not of my blood." Her expression was challenging. Gordon suspected that issues of race had complicated her life in Jamaica. But clearly she loved her stepchildren, and he wanted to know more.

"I'd like to hear the whole story," he said quietly. "My curiosity hasn't faded with the years."

She smiled a little. "Does it still get you into trouble?"

"All the time," he said promptly. "But I've come to realize that curiosity is incurable. Haven't you learned the same?"

"I've probably had less opportunity to indulge my curiosity than you, but it hasn't gone away," she admitted. "Merely been suppressed."

He supposed that her responsibilities had caused that. "So what is the long, complicated story about your children?"

Her brow furrowed. "I'll have to talk about my marriage, which is at the root of the complications."

"I heard you swear to your father that you'd be a good, docile wife in order to stop him from beating me to death," he said. "You paid a very high price for our mutual foolishness that night."

"We both did, but yours was higher." She brushed a strand of red-gold hair from her cheek. "I wouldn't have chosen to marry Matthew, but he was a decent man. From things he heard me say when he visited my father, he deduced that I was a rebellious sort who might welcome moving away to an exotic new home. He was ready to remarry and he liked my looks, so he offered for me."

"And your father was keen to get rid of you at a profit," Gordon said dryly.

"Exactly. Luckily, Matthew was a much nicer man than my father. Speaking of which, is my father alive, or has an apoplectic fit carried him off?"

"I don't know. I don't even know my own father's fate," Gordon said. "I've heard no news from Kingston Court or Rush Hall since I was dragged off and imprisoned." He'd been so badly beaten that he wasn't aware of much until he was deposited on the ship that would take him to the prison colony. "It was years before I made it back to England, and by then I had no interest in my family."

"With any luck, both our fathers have gone to their eternal rewards in a place much hotter than Jamaica," she said tartly. "To return to my story, I found the Caribbean interesting and beautiful, but the slavery there appalled me."

Gordon grimaced. "The shipping of slaves from Africa has been abolished and it's high time slavery itself was made illegal, but so many plantation owners have so much of their capital tied up in slaves that they claim they can't afford to free them. It's a damnable situation."

"That's what Matthew said when I tried to persuade him to free his slaves. The plantation adjacent to ours was owned by Quakers who freed their slaves and paid the ones willing to stay fair wages. Matthew said he didn't have enough money to do that." She sighed. "As slave owners went, he was better than most. He let me have the money to build a church for the workers and looked the other way when I went to the slave quarters to teach them reading and writing."

"That's illegal, isn't it?"

"Yes, but as I said, he didn't interfere. Matthew and I became friends. He enjoyed having a pretty young wife as a hostess, and he wasn't very demanding. We got on well enough until I discovered his mistress and her children. That was . . . a shock."

Gordon frowned. "Many men have mistresses, but it must have been distressing to unexpectedly discover her. How did that happen?"

"One day I rode in a different direction from usual and came across a pretty little cottage tucked away in an area that was difficult to find even though it wasn't far from the main house. Matthew was at the cottage with Susannah and the children. She was so beautiful and they were so obviously a happy family. . . ." She took a deep breath. "It was one of those moments when one's life changes forever."

Gordon nodded, understanding. "I see. In a place like Jamaica, a slave is acceptable as a mistress, but she could never be his wife. How did you deal with the revelation? That's probably too personal a question, but we've both established that we're curious beasts."

She laughed ruefully. "I was so startled that I jerked on the reins and my horse almost threw me."

"A good thing you're a fine rider."

"Indeed. Getting my mount under control gave me a moment to collect myself. When the horse was settled, I saw that Matthew looked embarrassed and belligerent and Susannah and her beautiful little children looked terrified."

"Why terrified? Did you look murderous?"

"Possibly," she admitted. "I'd developed a reputation for being forceful, so Susannah feared what I might do.

Actually, what influence I had with Matthew I used to improve conditions for his slaves. I persuaded him to discharge a brutal overseer and I made sure the workers had decent food and medical attention. That doesn't mean she wasn't justified in fearing what I might do under such circumstances."

"Was Matthew also terrified of you?"

"Very likely," she said wryly. "I was always civil and respectful of him, but I had a stronger personality than he. I think I made him nervous."

Fascinated, Gordon asked, "What did you do after discovering your husband's secret family?"

"I told Susannah she and her children had nothing to fear from me, and said to Matthew that we would discuss the matter later."

He was about to ask Callie how that discussion with her husband had gone when harsh voices intruded from the street. He crossed the room in two steps and dowsed the lamp. Callie drew a breath to ask what he was doing, so he swiftly put a hand over her mouth. In a whisper, he explained, "British soldiers are out there and looking for loot, I suspect. Better they not discover this cottage or my horse."

She nodded and he removed his hand, but he didn't move away. In the heavy darkness, he was acutely aware of her. He felt her anxiety, and also her courage.

Coarse words were becoming clearer as the looters came closer. Gordon's mouth tightened as he realized the soldiers were speculating on the best houses to rob. In a breath of voice that couldn't have been heard more than a yard away, he whispered, "Not troops who entered Washington with Ross. Probably they came from the British camp just outside the city."

A cockney voice cut through the babble. "The white 'ouse with the blue trim. Let's break in there. Whatever traitor owns it has plenty of blunt and we deserve a share!"

Callie breathed an anguished sigh. "The Marquands' house! They've always been good neighbors to me. Can you do anything to stop those men?"

Because it was Callie asking, he actually considered for a moment before saying with regret, "Sorry, but the odds of facing down soldiers who may be drinking and are far from their commanding officer are not good. The risk might be worth it to save a life, but not possessions."

"You're very pragmatic for a bold adventurer," she said, her voice dry.

"That's how one has a chance of becoming an aged adventurer, which is my goal," he said firmly. As the loud voices continued, he rested one hand on her shoulder, offering the comfort of touch. It seemed right to comfort his old friend Callie, though it would be easier if she wasn't now grown-up, alluring Callie.

CRAAASH!!! A shocking clamor of sounds, frighteningly close, sent heat and debris blasting through the night. Blows hammered the roof like an angry giant and the soldiers outside bellowed shocked curses. Callie made a strangled noise and Gordon caught her into an embrace.

"It's all right," he murmured as he held her trembling body. "That was the sound of the frame and walls of your house collapsing from the fire damage. The thumps on the roof were probably bricks thrown by the collapse. Luckily this cottage is far enough away and protected by the trees so there was no real damage. With the ground wet from recent rains the fire shouldn't spread."

"Sorry, I'm not usually such a nervous rabbit," she said in a shaky voice. "I'm so glad I sent the rest of my household away!"

She made no move to leave his arms, and he was in no hurry to release her. "After a day like this, you've earned the right to have strong hysterics. But this night will end, and tomorrow will be better."

The soldiers noisily agreed to find a different house to loot. As the voices faded, Callie exhaled softly and stepped away from Gordon. "You're right. There's no point in staying here and mourning what I've lost. I'll be off to Baltimore in the morning."

He found the wine by touch and poured two glasses, pressing one into her hand before drawing her down to sit beside him on the old sofa. In the dark quiet, he was very aware of her warm body mere inches away. He swore silently to himself. The problem was that he hadn't been with a woman in far too long, so his body was reacting too strongly to her alluring femininity.

But this was no random widow with a roving eye and an interest in mutual pleasure. This was his friend Callie, who had endured a shattering day and by the sounds of it, a rather trying life.

He took her hand for comfort, no more. "How did your life change after you discovered your husband's mistress?"

"I kicked him out of my bed," she said succinctly. "Matthew's first English wife sounded dreadful, which is likely why he took up with Susannah. I told him I'd continue as his hostess and mistress of the plantation, but he had broken our wedding vows, so he'd lost his marital rights where I was concerned."

He smiled into the darkness. Now that was the bold, defiant Callie he'd grown up with. "Most men would not take that well."

"I think Matthew was rather relieved to no longer be living a double life," Callie said thoughtfully. "He truly did love Susannah and their children, and they loved him."

"Did you consider going back to England then?"

"To the hell of my father's house? Or as a pathetic grass widow with no children or purpose for living? No," she said flatly. "In Jamaica, I was busy and did useful work. Matthew and I rubbed along very comfortably after the dust and emotions settled down."

"It sounds like a less than ideal marriage."

She shrugged. "There are many worse. Matthew treated me with kindness and respect and I was able to do what I wanted most of the time." A smile entered her voice. "That part I liked. Life is much more rewarding when a woman doesn't have a man causing her problems."

"Should I be offended on behalf of my sex?"

She laughed. "You've always made my life better, not worse. But you are not a normal man."

"I'm fairly sure I'm offended," he said with amusement.

"Think of my remark as a compliment," she said reassuringly. "Matthew was a rather weak man, but he had a kindly nature. I was fortunate that he wasn't a hard-drinking brute like too many of the other plantation owners."

"And he was fortunate that you were able to accept the situation and adapt your marriage in ways that benefited you both."

"I was much happier when I stopped thinking of Matthew as my husband. Once the truth was out, Susannah and I became good friends. She was a lovely, kind woman, and I fell in love with the children. I made sure they received an education equal to what a plantation owner's legitimate children would have." She halted for a moment, then continued with a catch in her voice. "When Susannah was dying, I promised her I'd look after them as if they were my own."

"I assume Matthew emancipated Susannah and his children?"

Callie said a rude word. "He said he would, but he never got around to it. He died not long after Susannah, and his death put his children at risk."

"Which is why you fled Jamaica with them?"

"Yes, and I brought Susannah's parents with me. Sarah and Joshua were both half European, the children of plantation owners by slaves. They were the butler and housekeeper at the plantation and they love Susannah's children as much as I do. I asked them to come with us and gave them emancipation papers immediately. But there might have been legal problems since Matthew had a legitimate son by his first wife. Henry was the heir, and he was not the sort of man to free valuable slaves."

Finally understanding, he said, "Which is why you came here and changed your name so he couldn't find you or the children."

"Exactly. Matthew brought me to Washington and Baltimore several times over the years, so I knew both cities." She laughed a little. "Well, Washington is more town than city, but it has aspirations, or did before the British decided to burn down everything important. Baltimore is much larger and Matthew owned a warehouse with living quarters above, so I sent my household to stay there. Now I need to join them to make sure everyone's safe."

"How do you plan to reach Baltimore when most of Washington has fled, taking virtually all of the horses, carriages, and wagons with them?"

"I'll walk if I have to," she said calmly. "I can reach the city in two or three days. With luck, a wagon or carriage might take me along."

He winced at the thought of her hiking the distance through a war-disturbed countryside. "*Not* a good idea. I came here from London on a ship that is now tucked into one of the creeks off the Potomac, so we can sail to Baltimore."

"That could be problematic, too, but I'll think about it in the morning. I'm so tired my mind is refusing to work." She sighed wearily. "Perhaps we can take turns sleeping while one person watches in case roving soldiers turn up."

"Don't worry about that." He stood, then scooped her from the sofa. "I'm a light sleeper and haven't had as tiring a day as you, so I'll keep watch. Now you must sleep."

She squeaked with surprise, then relaxed in his arms as he carried her to the small bedroom. Since there wasn't much furniture, he managed to avoid tripping and dropping her, which would have interfered with his manly attempts to sweep her away.

He laid her on the side of the bed that was against the wall so she was securely tucked in. She murmured, "There's a light coverlet folded across the foot of the bed."

It had cooled a little, so he found the coverlet by touch and spread it over her. She was already asleep. He had been telling the truth about being a light sleeper, and he put his brain on alert for any threatening sounds.

That done, he couldn't think of a good reason why they shouldn't share the bed, which was a damn sight more comfortable than the floor or the sofa. Quietly he lay down beside her, releasing his breath in a long sigh as he rolled onto his side and laid his left arm over Callie's waist.

They were perilously close, especially since she wore only a shift and he was in shirt and drawers, but no matter. For the first time in more years than he could count, all seemed right with the world.

Chapter 8

Callie was jarred awake by cannon fire. No, not artillery but thunder, because a blaze of nearby lightning briefly glared through the room. She relaxed, much preferring a violent thunderstorm to an attacking army.

She drowsed, feeling wonderfully relaxed in every fiber of her body. Another flash of lightning and almost instant thunder rattled the roof and brought her more awake. Memory returned with a shock as she realized that she was not home in her own bed because her house had been burned to the ground by the British.

She was in the guest cottage, and she was not alone in the bed. She jerked to full wakefulness, momentarily panicked. Then she relaxed. It was Richard, miraculously alive. He lay on his side behind her with his arm resting on her waist. Even in the darkness, she recognized him by his scent and some mysterious essence of her old friend.

To her relief, Richard stirred and removed his arm

from her waist. "Your thunderstorms are as extreme as your heat."

"True, but the rain that's pounding down should put out the fires, and that's a blessing." She stretched luxuriously, arching her back and extending her arms over her head. "I can't remember when I've slept so well. You make me feel safe. Remember when we decided to use each other's middle names?"

"It was raining, though not as fiercely as now," he said immediately. "We were very young then, barely out of the nursery. We'd walked out to the lake at Kingston Court and were on our way home when the storm struck, so we took shelter in a hay barn. You said I didn't look like a George, and asked what other names I had."

She laughed. "I liked the name Gordon better, but the sound is too hard, and Augustus is pompous. Richard is softer and warmer. More like you." Ever since that day in the hay barn, he'd been Richard to her.

"There are few who would consider me soft or warm," he said with amusement. "Apart from my nurse, no one else has ever called me Richard. But I liked the idea of us having private names for each other, so we picked through your names as well."

"You said Catherine was too dignified for an unruly chit like me. That left Callista, which you promptly shortened to Callie."

"The name is unusual, like you, but the nickname Callie is more mischievous," he explained. "I liked that Callisto was one of Artemis's huntresses in Greek mythology."

"I liked being a huntress, but I later learned that the name means 'most beautiful.' I'm sure you didn't intend that."

He chuckled. "Thinking back, you were a remarkably pretty little girl, but I never noticed because of the tangled hair and mud on your face."

"Ha! Were you any better?"

"Worse," he said promptly. "We spurred each other into trouble."

"We were never mean to other children, though. It was innocent fun." She sighed nostalgically. "I'm so glad to have my brother back."

A flare of lightning briefly illuminated the room and she saw that Richard had arched his brows. "You have a brother and I am not he."

"I scarcely remember Marcus. He was so small when I left England. Still in the nursery. He turned twenty-one recently. I expect my parents gave a grand ball to celebrate the heir's coming of age."

"Very likely," Richard agreed. "But here and now, I want to make the point that I am not your brother, and I do not regard you as a sister."

"But we were brother and sister to each other," she protested. "You had no sisters and my brother wasn't old enough to be a playmate, so we shared sibling ways of getting into trouble. Getting muddy in the creek together, riding and learning to jump fences, and covering up each other's crimes. Being punished together, too. You were a much better brother than my actual brother."

"I am *not* your brother," he said with an edge to his voice.

"No?" She blinked as another flash of lightning briefly illuminated his silhouette and strong, elegant features. She felt a sense of loss, as if his denial of their childhood relationship took away a treasured part of her past. "I liked having you as a brother."

"I am *not* your brother!" he repeated, his voice rough this time. And he leaned forward and kissed her.

As his lips covered hers with warm command, shock jolted through her. This was not the way things were supposed to be!

Her startled reaction was swiftly followed by sensations different from any she'd ever experienced. Heady, disturbing feelings curled through her from head to toes, bringing alive all parts in between.

She'd barely started to feel interest in the male half of the species when she'd been married off to a man three times her age. Matthew was always gentle with her, even in his brief, ardent honeymoon phase, but she'd never felt more than mild curiosity and dutiful acceptance in their marital bed.

This—*this* was different, and for the first time she understood why women ruined themselves with men. She felt a promise of something wild and compelling in Richard's touch, and it terrified her. When he moved a warm hand to her waist, mere inches from her unbound breasts, she shoved herself away from him, ending up plastered against the wall beside the bed. "This is a really, really bad idea!" she said in a choked voice.

"You're undoubtedly right." Seeing her reaction, he made no attempt to move closer or kiss her again. "But I wanted to make it clear that I am not your brother. Though I never had a sister, I'm sure I wouldn't feel this way about her."

"I should hope not!" Another bolt of lightning lit Richard's composed features. He didn't look like a menacing brute, but he was a great deal more than her childhood friend. She'd bought a large bed so married guests could be comfortable, but now it was filled with Richard, who dominated the space and the

very air she breathed. He was all strength and power
and she was acutely aware that she wore only a whisper
thin muslin shift and he wasn't wearing much more.

She started to scramble from the bed, but he caught
her wrist. "Stay, Catkin," he said softly. "Dawn is still
some time away, and I promise that nothing will happen that you don't want to happen."

She hesitated, then realized that she believed him.
Besides, at this hour of the night, with rain thundering
down on the cottage, there wasn't really anywhere else
to go. She lay back on her pillow, still tucked in the corner between bed and wall, and pulled the lightweight
coverlet over her.

She couldn't, *wouldn't*, believe that her friend Richard
would harm her, but she feared the male aggression and
dominance he radiated. She'd been suppressing fear
ever since she fled Jamaica. The day just past had
brought those fears to the surface, so she ruthlessly
suppressed them again. Her situation was difficult but
not disastrous, and she must focus on her real problems, not let herself be flustered by a man. "What I
want to happen is a swift, safe journey to Baltimore,"
she said coolly. "With no complications from you."

"Understood." He settled down again on his side,
facing her. He took up less space that way. "But I do
hope I've been reclassified from being your brother."

"You have. I'm not sure if that's good or bad," she
said, wishing he really was her brother. That would be
so much easier.

"Not good or bad, it just is," he said. "We aren't children anymore, Callie. We have a foundation of deep
friendship, but we're adults now."

She'd never thought about his voice when they were
children, but she realized that his adult voice was quite

lovely. Rich and flexible and dangerously persuasive. "Very true. Adults have less trust and time, and more doubts and fears and responsibilities."

"Yes, and my responsibility is to keep you safe from the dangers of war, which includes reuniting you with your family," he said peaceably.

"My English family, or my real family?"

"Your English family is paying for this mission, but where you go from here is your choice. When I was asked to take this mission, I made it clear I wouldn't try to coerce you to travel back to England against your will. Though I do wonder if you've ever considered returning there."

"I dream of England sometimes." And when she did, it was usually the joyful hours with Richard. "Cool. Green. Home in a way that the New World has never been. But I won't return to England and live as a poor relation. I like having the freedom to live my life as I think best. I'll start another dressmaking business in Baltimore. It will take time to build a clientele, but the city is far larger than Washington, and it's wealthy. I'll manage, and I'll do it on my terms."

"The traditional way for a woman to support her household is through marriage," he observed. "Beautiful women like you seldom lack for male interest, yet I gather you took no lovers after you banished your husband from your bed?"

The faint lift at the end of the sentence made it a question. She was grateful for the darkness that hid her flush. "I would not dishonor Matthew by being unfaithful. Nor was I tempted by any of the available men."

"There is nothing like lack of temptation to promote virtue," he said dryly. "But you're a widow now and marriage would make your situation much easier."

She snorted. "That's a very male way of thinking! One marriage was more than enough. I will not repeat the experience. I'll manage very well on my own."

After a thoughtful silence, he said, "Part of my mandate is to make sure that you're not in dire financial circumstances. Money would be very useful for rebuilding your life if you decide not to return to England, and I have a good deal of money at my disposal."

Surprised, she said, "Andrew Harding must be a very wealthy man to spend all this on a woman he's never even met!"

"He's wealthy, and I presume his wife is very persuasive."

"I have trouble imagining any of my sisters being that persuasive, but I haven't seen them in fifteen years." She had a brief mental image of how they had all looked dressed up for Callie's wedding, just before she'd left Rush Hall forever. "If I went back, it would be a shock to see them all grown up."

"I sometimes wonder about my various brothers, but not enough to actually find out what they're doing," Richard said. "The two older ones were rather rotten, and the youngest were still schoolboys. Since three different mothers were involved and we were sent to different schools, I don't know them well. Particularly not the two younger ones."

"My children know and love each other. That's the way families should be. Which is another reason not to marry. I could never, ever take a husband who would look down on them because of their mixed blood."

"That does call for caution in marriage," he agreed. "People are usually on their best behavior when courting. Reality may come as a rude shock after the wedding."

"So many good reasons not to marry." Since it was

easy to talk in the darkness, she asked, "What about you? Are you married? Or have you ever been?"

"Good Lord, no!" he said, clearly startled by the idea. "I've led far too irregular a life for marriage. No sane woman would want to take me on."

But his looks and charm could easily make a woman forget her sanity. Curious, she asked, "What do you wish for? Are you rooted back in England? Do you want a wife and children? Do you want to fulfill the Englishman's dream of owning your own estate and becoming the local squire?"

He huffed out a breath and she heard him roll onto his back. She guessed he was staring up into the darkness when he replied. "Once I would have said no. I've led an erratic life, and while some parts were terrifying and painful, others were very rewarding. I wouldn't trade my past, even the parts I regret. But . . ."

When his voice trailed off, she prompted, "But what?"

"I'm over thirty now. Five years ago I had an experience that made me take a closer look at my life. I'd done too many things I'm not proud of. Sowing wild oats is relatively acceptable when one is young, but eventually, it becomes—unseemly. Since then, I've tried to be a better person. To help others where it's needed."

Fascinated, she asked, "What was the experience that changed your direction?"

"Imminent execution," he said succinctly. "I was in northern Portugal when the French were overrunning the place. Five of us ended up imprisoned in a damp cellar and condemned to be shot at dawn as English spies. We drank bad brandy and talked about how we would reform our lives if by some miracle we survived."

He sounded so *casual* about a sentence of death! "Obviously you survived. You lived up to your resolution?"

"Yes, that's how I took up my present line of work. I find solutions for people who don't have the means to solve certain problems themselves."

"That sounds admirable," she said. "And so you are here, rescuing a prodigal widow on behalf of a very rich man."

He laughed a little. "The work is worthy and the pay is very good. But as I said, since reaching the great age of thirty, I've started to think there must be something more. I just haven't figured out quite what."

"Marriage, family, and a manor house?" she suggested. "As I recall, you had an inheritance from your godfather. Might that be enough to become a country gentleman?"

"I imagine it would be, though contacting the family lawyer would mean the risk of actually meeting my father or brothers," he said without enthusiasm. "My interactions with the noble Audleys have consisted of occasionally sending a note to the family lawyer saying something like, 'Sorry to inform you that I'm still alive!' "

She laughed out loud. "I see you haven't entirely outgrown your desire to irritate your relations."

"No, so it's just as well I don't see them," he said without regret. "If I ever do become a country squire, I'm unlikely to run into my grand relations since they're such snobs and prefer to avoid the lower orders. Personally, I find the lower orders so much more interesting than most members of the beau monde."

"You're Lord George Gordon Richard Augustus Audley, third son of the Marquess of Kingston," she said with a smile. "Not precisely one of the lower orders."

"My father would disagree," he said dryly.

"Your father is hopeless, but it might be possible to become friends with your brothers. Surely one or two of them are worth knowing?"

"Perhaps," he allowed. "It would have to be one of the younger brothers since the two older ones are deeply unpleasant. I prefer friends to family because we get to choose our friends."

"If you decide to marry and settle down, your wit, handsome face, title, and a moderate fortune will make it easy to find a wife who can be both friend and lover."

"Finding a good mate is the most difficult thing on earth, I suspect," he said pensively. "My title isn't much use since it's merely courtesy. You didn't seem to be very impressed by becoming Lady George Audley."

She chuckled. "I was too surprised to be impressed. Besides, I don't like the name Lady George any more than I liked you being Lord George."

"With luck, you won't have to pretend to be Lady George again." He took her hand casually, his fingers lacing through hers. "We should be able to get another hour or two of rest before facing the new day, which is apt to be a busy one."

She covered a yawn. "That's a good plan. Sleep well, Richard. And dream of a suitable wife who is a friend, along with a happy, uneventful life."

As she drifted off, she heard him murmur, "I don't know if that's possible, Catkin. Because the only woman I've ever come close to marrying is you."

Chapter 9

Morning had arrived when Gordon woke up, though the soft light said it was still early. The odor of burned wood was in the air, but the temperature was relatively cool for the moment.

Callie had moved during the night and rolled into him, her head tilted against his upper arm and her soft curves pressed along his side. She looked much younger and thoroughly irresistible in the pearly light. A few strands of apricot hair had curled loose against her fair skin. He felt a surge of pure, mindless desire, a need to bend over for a kiss and caress her into joyful morning passion. . . .

Except that he damned well had to resist for more reasons than he had fingers and toes to count on. Reasons that started with "war zone" and continued to Callie currently having zero interest in him or any other man. Maybe later, when she was safe and her life sorted out, she'd be more open to dalliance. Or maybe that would never happen. She seemed quite determined to keep men out of her life, and he understood why. The men in her life had not done well by her.

Thinking of all she'd endured produced a deep tenderness shadowed by past, present, and future. The past was bright memories of playfulness and long conversations right up till they'd been wrenched apart and sent into different forms of exile. The present was delight, danger, and an absolute duty to get her safely away from this cursed city and reunited with the children who gave her life meaning.

The future was a mystery—except that he knew Callie had to be part of it. What that meant for him, he couldn't guess, but no matter. He'd work it out as it came along. Today, escape to Baltimore, collect her family, then off to England posthaste.

He knew in his bones it wouldn't be that easy.

Callie stirred and her eyes snapped open as she remembered where she was. Her hazel gaze was golden in the dawn, and the intimacy between them stabbed with rapier depth and intensity. He wanted to bolt from the bed like a scalded cat.

He didn't have to because Callie beat him to it. She scrambled along the wall and off the end of the bed. When she stood, the coverlet fell away to reveal her body backlit by a shaft of sunshine that turned her shift translucent. Desire stirred again, but it was no match for his panic. Where the devil did that reaction come from?

He'd think about it later. For now, he slammed the door on his wildly veering thoughts and swung his feet to the floor. "How much needs to be done before we can leave? I presume you want to say good-bye to Mrs. Turner. Do you have any possessions in this cottage to carry away?"

"I do want to say good-bye to Edith, but otherwise

I'll be traveling very light," she said ruefully. She pulled her blue gown from the clothespress. "All I have is the clothes I wore and my pistol. Luckily the skirt on this gown is full enough for me to ride astride behind you without being too indecent."

"I have a better solution." He stepped into the sitting room and opened one of the saddlebags he'd left by the door the night before, then removed two neatly folded garments. He handed them to Callie, then extracted a flattened hat, which he shaped into a wide-brimmed sun shade suitable for gardening or field work. "Wear these clothes. They'll be loose, but not as loose as anything of mine."

Her brows rose as she accepted the tan trousers, linen shirt, and hat. "You regularly carry around clothing that doesn't fit?"

"When I'm going to rescue widows from war zones, yes," he explained. "There are women who would rather die than wear male garments, but I like to be prepared. Female clothing isn't well designed for escaping trouble. Climbing out of windows or riding astride are much easier in breeches. Because I wasn't sure what size my widow would be, I erred on the side of large."

She shook out the shirt, which fell to midthigh. "You certainly did. But it's smaller than one of yours."

"You'll look like an urchin, but that's not a bad thing in these circumstances." He thought a moment. "You were wearing sturdy half boots, weren't you? That's good. Much better than delicate little slippers."

"Like you, I was thinking ahead in case I might have to run for my life. Will you pack this in your saddlebag?" She handed over the blue gown, then disappeared into the bedroom to change.

He dressed also, pulling on his trousers and boots

and tucking his shirt in. The heavy London coat could wait till they left. He explored the food basket Mrs. Turner had provided the evening before and found crumbly biscuits, a medium-sized chunk of cheese, and a bottle of tepid but flavorful lemonade.

Callie emerged from the bedroom in her shirt and trousers, her hair braided and pinned up so she'd look like a boy when wearing the hat. As she settled at the table to eat, she said, "I gather you'll be in full lordly array."

"Yes, and envying you for being lightly dressed," he said feelingly. "But if we run into British troops, I may need to become all lordly again." He sat opposite her and split a biscuit, then laid a slice of cheese in the middle.

When they'd finished eating, Callie packed the empty bottles into the basket along with the remaining food. "I'll take this back to Edith when I say good-bye. I'll miss her."

Gordon rose and pulled his coat on. "I'll saddle Samson while you take a last look around."

"There's nothing here worth carrying away." She moved into the bedroom and returned with a folded blanket and her pistol. "It's going to be awkward riding on your saddlebags. This blanket can be used as a pad so I won't be so uncomfortable."

He accepted the blanket and pistol. "I presume this is loaded from yesterday. Rather than pack it away, better to ride with it ready to hand."

"It's loaded. Perhaps it will be more useful today than last night." She bit her lip as she gazed at the weapon. "But . . . I don't know if I can shoot a man. Though I'm a good shot, last night when those soldiers broke into my house I couldn't bring myself to pull the trigger. Since shooting only one man wouldn't save me and would probably get me killed, I was spared from having to fire, but today . . . might be different. I'm afraid I won't be able to do what is needed."

"It's hard to deliberately choose to kill another human being," he said seriously. "I've had to do so, and it wasn't easy. It's not something I make a habit of. But a warning shot can have a sobering effect on attackers, and if anyone really needs to be killed, I'll take care of it."

She smiled wryly. "As much as I like to proclaim how capable I am, that's one responsibility I'll gladly leave to you."

"I learned such skills the hard way, so I'll do what's needed. But sparingly." He lifted the saddlebags and added her folded blanket. "I'll saddle Samson. We can walk him down to Mrs. Turner's house for your farewells."

She lifted the basket. "I'll look around to see if there's anything Edith might be able to use, then join you out in the street."

He nodded and headed outside. The acrid scent of smoke was much stronger there, but the storm in the early hours had saturated the ground and smothered some of the odors.

Samson had made good use of the fodder and water and looked ready to face the day. Callie's idea of the blanket pad was good and Gordon secured it across the saddlebags on Samson's broad back. When he led his mount from the shed, he saw that Callie was in the street but had turned right toward the remains of her house rather than left toward Mrs. Turner's.

Leading Samson, he followed her. She stopped and stared at the ruins of her home, her face like granite. Charred bricks and blackened timbers had collapsed into rough piles, and rain had turned the ashes into a filthy mess. At the far edge of the wreckage, a thin wisp of smoke rose.

Abruptly she pivoted and walked toward him, her jaw set. "I'm sorry, Catkin," he said quietly.

Ignoring his sympathy, she said, "Thus ends one act of my life. We'll see what comes next."

He fell into step beside her, Samson ambling obediently behind. He realized that they'd avoided looking each other in the eyes since that disturbing moment when they woke up. The relationship between them was compelling but impossible to define.

"I had concealed holsters built into the front edge of the saddlebags." He tapped the left bag. "Your pistol is in here, not visible but easy to draw if necessary."

"You remembered that I'm left-handed," she said, surprised.

"Of course, since I am, too." He chuckled. "Sinister, which means 'left' in Latin. It gave our fathers another reason to believe we were limbs of Satan."

She smiled, much of her tension fading. "They never lacked for reasons to believe that. Nor did they ever realize that treating a child as if it's wicked will make it genuinely wicked in time."

Interested, he asked, "Is the opposite true? If you treat a child as if it's good, does it become so?"

"Probably, but I'm not sure. My children have always been good."

Their conversation ended when Edith Turner saw them and came outside. She stared at Callie. "I'd not have recognized you, Lady George! Are you leaving now?"

"Yes, I came to say good-bye and to leave you the key to the cottage. Feel free to use it if needed." Callie set the basket on the ground and gave her friend a hug. "I don't know if I'll ever come back here."

Since tears seemed imminent, Gordon said, "I'll take good care of her, Mrs. Turner."

"I'm sure you will." Hug ended, Mrs. Turner dabbed at her eyes. "Your beautiful house is gone, but the land is very well situated. Will you sell it?"

Callie looked blank. "I hadn't thought of that, but you're right. It's a good location. I suppose Washington will still exist no matter how this beastly war turns out, and the property is of no use to me anymore."

"If someone is interested, do you have a lawyer I can refer them to?"

Callie frowned. "A lawyer over in Georgetown has handled several small matters for me. Mr. Key, Francis Scott Key. Do you know him? I made some gowns for his wife and became friends with both of them."

"I know the name and will send any interested buyers to him," Mrs. Turner replied. "Take care, my dear, and write when you're properly settled again."

Callie promised to do so. Gordon mounted, then offered Callie a hand. She took it, set her foot on his stirruped boot, and swung up behind him. "Please say good-bye to my other friends for me, Edith."

"I will. They'll miss you and your wonderful gowns as well. Have a safe journey!"

Gordon couldn't agree more.

Chapter 10

～❧～

The streets of Washington were quietly tense. A few people went about their business, their gazes wary. Callie saw a peddler, a free black named Harry, driving from house to house in his pony cart filled with fresh produce. She'd often bought fruit and vegetables from him. The sight was comforting. Washington might be an occupied city, but life was going on.

Better to wander about the city than to think how close she was to Richard's very masculine body. Waking up in the same bed with him this morning had been deeply unnerving because part of her found it very natural. Desire had never been part of her life, but apparently it had been lying dormant and was now beginning to stir. The timing was not good.

They turned a corner and saw a large number of British troops marching toward the burned-out President's House. Nearby was a large brick building that had been untouched. Callie said, "It looks like they're

heading toward that building, which has the head-
quarters of the State, War, and Navy Departments."

"Judging by the men carrying powder and rockets,
those departments are going to get the same treatment
as other government buildings," Richard said grimly.
"Perhaps another route would be wise."

Before Callie could reply, a man galloped from an
alley shouting insults at the British in a wild one-man
attack. He raised a pistol and shot—and was immediately brought down by a barrage of return fire. As the
rider fell bleeding, Richard turned Samson and spurred
the horse into a canter. "Definitely another route! You
know this city. Give me directions."

"Go to the end of this block and turn left." She swallowed hard, shaken by the swift, unexpected violence.
"Why would a man do such a suicidal thing?"

"At a guess, he hates the British and got drunk
enough to behave stupidly," Richard said tersely. "With
the results you see."

He was probably right, but she was reminded how
deadly an occupying army could be. A few minutes later
they came on another group of soldiers smashing up a
business while a fire burned behind the building.
"That's Admiral Cockburn supervising," Richard said.
"Do you know what the business is?"

"A newspaper, the *National Intelligencer*. The editor
has been writing inflammatory articles about the British
in general and Cockburn in particular," Callie said. "It
looks like the admiral is taking a personal revenge.
Turn right at this corner."

Richard silently obeyed. By keeping to smaller streets
with no government buildings, they avoided any more
ugly conflicts.

They were nearing the edge of the city when a patrol
of British soldiers led by an officer on horseback

emerged from a cross street and came straight for Callie and Richard. The officer barked, "Halt!"

"Should we try to outrun them?" she asked in a voice that surprised her with its calmness.

"If we did, they might think we have reason to run and shoot us down. Better to bluster it out. We are English, after all. Not their enemy."

"Speak for yourself," she said flatly. "I live and work here. I could be considered treasonous."

"Urchins are beneath the notice of British officers," Richard assured her before pulling Samson to a stop and waiting for the officer to intercept them.

"Who are you and what is your business?" the lieutenant asked in a menacing tone. Callie surreptitiously laid her left hand on the butt of her pistol, but she didn't draw it out.

"My name is Lord George Audley and I'm busy about the king's affairs," Richard replied with an aristocratic accent sharp enough to cut glass.

"So you're a lord," the lieutenant sneered. "And I'm bloody Bonaparte! You sound English, all right, but I'm betting you're a treasonous Yankee."

"A bet you'll lose," Richard said in full lordly mode. "Shall I show you my letters of introduction?"

"You can, but that doesn't mean I'll believe them."

Richard reached inside his coat and produced an oilskin pouch, opening it with great deliberation. "This should do." He handed over a folded piece of paper. "Be careful with it."

The officer opened the letter and scanned the brief lines, then gasped. "Lord Liverpool? The prime minister?"

"Yes. Would you prefer a letter from Lord Castlereagh? As foreign secretary, he might be appropriate under these conditions." Richard smiled with knife-

edged arrogance. "Or if you hold on a moment, I believe I have a letter from the Duke of Wellington, who
is most relevant of all."

Suppressing his rage, the lieutenant handed back
the letter from Lord Liverpool. "What are you doing
in a conquered enemy capital?"

Richard folded the letter, tucked it in the oilskin
pouch, and returned it to his inside pocket. "That, Lieutenant, is none of your damned business. Now let us
pass!"

The officer gestured to his men and an aisle opened
up through the middle of the patrol. Callie's skin crawled
as they rode through the group of scowling soldiers.
One exclaimed, "That's a bloody woman riding behind him!"

"You brought your own whore?" the lieutenant
snarled.

Richard whipped around and said with lethal intensity, "The lady is my *wife*. Last night a group of British
soldiers attacked Lady George and I barely rescued
her in time. Since our troops cannot be trusted to behave properly, do you blame her for going in disguise
for her own safety? Now, let us pass or there will be
blood!"

The lieutenant paled. "Get yourself gone and stay
away from British patrols!"

"Believe me, I intend to." Richard turned again and
they continued through the patrol and down the
street. Callie's back itched as they rode away from the
soldiers. She murmured, "What are the chances that
one of those soldiers will fire?"

"Slim, but not impossible," was Richard's honest
reply.

"I was afraid of that," she said grimly. "That horrid

lieutenant looked ready to do murder just because he could."

In an impeccable aristocratic accent, Richard said, "May all his rabbits die and he can't sell the hutches."

After a moment of shock, Callie burst into tension-relieving laughter. "I haven't heard anyone say that since I left Lancashire!"

Richard chuckled. "One reason I like 'the lower orders' is because they often have such wonderful turns of phrase."

"I miss the directness of northern England."

"Cooler there, too. The rain this morning did nothing to ease the temperature." He ran a finger around the edge of his cravat to loosen it a little. "I'll be glad to get back to the *Zephyr* so I can take this blasted coat and cravat off."

"They must be very uncomfortable," she said sympathetically. "But looking and talking like a lord does help when dealing with the British soldiers. It wouldn't work as well with Americans."

"I've noticed," he said, his accent moderating to one that would suit an educated man on either side of the Atlantic.

"Americans are odd," she mused. "They both despise and are fascinated by the British nobility. Since I had no desire to be noticed, I never mentioned that my father was a lord."

"Or that you were married to one," he said teasingly. "You handled our reunion scene very well. Most touching."

"The playacting we did as children came in handy then. But usually I prefer a combination of honesty and saying as little about myself as possible."

"Truth has the advantage of being easier to remem-

ber than multiple lies." He guided Samson to one side
of the road as a British military wagon rattled by with several soldiers inside. They gave Richard curious glances
but no more.

He continued, "We didn't finish our name discussion. I noticed Mrs. Turner called you Catherine,
which is common enough not to draw attention."

"I asked my husband to call me Callista, not Catherine, so I was Miss Callista in Jamaica. What name do
you generally use? Or have you had dozens over the
years?"

"Not *dozens*," he protested. After a moment of
thought, he said, "Well, maybe two dozen, but I've
only created false identities when it was useful. Mostly
I've gone by Gordon. As you say, it has a harder,
tougher sound than George or Richard, and Augustus
was never in the running. Gordon can be either a first
or last name, so it's nicely ambiguous."

"Like you."

"I like being ambiguous. It's safer that way."

She could understand that need for safety. After all,
she'd created a new identity for herself when she moved
to the United States. "With all your traveling and shifting identities, is there any place you call home?"

She was surprised when he said, "After returning to
England, I bought a house in a pleasant London neigh-
borhood, not far from Mayfair but less grand. I found
that I liked having a place to call home." After Samson
had taken another dozen steps, he added, "I was surprised to find that I look forward to returning when
I've been away."

Given all the challenges he'd survived after being
transported to New South Wales, she liked hearing
that he had matured to the point where he craved a
real home. Everyone needed a home. She felt a deep

pang for the house she had loved and where she had known happiness, but ultimately, it was just a house. The people who made it a home were waiting for her in Baltimore.

An ear-numbing explosion shattered the air. Placid Samson was so startled that he shied and jerked sideways. Callie instinctively grabbed Richard's waist for balance and for a moment they were in danger of being thrown.

"Hold on!" After several nerve-racking moments, Richard brought the horse under control again. He patted the sleek neck soothingly. "Samson doesn't like sudden loud noises."

"Neither do I!" Nerves jangling, Callie released her grip on his waist. "Do you have any idea what that might be?"

"An explosion that large is likely an American powder magazine, and it could have been set by either side to keep it from the hands of the enemy. I hope no one was nearby when it exploded." Richard set Samson into a fast walk. "I'll be glad to get out of Washington. Too many unpredictable things are happening."

Callie agreed wholeheartedly. Her tension eased when they left the city and headed east along a pleasantly rural road through heavy woodland. The tall trees kept the road cooler than the city, though the air was still heavy and ominously still. "How long a ride is it to our destination?"

"About two hours to Tucker Hall if nothing delays us. The ship should be waiting in Tucker Creek near the plantation."

She eyed the dark clouds roiling on the horizon. "There's a storm coming. I hope we reach our destination before it hits."

"Another storm?" He glanced up and saw the gathering clouds. "What a jolly place your Maryland is!"

"Afternoon thunderstorms are common here in high summer, but they're usually limited in scope. It can be pouring rain on one side of Washington and dry on the other. With luck, this storm might miss us." She studied the breadth of the dark, roiling clouds. "But I'm not optimistic."

Richard set Samson to a faster pace. "Neither am I. Though rain only makes us wet, which is mild compared to being threatened by armed soldiers."

"Rain would feel pleasantly cool about now," she said. "But summer storms can be fierce in this part of the world."

Swift flickers of lightning were visible in the approaching clouds, which suggested the storm would be a bad one. She wished they could take cover in a building, but the road was isolated and buildings were few and far between.

The sky darkened so much that Richard slowed Samson down so he could watch the footing on the rutted road. A breeze began to stir the heavy air. Gradually it strengthened to wind, and then to near-gale strength. Small branches and dead leaves from the previous autumn whirled through the air, occasionally hitting with stinging force. Fat, heavy raindrops began to fall.

At first there was just a spattering. Then trees began crashing in the woods and all hell broke loose.

Chapter 11

❧

In an instant the rain went from sprinkles to blowing sideways in sheets, soaking Callie and Richard to the skin. At first the water was blessedly cooling, but as the wind picked up, she began feeling chilled.

Raising his voice against the roar of wind and rain, Richard called over his shoulder, "I wish now we'd taken shelter earlier, but I'd hoped to reach Tucker Hall before the storm. We're not far now, so hang on. We'll be safe indoors soon."

"Getting wet feels good, though it isn't doing your beautiful coat any good!" she said cheerfully. "The rain could stop as suddenly as it started. These storms pass over quickly." At least, they usually did. This was the most violent storm she'd seen since a hurricane hit Jamaica. Or maybe it just seemed worse because usually she wasn't outdoors when such weather struck.

She flinched as lightning blazed overhead and bone-rattling thunder followed almost immediately. Samson shied again and Richard had to use his considerable riding skill to keep the horse from bolting. "Samson is terrified by all these loud noises," he said as he slowed their pace to soothe the horse.

GA-GA-BOOOM! Searing lightning and thunder were now simultaneous. A tree crashed down across the road behind them and Samson panicked. He reared and bucked wildly. Falling, Callie released her grip on Richard's waist so she wouldn't drag him from the saddle along with her.

Experienced in falls, she tucked and rolled when she hit the ground. More lightning and thunder and more trees crashing in the adjacent woods. Nature was showing her what it was like to be inside an artillery barrage, she thought dizzily.

Richard managed to keep his seat, but as soon as he brought Samson under control, he swung from the saddle, asking urgently, "Callie, are you all right?"

"I'm fine." She accepted his hand up. "The ground is so soft that I won't even have bruises. But God be thanked we weren't a few yards farther back along the road!"

She stared at the great tree that had fallen, its leafy branches still vibrating from the impact with the earth. The trunk was easily a yard thick. They would have been dead if they'd been underneath when it crashed over.

Richard swore, but since he was standing at Samson's head he did it in the same soft, soothing voice he used to calm the horse. "It's not safe to stay here. There's a bridge over a creek just around the next bend. When I crossed yesterday, it felt sturdy, so I hope it's still passable. On the other side there's a small barn where we can shelter if the rain doesn't let up by then."

"Agreed. Will Samson cross the bridge?"

"I think so if I lead him. I don't blame him for being

frightened." He stroked the horse's neck, then started walking the muddy road again, Samson obediently falling into step beside him. "Stay close. Visibility is only a dozen feet in this rain."

"It beats bullets. I'll walk on Samson's other side and keep hold of a stirrup."

"Good lass. At least the rain will quickly wash the mud off you." He grinned at her over the saddle. His hat had been blown into the woods and his blond hair was darkened by the rain and he was the most beautiful, dashing man she'd ever seen.

Suddenly this was an adventure, not sodden drudgery, and she laughed out loud. "I'll be the cleanest woman in Maryland!"

Clean but windblown. Twigs and leaves banged into her, blown by the force of the wind. She reminded herself that this wouldn't last much longer. The hurricane in Jamaica had gone on for hours, but this wasn't Jamaica.

As Richard had predicted, the bridge was around the next bend in the muddy road. Vague outlines of a barn were visible on the other side of the creek. The building looked intact and it sat in a meadow with no trees close enough to crush the structure if they were blown over. She found that reassuring.

But first they had to cross the bridge, and the creek was close to overflowing with water raging downstream like wild horses. "I'm guessing that the water level wasn't this high when you came through yesterday!"

"It was four or five feet lower and the current was lazy by comparison," he said grimly. "The bridge still looks sound, though. It's made of several large logs laid across the creek with boards nailed on top to level it off. With pilings at both ends and railings, it should be safe if we cross before the water rises any higher."

Another tree crashed behind them, this one close

enough for leaves to brush Callie's heels. "Do you want me to walk across the bridge to test that it's still sound?"

"I'm heavier, so I'll do the testing. Take Samson."

She took hold of Samson's bridle, petting his neck and murmuring words of comfort. The horse was skittish at the sight of the bridge and rushing water, but he didn't look panicked. They should be able to lead him across safely.

Richard proceeded onto the bridge cautiously. Despite being hatless and saturated, he seemed still very much the gentleman.

As he'd told her, he was a pragmatic adventurer, not taking unnecessary risks, so he started by gripping the left side railing and shaking hard. It was merely a long, thin tree branch, irregular but solid. It didn't move.

Holding on to the railing, he stepped onto the boards of the bridge, stamping with one foot while keeping the other on land. The bridge vibrated from his stamping and the water beating against the pilings, but it was solid enough for safety.

The bridge was short, perhaps thirty feet long. After crossing with care, Richard returned at a much quicker pace. "That's a good piece of bridge building. Now let's get across into that barn before lightning or a flying tree hits us! You go first. Once you're safe on the other side, I'll bring Samson across."

Callie waited till Richard took control of the horse, then cautiously started across the bridge. After a brief lessening of intensity, the rain was again so heavy that she could barely see the opposite bank. Though the bridge felt solid, the shaking of the structure seemed much stronger now that she was actually walking on it. Water was starting to splash across the boards. A few more minutes and the bridge would be flooded.

She reached the other side and stepped gratefully onto land. Turning, she called, "Your turn!"

Samson was clearly nervous, but he'd been well trained. With Richard at his shoulder, he stepped warily onto the bridge and started to cross. Callie's gaze was so intent on man and horse that she didn't see a massive, uprooted tree sweeping full speed down the creek. Just before it slammed into the bridge, she recognized the danger and screamed, "Richard! Look out!"

Before she could say more, the tree's huge root ball slammed into the middle of the bridge, smashing the boards and tearing the underlying logs away from the pilings that had secured them. Samson reared in panic and tore free of Richard's grip. Callie instinctively tried to catch the horse as he galloped past her, but she failed and barely escaped falling under his thundering hooves.

Richard, where is Richard?

Dear God, he'd fallen into the raging current and was being swept away! One of the bridge railings had torn loose and was about to be dragged into the water. She grabbed hold before the water could take it and raced along the bank of the creek, the long railing dragging behind her.

A sapling tree had fallen into the water, its roots still tenuously connected to the bank. Richard managed to snag one of the upper branches, which reached almost the middle of the creek. The thin upper branches bent and the sapling's roots started to pull from the bank, but his hold slowed him down long enough for Callie to catch up with him. She shouted, "Grab this!"

He looked up and saw her shoving the railing through the water toward him. He released his hold on the sapling's branches just as the young tree was wrenched from the embankment. He was just able to catch the end of the railing before he was swept out of range. His weight almost pulled Callie into the water. She dove flat on the muddy embankment, holding grimly to the railing.

The slippery wood almost tore from her grip, but she managed to hang on while Richard hauled himself hand over hand along the railing toward her. There was blood in his hair and she guessed he'd been hit by floating debris. But he doggedly fought his way through the chaotic currents until he reached the bank.

She helped pull him onto land and for a long moment, they lay side by side gasping for breath as the rain pounded on their thoroughly saturated bodies. Richard said in a breathless voice, "I am really beginning to *loathe* this country of yours!"

She couldn't help but laugh. "I'm not that fond of this piece of America just now, either. Come on, we need to get to that barn."

She pushed herself to a sitting position and stared at the creek. The bridge was gone except for the pilings. "Are you hurt?"

He cautiously moved his arms and legs, then rubbed the bleeding area on his head, wincing a little. "Bruised, but I don't think anything is broken." He sat up, moving gingerly. "I assume Samson is halfway to his home barn by now."

"If I had four legs I'd be right behind him," she said wryly.

"Shall we get a roof over our heads?" He stood and offered her a hand. When they were both upright, he slung an arm around her shoulders and they wove their way to the barn, battered by the still falling rain.

"I think it's letting up a bit." She stumbled in a rut and he kept her from falling.

"Optimist. I think this is the first of forty days and nights that will drown the world." He lifted the iron latch that secured the doors and swung one open for her. She stepped inside, grateful to be out of the pounding rain.

He closed the door behind them, putting them in darkness except for the light coming in the ventilation holes under the eaves, which wasn't much because of how dark it was outside. Darkness heightened the fragrance of fresh green hay. She made an involuntary sound as the distinctive scent snapped her back fifteen years to the night when they'd taken shelter in a hay barn during their doomed elopement.

Richard's gaze moved around the familiar farm tools, rough beams, and stored fodder and he exhaled softly. "You're thinking of the barn we stayed in when we eloped, aren't you?"

"How could I not?" she said as she gazed at his dark outline. Because that was when everything in her life had changed.

Chapter 12

That Lancashire barn had been half a lifetime and thousands of miles away. He'd been a young fool not to recognize how disastrous their impulsive actions could be. And he was the damned fool who had suggested that they run away together.

He drew a deep, slow breath as he peeled off his heavy, saturated coat and dropped it on the floor in a soggy pile. Then he caught Callie's hand and drew her toward a soft, fragrant pile of hay. "Let's see if American hay is as comfortable as the British variety."

She went willingly, exhausted by the day and the danger. He lay on his side, studying her face. The dim light emphasized the delicacy of her features. Her hat had vanished as his had, and her long braid of red-gold hair had darkened with the rain.

"You look like a drowned rat," he said affectionately. "A very pretty drowned rat. Thank you for pulling me out of the water."

He bent his head, meaning to brush a light thank-

you kiss on her mouth, but her lips moved under his
and he found he couldn't stop because she was kissing
him back. His mind became as turbulent as the roar-
ing waters that had almost drowned him. He moved
closer and her arms came around him as she gave a
breathy little sigh.

Callie, Callie . . . His hand slid down to cup the soft
breast concealed under her wet, baggy shirt. She was
sweet and strong and deeply feminine, a woman like no
other. . . .

Abruptly she pulled away, crushing the hay and releasing a fresh clover scent. "No! I need you as a friend,
Richard! I don't have room in my life for anything else!"

He wanted to kiss her again and change her mind,
but he'd learned a few things over the years. "Sorry!
That was a grateful impulse gone awry. It shouldn't
have happened."

He rolled onto his back, his gaze fixed on the dim
patterns of light from the ventilation holes. "I didn't
mean anything more than a thank-you kiss, but you
have an . . . unfortunate effect on my common sense. I
keep forgetting that I'm here to help you, not make
your life more complicated."

"More complicated, but better." She drew a deep
breath, and he was pleased to see that he was affecting
her also. "Much of the blame is mine. I shouldn't have
kissed you back, but for a few moments there, it . . .
seemed like a good idea."

He'd thought it a splendid idea. But . . . "You terrify
me, Callie."

"Me?" She blinked at him. "I'm not even armed at
the moment!"

He laughed and the tension eased. "I'm reasonably
sure I could beat you in a fair fight, though probably
not an unfair one."

"The only kind I would attempt," she said promptly. "Why fight fair with someone twice my size?"

"That's my girl." He took her hand, making no attempt to move closer. "You're terrifying because—" He hesitated as he thought about it. "Over the years I've had my share of friends and enemies, but . . . I haven't been really close to anyone since I was a boy. And it was you then, too."

"I'm sorry," she said softly. "I can see why that would be disconcerting." After a long silence, she said, "I've been close to others, particularly the children and Sarah and Josh. But my friendship with you was a different kind of closeness. A kind I haven't known since our ways parted."

"Who could have guessed how far our lives would diverge given that we started in such similar places? I'm finding it very interesting." He squeezed her hand briefly. "Rest now, Catkin. I think the rain is letting up some. When it ends, we'll walk the last distance to Tucker Hall."

She exhaled roughly. "That's a good idea. Rain on the roof is much more soothing than rain beating down on one's head."

She closed her eyes and her breathing slowed. Still holding his hand, she rolled on her side so she was facing him, her features peaceful.

With sudden pain, he realized why Callie terrified him. It wasn't just that he'd not been close to anyone for fifteen years, but that he was no longer capable of such closeness. He'd survived by cultivating cool, ironic detachment.

He was capable of enjoying life and other people, but never so much that he couldn't leave without looking back. The capacity to feel deep emotional connection had died when he'd been convicted of theft and kidnapping and shoved onto a hell ship bound for the far side of the world.

On the whole, he thought he'd adapted well to the new life that had been forced on him. He'd survived and, while he'd done things he wasn't proud of, he hadn't become evil. But somewhere along the way, he'd lost his youthful capacity for hope and deep feeling.

Not the capacity for desire. That was alive and well, and he desired Callie with embarrassing intensity. But he cared for her enough not to want to do any damage. She'd suffered enough. She needed a friend.

He could manage that. She didn't need the complications of an affair, and he didn't need his life to be shattered again. Desire was a different matter, and he could control that. They'd be friends.

Forever friends.

He dozed as well, coming awake when he realized the rain was falling more gently and there were no more rumbles of thunder. He hadn't slept long, less than an hour, but he felt recovered from his most recent escape from death. The darkness in the barn had lessened as the storm passed, and when he opened his eyes he saw that Callie was also awake and watching him with thoughtful hazel eyes.

He smiled at her. "Hello, Catkin."

"I should call you Lion," she murmured. "Larger than a cat, but of the same nature. And the courage of a lion."

"Richard the Lionheart?" he asked with a chuckle.

"You have the tawny coloring for it."

"More or less. Didn't the Lionheart spend years kicking around the Holy Land getting into trouble rather than staying home in England and taking care of his responsibilities?"

She grinned. "The resemblance grows stronger."

He laughed. "The difference being that I'm not king of England and I have no responsibilities to the nation."

"But now you do have a home there," she said softly.

Yes, he had a home in London and he was bemused by how much he wanted to return to it. "It's a rather modest house, not a Plantagenet castle. There's not much damage I can do to England."

"Maybe not the nation, but just as the Lionheart was irresponsible to leave England at the mercy of his brother, now known as Bad King John, you have a bad brother, too. When the appalling Viscount Welham inherits and becomes Marquess of Kingston, he'll be the equivalent of Bad King John." Callie's nose wrinkled. "He was a nasty piece of work. He regularly tried to get me alone so he could paw me."

"*What!*" Gordon jerked to full wakefulness, shocked by her casual words. "Why didn't you tell me?"

"Because I thought you might kill him," she said flatly. "I didn't want to see you hanged."

"You're probably right," he said, trying to clamp down on his fury. He'd never liked Welham, the oldest and most bullying of the Audley brothers, but now he felt murderous. How *dare* that obnoxious brute try to molest Callie! "If I had killed him, I'd have been very careful to make it look like an accident."

"I should have thought of that," she said with a wry smile. "He might deserve killing for any number of reasons, but I prefer to think of people who wronged me the same way my nanny did." She grinned. "She always said, 'Get on with your business secure in the knowledge that God will get 'em eventually.' "

He chuckled and began to relax. "It's a wise philosophy. These days I usually do just that, but if Welham was here, I'd beat him bloody for what he did to you. I chased him away from housemaids, but I never thought he'd go after a well-born neighbor."

"I was good at avoiding him, so he was merely a nuisance, not a threat." Callie's expression changed. "You said earlier that you haven't been really close to anyone in years. What about bedmates? I don't imagine that you took any vows of chastity."

The unexpected question made Gordon roll onto his back and gaze up at the rough-hewn beams. Callie said with amusement, "I assume that means you don't want to discuss your romantic life."

"It's not a topic a gentleman, even a tarnished second-hand version like me, discusses with a lady." He slanted his gaze over to her. "But you're not a lady, you're Callie, and we've always been open with each other."

"I'll try to look on that as a compliment," she said. "How about if you tell me the truth, but not the whole truth? We all have our secrets."

"That's a good approach." He preferred not to think about the whole truth even in the privacy of his own mind. "Unlike Welham, I never touch unwilling women."

"That I've always known. You're much nicer than you look, Richard."

"No, I'm not," he said wryly. "But since I grew up with a female as my best friend, how could I go on to mistreat other women?"

"So I get the credit for your treating the fair sex well? Good."

"There's a vast distance between not actually abusing women and always treating them well," he said soberly. "Because I moved around a great deal, for years I chose unhappy wives as bedmates. They knew the relationship would be limited and that I would never betray them. In return, I did my best to give them pleasure so there would be some happiness in their lives for at least a brief time." He drew a slow breath. "Then I realized that I might not mean to inflict pain, but I did."

"Because some of those foolish women fell in love with you?"

He turned his full gaze to her. "How did you guess?"

"How could they not?" She twirled a pinch of hay absently between her fingers. "For a woman trapped in an unhappy marriage, a handsome man who treats her kindly and wishes to give her pleasure is a dream come true. Such a woman would want you always in her life, not merely as a brief, passing affair. I hope no married woman quietly murdered her husband in hopes that you'd marry her."

He frowned. "I certainly hope not! But it took me years to realize that I was causing pain because I always moved on to some other place."

"You implied that you changed your behavior at some point. How did that happen?" Her brows arched. "Slowly dawning maturity?"

He smiled ruefully. "By chance, I ran into a woman I'd had an affair with several years before. I was pleased because my memories of our time together were good ones. I discovered my error when she walked up and returned my greeting by punching me in the jaw. She threw a good fist, too. I asked her what I had done and she explained. I apologized for my criminal thoughtlessness and said I would do better in the future."

"Did she believe you?"

"I don't know, but I did change." He glanced at the ventilation holes at the end of the barn. "It looks like the rain has stopped, so we can proceed on our way." He stood and brushed off his damp breeches, then offered her a hand up from the hay.

She came up, wincing. "I was wrong that I wouldn't have any bruises from coming off the horse! Nothing serious, though."

Gordon opened the door, then retrieved his sodden coat from the floor and checked the inside pocket. "Good, the oilcloth preserved my letters of introduction. We may still need them." He wrung as much water from the coat as he could, then tied the arms around his waist rather than wear it.

Outside, the saturated soil was steaming under the rays of the sun. The temperature had dropped with the storm, but it was still hot and as humid as any tropical country he'd ever visited. The bridge had completely vanished and the creek had overflowed its banks in some places.

"I'm glad we made it over the creek while there was still a bridge," Callie observed. "How much farther?"

"Less than a mile, I think." He smiled encouragingly. "Then we're ready for the next stage of this adventure."

"Speak for yourself, Lionheart! I don't want an adventure. I want a thoroughly boring journey to Baltimore."

"Where we will then await the invasion of the most powerful army in the world. That will be very boring, I'm sure," he said dryly.

Callie laughed. "A lady can hope!"

Chapter 13

━━◆◆◆━━

They found the owner of Tucker Hall, Thomas Green, in his stables grooming Samson. He looked up warily when they entered, then relaxed when he recognized Richard. "I'm glad to see you're safe. I started to worry when Samson galloped in here." He fed the horse a carrot, then left the loose box and latched the door as he came out to greet his visitors. "He's a good steady beast most of the time, but he doesn't like thunder."

"So we discovered," Richard said as he shook Green's hand. "I was leading him across the bridge when an uprooted tree smashed the bridge dead center. Samson was already anxious, so he bolted to solid ground and headed for home while Mrs. Audley here fished me out of the creek. We took shelter in that barn till the storm passed."

Green grimaced. "I thought the bridge would be all right, but we didn't build it to survive a floating battering ram. I'm glad you made it over here safely." He offered a hand to Callie. "It's a pleasure, Mrs. Audley.

I'm glad Lord George was able to find you. Are you heading back to England now?"

"I have no idea," she said as they shook hands. "I sent my family to Baltimore for safety. I didn't expect the British to burn my house down, but they did. My main concern now is to get to my family and hug them all."

"I'm sorry about your house." He sighed. "I want my family back, too. I hope they'll be able to return soon. Any idea whether the British plan to occupy Washington?"

"I suspect that they intended a raid, not an occupation," Richard replied. "They must have been shocked to find that after Bladensburg, there was no attempt to defend the capital. It probably won't be long until some competent American officers organize a counterattack, and the British might not want to wait around for that."

"I hope that means the British troops leave soon!" Green said fervently. "Infamous to burn our capital city! It's time America stopped relying on inexperienced militia volunteers and trained more regular army soldiers like Britain has."

"Surely that will happen," Callie said. "Our military defeats have been appalling. We can do better." Yet as she said the words, she wondered if she had the right to think of herself as an American. She'd been in the country for little more than three years, and being around Richard was making her feel more English.

Richard asked, "Is the *Zephyr* out in Tucker Creek? I didn't see any masts when we came in."

"When the storm hit, the ship sailed out into the open river rather than risk being smashed up in the creek," Green replied. "I assume it will return now the storm has passed."

"I guessed that's what Hawkins would do. The current

down the creek now is ferocious, so he'll probably wait until the floodwaters subside."

"He might not return till tomorrow," Green agreed. "But I'm being a poor host. Come into the house and I'll find you dry clothing and food."

"Something dry would be lovely!" Callie gestured at her wet, clinging trousers. "And a proper dress would be nice if you can spare one."

"For saving Lizzie, you're welcome to anything in the house." Green led them from the stables to the spacious, airy house and summoned a pair of servants.

Within half an hour, Callie was dry and her hair was combed out loose over her shoulders so it could dry, too. When offered her choice of garments from Mrs. Green's wardrobe, she chose a plain old cotton gown that was faded from washing since Mrs. Green probably wouldn't miss it much.

The sun was setting and she enjoyed the cooler air when she joined the two men for a simple supper. As she met them in the dining room, she smiled at the sight of Richard. He wore an ill-fitting shirt and trousers, yet he still looked every inch an English gentleman. She must ask him how he managed it.

Tom Green proved to be an exemplary host. The clothing he'd offered Gordon from his son's wardrobe was clean and dry and the fit wasn't bad. A servant took charge of Gordon's expensive and much loved boots, promising that by the next morning they'd be almost back to normal. His coat, minus the precious introductory letters, was also taken away, though the servant wasn't optimistic about how well it could be restored.

When Callie entered the dining room to join the

men, she wore a faded gray gown, but with her damp, shining, red-gold hair falling over her shoulders, she looked like the girl he'd run away with. Except for her eyes, which were old beyond her years.

The meal was light and pleasant, with cold roast chicken, warm crumbly biscuits, and a fresh vegetable salad. Callie said little as they ate. He'd have thought she was a demure young lady, except that this was Callie. He guessed that her thoughts were complicated and troubled.

After tea and a delicious fresh peach cake, Green pushed his chair back from the table. "If you'll excuse me, I need to return to my office for a couple of hours. I must catch up on my accounts."

Callie asked, "Did you send some of your people across the river to safety?"

"No need. My blacks are safe here. The British leave them alone." Green grimaced. "Except for luring some of them away and giving them uniforms and weapons and calling them Colonial Marines."

Gordon wouldn't have touched that topic, but Callie said, "I freed my slaves. Have you considered doing that? Then they wouldn't need to run away to the British."

"You're not running a great plantation like I am," Green said in a patronizing voice. "I can't afford to free my slaves. I'm already shorthanded because of the ones who ran off to the British to fight Americans."

"One can see why they're tempted into running," Gordon said, keeping his voice relaxed and conversational. "If you were a slave, wouldn't you do the same?"

Green started to protest, then closed his mouth with a scowl. "I suppose I would. But Africans are different from us. I treat my slaves well, better than most owners. If they had any sense, they'd stay with me."

"The desire for freedom is powerful," Callie said in

a soft voice. "As powerful as the desire for love and family. Men and women of all races will risk their lives for those things."

Green looked acutely uncomfortable. "I don't disagree, but I can't run this plantation without slaves."

Voice still soft, Callie said, "Why not treat them like indentured workers? Let your slaves get their freedom after a certain number of years of work. If the slave agrees, draw up a contract explaining the terms, and have it witnessed by a local preacher or abolitionist that the slave trusts. That would give your finances time to adjust, and I think many of the workers would stay on after they're freed."

Green opened his mouth, then closed it again as he considered. "Perhaps that would be possible. When this crisis is over and my wife and son and his family are home again, I'll discuss the matter with them."

Callie gave Green a shining smile so potent that it almost knocked Gordon from his chair even though it wasn't aimed at him. Green looked stunned for a moment, then said, "I will indeed consider this seriously, Mrs. Audley. Thank you." He rose from his chair. "But now I must return to work."

After Green left the room, Callie also stood. "Good night, Richard. I'm going to get a bit of fresh air on the veranda and then go to bed. It's been a tiring day."

He stood courteously. "That it has. Do you mind if I join you?"

"Not at all." Her smile was wry. "You can tell me which direction Washington is so I can see if anything is still burning."

"Probably nothing after that rain." He followed her outside. There was enough moonlight to dimly illuminate the wide veranda that ran around three sides of the house. Wooden rocking chairs were clustered in groups on all sides, and it was easy to imagine the Greens and their guests sitting out and enjoying the beautiful scenery with chilled drinks in hand.

He guided her to the western side of the house. "The city is that way." He pointed. "No signs of flames."

"Thank heaven for that!"

The veranda overlooked the moon-touched currents of Tucker Creek. Unlike the bridge, the sturdy pier that jutted out into the creek had survived. Gordon observed, "The pier was submerged when we arrived, but the water has dropped a couple of feet since then. By tomorrow morning, the creek should be close to normal level."

"So we can set sail for Baltimore." Callie crossed her arms and leaned against one of the tall wooden columns that supported the roof of the veranda. Her hair was mostly dry now and it fell over her shoulders in a shining veil.

She looked as young as when they'd eloped together and was so beautiful it hurt to see her. More than anything on earth, he wanted to sweep her into his arms and keep her with him forever.

But Callie's thoughts were far different. "Do you think Mr. Green will take my suggestion to convert his slaves into indentured servants and eventually free them?"

"He might." Gordon hesitated, not wanting to be falsely optimistic. "But I've not spent years living in a slave society as you have. Your guess is better than mine."

"In Jamaica, most people simply assumed slaves were necessary and must be kept subjugated. Some are less comfortable with slavery and would welcome an alternative that won't bankrupt them. Mr. Green might be one of those." She exhaled roughly. "But I haven't the energy to worry about great societal problems just now. What I really want to do is go to Baltimore and snatch up my family and keep them close and safe."

Not unlike his desire for her. He gazed at Callie's graceful silhouette and knew that he wanted her more than anyone or anything in his life before. But he'd have to be a flaming fool to think now was a good time to try to engage her interest.

All the same, he could offer comfort. He looped an arm around her shoulders and drew her to his side. "Your family is fine and you'll see them soon," he said reassuringly.

After an instant of resistance, she settled against him with a small sigh of relaxation. "I'm sure you're right, but with all that's happened, I won't be happy until we're together again."

The soft, well-worn gown she wore had been stored with lavender and the lovely scent made her even more Callie-like. He swallowed hard and told himself not to draw her so close she took flight. "Tell me about your children. I know nothing except that they're quadroons. Surely there is much more to say about them."

She chuckled. "You may regret asking because I can talk about them for hours! I'll try to keep it brief. Molly is sixteen. Her real name is Mary, but Molly suits her lively spirit better. She's even more beautiful than her mother, which is saying a great deal. She's very clever and has been a wonderful assistant in my dressmaking business. When the children were little, I told them stories of England and she wants to visit there someday, when the war is over."

"She'll have her chance soon," he promised. "What about the other child? I don't even know if it's a boy or a girl."

"Trey is fourteen and all boy, for better and worse.

He's well grown for his age and full of energy and charm and curiosity. His real name is Matthew, after his father and grandfather. As the third Matthew, he was nicknamed Trey when he was in the cradle."

"The legitimate son wasn't named Matthew?" Gordon asked curiously.

"His mother, Matthew's first wife, insisted that her son be named Henry for her father," Callie explained. "I gather she was a difficult woman to argue with."

Gordon wondered if Matthew Newell thought marrying a sixteen-year-old girl would give him a more docile wife. If so, he'd been wrong, but at least Callie would have listened and discussed, not bullied him. "From the way you talked of your children, I thought they'd be younger, but they're close to grown."

"Yes, and I'm learning the age-old lesson that there are new worries as children grow older," Callie said ruefully. "Molly already attracts too much unwanted attention from men, so I've taught her a few ways to protect herself if necessary. Luckily she has a good head on her shoulders and she isn't likely to fall for a smooth-talking rake."

He loved the feel of her against him. Gently he stroked her outside arm, bringing her even closer. "What would Trey like to do in his future?"

"He loves machinery and ideas and working with his hands. I'd apprentice him to an inventor if I could find such a thing. Or perhaps to a printer who produces newspapers."

"Will they receive inheritances from their father?"

"That is a whole other story," she said tartly. "Matthew drafted a will that left the plantation to his son Henry and generous legacies to Molly and Trey. At my request, he also freed all his slaves after his death. I would be guardian of both children until they came of age. He gave me the draft to read. I made a couple of suggestions that he said he'd incorporate. But he died soon after, and if there was an updated will, it vanished."

Gordon sucked in his breath. "Let me guess. The only will that could be found was an older one leaving everything to his legitimate son."

"Exactly. I think Henry destroyed the new will. It wasn't enough to inherit his father's property. He wanted the slaves and every penny of his father's money as well."

"I suppose there was no legal recourse since you didn't have a copy of the new will."

"The story gets worse. Not only was the will gone, but he told me that he intended to sell his brother and sister. Molly would be worth a pretty penny, he told me." She laughed bitterly. "He generously said I could stay on as his mistress."

Gordon swore out loud, wishing he'd been around to kill the bastard for her. "So you vanished, and you can't touch your jointure because that would mean revealing your location. It's damnable!"

"I try not to think about any of that because it makes me feel murderous and there isn't anything I can really do except pray that he isn't looking for us anymore. He has everything now and nothing to fear from me. But I hate that Molly and Trey won't receive what they're entitled to." She sighed. "They might be safer in England."

"I was sent to take you and yours there," he said mildly. "All you have to do is say that's what you want."

"England is expensive. I don't know if I can earn enough to support the household," she said. "I'd be starting all over again, and I don't want charity from my family even if any is offered."

"You can marry me," he suggested. "I'm not hugely wealthy, but I have enough to keep you and your family comfortably. I can dower Molly and help Trey achieve what he wants. Perhaps he might want to go to university."

She glanced up at his face, startled. "Thank you, but I'm not that desperate."

He burst into laughter. "Callie, if I ever deluded myself into thinking I'm attractive to women, you've thoroughly destroyed the notion."

"Sorry!" She joined his laughter. "It's a kind offer, but well beyond what you were hired to do. I don't want to marry anyone, and I'm sure you can do better than me if you decide you want a wife."

No, he couldn't. But now was obviously not the time to say that. "The offer is open," he said casually. "Should you become sufficiently desperate."

"I keep telling myself not to worry. My world is in flux and no great decisions can be made until I see what happens."

"Every family has a designated worrier, and usually it's the woman."

"You're suggesting that even if I can't stop myself from worrying, I should try not to make myself insane with it?"

"That's about it," he agreed. "Time for bed now. Though perhaps warm milk with sugar and brandy would help you sleep better."

She smiled. "That will take me back to my childhood. Did my nanny give yours the recipe, or did your nanny give it to mine?"

"I forget. Shall we look for the kitchen and see if we can stir up a couple of mugs of relaxation?"

She looked tempted, but shook her head. "Too complicated to do in a strange household, particularly one in crisis mode." She smothered a yawn. "Besides, I'm tired enough not to need it."

"A tiring and bruising day." He thought of his simple, pleasant guest room upstairs. "Last night we shared a bed."

"We only had one bed," she pointed out. "Sleep well, Richard."

"And you also, Callie," he said as he opened the door into the house.

Chapter 14

The sun was barely up when Gordon woke the next morning. As soon as he started moving around, two servants arrived, one carrying a pitcher of hot water and the other his boots and coat. As promised, the boots were in good shape. His dark blue coat would never be the same, but it was wearable.

After he washed and dressed, he swiftly packed what few possessions he had in the battered canvas satchel he'd used to bring the same items to Tucker Hall. He'd transferred everything to Mr. Green's saddlebags before riding into Washington to find the mysterious Widow Audley. Both pistols would need cleaning since they'd been rained on, but everything had survived.

Satchel in hand, he headed downstairs and found Callie standing at a window staring out at the creek. This morning her hair fell in a braid down her back. In her soft gray gown, she looked like an unusually pretty servant. She turned at the sound of his footsteps. "No sign of your Captain Hawkins yet."

"It's early and he couldn't sail the *Zephyr* this far up the creek anyhow. He'll send a small boat." Gordon scanned the horizon, but couldn't see any masts or sails.

"May I put my clothes in with yours? All I have is what you gave me."

"Of course." Gordon tucked the folded garments inside. By the time he fastened the satchel again, Mr. Green had joined them, carrying a pair of wide-brimmed straw hats in one hand. "To replace the hats you lost," he explained as he gave them each one. "These aren't stylish but they'll keep you from burning in the sun. For now, though, breakfast."

The food was excellent and Mr. Green was a very gracious host, but Gordon sensed that he was anxious to see the last of his guests so he could return to his usual responsibilities. Callie was probably even more impatient to be off for Baltimore. Over the years, Gordon had learned to live in the moment, so he enjoyed the food and the sight of Callie across the table from him.

She sat opposite a window that overlooked the creek, and as they finished eating, she jumped to her feet. "A small boat is approaching your dock!"

Mr. Green also stood. "No one inside wearing a red uniform, I hope?"

"No, that's Hawkins on board." Gordon got up and donned one of the straw hats, handing the other to Callie. Picking up his satchel, he said, "Thank you for your most welcome hospitality, Mr. Green. Shall we see if Hawkins has news?"

That thought propelled them all from the house and down the path to the dock. Hawkins greeted Gordon with a firm handshake. "Glad to see you're still alive!" His interested gaze moved to Callie. "You succeeded in finding your widow?"

"Indeed I did," Gordon replied. "Mrs. Audley and

Mr. Green, who is head of the family you carried over to Virginia."

After handshakes all around, Green said, "We've had breakfast, but there's food to spare if you'd like to come inside."

"Thank you, but I've eaten and I expect my passengers are anxious to get away."

"That I am." Callie gave Mr. Green a swift hug. "Stay safe, and may your family be home with you soon!"

He hugged her back. "From your mouth to God's ears! Captain Hawkins, do you know what's going on out there?"

"The British troops have withdrawn from Washington," Hawkins replied. "I imagine that the government officials are on the way back to restore order."

"Thank God for that!" Green said fervently. "Does anyone know where the British forces are going next?"

"The best guess is to Baltimore," Hawkins said. "But it's too soon to tell. They might decide to burn Annapolis on the way."

Green nodded soberly. "It's selfish of me, but I'm glad they're heading elsewhere. I hope our troops are better prepared for the next battle."

After final farewells, the captain ushered his passengers back to the dinghy. Gordon was amused to see the blushes of the two young sailors who had been rowing the boat. Callie was a potent feminine force.

After he helped Callie into the boat and settled on the bench seat next to her, he asked Hawkins, "Did you escape the force of the storm?"

Hawkins growled, "No, dammit. The *Zephyr* took major damage to the masts and sails. There were hailstones the size of musket balls. If I hadn't been able to get her into the Potomac, she would have been destroyed. She can still sail, but I couldn't outrun a rowboat, much less a British frigate. We can't cross the Atlantic until repairs are made."

Callie tensed. "Can you make it as far as Baltimore? I must go there!"

"You want to go to Baltimore?" Hawkins looked pained. "I can't recommend it."

"If you can't do it, set me ashore," Callie said stiffly. "I'll make my way by land."

"I *really* do not recommend that!" Hawkins exclaimed. "The countryside is badly disturbed and you'd risk bandits, looters, frustrated American militiamen, and possibly British Army patrols."

Before Callie could say that she'd risk it, Richard said, "It's not an easy destination, but Mrs. Audley must go there to find her family since she sent them away from Washington for safety. What do you suggest as the best way of reaching the city?"

Hawkins's brow furrowed as he considered. "I plan to take the *Zephyr* to St. Michaels, a shipbuilding town on the eastern shore of the bay. My pilot, Landers, grew up there and his father owns a first-rate shipyard. While my ship is being repaired, I can hire a small boat and sail you up to Baltimore. A vessel the size of a fishing boat will be too small to attract unwelcome British attention. It's the best chance for you to reach Baltimore in one piece."

As Callie ached at the thought of how long that would take, Richard enfolded her hand in his large, warm clasp. "It's good to listen to people who know what they're talking about, Catkin," he said quietly. "You'll do your family no favors if you get yourself killed."

She exhaled slowly, struggling to control her anxiety. "I know you're right. But I don't like it!"

"Mrs. Audley, there are many things I don't like and

can't change," Hawkins said tersely. "This is one of them. But I promise to do my best to make sure you reach Baltimore safely."

She looked at the two strong, capable men who were risking so much to help her, and bit her lip. She'd also learned hard lessons about accepting what could not be changed. It was time to act like an adult. "I'm sorry for being unreasonable," she said apologetically. "You've suffered grave damage to your ship, Captain, and Richard risked his life to find me in Washington. I am deeply grateful to you both."

Hawkins nodded acknowledgment, but glanced at Richard quizzically. "Your given name is Richard?"

"It's one of my names. I was shocked to discover that the Widow Audley was a childhood friend from England." He gave her an intimate smile. "We grew up as neighbors, but lost track of each other years ago."

"I thought he was dead," Callie added.

"That he's still breathing is not for lack of trying to get himself killed," Hawkins said dryly.

She almost laughed. "He's not the only one! Richard told me about a certain cellar in Portugal. The one with bad brandy."

Hawkins's brows arched. "It's not one of my fonder memories."

"Yet men often seem to love danger and mystery." Curious, she added, "You didn't know any of Richard's given names, Captain Hawkins. What are yours?"

"If you ever need to know, I'll tell you," he said, an amused gleam in his eyes. "But for now, I prefer to be mysterious."

Callie smiled, then caught her breath in shock. The dinghy had just rounded a wide bend in the creek and they could now see where the *Zephyr* waited quietly at

anchor. Two of the masts were broken and some of the
sails were shredded. Sailors were working to replace
one of them.

Richard gave a soft whistle. "You weren't joking
about the damage!"

"She's suffered worse," Hawkins said tersely. "But
you can see why I'm in no shape to whisk you back to
England."

"That's all right," Callie said, knowing it was time to
reveal her uncertainty. "I haven't decided if I'm going
to stay here or return home." As she said the words,
she realized that England did feel like home. But that
would not be the only factor in her final decision.

"I should have known that rescuing a woman wouldn't
be straightforward," the captain said dourly.

"This has more to do with being in the middle of a
war than it does my gender. I've learned how quickly
and disastrously life can change, and how uncertain the
future can be." She frowned. "I can't decide if I'm so
anxious to get to Baltimore just on general principles,
or if my maternal instincts are whispering that something is wrong. But worry isn't helping. All I can do is
wait and see."

"Patience is one of the most irritating adult virtues
to acquire," Richard said ruefully. "But I swear that I'll
stay with you until you know what you want to do."

"In the meantime, you're giving us ample opportunity
for danger and mystery," Hawkins said, wryly amused.
"Remind me to thank you if I live long enough."

Chapter 15

◆❧◆

Callie's excitement at finally reaching Baltimore was muted by the time their sailboat entered the city's harbor. It was late afternoon and golden light poured over boats and buildings. They'd already passed Fort McHenry, a small brick fort that Hawkins said was sometimes called the Star Fort because of its shape.

The fort and harbor were rife with military activity. Their small vessel, the *Sally May*, had passed over a boom designed to prevent enemy warships from entering the inner harbor, and it was backed up by barges bristling with cannon.

Closer to the waterfront a strange structure crossed the harbor, rising and falling on the waves. "What is that?" she asked.

"They've used barges to create a temporary bridge to move men and supplies over to the fort," Hawkins replied.

Richard studied the connected barges. "I can't help

but think about the bridge of boats in Porto on that fatal day we met."

"This bridge of boats is sturdier and it's not crowded with fugitives," Hawkins said. "But I'd rather not risk my life on it."

Callie stared at the chained barges and made a mental note to ask Richard more questions later. But for now, her attention was on this reunion. She'd burned with impatience for the last week, but finally, she was here.

It had been almost a fortnight since she'd sent her family north. The journey to St. Michaels had been slow in the damaged *Zephyr*, and twice they'd had to shelter in one of the many creeks and rivers that ran into the bay when they saw the clustered masts of Royal Navy ships.

St. Michaels had proved to be a charming town, where memories of the previous year's British attack were vivid. The owner of Landers Shipyard was happy to undertake repairs to the *Zephyr*; he and Hawkins had done business before. Landers also negotiated the hire of a swift sailboat that was small enough to be overlooked but large enough to carry all of Callie's family.

Hawkins clearly enjoyed having a small, responsive boat he could sail with his own hands. He'd brought one of his sailors to help and Richard also acted as crew. To Callie's inexpert eyes, Richard seemed as skilled as Hawkins. She supposed he'd qualified as an able seaman by the end of the long voyage from Britain to Botany Bay, and he'd been on and off ships ever since.

Now, finally, her journey was over. She sat on the right of Hawkins, who was at the tiller to guide the boat in. "Newell's is right on the waterfront." She scanned the solidly built warehouses that lined the harbor.

"There!" She pointed. "That tall building with a hoist at the top and a church spire beyond."

Richard sat on Hawkins's other side, intently studying the streets and buildings. "There seems to be a lot of preparation for a possible attack, but not a mass evacuation as there was in Washington."

"This city is larger, better defended, and has more to lose," Hawkins said. "There also must be a competent military man in charge, which Washington didn't have."

"I hope you're right!" Callie said fervently as they glided gently to the pier nearest Newell's warehouse. Richard and Hawkins's sailor attached the mooring lines, then Richard climbed onto the pier and extended a hand to Callie. "Almost there, Catkin," he said encouragingly.

She scrambled up onto the pier, thinking how much easier this would be if she wore the trousers Richard had supplied. But now that she was in Baltimore, she needed to look and act like a woman of authority.

Hawkins said, "I'm going to call on a fellow I've done work for in the past. Later we can determine the next step."

Callie nodded, wishing she knew what that was. Then she set out for Newell's warehouse at a fast walk. When Richard fell into step beside her, she said, "You needn't escort me. The warehouse is just a few steps away."

"The city is in turmoil, so you're stuck with me until your situation is settled." He gave her a half smile. "You'll be rid of me soon."

The knowledge was painful, but also a relief. Richard was too disquieting for her peace of mind.

Her step quickened as she approached the ware-

house. The wide loading doors were closed, but she saw
a light from the small office in one front corner of the
building. She stepped inside, blinking at the loss of sunlight. The office looked much as she remembered it,
with a counter, several chairs, and drawers and a table
behind.

The place seemed unoccupied. Then she saw a figure
behind the counter. It was a woman making a rag rug
with braids of scrap fabric spread over a table.

Not a woman, a girl. Her stepdaughter. Callie recognized her an instant before Molly looked up. "*Miss
Callista!*" she exclaimed, racing around the end of the
counter.

The girl tumbled into her arms, gasping, "We were
so afraid you were dead!"

Callie hugged her hard, trying to remember when
Molly had become taller than she was. "I'm so glad to
see you! Why did you think I was dead?"

"News reached us that our house was burned down
by the British and no one knew what had become of
you. We were afraid that you were trapped inside when
the fire was set." She hugged Callie again. "The last fortnight has been horrid!"

"You must tell me everything that has happened.
But first I want you to meet an old friend of mine who
escorted me here from Washington." She gestured at
Richard, who waited quietly inside the door, then hesitated, realizing that she didn't know how to introduce him.

He solved that by saying, "I'm Gordon." He extended
his hand. "Callista said you were beautiful, Molly, and
she did not exaggerate."

Molly smiled and took his hand. "Thank you for
keeping her safe."

Callie realized that after a mere fortnight of separation, she was much more aware that Molly was a young lady, no longer a girl. Her stepdaughter was stunning, with dark wavy hair and golden skin that complemented her lovely face and figure. And like her beautiful mother, she had warmth in her eyes. She'd also learned to accept a compliment graciously without having her head turned.

Callie asked, "Why are you here in the office, and why has the last fortnight been a nightmare? Has something gone wrong beyond being uprooted from our home?"

"I'm keeping an eye on the office because the manager and warehousemen have joined their militia companies and are drilling all day and into the night," Molly explained. "There's no one else to do it. Grandmother came down with a horrid fever and frightened us to death."

"Sarah is ill? I must go to her!" As Callie turned to find the stairs, Molly raised a hand.

"The crisis is over and she's doing well, but she's resting now. There's no need to rush upstairs. Come behind the counter and we can exchange news."

Callie halted reluctantly and followed Molly into the sitting area in the back of the office. Richard came along, silent but interested.

"Where's your grandfather?" Callie asked.

"Once Grandma started to get better, Grandpa volunteered to help dig fortifications east of the city. They say it's the most likely place for a British attack," Molly said. "General Sam Smith is in charge of the city's defense, and he called for every man who had a pick, a shovel, or a wheelbarrow to start digging earthworks on Hampstead Hill."

"Working together to defend the city is promising," Richard said. "Not like in Washington."

"I hope you're right. Most of us have nowhere else to go," Molly said soberly.

"What about Trey? Is he also out digging?" Callie asked.

"He's joined a Maryland militia regiment and is drilling with them," Molly said, her voice flat.

Callie gasped. "He's only fourteen!"

"Almost fifteen, tall for his age, and he knows how to handle firearms. He's not the youngest to enlist." Molly turned her hands up in a gesture of helplessness. "How could I stop him?"

"You couldn't have," Callie said, not wanting Molly to feel guilty. "I don't know if I could have, either. He's a stubborn lad, your brother."

"And of an age where boys are anxious to become men," Richard said quietly. "Joining the militia doesn't necessarily mean he'll be sent into battle; it's too soon to know. But his willingness to defend his family and home is admirable."

"I keep telling myself that," Molly said, her smile crooked. "What happened to you, Miss Callista? Why was our home burned down when they say most houses in Washington were spared?"

"Pure bad luck." Callie gave a succinct explanation about the snipers, the shooting, and the fire.

Molly bit her lip. "Everything is gone? My clothes and my room?"

"I'm afraid so," Callie said gently. Molly loved pretty things and had worked hard sewing her gowns and decorating her bedchamber. She'd thought she would be returning to them. "I was dragged out by some soldiers so I escaped the fire, but"—her gaze went to Richard—"if my friend here hadn't come when he did, it would have been very bad."

Molly was not a sheltered innocent, and she could

guess at what might have happened. Horrified, she exclaimed, "You're all right? You weren't hurt?"

"I'm fine." Callie smiled reassuringly. "My knight on a white horse rode to the rescue in the nick of time. Very like the Gothic stories you enjoy."

"*Thank* you!" Molly said to Richard. She looked like she wanted to kiss him, but she refrained. "Would you like to see Grandma? She might be awake by now."

Callie jumped to her feet. "The sooner the better!"

Molly locked the front door, then led the way from the office to a staircase in the adjoining corridor. There were a lot of steps since two floors of storage space separated the ground floor from the living quarters. As they climbed, the close air became stifling.

Callie hadn't seen the upstairs apartment on her previous visit to the warehouse, only heard it mentioned, so she didn't know what to expect. She vaguely recalled hearing that there was a sitting area and a pair of bedrooms, but some of the space was used for storage when the warehouse was too full.

The door at the top of the stairs opened into a long, narrow area that extended the length of the warehouse, though the available space was diminished by a cluster of massive barrels. A faint, not unpleasant scent of tobacco permeated the air.

The apartment was crude, with worn furnishings and walls of rough planks. But a sitting area had been set up with chairs and a high-backed bench arranged around a worn rag rug, and windows in front and back allowed ample light.

The two bedrooms were carved from the back of the space and jutted into the main area with a primitive kitchen in between. The sitting area in front had a door leading to a strip of flat roof that had been turned into a balcony with a view over the harbor. Callie glanced out, then away as her imagination produced nightmare images of Royal Navy warships sailing in to occupy a shattered city. "Sarah is in one of the bedrooms?"

"Yes, the one on the right." Molly gestured.

The door to the bedroom was open. The window at the back had been raised so there was a bit of a breeze, though not enough to freshen the stale air and lingering scent of illness. It was a far cry from their luxurious home in Washington.

Sarah lay on a straw mattress on a simply constructed bed, her eyes closed and her face drawn. Her nightgown and the light coverlet over her were damp and wrinkled and she looked frighteningly fragile. Chest tight, Callie knelt beside her. "Sarah, are you awake?" she whispered. "I'm here, safe and sound."

Sarah's eyes fluttered open and she gave a sweet, tired smile. "Miss Callista! I knew you must be all right. You're like a cat with extra lives." She tried to lift a hand, but it wavered until Callie caught it. Her friend's bones felt frail.

"You must be going mad lying here," Callie said affectionately. "At home you're never still."

Her friend made a face. "I surely am tired of this room. But when Josh gets home tonight he'll take me out to the balcony for a bit of fresh air, and in a day or two I'll be able to walk around again."

A soft male voice said, "Would you like me to carry you out to the balcony now? It's cooler there and the view is better."

Wary of a strange man, Sarah jerked her attention to Richard, who stood in the doorway. He had the ability to look both elegant and self-effacing.

Callie said reassuringly, "This is Gordon, an old friend

from Lancashire. He rescued me from Washington and escorted me here."

Deciding that was a good enough recommendation, Sarah said, "Indeed I would like some fresh air. If it's not too much trouble."

"Of course it isn't." He grinned at her. "I like sweeping lovely ladies away."

Sarah laughed. "Your old friend is a sweet-talkin' ladies' man, I see."

"We all need a skill," he said as he bent to the bed.

"I'll put a folded quilt on one of the long chairs," Molly said.

Leaving the coverlet over Sarah, Richard carefully slid one arm under her back to help her sit up. Then he moved the other arm under her knees. "The worst thing about fevers is the way they leave a person feeling weak as a tired baby," he said sympathetically. "I had one fever that left me almost paralyzed for a fortnight. I wondered if I'd ever recover."

He punctuated his light sentences by carefully lifting Sarah, no easy feat when she was lying on the floor. Callie stood by in case help was needed, but he managed smoothly. That lean build concealed strength.

He carried her sideways through the door so he wouldn't knock her against the frame. Molly held the door to the balcony open. Several of the wooden chairs had high backs and extended seats so legs could stretch out comfortably. With the quilt for padding, the one Molly had prepared made a cozy nest.

Once Richard settled Sarah into place, Callie smoothed the coverlet over her and adjusted a small pillow behind her head. "How is that? Are you comfortable?"

Sarah sighed and leaned her head against the high

back of the chair. "Oh, yes. The fresh breeze from the harbor is so fine."

Molly came out on the balcony carrying a tray with a pitcher and several small, dented pewter cups. "Grandma, here's some of that cool mint tea you like." She set the tray on the table and poured a cup, then handed it to her grandmother.

"Thank you, Molly." Sarah was now strong enough to hold a cup and sip. "You're such a good girl."

"I try. Here, there's enough for all of us." Molly poured three more cups and passed them around.

Callie accepted hers and settled into one of the plain wooden chairs. The tea was cool and sweet. Richard accepted a cup with every evidence of pleasure and chose a chair by Callie. She sipped her tea, relaxing into this moment of peace.

"There's quite a view from here," he said. "We can see all the way to Fort McHenry."

He was right about the view. She just wished that so much of the activity wasn't war related.

For several minutes, they all silently savored the peace. Then Molly stood and looked over the railing. "Look, Trey and Grandpa are coming this way! Wait until they see you, Miss Callista!"

Callie also stood, drinking in the sight of the men in her family. Josh looked muddy and tired, but he was his usual strong, utterly reliable self. Dear God, Trey was the young soldier beside him! In his uniform jacket, he had the confidence and swagger of a man. She bit her lip, proud but also sad that her beautiful little boy was only a memory.

Molly called, "Grandpa, Trey, look who's here!"

The two men raised their heads and Callie waved to them. Josh grinned widely and Trey gave an exuberant shout. "Miss Callista, you made it here safely!"

"Yes," she called down. "Now get up here so I can hug you!"

In just a couple of minutes, she was doing exactly that. Hugging Trey felt so right and good. When they released each other, he smiled mischievously. "You've become just a bit of a thing, Miss Callista."

"I'm average height!" she retorted.

"And we Adamses are all above average!"

It was sadly true; she was the shortest person here. In Washington, she'd not really noticed. With a twist of her heart, she realized that there she had been the linchpin of their household. She owned the house and earned most of the money that supported them. But everything had changed, including the patterns of her family.

While she'd been hugging Trey, Richard had introduced himself to Josh, offering his hand. She saw that they were doing the male measurement ritual of sizing each other up. Approval seemed to be mutual.

Josh said, "Miss Callista, have you snuck a British soldier in here? He talks just like you."

She laughed and introduced Richard to Trey. His easiness with the Adamses spoke to how varied a life he'd lived.

"So you rescued Miss Callista?" Josh said.

"Yes, a member of her family sent me to find her and make sure she was safe." He paused, and Callie was suddenly certain that he was going to toss a bombshell into their midst.

"And then to bring her home to England."

Chapter 16

Gordon wasn't surprised at the appalled expressions that greeted his words. But the situation needed to be explained to her family. The protective side of him wanted to sweep Callie away from this city before the combined forces of the British Army and Royal Navy attacked. But he couldn't do that if she wasn't willing. Callie needed to decide what she really wanted—and so did he.

"You're going to take her away from us?" Sarah asked. She and her husband were obviously of mixed race and they had the quiet wariness of people who were born and raised in slavery. A man like Gordon, with confidence and fair coloring, had the potential to be their worst enemy. He made a conscious effort to look unthreatening.

"Only if she wants to go," he said steadily. "I can take all of you to England to new lives if you wish. We could leave tomorrow morning."

"What kind of lives?" Josh asked. "Field hands? Not going to happen."

"You would get to choose what you wanted to do, and I promise you'd be comfortable while you established yourselves. If you wish to set up a business, perhaps own an inn or a carpentry shop, that could be done." Gordon's gaze moved around the group. "Molly, there would be a dowry for you when you're ready to marry. Trey, you can go to university or study a trade if you like. You will all have choices."

Callie was watching Gordon with narrowed eyes, probably wondering if he had authority to make such broad promises. Or if he was assuming she'd be willing to marry him to get those benefits for her family. A suspicious girl. He liked that in a woman.

"They say it's cold and wet in England," Sarah said, frowning.

"They say rightly," Gordon admitted. "It is colder, but it doesn't get miserably hot like this, and winters are fairly mild."

Callie said hesitantly, "Molly, you've always wanted to see London. I'd love to take you there."

"I'll never go!" Trey said fiercely. "Britain is the enemy. I want to kill them all!"

Shocked, Callie exclaimed, "Including me?"

He flushed. "Of course not you! But you're an American, like me. No one has to be born here to be an American."

Not liking the hurt on Callie's face, Gordon said, "This is a damnable war, one that no sane person likes. You can dislike the war without thinking that everyone on the other side deserves death."

"This might seem like a stupid war to you, but England hasn't much to lose except some soldiers and money," Trey said flatly. "America risks everything."

As Gordon thought about it, he realized the boy was right. "The stakes are uneven," he admitted. "Britain pays in lives and treasure, which is bad enough, but the United States risks losing its very identity. Yet this country still has slaves. England doesn't. Is that a factor to weigh in the balance?"

Trey hesitated, then shook his head. "Maybe there aren't slaves in England itself, but the British are perfectly happy to own slave colonies like Jamaica. I'm free here. Baltimore has more free blacks than any other city in America. I like this place."

"No one has to decide tonight," Gordon said peaceably. "It's a huge and alarming opportunity. You need to think and discuss it as a family."

Sarah said softly, "I'd like to see London some day. But I'm too weak to travel, and I'm not going so far from my family. I want to see my son and his children."

"Your son?" Callie asked, startled. "Susannah wasn't your only child?"

Since Sarah was so drained, Josh answered. "Our son, Joshua. He's named for me. He escaped from Jamaica before you came to the island. He's living in Philadelphia. He's married and has three children we've never seen. We've been talking about going to visit them when the fighting is over here. Give the cousins a chance to meet each other."

"Why didn't you tell me about him?" Callie asked, baffled.

"It wasn't needful," Josh said simply.

The hurt deepened in Callie's face. Gordon guessed that her ignorance of something so important made her feel less like they were all family. "We need to talk, Callie. Down in the office?"

Her expression numb, she nodded and headed to the stairs. Molly said, "When you're done talking, please join us for supper, Mr. Gordon. I bought a nice pork pie and made a potato and carrot salad."

He smiled at Molly. "Thank you for the invitation. I may take you up on that, but now I have to have a discussion."

Callie descended the staircase with quick, tense steps, and Gordon didn't catch up until she was in the office. She leaned against the counter with her arms crossed on her chest, looking ready to bite someone, starting with him. With her flawless profile and graceful posture, she looked like an angry angel.

Narrowing her eyes, she asked, "Was the offer to support the Adamses in England dependent on my marrying you?"

She'd always had a deep aversion to coercion. "No," he replied. "Those are two separate issues."

She tilted her head to one side. "Then why did you make that offer to people who are virtually strangers?"

"You mean what's in it for me?" He mirrored her stance by leaning against the door frame with crossed arms, but in a much more relaxed fashion. "I can afford to help them get established in England, so why not? They're good people and they deserve a chance to build the lives that they want. Plus, you care about them and they care about you." He avoided using the words "love" or "family" since he suspected they were both fraught at the moment.

"I thought of them as family," she said in a tight voice. "Yet I didn't know that Josh and Sarah had a son and another whole family here in the United States. Why didn't they tell me?"

The pain in her face was the reason he was glad he'd lost any ability to love. Exiled from her birth fam-

ily, Callie had created a new family of her own, and
now she was finding that she was more of an outsider
than she'd realized.

Choosing his words carefully, he said, "They were
slaves, Callie. You always saw them as people who mattered and you freed them legally, but most of their lives
were shaped by slavery. As a matter of survival, slaves
learn to be very careful of what they say. That self-
protection becomes an essential habit."

"But they've been free for three years, since we came
to America," she said plaintively. "Didn't they know I
would have helped them visit their son and his family?"

He frowned, trying to come up with an explanation
that would make sense to both of them. "When you
came to Washington, you were the master. You *gave*
them their freedom, you provided their home and
their work and their money. You were their beloved
friend, but you also held the power. It was second nature for them not to tell you more than was necessary."

"And coming to Baltimore broke that pattern," she
said slowly. "That makes sense. The world has turned
upside down, the children aren't really children anymore, and their grandparents are coming into their
own as independent individuals." She smiled ruefully.
"I think I understand, but change hurts."

Despite the pain in her eyes, she was adjusting surprisingly well. A lot of women would be weeping with
devastation. "They are all becoming butterflies, free to
soar," he said encouragingly. "That's good."

"Yes, and they're flying away from me," she said wryly.

"That's what usually happens with children even
under normal conditions."

"And my life hasn't been normal." She sighed. "I
unconsciously assumed that we would continue on
as we have the last three years, living together as a fam-

ily. But now I realize that was inherently a temporary situation." She swallowed hard. "Because I was happy, I didn't look far enough into the future. Now I am looking, and I have no idea what is there."

"You're already a butterfly. Choose your flower!" he said lightly. "But don't survey a whole meadow full of flowers all at once. It's too confusing."

She smiled. "It's a good metaphor, but I'm not sure how far it can be pushed."

"All right, start with this. Take away considerations of family and think about where you would like to live. Here? Go back to Washington? England?" He held his breath, wondering what she would reply.

Her forehead furrowed. "There is much I love about America, but my roots are still in England. That's what I would choose if life was simple." She smiled humorlessly. "I thought my family was here, but now I must rethink that."

"The core of your relationship to the Adamses hasn't changed," he said gently. "You love them and they love you. Soon you will no longer share your lives in the same way as in the past. But you will still be dear and much loved friends."

"Not family, though. Blood matters." She bit her lip. "Maybe I should return to England. Learn what relative of mine cared enough to send you. Perhaps start a dressmaking business in a place like Bath. If I can sell the property in Washington, I'll have enough money to set up a shop and cover my costs until I get back on my feet."

"That would work well." He paused a beat, then said, "Or you could marry me."

Chapter 17

Callie studied Richard where he leaned against the door frame, looking like a lounging lion. Too handsome to be real. Richard, both friend and stranger. "If you say that often enough, I might start to believe you and accept. Then you'd be stuck with me."

He smiled. "I wouldn't ask if I wasn't prepared to accept the consequences."

Needing to know, she asked, "Why me, Richard? With your looks and birth and a comfortable fortune, you can easily find a wife if you want a family."

"Yes, but that would be so much work," he said promptly.

She grinned. "So I'm easiest? But I'm not an easy woman, and I won't accept an easy answer. You can do better than that."

His levity vanished. "I'm ready for a change, Callie. I've never met any other woman I'd want to marry, but I've seen marriages I envy. Couples who truly enjoy each other's company and who are completely loyal to each other. I'd like that too."

"And I'm here and you know my flaws, so you wouldn't have to put much effort into getting acquainted?" she said dryly.

"Exactly. We were best friends once and I think we could rub along comfortably."

"That is the least romantic proposal I've ever heard of," she said with a half smile.

"There would be much to disappoint you in me," he admitted. "As an adventurer, I'm boringly cautious and practical. As a husband, I'll be incapable of poetic declarations of love. But I will always look out for you. And"—his voice dropped—"I rather like the idea of marrying my best friend."

As she studied his face, she realized that under his strength and confidence was loneliness. Her life had not been easy, but his had been worse.

As a girl, she'd had the usual romantic dreams of falling madly in love with a worthy man who would love her equally. Perhaps only the young and idealistic could know that kind of love. Even if it didn't last, they would have it for a while, at least.

But if a great romantic love wasn't going to happen, friendship wasn't a bad substitute. "You're making marriage seem . . . possible. But not when a battle may fall on us in the next few days."

"We could sail away with Hawkins and wait out the Battle of Baltimore in peaceful St. Michaels, but I doubt you'd agree to that. The marriage offer is open, dependent on events. For now, let's go out and see if Hawkins is back on the *Sally May*."

She stood and headed toward the front door. "Are you going to ask him to wait while my complicated affairs are sorted out and decisions are made? That will take time."

Richard took the key to the outside door from a nail where Molly had hung it earlier, then opened the door for her. "Hawkins has more than fulfilled his part of our initial bargain. I suspect that he'll be keen to get away before the Royal Navy knocks on Baltimore's door. Any sane man would be."

"So we're not looking very sane, are we?" she said as she stepped onto the street.

He gave her an intimate smile that did strange things to her pulse. "Sanity was never a strongpoint with either of us, was it?"

He locked the door behind them, then escorted her the short distance to the *Sally May*, a light hand at the small of her back. She felt . . . claimed, and wasn't sure if she liked the sensation or not.

Hawkins was sitting in the *Sally May*'s cockpit puffing absently on a pipe as he studied the activity in the harbor. He looked up when Richard hailed him from the pier. "Hello there." Moving with the balance of a sailor, he rose and offered Callie a hand down into the sailboat. "Did you find your family safe and happy? Are you ready to leave now?"

She stepped carefully down into the cockpit and seated herself on one of the polished wooden bench seats. "Sorry, no. Naturally everything is more complicated than expected. We can't leave now, so it's probably time to say good-bye and Godspeed."

Richard followed her down into the cockpit. "You've fulfilled your end of the bargain, Hawkins. You're free to head for home."

"Just how complicated has everything become?" Hawkins asked.

"My stepson joined the militia and flatly refuses to

leave, his grandmother is recovering from a fever and too weak to travel, and no one in the family is sure about going to England." She gave Richard a sidelong glance. "I'm not sure, either."

Hawkins's eyes showed sympathy for complicated situations. "What about you, Gordon? Seems to me you've done your duty also."

Richard shrugged. "I'm not leaving Callie on the brink of a major battle. I can arrange transport home later."

Hawkins frowned. "When I talked to the man I do business with here, he told me of a couple who desperately want to get to Norfolk, where their daughter and her family live. I said I'd take them there. It's a good long sail down the Chesapeake in a small boat, so it will take several days to reach Norfolk, several more to return to St. Michaels."

"By then, it might be clear what will happen here in Baltimore," Richard said thoughtfully.

Hawkins nodded agreement. "I can't wait indefinitely, but my ship is still undergoing repairs, so I can stay longer in St. Michaels while events unfold. After the battle, if there is one, I'll sail back here if that's possible to see if either of you want to return to Britain."

"That's more than fair," Callie said warmly. "I'm sorry this mission has become so complicated for you."

The captain chuckled. "It's complications that make life interesting. I'll be off on the early morning tide. You take care of yourselves."

He extended a hand and Richard shook it. "The same to you. I'll go below and collect my possessions."

As he did that, Callie stood and brushed a kiss on Hawkins's cheek. "Thank you. I appreciate all you've done."

He said quietly, "I hope you find what you're looking for, lass."

Richard emerged from the cabin with his satchel of possessions, then vaulted onto the pier and offered Callie his hand.

"Do your attic quarters have space for me if I stay out of the way?"

"Of course." She smiled. "You can rearrange the tobacco barrels to create a nice private space for yourself."

"That's not a bad idea, actually." As they made their way back to the warehouse, he took her hand casually. She should have pulled away, but in a world where everything was shifting, Richard was solid. Reliable. A connection to a past that was simpler than the present.

The waterfront was busy even this late in the day. Some merchants had found wagons to carry their goods out of town. Other people were clutching their possessions and boarding small boats. Though Baltimore wasn't emptying out as Washington had, some residents were evacuating. But most were going about their business or wearing uniforms.

Callie abruptly gasped and came to a stop, halting Richard because she held his hand. "What's wrong?" he asked.

"Sorry." Callie scanned the people ahead, then started walking again. "I caught a glimpse of a man who looked like my stepson, Henry. That happened a lot when I first came to the United States. Not as much lately, but all the uncertainty is making me jumpy."

"Are you sure it wasn't him?"

She nodded her head. "He lives in Jamaica and I can't imagine him coming here in the middle of a war. I'm just on edge because of all that's going on."

They reached Newell's and Richard unlocked the door. Callie asked, "What will you do with yourself while we wait for the war to come to us? I can't imagine that you want to join one of the Maryland militia units."

"I won't fight my own people. Nor would I fire on Americans if I was with British troops." He grinned at her. "But I can dig ditches."

"So you'll work on defense but not offense," she said thoughtfully as she headed up the stairs. "Fair enough."

"If the defenses are good enough, the British forces may choose not to try to invade the city. They haven't a huge number of troops and Ross isn't fool enough to throw lives away by attacking entrenched forces that won't run this time."

"A British retreat is possible?" she asked hopefully.

"Yes, but I don't know how likely it is. We can ask Josh how the earthworks are coming." They reached the top of the stairs and he held the door open for her.

When they entered the main living space, Richard announced, "I'm going to be staying here for the duration. I'll try not to be too much trouble."

Josh was setting a table with Trey's assistance, but he cocked a quizzical brow at Richard. "Idle hands are the devil's workshop. Need something to do?"

"I told Callie I'd volunteer to dig trenches east of the city if idle hands are still needed," Richard said.

Josh looked shocked that a man so obviously aristocratic would do such work, but recovered quickly. "You look like you have a strong back, so I expect you'll be welcome. If you don't want to ruin your London tailoring, I can lend you some clothes. We're near the same size."

"That would be welcome." Richard indicated his satchel. "I've been traveling with very little."

"Rather than digging ditches, you should join the militia." Trey grinned. "It's more fun and the uniform is better. Do you know how to shoot?"

"I'm a tolerable shot, but I don't want to kill either British or American soldiers," Richard explained. "Digging ditches should keep me out of trouble."

Callie knew that he was a superb shot, so all the more reason to avoid active military duty. From the murmur of voices in Sarah's room, she knew that Molly was tending her grandmother, but she was surprised to see a young, blond militiaman enter from the balcony. She smiled at him. "You must be a friend of Trey's?"

"Yes, ma'am," he said shyly. "I'm Peter Carroll. Usually I read law, but this week I'm a soldier. Trey said I could come for supper and gawp at his sister."

He was a nice-looking young man a couple of years older than Trey, and he blushed charmingly when Molly emerged from Sarah's room. Interestingly, Molly seemed equally taken with him. "Hello, Peter! I'm so glad you could join us. The guest list is expanding so it's lucky I bought a loaf of bread to go with the pork pie and salad!"

Molly looked tired, but she was taking on the duties of cook and lady of the house very well. Callie realized that she herself wasn't really needed, not anymore. With a mental sigh, she tucked that knowledge away with all the other realizations that her life was changing.

They sat down to their supper a few minutes later. The meal was one of the most enjoyable Callie had ever experienced even though the food was plain and the people sitting around the table were very diverse. Perhaps imminent danger made such moments of shared pleasure special.

Trey and Peter returned to their regiment when the meal was over. It didn't take long to sort out their new living arrangements. Josh and Sarah had slept together until she became ill, but then they'd split the two bedrooms into male and female quarters. Molly slept on a pallet by her grandmother to look after her while Josh and Trey had turned the other bedroom into a male dormitory. That way Molly was on call for nursing duty and Sarah wasn't disturbed when her husband left early to work on the city's fortifications.

Since it was summer, a blanket and an improvised pillow sufficed to make up a pallet for Callie on the other side of Sarah's bed, with the same for Richard beside Josh. Josh tried to give him the bed, but Richard cheerfully pointed out that he wasn't the one with the old bones. Trey would sleep in that room if he had an overnight visit home.

Despite her disquiet over the way things were changing, Callie slept well and happily. Except for Trey, all the people she loved best were under this rough-beamed roof. She prayed that a month from now, they'd all be equally hale and happy.

Chapter 18

❧

Digging ditches was extremely hard work. Gordon had known that, of course, and he was not unfamiliar with heavy labor. But building earthworks was its own particular form of exhausting.

By the end of the day, he was covered with mud and had sore muscles in places where he hadn't known he had muscles. Josh noticed, but had the tact not to point out that Gordon looked as if a field of derby horses had raced over him. Several times.

By the time they reached Newell's, he barely had the energy to eat a few mouthfuls of bread and cheese before he headed for his pallet, stripped off his muddy garments, and collapsed. Before consciousness slipped away entirely, he heard Josh say with a chuckle, "Gotta give that white boy credit. He knows how to work."

"Oh?" Callie's voice had a tart edge.

"That was a high compliment, Miss Callista. You'd hardly know he was a gentleman when he was digging away with his shovel."

Gordon smiled as he drifted off to sleep. Apparently he'd passed Josh's test.

He rose the next morning to find that someone had taken his muddy clothing and boots and brushed them off and laid them out to dry in the warm air. He was touched that someone was looking out for him. Callie? Molly? Josh? One of the women, he guessed. Josh had already put in a long day of work.

The digging was just as hard as the day before, but his body was adjusting. After supper, he suggested to Callie, "Shall we take a walk? I'd like to see more of the city."

She hesitated before saying, "I'd like that. I don't know Baltimore well, either."

They descended to the street and she took his arm as they strolled east along the waterfront. Her light clasp felt right and proper. Feeling tired but generally pleased with the world, he asked, "How did you spend your day?"

"Sewing." She smiled. "It's what I do best. Since I have almost nothing to wear, I found a used clothing shop and bought a couple of gowns and a cloak and a few other necessities. I altered this dress today and will do the other tomorrow. I also bought fabric to make some new things."

He realized that she wasn't wearing the rather shapeless dove gray gown from the Greens, but a quietly elegant garment in pale green sprigged muslin. "I must be very tired not to notice that you've improved your wardrobe. Of course, you're always lovely, so it's easy to overlook what you're wearing."

"Flatterer," she said, amused. "How is life as a ditch digger?"

He showed her his hands. "Blisters are flourishing, but this will make a good entry on the list of strange and interesting things I've done."

He hadn't had pampered hands to start with, so the blistering could have been worse, but there were raw patches where blisters had formed, then broken. She frowned. "Remind me to put salve on those tonight so they don't become inflamed."

She took his arm again and they resumed walking. "I can understand why digging fortifications is strange, but what makes it interesting?"

"The men," he replied. "White and black, slave and free, rich and poor, and all in between. Working for a common, vital goal has created a wonderful spirit that binds everyone together. There's a boy who can't be more than eleven or twelve years old. His name is Sam Smith and he's the grandson of the General Sam Smith who is commander of the city's defense. The boy works till he's ready to drop, and he's proud to be doing it."

Her hand tightened on his arm. "There is nothing like a shared threat to lives or homes to bring people together."

He'd learned that truth in places like that cellar in Portugal where five strangers faced a firing squad in the morning, but this was larger and involved the fate of a nation. "No one has even commented on my English accent. There are a couple of other Britons out there in the trenches, too. As long as we're digging, we're accepted as Baltimoreans."

"Do you enjoy being part of something greater?"

"I do. The feeling is temporary, but powerful."

She was about to say something when she flinched, then muttered an unladylike curse under her breath. He asked, "What's wrong?"

"I caught another glimpse of the man who looks like my stepson, Henry. He must live near here, because I've had a couple of other sightings out of the corner of my eye. Not a clear view, just enough to set off my alarms."

He looked in the same direction she did, but didn't see anyone who seemed to be watching them. "What does he look like?"

"Henry is rather tall, brown hair, watery blue eyes. He looks like a man who is supposed to be skinny but has plumped up because of self-indulgence," she said acidly.

"You still have a wicked tongue on you," he said with a chuckle. "But I'm a great believer in intuition. Given your reaction, are you sure that man you've caught glimpses of isn't your stepson? A different man might make you twitch less."

She shook her head. "If it was Henry, he'd be causing trouble."

"Could he be here because of Newell's warehouse? I assume he owns it, and in more normal times I gather it does quite a good business."

"The ownership is complicated," she replied. "Remember I said that Matthew's revised will had mysteriously vanished?" When he nodded, she continued, "The revised will left me the warehouse and several other business ventures that would produce regular income. Not a great fortune, but enough to keep me comfortable."

"But you can't prove that without the revised will."

"True, but I do have the draft version that Matthew gave me to study. It has notes I made and which he initialed to show his intention to make those changes. He took it away to have a fair copy made and properly signed, but then he died very suddenly. I believe he did have the final copy made, but I never saw it. If it was done, Henry probably burned it as soon as Matthew drew his last breath."

"But if Henry does show up, you might be able to use the draft will as evidence that your husband meant to give the warehouse business to you?"

"Exactly. I don't know if it would work, but if Henry stamps in and demands we leave, he's so obnoxious that a judge might be more willing to believe the property is mine. I have my marriage settlements, which state that Matthew promised to give me certain properties as my jointure to support me in the event of his death."

"It sounds complicated enough to keep a lawyer fat and happy for years," he observed. "You actually have the papers to support this?"

"Yes, and I sent them to Baltimore with Josh and Sarah. All the important documents are here." She shivered. "I'm glad I obeyed my intuition with that. If Henry does cause trouble, at least I'll have some ammunition."

"Just how close to the final will was the draft?"

"Quite close, as far as I know. Matthew wrote it with his own hand and it has several words scratched out, but his provisions for me and his children were very clear."

"I'm a fair hand at forgery," Gordon said. "If you have a copy of Matthew's signature, I could easily add it to the draft will. It would seem more legitimate if there were witnesses, though, and I assume that Josh and Sarah wouldn't be allowed to witness because they were slaves at the time."

She stopped in the street and stared at him, her hazel eyes wide. "Have I shocked you?" he asked.

"I think that's a *wonderful* idea!" she exclaimed. "I've

hated that Molly and Trey haven't received the inheritances they deserve and that their father wanted them to have."

"You're entitled to your jointure, too," he pointed out. "In a complicated situation, you were a good wife to him and mother to his younger children."

"It would be nice to have an independent income," she agreed. "But not as important as Molly and Trey being given good starts in life." Her brow furrowed. "As for witnesses, Matthew had a good friend called Frederick Holmes. They would regularly get together to play cards and smoke cigars. Mr. Holmes was very old, and he died only a week or so after Matthew. He was a respected local planter and could have signed the will." Her smile turned wicked. "And I have a copy of his signature on a condolence letter he sent me after Matthew's death."

"Brilliant!" Gordon exclaimed. "I don't suppose your husband had any other friends who conveniently died."

"Luckily for them, no. Will one witness be enough?"

Gordon resumed walking as he thought. "It would be a little irregular, but you could sign it in a personal way. Something like, 'This seems very fair, Mr. Newell. Your loving wife, the Honorable Catherine Callista, et cetera, et cetera.' And date it."

"If the will looks legitimate, won't a judge wonder why I didn't produce it earlier?"

Gordon grinned. "Blink your beautiful eyes and say that you hadn't thought it was legal because there were words scratched out and only one witness had signed. Look lovely and vulnerable and perhaps not very intelligent and you'll have the judge eating out of your hand."

She laughed and squeezed his arm. "I love this

idea! My lawyer, Francis Scott Key, is one of the best in Washington. I have no idea where he is now, probably staying at the family estate in central Maryland, where it's cooler. But when all this madness is over, I'll write him to see what can be done. He might know of lawyers in Jamaica who can file the will and get justice for Molly and Trey."

"It's certainly worth trying," Gordon agreed. "You're not attempting to steal something you aren't entitled to. You're just making it possible for your husband's wishes to be carried out."

"That is both true and an elegant rationalization." She chuckled. "I'm so glad for your varied talents."

"All of them at your service, Catkin." His gaze shifted to the waterfront ahead of them. Sleek two-masted Baltimore clippers were moored at the wharves, and a similar ship was under construction in a shipyard. A ship's bell tolled mournfully nearby. "This is obviously Fell's Point, the shipbuilding community."

"The birthplace of so many of the ships that harassed British shipping. I've heard that over a thousand British ships have been taken by American privateers."

Gordon whistled softly. "No wonder the British call Baltimore a nest of pirates!"

"Yes, it's become a badge of honor here." Her amusement faded. "If the British do manage to conquer the city, Fell's Point will surely be razed to the ground."

"I don't think the British will get this far. You should see our earthworks!"

She laughed, and by mutual consent they turned to retrace their steps. It was almost dark by the time they reached the warehouse. As Callie felt her way up the long staircase to their living quarters, she said, "One of the first things Josh did when they moved in was put railings on both sides of these stairs. Very useful when climbing them in the dark without a lantern."

"He might do well starting a carpentry shop. Baltimore is a growing town, so good carpenters are in demand."

"I think he'd love to have his own business."

They had nearly reached the top of the steps, so it was time to make a move. "Callie?"

"Yes?" She stopped and turned to him. In the darkness, she was a shapely shadow, a faint scent of lavender, and a pale face. "What do you want?"

He was two steps below so he moved one step higher, which put their faces on the same level. "Only this."

Keeping one hand on a railing for balance, he leaned forward and kissed her. In the darkness, his lips first touched her cheek, but it was easy enough to find her mouth.

She sighed, her mouth softening and one hand rising to rest on his shoulder. He didn't try to deepen the kiss, but he circled his other arm around her waist and drew her closer so that their bodies touched. She was soft and warm, molding to him.

It was an effort to keep the kiss gentle, but he'd be a fool to risk driving her away. The tender kiss went on and on, until she swayed away from him and said in a breathy voice, "Are you trying to seduce me, Lord George?"

"Not at all. I thought that was a very gentlemanly kiss," he said as he struggled to regain a lighter tone. "Seduction would be ungentlemanly." And to say he was courting her would be moving too fast.

"So just a gentlemanly good-night kiss." She leaned forward and her lips briefly brushed his. "Good-night, then."

She turned and climbed the last steps at a brisk pace. He followed, and just before she opened the door at the top, he said, "That kiss will send me to my night's sleep with happy dreams. And you?"

She opened the door and light from the lanterns inside flowed over her, illuminating the enigmatic smile she sent over her shoulder. Then she was gone.

He guessed that they would both have sweet dreams this night.

Chapter 19

"They say that from the top of Federal Hill, we'll be able to see halfway to Washington," Richard said as they climbed the hill together. "Though that may be an exaggeration."

Callie and Richard had ended each day of this long week of preparation and waiting with a walk to a different part of the city. Baltimore was the third largest city in the United States, but they were coming to know it well.

"Is Federal Hill as high as your Hampstead Hill? The one you're digging ditches on?" Callie asked, panting a little from the climb. "That gave a most splendid view of the city and your earthworks."

"I don't think this hill is as high, but it does have fine water views." They crested Federal Hill and looked out past the forts and down the Patapsco River, which led to the bay. Richard stiffened and muttered an oath under his breath.

Callie followed his gaze. In the misty distance were

the clustered masts of sailing ships. A cold hand seemed to clench her heart. "The Royal Navy?"

Richard laid a comforting palm on her lower back. "I think it must be." His voice was stark. "In the next few days, Baltimore's people and resolution will be tested."

"Trey." She swallowed hard. "If General Ross lands his troops, Trey's regiment will surely be called to action."

"Perhaps, perhaps not," Richard said calmly. "Militia, volunteers, and seasoned soldiers have been pouring in. The city is filled to the brim. The British can't match the American numbers, and given the very fine fortifications we've built, the militia won't be routed like the troops at Bladensburg were."

She guessed he was right. Sarah had told her that after the burning of Washington, Baltimore had collapsed into flat panic, but within a couple of days, the city had rallied and grimly dedicated its resources to resisting the likely British attack. She gave a silent prayer to keep Trey safe.

Burying her anxiety, she said, "I've heard that the British can't sail into the harbor unless they turn Fort McHenry into rubble. Do you think that's true?"

"The Hampstead Hill digging crews certainly believe that." Richard gestured at the star-shaped brick fort at the end of a peninsula that pointed directly at the distant warships. "According to the sailors I was working with, the fort is well positioned and the river is too shallow for the largest warships to come all the way in. Only the smaller naval vessels can get within firing range."

"Meanwhile, General Ross's army will land and invade from the east." She realized her hand was locked in his with numbing force. She consciously eased her grip. "I wish this damnable war had never begun!"

"I agree." Frowning at the fort, Richard continued,

"I've realized that while I don't stand against my own country, I want the United States to come out of this war stronger and more sure of its identity." His gaze slid to Callie. "I never could resist cheering for the little fellow."

She smiled. "Neither can I. How imprudent of America to take on the greatest military power in the world! They've made dreadful military mistakes in the war, but here they are literally digging in and making their stand."

"And more power to them." He turned, taking her with him, and by mutual consent they headed silently back to the warehouse.

She enjoyed these after supper walks because it gave them private time together. These shared hours were like their childhood friendship, except for the nightly kiss he claimed on the stairs up to their living quarters.

Callie could have eluded him if she'd wanted to, but she'd discovered that she didn't want to. He didn't attempt to seduce her, but the kisses became longer and more intoxicating every night. She suspected he was courting her, but didn't want to ask. A week from now, the battle might be over and it would be possible to think about the future.

But not yet.

After such intense preparations, Baltimore had started to become complacent, but having British ships within view brought the city back to a state of high anxiety. Troops garbed in everything from official uniforms to scruffy sailors' clothing churned through the streets, complicated by the number of people who'd decided that the time had come to visit out of town relatives.

Trey was home on an overnight leave, but he bub-
bled with excitement. "We'll be mobilized in the morning, I'm sure of it!" he exclaimed.

Gordon considered enlightening him about the ugly
realities of combat, but decided against it. Trey wouldn't
believe him, and he'd learn the truth soon enough.

Callie said, "Let's make a rope ladder tonight, just
in case. Josh, do we have enough cordage to make a
ladder that will reach the ground from this floor?"

Josh considered, then gave a confirming nod. "We
do, and I have wood that would do for solid crossbars."

Molly asked, "Do you think we'll need to escape that
way, Miss Callista?"

"Probably not, but having had one house burned in
this war, I want to be prepared," Callie explained. "These
buildings are all wood, and they'd go up in flames very
quickly if the British decide to torch the city."

Gordon agreed with Callie, and also recognized
that having a joint project to work on was a good distraction from the uncertainty looming over them.

Callie lit all their lanterns to provide working light,
and even Sarah helped now that she was feeling stronger.

Like most men who spent time at sea, Gordon knew
a great deal about knots, so he was designated the knot
master. With everyone working together, in a couple
of hours they had a sturdy rope ladder long enough to
reach the ground from either the front or back of the
warehouse.

The ladder made quite a large pile when finished.
As Gordon and Trey rolled it into a fat cylinder almost
the size of a tobacco barrel, Molly asked worriedly,
"Will you be able to manage the ladder if we have to
use it, Grandma?"

Sarah laughed. "If it's the ladder or turning into bar-
beque, I'll manage!"

Josh nodded approvingly. "I won't let you fall, sugar. In the morning when it's light, I'll put anchors for the ladders in the front and back." Josh covered a yawn. "Now I'm ready for some sleep."

"I'm going to sleep on the balcony," Trey said. "So I can hear if they give the signal calling the troops to assemble."

"I think I'll join you out there," Gordon said. "It will be pleasantly cool."

Molly smiled. "If Miss Callista and I sleep outside, too, Grandma and Grandpa can have their bed back."

Josh chuckled. "A mighty fine idea. I'm not fond of sleeping alone."

"Me neither," Sarah said with a smile. "I miss your snoring."

Gordon wouldn't miss Josh's snoring, but he envied the older couple the deep affection that bound them together. He and Callie had great affection, but it was an open question whether it would be enough to hold them together.

The balcony was indeed pleasantly cool, though there was more activity in the streets than usual. Trey and Molly spread out their blankets on the left end while Gordon and Callie took the right end. Gordon was pleased when she spread her pallet beside his. Not close enough for trouble, but close enough that when everyone had settled down, her hand was able to glide over and take his.

He lifted her hand to brush a kiss on her fingers, then settled down into sleep. He was grateful for both his self-control and his fatigue. If he'd given in to temptation and seriously tried to seduce Callie this strange week, she'd probably have brained him with the barrel of her pistol.

Instead she was becoming increasingly relaxed around

him, and encouragingly responsive to his kisses. Next
time he asked her to marry him, she might actually give
the question serious consideration.

If not, well, he'd bide his time and ask her again
later.

Callie awoke at dawn to find that she'd migrated
over to Richard's side and burrowed under his arm to
rest her head on his shoulder. She tilted her head up
and saw that he was watching her with amusement in
his gray eyes. Seeing she was awake, he gently stroked his
palm down her arm to the side of her hip. It felt dreadfully wonderful. He didn't say a word when she silently
scrambled away, but the amusement deepened.

She lay on her back, and remembered that today
war would surely come to Baltimore, and her stepson
would be part of it. Her hand moved back to take
Richard's and he threaded his fingers between hers.
Her feelings for him were complicated, but at the moment, she'd take any comfort she could get.

They lay like that until Trey began to stir. "Today's the
day!" he said in a husky voice. A man's voice, not that of
a boy.

Molly, who was not an early riser by choice, said
crossly, "I accept that you're keen to get yourself killed,
but can you be quieter about it?"

Callie smiled at the familiar sibling banter. "Time
we all got up, I think." She suited her actions to her
words and sat up with a yawn.

"Time all you sleepyheads got moving," Sarah said
from the balcony door. She sounded like her usual
healthy self. Sleeping with her husband's warm body
next to her must have improved her energy. She continued, "I'll make us some breakfast, and then I think

we all should go to the nearest church and do some prayin'."

"Hard to argue with that," Richard said as he stood and rolled up his pallet. "I just hope God remembers my face when I set foot in that church. It's been a long time!"

"Then a good thing you're going this morning, because I guarantee the devil knows your name!" Chuckling, Sarah returned to her cooking.

Beginning the day with laughter was not a bad thing, Callie decided. Laughter and prayers. They needed both.

Chapter 20

❧

The nearest church was Methodist and only a few blocks away. The streets were crowded with people dressed in their Sunday best to attend services, restless militiamen waiting for their summons to war, and packed wagons as some households decided it was time to leave the city.

Seeing how many were heading to the same destination as they were, Gordon observed, "The church will be full to overflowing. I assume this isn't usual?"

"No," Sarah replied soberly. "We aren't the only ones asking God for some extra protection today."

Gordon tried to remember the last time he'd been in a church. Probably it was when an old classmate, Daniel Herbert, had married in London the previous year. The ceremony had taken place in the very grand St. George's, Hanover Square. The church they were approaching today was far more modest in design and materials, though the steeple had aspirations.

Since Callie and Molly were chatting together and

Sarah had Josh's arm, Gordon fell in beside Trey. The young man wore his militia jacket and carried his rifle and pack, ready to be called at any moment. He asked, "What outfit are you with, Trey? That dark green you're wearing is similar to the rifle brigades of the British Army."

"Exactly, sir! I'm in Captain Aisquith's Rifles because I'm such a good shot. I'm the youngest in the company." His voice lowered. "They think I'm seventeen and a couple of other boys are about that age, but I'm actually younger."

"Maybe the other boys are lying, too?"

"I hadn't thought of that," Trey said, looking crest-fallen.

"It's an honor to be in such an elite group no matter what your age," Gordon assured him. "But I haven't heard anyone in your family mention that you're in a company of sharpshooters."

"I didn't explain because they'd worry even more than they do now," Trey said. "A lot of the militiamen will be stationed in the earthworks you worked on, but special troops like us will be sent out in advance. We'll get to do real fighting!"

"There's good reason why your family wouldn't be enthralled with that knowledge," Gordon said dryly. "Real fighting can lead to real dying."

"I'm not going to be killed," Trey said confidently. Seeing Gordon's raised eyebrows, he added, "But if I am, at least it's for a good cause."

Hoping the boy's confidence wasn't misplaced, Gordon asked, "Where did you learn to shoot so well?"

"My father taught me. He said I was a natural marksman." Trey looked wistful. "I miss him. It wasn't right, him having my mother and Miss Callista as well, but he treated all of us well."

"What about your half brother, Henry?"

Trey's good nature vanished into a scowl. "He's mean. A bully. I don't think my father much liked him, but he was the oldest and legitimate, so my father had to make him the heir. Henry was mostly away at school in England, but when he came back, he was always after my family. My mother and Molly and I were all scared of him. That's one reason I figured I should learn to be a good marksman."

"Henry was dangerous?"

"Oh, yes." The youthfulness left Trey's expression. "He wanted to sell all of us, me, Molly, and my grandparents, to another island. On Jamaica, my father had friends who might have helped me and Molly for my father's sake, but on another island, we'd just be more slaves."

Gordon now understood how Trey had developed the tough-mindedness a soldier needed. "A good thing Miss Callista was there to take you all away."

"She's our angel," Trey said in a low voice. "Without her . . ." He gave Gordon a hard look. "You know how special she is?"

"I do. I always have." And she was becoming special in new ways now.

When they reached the church, they saw that soldiers were stacking their weapons outside, with a corporal from the City Brigade keeping watch over the weapons. When Trey hesitated, the guard said, "Don't worry, no one will steal it. But you can't enter if you're armed."

Luckily, Gordon's pistol was concealed. Trey reluctantly laid his fine rifle on the far side of the pile between the other weapons and the wall, and they joined the rest of their party inside. The last pew on the right had space for the six of them, though it was a tight squeeze.

Gordon generally found church services boring, but on this particular Sunday, the singing was heartfelt and the atmosphere was electric with fear and anticipation. The silver-haired minister gave a rousing sermon based on a biblical passage about the Israelis conquering a much greater force.

The sermon was interrupted when a cannon boomed from nearby. A second shot sounded, then a third. Trey leaped to his feet, burning with excitement. "That's it, the assembly signal from the courthouse!"

A clamor filled the church as voices cried out and people leaped to their feet. The minister slammed his Bible shut and raised his voice. "My brethren and friends, the alarm guns have just fired!" he roared, his trained voice cutting through the cacophony. "The British are approaching, and commending you to God and the word of His Grace, I pronounce the benediction, and may the god of battles accompany you!"

Gordon gave the minister top marks for drama and appropriateness. Trey was in the middle of the church pew, and he had to work his way past all of his family. He hugged the womenfolk and shook hands with Josh and Gordon. Then he was away, scooping up his rifle outside and heading off to assemble with his sharpshooter company.

Callie got to her feet and said in a voice that was almost steady, "Time to head for home now. We can keep praying wherever we are."

Sarah also stood, looking very weary. "Can, and will."

As they merged into the crowd flowing slowly toward the church exit, Gordon was behind Callie and saw her glancing around, her expression wary. He asked quietly, "Is something wrong?"

She smiled apologetically. "I keep feeling that I'm being watched. It's probably just general nerves."

"Perhaps, perhaps not. I've learned to listen to my intuition." He rested his hand on her shoulder. "Maybe Henry Newell wouldn't come all the way from Jamaica, but the warehouse business is here and there is a potential dispute about ownership. Might he have hired men to watch if you or the rest of the family came to Baltimore?"

"I suppose it's possible," she said uneasily. They moved through the front door onto the street, and she drew a deep breath of fresher air. "Thanks so much for giving me still more to worry about!"

He chuckled and squeezed her shoulder before releasing it. "I've always found that having many worries reduces the anxiety about any individual concern."

"I'll bear that in mind." She took his arm as he moved forward beside her. "What do we do now? I'll go mad with waiting!"

The center of the street was full of militiamen streaming toward their gathering points. Like other civilians, their party drew to the sides of the street to let the soldiers through. "I'm not good at waiting, either. Usually if there's action, I'm stuck in the middle of it, keeping my head down and trying to stay alive."

"I'm glad you aren't this time. I have enough worries." Her grip tightened on his arm. "This isn't your fight."

Perhaps not. But it felt wrong to watch a boy who wasn't yet fifteen go off to fight and perhaps die. "We need to keep busy, and one way to do that is to prepare for the worst. The worst won't happen because there are a lot of troops here, they have more experience of the terrain than the British and better defensive positions, and many are Baltimoreans. They're fighting for their homes and they're as dangerous as cornered wildcats. But preparations will help keep us sane."

Callie smiled. "In other words, busy is better."

Gordon agreed. Not only would busyness distract them, but it would help him keep his hands off her. The sooner this crisis was over, hopefully with a minimum of damage, the sooner he could move his covert courtship into the open.

Chapter 21

⤐

"Hello! Hello?" Hammering sounded on the warehouse street door, and a young voice called, "Mr. Gordon? Mrs. Newell?"

Callie froze. She was sitting on the balcony resting after a day of collecting and storing water and other provisions so they would be ready for a possible siege or occupation by British troops. Richard and Josh had hauled up casks of water and cooking fuel, using the hoist on the back of the building.

Josh had built sturdy anchors for the rope ladder, and Sarah had sent Josh out for medical supplies. Josh said wryly it was a pity none of them smoked since they had a lifetime's supply of tobacco sitting in the middle of their drawing room.

Early Monday morning, three cannon shots had announced that the British were landing at North Point, the peninsula east of the city that lay between the Patapsco and Back Rivers. As General Sam Smith had predicted, the land attack would come from the east and would have to get past the massive earthworks that Richard had helped dig.

The city hadn't emptied out as Washington had, and the remaining residents were quietly determined to face what might come. Sporadic cannon and gunfire barked from the east, and word spread that General Stricker has set up skirmish lines of his best troops across the narrowest part of the peninsula in hopes of blocking a British advance.

But that was all at a distance. With Trey's friend Peter Carroll shouting from below, danger had become very personal. Callie leaned over the railing and called, "I'll be right down to let you in, Peter!"

She was fast but Richard was faster. He risked life and limb by racing down the steps three at a time, and by the time Callie reached the bottom of the staircase, he'd already let Peter in to the small hallway. Peter's uniform was dusty and the right sleeve was torn off and turned into a sling to support his crudely bandaged right arm.

"What's wrong?" she asked sharply. "Where is Trey?"

Peter wiped his sweaty face with his left hand, visibly trying to collect himself. "He's alive, but wounded. He needs help."

"How seriously is he injured?" Richard asked. "No, come upstairs first so everyone can hear at once."

Callie knew that made sense, but her heart hammered with anxiety as she followed Peter up the stairs. He was weaving from exhaustion.

When he emerged into the main sitting area, the three Adamses converged on him, Molly carrying a tankard of chilled lemonade because Richard had brought up ice earlier. "Here, drink this, then tell us about my brother!"

Peter sank into a chair and emptied half the tankard with one long swallow. While he drank the rest more slowly, Sarah came to him with the medical kit she'd assembled earlier. She removed the improvised sling and examined his arm. He winced under her gentle fingers, but she said soothingly, "Nasty and bloody but only a flesh wound. I'll pour whisky over it, which will sting, but make it less likely to fester. When it's bandaged properly, you'll be able to use it a little."

He inhaled sharply as she applied the whisky. "Trey has a leg wound and another in his shoulder. There don't seem to be any bones broken, but he's lost a fair amount of blood, and even with my help, he can barely hobble along."

"What's been happening?" Richard asked. "We've heard artillery and gunfire, but it didn't sound sustained enough for a pitched battle."

"Skirmishes, not battles, sir," Peter replied. "General Stricker sent a group of us sharpshooters ahead to provoke a fight before more British soldiers landed. It worked. Trey was one of the shooters and I was his spotter." He swallowed hard. "The British commander, General Ross, is seriously wounded or dead. I think dead."

There were shocked noises from everyone. If Ross was dead or incapacitated, it might end the land attack. At the least, the attack would be blunted. Ross was an outstanding officer and his next in command was unlikely to be as capable.

Face pale, Callie asked, "Where is Trey now?"

"Since I'm no use with this arm, our lieutenant said to help him behind the lines to a surgeon. I had to half carry him, and it got to be too much for both of us. I left him at an empty cabin off the Philadelphia Road. Trey said you have a cart and a pair of horses. Can you come and bring him home?"

"Of course," Richard said, sliding naturally into command. "Josh and I will go. Peter, you'll need to ride with us to guide us to Trey."

"I'll go," Callie said. "I have more nursing experience than any of you men."

"And I have more yet," Sarah said belligerently as she bandaged Peter's arm. "I want to go to my grandbaby!"

Before Josh could protest, Richard said, "You haven't fully recovered yet, Sarah. You need to be here and fit to patch him up." His gaze shifted to Callie and Molly. "I know you want to come, but you're both too pretty to take into a war zone. The potential for trouble is too great."

"You surely make a refusal sound good!" Molly said ruefully.

"He has a very talented tongue," Callie agreed before she realized how suggestive her comment was.

Mercifully not taking the innuendo up, Richard said, "We won't be back for hours, so keep your pistol close to hand just in case."

"I will." Reluctantly she accepted that he was right; she and her pistol should be here since neither Sarah nor Molly knew how to shoot. "Sarah, do you need to replenish anything in the medical kit before they take it?"

"As long as they don't decide to drink the rest of the whisky, there are enough supplies." She closed her medical kit and handed it to her husband.

"I'll collect blankets to pad the cart," Josh said. "Gordon, will you go to the livery stable and get the horses harnessed and bring them to the back of the warehouse? The cart is stored back there."

"Of course."

Callie asked, "Peter, how far is it to where you left Trey?"

He thought a moment. "Maybe four miles or so.

About halfway back from where we shot Ross and this side of the fighting unless our troops retreat like they did at Bladensburg. We should be back by nightfall."

"There will surely be delays," Richard said. "Don't worry, we'll return with Trey as soon as is possible." He moved to his satchel and pulled out his pistol. It was on top of his other belongings and already loaded. He holstered it, then slung a powder horn and a pouch for shot on the other hip.

His expression had changed and he was no longer her amiable Richard, but the menacing Lord George Audley who had thundered out of the night in Washington to rescue her. A dangerous angel.

"You all be careful!" Sarah kissed her husband hard.

Richard stepped up to Callie and drew her into a full body kiss. Not a polite brushing of the lips but mouth and tongue and pulling her hard against him, his hands moving hungrily over her back and hips.

After an instant of resistance, she fell into the embrace with equal hunger. Fire burned through her veins and her brain, eradicating awareness of where they were and the crisis they faced. Her trusted friend, the man she cared for most in all the world . . .

Then he released her, his breathing rough. With his steadying hands on her arms, he said forcefully, "I'll be back, Callie. Never doubt it. And we'll have Trey, so don't worry. *I will be back!*"

He spun on his heel and left. Callie stared after him, touching the fingers of her left hand to her lips. *What had just happened?*

Her life had turned upside down. Again.

Round eyed, Molly exclaimed, "I thought you were just friends!"

"We were." Callie moistened her lips with her tongue, still shaken. "That's changing."

Sarah gave a deep chuckle. "Next time that boy asks you to marry him, you need to say yes!"

Maybe she would. The idea was starting to make sense.

The apartment felt very empty after Richard and Josh and Peter left. In the silence, Molly said uncertainly, "Trey will be all right, won't he?"

"He will." Sarah put a comforting arm around her granddaughter. "Peter Carroll didn't sound too worried. It's just that a leg wound makes it hard to walk, and it's a mighty hot day. The boy is tired."

Callie didn't disagree with any of that, yet a pall of anxiety hung over her. Was danger really threatening, or was she generally tied in knots of anxiety? It felt like real danger coming at them. Maybe a small group of British soldiers would make their way into the city. Or British sailors might come ashore in a small boat to wreak havoc.

Both ideas were highly unlikely. Yet her unease wouldn't lift.

A tired Sarah relaxed in the padded, extended chair. Eyeing Callie, she said, "You look like a cat dancing on hot coals, Miss Callista."

Callie took a deep breath to steady her nerves. "It feels like something is about to happen. Not the British invading the city. At least not yet. But *something*."

"There could be plain old criminals," Molly suggested. "With so many men off in the militia, looters might break into houses that don't have men to defend them."

"Maybe that's what I'm feeling," Callie said slowly. "As a way to keep busy until the men return, how about if we practice what we'd do if thieves did break in? Like the drills that soldiers are always doing."

"I like that idea," Molly said. "Trey told me that's why soldiers drill all the time. So they'll know what to do when they face danger. Most people just freeze when something terrible happens. We'll do better if we've practiced how to react."

"Exactly!" Callie said, struck. "When the British soldiers broke into my house in Washington, I felt paralyzed, like a terrified rabbit. I don't think I could have done anything more since they outnumbered me, but I hate myself for feeling so helpless."

"No one likes feeling helpless," Sarah said with a touch of grimness. "Let's work out what we'll need to do if we have to defend ourselves."

Callie regarded her pistol thoughtfully. "In Washington, I knew a single shot wouldn't be enough to save me from a squad of angry soldiers. But if there was a break-in here, it would probably be only a few men. I need to put the pistol in a convenient place, along with powder and shot for reloading."

"How about this?" Molly pulled a small table to a position with a clear shot to the doorway. Then she put a basket with her rag rug materials on the edge toward the door. "You can put your pistol and ammunition there and someone coming in won't see them."

"Perfect! What about knives? We have Sarah's good sharp cooking knives, but it would be hard to throw them accurately without a lot of practice."

Molly considered. "Knives work best close up. I don't want anyone to get that close to me!"

"I certainly hope not, but if several drunks break in and see three females, they might decide they want to amuse themselves." Callie swallowed hard. "Which means they would get far too close."

They all fell silent, too aware of the possibilities. Molly said, "I have a good-sized scrap of tanned leather. I could fashion it into a couple of sheaths for the smallest knives that could be worn on a thigh."

"You have a delightfully wicked mind!" Callie exclaimed. "Let's get to work on those."

"Don't forget tobacco," Sarah said. "We've got great barrels of it just sitting here. They're nice and stable on their flat ends, but if we turned a couple on their sides, they'd roll fast if pushed, and they're heavy."

"Brilliant, Sarah! Molly, let's start by tipping a couple of the barrels on their sides and aiming them toward the doorway. After that, we make sheaths for the knives."

Her stepdaughter smiled. "This is fun, in an alarming way."

"I'm sure it will come to naught," Callie said. "But the preparations will keep us busy." She laid her loaded pistol, her powder, and her extra balls on the table behind the rag basket. She'd told Richard earlier that she wasn't sure she could try to kill someone. But her opinion on that was changing.

Chapter 22

"The cabin is down here." Peter directed the cart into a bumpy track that wound through a tunnel of trees. "I brought Trey as far as I could so we'd be beyond the battle." His words were underlined by the blasting of artillery just east of them.

The lane ended at a weathered log cabin. Chickens scrabbled around the yard, glancing up incuriously before returning to their hunt. Gordon guessed they'd been turned loose from their cages so they wouldn't starve before the cabin's owners could return.

"If the redcoats find this spot, those chickens are history," Josh remarked as he halted the cart in front of the cabin. "Did you have to break in, Peter?"

The young man nodded, looking apologetic. "The lock was very simple. I didn't want to leave Trey lying out in the open. I left some money and a note of apology. I also left both of our rifles under the table. I didn't feel strong enough to carry them."

Gordon and Josh followed Peter inside. Trey lay with

his eyes closed on a simple pallet of old blankets that his friend had fashioned in front of the cold fireplace. The crude bandages on his left shoulder and leg were stained with blood, but he opened his eyes when they entered. "Grandpa!" He looked ready to weep with relief.

"Don't worry, Trey," Josh said in his deep, comforting voice. "This is a good friend you have here. He came straight to the warehouse, then guided us back."

Trey's exhausted gaze moved to Peter. "He saved my life. If the British had found me, I'd be dead, like Hank McComas and Danny Wells." He swallowed hard. "I really liked them both."

"Were they the ones who shot General Ross?" Gordon asked sympathetically.

"I'm not sure who fired the shot that took him down," Trey said painfully. "Three of us fired at once and we're all sharpshooters, so it could have been any one of us. General Ross was knocked from his horse and an aide caught him before he hit the ground. His troops gave a kind of howl of anguish and rushed forward to attack us. Hank and Danny were both killed under the tree they'd used as a shooting platform. I . . . I'm sure they're dead. I was hit twice but I was farther away so it wasn't so bad." His face screwed up and he looked very young. "I'm not dead yet. Am I going to die?"

Gordon removed the leg bandage, poured on whisky to clean it, then applied a fresh bandage. "Some day, but it won't be today. The musket ball that struck your left thigh went straight through the muscle without hitting any major blood vessels."

Trey's jacket was already off, so it was easy to examine the shoulder wound. "A ball grazed over your shoulder." He poured more brandy, then fashioned a pad and bandage. "Inflammation is always a danger, but you're

young and strong and you'll be home with your grandmother very soon. You should be fine. In the future
you can brag to girls that you're a hero of the Battle of
Baltimore." Which was no more than the truth.

Trey gave a rusty little laugh, then gasped when
Josh and Gordon carefully lifted the blanket he lay on
from both ends, using it as a stretcher to carry him outside to the cart. As Peter fashioned a blanket canopy to
keep the sun out of his friend's eyes, Gordon returned
to the cabin and added to the money Peter had left.

Then he collected the rifles, powder, and ammunition, and closed the door. With luck, the owners would
return to find their cabin intact and the money sufficient to excuse the home invasion.

They set off at a slower pace than when they'd arrived so Trey wouldn't be jolted more than absolutely
necessary. Josh drove while Peter gave directions. Gordon sat in back with Trey and loaded both rifles, then
concealed them under the blankets. He could pull one
out and shoot quickly, but hoped he wouldn't have to.

Shortly after they turned onto the main Philadelphia Road, a squad of American soldiers led by a lieutenant stopped the cart and brusquely demanded an
explanation of what they were doing so close to the
battle lines.

"My wounded friend and I were in the advance
guard of sharpshooters," Peter explained. He indicated his bandaged arm. "I'm no good now, so I was
told to take my friend Trey back for medical treatment."

The young officer peered into the back of the cart,
seeing the bloodied bandages. He asked Gordon, "Who
are you?"

"A surgeon, George Gordon." He showed his blistered hands and Americanized his accent. "But I've put in time digging fortifications this last week, too."

The lieutenant accepted that and waved them on. "Best get out of here fast. The City Brigade is holding off the British so far, but if they break . . ."

He shook his head wordlessly, then continued with his patrol. He'd barely noticed Josh, probably considering him a slave and of no account.

As they headed west toward Baltimore, Trey said, "You tried to warn me that war isn't glamour and glory."

"Yes, but it's one of those things that must usually be learned firsthand," Gordon said. "At least you survived your baptism by fire."

"So far." Trey gave a crooked smile. "Were you an officer in the British Army? I heard Miss Callista call you Captain Audley once."

"I've commanded a ship or two, but I've never been a formal soldier with a rank and uniform. Obeying orders is not my strong point," he replied. "But I've had to fight for my life more than once. Surviving pirates in the South China Sea is serious combat."

"Really?" Trey's eyes opened wide. "That's not just a story you're telling to distract me?"

"Entirely true. I've fought on other occasions, too. Usually against bandits or pirates. Not fighting for my country, just defending myself and my friends from vicious people who wanted to kill us for whatever reason."

Trey closed his eyes and was so silent that Gordon thought he must be asleep or unconscious. They were halfway back to the warehouse before he asked in a thin whisper, his eyes still closed, "They say General Ross was a good and honorable man, and I might have killed him. Am I a hero or a villain?"

Gordon laid his hand on Trey's. "Both. Neither. The hell of war is killing strangers, many of whom are decent, honorable men with friends and family who love them. Ross is such a man. But the British Army has no other officers here who are his equal. With him gone, they may withdraw, or if they attack our fortifications, they may not do as good a job of it. That could save many American lives."

After another long silence, Trey said, "I thought soldiering would be grand and honorable. Now I don't think I like it very much."

"Which proves you're wise beyond your years. You've done your duty. You can take pride in that even if you don't like what you did."

"Thank you," Trey whispered. He said no more on their trip back to the warehouse, but Gordon saw a glint of tears under his eyes.

Being yanked into adulthood wasn't easy.

Chapter 23

❧

Arranging their defenses was a good distraction for Callie, Molly, and Sarah. Sarah's energy was still low, but she assured the younger women that she was quite capable of rolling a tobacco barrel into invaders.

Molly's tanned leather was easily fashioned into a pair of thigh sheaths that would safely conceal the two smallest kitchen knives. Callie felt like a dashing lady pirate when she tied the sheath to her left thigh and practiced swiftly pulling it out from under her skirts.

Sarah dryly asked her not to kill anyone with the knife because she wouldn't want to use it in the kitchen after that. Despite the heat, Sarah was making a beef, barley, and vegetable soup that Trey liked, saying it would be strengthening. Even more strengthening would be the grandmotherly love Sarah put into it.

It was hard to ignore the noise of artillery and gunfire sounding in the east, but Callie became somewhat used to it. People really could become accustomed to anything.

Their preparations were complete by dusk. Callie and Molly settled on opposite sides of a lamp, Molly working on her rag rug and Callie altering another secondhand gown. As Callie unpicked a seam, it occurred to her that the two of them were more like sisters than mother and daughter. Being a sister seemed to carry less responsibility than being a mother.

Molly wasn't much younger than Callie's smallest sister back in England. Annie had been in leading strings when Callie went to Jamaica. What would she be like now?

She felt a stab of longing for her childhood home. Her father was a bully and probably her next younger sister had betrayed Callie to their father when she'd tried to elope with Richard. But by and large, she got along well with her sisters and little brother. Had they missed her? Would they even remember her after all these years?

CRASH! A thunderous blow on the door yanked Callie from her thoughts. She leaped to her feet as fear lanced through her. Another blow smashed into the door, wrenching it halfway off its hinges. This was it, the menace she'd felt approaching!

After a paralyzed moment, she remembered the pistol. But before she could even leap from her chair, a third blow shattered the door into jagged fragments and three men surged into the sitting room.

And in the lead was her brutal stepson, Henry Newell.

A triumphant sneer twisting his features, he hissed, "I've got you now, you bitch!"

Sarah was in the kitchen stirring her soup. She and Molly both froze, staring at Henry like rabbits hypnotized by a snake. They knew all too well what he was capable of.

Callie had thought it absurdly unlikely that her step-

son would come all the way to America to find her. Yet
now that he was here, there was a ghastly inevitability to
this meeting. According to Matthew's servants, Henry
had been a beastly little boy, never able to admit when
he was wrong or able to bear losing. He'd go to any
lengths to claim that he'd won, which meant that he
must hunt her down and destroy her.

Marshaling all her resources, she rose gracefully,
letting the gown she was altering slide to the floor. A
pity she'd moved out of reach of the table that held
her pistol in order to get better light for her sewing.
The table was between her and Henry, and her weapon
was tucked in the shadow of the rag basket where he
couldn't see it.

Callie moved a step toward him and said with lying
warmth, "Why, Henry, what a surprise to see you! Have
you come to insure that your stepmother and half siblings are safe and well? I would have thought you'd
have a wife and child to look after by now."

"No wife and no child, not until I've dealt with you!"
He yanked a pistol from under his coat and aimed it at
the center of her chest. The barrel looked as large and
deadly as the mouth of a cannon. "I've waited three
damned years for this moment!"

Callie had but one thought: buy time any way she
could. "How did you find me? I thought you'd have
given up by now."

"I never give up! I couldn't believe my luck when
the warehouse manager wrote a couple of months ago
and mentioned that Mrs. Newell was living in Washington and might want to move into the warehouse loft if
the British invaded." He smiled with sick anticipation.
"Finally, after three bloody years and having to sail
through the Royal Navy. Today we spent hours in the
alley while I studied the warehouse and waited to

make sure the men wouldn't be back soon. Now it's time to administer justice."

Clamping down on her panic, she drifted a couple of steps closer. "I don't understand why you need justice, Henry. Your father's final will mysteriously vanished, so you've inherited everything. Isn't that enough?"

His pale eyes glittered. "You ran off with all the money in my father's safe and four valuable slaves, not to mention my mother's jewelry! I want everything back!"

Even a war hadn't been enough to stop him. His hunt would have cost far more than the value of what he claimed to have lost. But Henry didn't care about logic. She'd always sensed that he had a dark obsession with her that must be satisfied, no matter what the price. "You know your father wanted to free all four of the Adamses. He told both of us that at the same time."

"But he was too lazy to ever get around to doing it. Since he didn't, they belong to *me* and you had no legal right to free them!" he growled. "I've come to take them back and to settle my score with you. With the city under attack, no one will even notice what happens here."

"What score is that?" Another step closer, keeping an eye on his men as well. They were a pair of surly brutes and they smelled like they'd just emerged from a distillery. One man was familiar and she realized it was Hoyle, the brutal overseer she'd persuaded Matthew to fire. Now she recognized that the other was a muscular but not very bright crony of Hoyle's called Goat, which was an insult to real goats.

Keeping her voice calm, she continued, "I've done you no harm. The money I took from your father's safe is far less than I would have been entitled to if I'd received my jointure. Even if you add the fair market value of the Adamses to what I took"—the very idea of a price on her friends made her want to vomit, but she swallowed and continued—"it would be far less than paying my jointure. You *won*, Henry. Why did you go to so much effort to track us down?"

"Not only did you take my property, but you treated my father's whore like she was a white woman!" he raged. "Neither of you were fit to touch my mother's skirt, yet there you were, cozening my father and plotting against me!"

"I treated your father with respect and affection, and I never plotted against you." Another step closer. The pistol was almost within reach, but in the instant it would take her to grab it, cock, and aim, he could shoot her since his pistol was already aimed and ready to fire. Misfires weren't uncommon, but she didn't want to bet her life on one.

"You gave ideas to the other slaves!" he added furiously. "After you left, several of my best field hands escaped from the plantation and joined the free Maroons in the hills. You took them from me!"

"Enough of that!" Hoyle, the fired overseer, said impatiently. "You promised us girls as part of this. That black girl over there? She looks ripe for it!"

"She's worth more as a virgin, if she is one. I can make a small fortune if I sell her in New Orleans. You can have that one, my father's widow, after I'm done with her." Henry waved the pistol toward Callie, then at Sarah. "The old one is a good cook and will fetch a fine price, too. Where's the boy?"

"My brother joined the militia to fight the British," Molly said fiercely. "He's out of your reach!" She also inched toward the invaders, a dangerous light in her eyes.

"I shouldn't have waited until the men left, but that blond fellow looked dangerous." Henry swore, his brow furrowed as he considered what to do next. "The boy may be out of my reach, but the old man is a good carpenter and worth something. We wait here till they get back." His gaze burned over Callie again. "We can amuse ourselves with the women, then ambush the men when they return. Who's the blond man, step-mama dear? Your lover?"

"Just an old friend from England," she said mildly. "No one you'd know."

"So I shoot him and tie up all my slaves and leave your bodies for the warehouse manager to find." He laughed. "Or what's left of you."

Goat, whose gaze had been flicking from one woman to another, swaggered toward the kitchen. "I don't wanna wait till you're done with the redhead. The old woman ain't bad lookin'. I'm willin' to give her a try while Hoyle stands guard." Leering, he reached for Sarah.

"Don't touch me, you swine!" Sarah flung a ladleful of boiling soup into Goat's ugly face. He screamed and leaped back, clawing at his eyes.

While he was off balance, Sarah shoved him furiously into the nearest tobacco barrel. It lay on its side, aimed toward the door. Goat's head hit the heavy barrel with an ugly crack, propelling it toward Hoyle.

"Watch the hell what you're doing!" the overseer barked as he dodged back out of the path of the barrel and collided with Henry.

"You clumsy oafs!" Henry roared as he stumbled and swung around to see what was going on behind his back.

In the instant he was distracted, Callie snatched her pistol from behind the rag basket, cocked the weapon, and held it with both hands as she took grim aim.

"You wanted justice, Henry? I'll give it to you!" In Washington she'd been unable to pull the trigger, but this time she didn't hesitate. She squeezed the trigger slowly so her aim would be true, and fired a pistol ball into Henry's black heart.

A deafening blast of sound and a cloud of eye-stinging smoke saturated the room when the kick of the pistol rocked her back. As blood sprayed out from the wound, she fought back her nausea. She felt sick—but not sorry.

"What . . . ?" His expression disbelieving, Henry slowly folded over, staring at her as blood gushed from his chest. With his last breath, he hissed, "*Bitch . . . !*"

Callie clutched the table as Henry fell, his pistol dropping from his hand. Fearing the cocked weapon might fire, she instinctively ducked back.

The weapon blasted more numbing sound and stinging smoke, and Goat shrieked. When Callie straightened, she saw blood blooming from the man's temple. He made a strangled sound as he fell into an ungainly sprawl and spoke no more.

Callie was frantically reloading when Hoyle wrenched the pistol from her hand and threw it aside. "You bloody hellcat! You'll pay for that!"

He grabbed her neck with both hands and dragged her toward him. Gasping for breath, she fumbled to pull her skirt up so she could reach the knife sheath on her left thigh. Molly had carefully sharpened both knives, and if she could just reach hers . . .

Molly screamed, "Let her go!" She scooped up Henry's empty pistol and hurled it into Hoyle's face, crunching viciously into his nose and cheeks. Then she reached for her own knife, fury in her eyes.

While Hoyle swore and clutched his nose, Callie

managed to yank her knife from its sheath. She slashed at the overseer, cutting the right side of his face. He swung at her wildly, but missed her knife hand.

More by instinct than design, she ripped the knife sideways with all her strength. The razor-sharp blade sliced across his throat and released a scarlet fountain of warm blood. He was so close that it splashed over her as he collapsed.

She gagged and almost fell herself, but Molly caught her arm and kept her upright. "It's all right now," Molly said wildly. "It's all right!"

From the time Goat had gone after Sarah to the death of Hoyle couldn't have been much more than a minute.

Callie stared at the blood and bodies. The loft looked like a battlefield. She began to shake, her eyes stinging viciously from the smoke. Then she heard heavy footsteps pounding up the stairwell. Blindly she raised the knife and steeled herself to face this new threat.

"Callie!" Richard's voice. "*Callie!*"

He blasted through the broken door, summed up the scene in one swift, horrified glance. "My God!"

"Henry attacked us," Molly said starkly through her tears. "It was my thrice-damned *brother.*"

Richard reached Callie in half a dozen swift steps and enfolded her in his arms before she had fully realized that he was there. "Callie, are you all right?"

Her body recognized his before her mind did. She sagged into his chest and clung with biting fingers as the fear and anguish of the last minutes rushed through her. She began to sob uncontrollably.

Josh barreled through the door, older than Richard but not much slower. "Sarah, Molly!" He stopped and stared down at Henry Newell's body. "Dear God, that brute came all the way here?"

"Grandpa!" Molly ran sobbing into his arms.

Sarah followed at a more moderate pace. Coolly she said, "That devil man came to rape and kill Miss Callista and take the rest of us back into slavery." She reached her husband and slid an arm around his waist, leaning into his solid strength since his arms were occupied by Molly. "Miss Callista killed him and Hoyle like the swine they were," she said with fierce satisfaction. "Fought like a tigress. Molly too." She gestured at Goat. "Henry's last shot killed that one and no loss."

Josh swore with words Callie had never heard him use before. Not releasing his womenfolk, he moved forward and kicked Henry in the head. "I wish I'd been here to do the killing!"

"I wish you had, too." Callie's voice was so thin she could barely hear it herself. "But he waited until you and Richard were well away because it would be harder to break into the loft with you here."

Richard smoothed her hair back with one large, gentle hand. "Come sit down, Catkin. You look ready to collapse."

Numbly she folded limply into the nearest chair. "Where is Trey?"

Richard knelt in front of her and took hold of her hands, his gaze searching. "He's down in the cart with Peter Carroll. Not badly injured, but weak. We were just pulling up to the warehouse door when we heard gunshots and a scream from in here. Josh and I left Peter in charge while we ran up as fast as we could." His smile was as warm as his hands. "But you didn't need us, Catkin. My warrior woman."

"I was terrified," she whispered.

"Of course you were," he said briskly. "Any sensible person would be. A hero does what needs to be done despite being terrified. You're a hero, Callie."

"I don't feel like one."

"But you are." His brow furrowed. "I need to go down and help bring Trey up here. Will you be all right for a few minutes?"

She summoned the remnants of her strength and resolve. "I'm fine." She squeezed Richard's hands, then released them. "Bring Trey up. After Sarah treats him"—she glanced at the bodies on the floor, then looked away—"we can decide what to do next."

Chapter 24

It was full dark now. Gordon left Josh to deal with the bodies and headed down to the cart, his heart still pounding from the panic that had consumed him at the sound of the gunshots. He barely remembered telling Peter to look after Trey as he bolted from the cart, unlocked the door, and raced up the stairway, Josh half a dozen steps behind him. The shattered door signaled that disaster had struck.

When he'd entered and seen Callie covered with blood, he'd felt his heart die inside him. He'd never forget the overwhelming relief of finding that she was unhurt, but her devastated shock was bad enough. Her hands had been icy when he sat her down and tried to warm them.

She'd rallied when he said he needed to help Trey, but she was deeply shaken. She would always do what was needed, but she had the soul of a nurturer, not a killer.

When he reached the street, Trey was struggling

against Peter's attempts to keep him in the cart. "What happened?" he asked frantically. "Is my family all right?"

"Everyone's safe." He glanced at Peter, wondering how much he should say in front of someone who wasn't family.

Guessing his thoughts, Peter said in a low, very adult voice, "I am a Carroll of Carrollton and I will do anything to protect Molly and Trey. If there are secrets, they are safe with me."

Gordon gave a short nod of acknowledgment. "Trey, your half brother, Henry, broke in with two thugs. Callie, Molly, and Sarah fought them off."

Trey blinked uncertainly. "Fought them off . . . ?"

"All three are dead," Gordon said bluntly. To Peter, he said, "You're part of this now. Tether the horses and we'll take Trey upstairs. You can learn the whole story there."

Peter nodded and secured cart and horses after Gordon helped Trey out. Though Peter kept his injured arm in the sling most of the time, he was able to do some things when necessary, such as bring up the two rifles. A good lad.

Since Trey could barely walk, Gordon locked an arm around his waist and half carried him up the narrow stairwell. The boy gasped from the pain when his injured leg was jostled, but he kept moving upward, hauling some of his weight by using the railing.

Finally they reached the living quarters, which were bright with lantern light and welcome. Sarah had already made up the bed in the men's dormitory for her grandson, and she ordered, "Bring my boy here!" when they entered the sitting room.

Trey almost wept with gratitude when he was lowered onto the mattress and could roll into Sarah's soft, welcoming arms. She silently shooed everyone else out and rocked Trey as if he were an infant, crooning words of comfort as she stroked his back.

Gordon and Peter wearily returned to the main room and found that Josh had dragged the bodies against a wall and covered them with a blanket. Molly was setting the dining table with food and drink, but she turned and came straight into Peter's arms. "Thank you for saving my brother!"

"I'm glad I was there to help him." He hugged her back and it was a mutual embrace of much more than gratitude.

Gordon had suspected that there was a strong attraction between the two, and that was now confirmed. They were both young, but if they developed a lasting attachment, it would establish Molly for life; Gordon had been in Baltimore long enough to know that the Carrolls were one of the first families of Maryland. Charles Carroll—Peter's grandfather, perhaps?—was a signer of the American Declaration of Independence and said to be the richest man in America.

Wealth usually married wealth, but Molly was beautiful, kind, intelligent—and the death of Henry Newell changed her financial situation dramatically. Now she and her brother would be heirs to the Newell estate. Given Gordon's skill at forgery, he'd make sure of that. Molly would be an heiress.

Since when had Gordon started thinking like a matchmaking mother?

Tactfully overlooking the embrace, he said, "Thanks for bringing out the bottle of good brandy I bought a couple of days ago, Molly. I think we all could use some."

"I certainly can." Callie emerged from the women's bedroom looking pale and shaky but under control. She'd washed off the blood and changed her dress and seemed almost normal, unless one looked at her eyes.

With difficulty, he refrained from embracing her since that might undermine her fragile control. "How are you managing?"

Her smile was crooked but genuine. "We're all alive and unhurt, and Henry and his brutes are dead. I consider that the best possible outcome." Her gaze went to the covered pile of bodies and she swallowed hard. "Now we must decide what to do with the . . . the remains."

"I have some ideas for that, but first, nerve tonic." Gordon poured brandy into the half dozen small glasses Molly produced. He tossed his off in one gulp and poured another. If the bottle were big enough, he'd have crawled inside and drunk it dry. Callie didn't drink quite as quickly, but was ready for a refill rather soon.

Molly choked a little on hers, but the spirits seemed to steady her. She said, "Now we eat. We'll think more clearly then."

Josh smiled fondly. "You're just like your grandma."

She gave a shy smile of thanks and brought in a serving platter of sliced ham and cheeses, then a pot of steaming soup with bowls, a large loaf of bread, and a pitcher of her lemonade. Gordon realized he was ravenous, and so were Josh and Peter. Callie and Molly tucked into the food also and Callie started to look less pale.

Sarah joined them a few minutes later. "Trey is sleeping. He'll be fine, I think." She sank wearily into the chair next to her husband and he efficiently filled a plate for her.

This was what family should be, Gordon realized. This sharing and consideration were nothing like the tense, miserable meals of his own childhood.

Molly finished first, then talked Peter out of his uni- While the men had been retrieving Trey, she'd washed the blood from the right sleeve, which had been taken off and turned into an improvised sling. Now that man, jacket, and sleeve were all in the same place, she started neatly reattaching the sleeve. Peter stared as if he'd never get enough of watching her.

When everyone was done eating, Callie asked baldly, "What do we do with the bodies?"

"I saw the Royal Navy masts out in the Patapsco River earlier," Peter said. "Within the next few hours, they'll start bombarding Fort McHenry. I don't know how long the fort will hold, but my guess is that quietly putting some bodies in the harbor within the next few hours will not draw much attention."

After a startled silence, Callie asked, "Are lawyers allowed to suggest such things?"

"The aim of the law is justice," he said in a steely voice that hinted at the man he would someday become. "Those three men broke in here to destroy three innocent women. Their deaths are just."

"That's very pragmatic," she said. "I admit that I'd rather not try to explain what happened here, especially not with a battle about to begin."

"Henry's two bruisers can be disposed of that way, but Henry's death must be officially confirmed," Gordon said. "If Henry died unmarried, Molly and Trey are heirs to the Newell estate."

Callie gave him a sharp glance. "He said in as many words that he would marry only after he'd dealt with me."

Gordon wished he could kill Henry all over again. "In that case, the codicil to the will goes into effect and the estate goes to Molly and Trey, apart from your jointure and some individual bequests. As you probably recall, you're their legal guardian until they come of age."

Callie knew he was bluffing about a codicil to the

will, but she must have had faith in his forgery skills. "I'm glad he chose me as their guardian, but does that mean I must take them back to Jamaica to run the plantation?"

"No!" The hoarse voice was Trey's. He'd risen from his bed and was now clinging to the door frame of his bedroom. "I won't go back there. Not ever!"

As Josh stood to help Trey to the table, Molly said in a voice quieter but no less emphatic, "Nor will I. Papa doted on us, but not enough to free us. We were slaves there. I will never, ever return!"

"I understand and agree. I don't want to go back, either." Callie frowned. "But that means the plantation will have to be put in the hands of a manager, which is often problematic for absentee owners, or it must be sold."

"We can't sell the plantation with its slaves," Molly said flatly. "They're our friends and they must be freed."

"Molly's right. I don't want things to go on as they were before," Trey said. Watching his grandmother warily, he poured a small amount of brandy into his glass of lemonade. Sarah didn't object, but her expression said that was all he was going to get.

"There's another possibility," Gordon said. "Callie, didn't you tell me that a neighboring plantation was owned by the Quakers and worked by free blacks? You could free the Newell slaves and sell the plantation to the Quakers with the provision that they keep on anyone who wanted to continue working there at a fair wage. It will greatly reduce the value of your inheritance, though."

Molly and Trey exchanged a long glance, then nodded. "Let's do that," Molly said. "We don't need to be rich, but we need to do the right thing."

Callie smiled mistily at them. "I am so proud of both of you. This will be complicated to do at long distance, though. Peter, once we have a death certificate for Henry, should I contact my lawyer? He might have connections with lawyers in Jamaica, or know someone who does."

"That depends on the lawyer," Peter said. "Many work only locally, but Baltimore and Washington have lawyers with international connections. Who is yours?"

"Francis Scott Key, of Georgetown."

"Mr. Key? Excellent!" Peter said enthusiastically. "I read law with my uncle, and he and Mr. Key are good friends. They've worked together on cases before. They'll be able to find a good, honest lawyer in Jamaica to handle the probate, free the slaves, and sell the plantation after your ownership is confirmed. It will take time, of course."

"I don't know where Mr. Key is at the moment, but surely the world will settle down eventually," Callie said. "Perhaps your uncle can start the process of declaring Henry Newell dead and let us know what legalities will be involved?"

"I'm sure my uncle will be happy to aid you." Peter's expression made it clear that any excuse to see Molly more often was welcome. "As for Mr. Key's present location, I believe he's currently a guest of the Royal Navy."

Callie stared at him. "Why would he be on a British ship?"

"Mr. Key and Mr. Skinner, the American prisoner of war agent, sailed out to Admiral Cochrane on a truce ship to ask for the release of an American prisoner, an elderly doctor whose health is not good," Peter explained. "They also wanted to get a list of other Americans who are being held prisoner by the British. My uncle said that because they are on board the British flagship, it's likely they will be detained until after Baltimore is defeated."

Trey made a growling noise. "And if Baltimore isn't defeated?"

"No matter who wins the battle, they should be released afterward. Mr. Skinner has been the American agent for some time and he has always been treated with great courtesy." Peter grinned. "He said British admirals set a very fine dinner table."

"That's good to know." Callie frowned. "But how do we get Henry declared dead without my being accused of murder?"

"I have an idea, though you'll probably all hate it," Gordon said. "We could say that he was concerned about his stepmother and half siblings so he came to Baltimore in hopes of taking them to safety. Learning of his young brother's injury, he accompanied us to the battlefield to help bring Trey home and was, alas, mortally wounded. There were enough bullets flying around North Point to make that plausible."

"You're right," Callie said with a wry smile. "The thought of a heroic, concerned Henry is *revolting*! But it would probably work if we all agree on the details of the story. It would even account for his body being here. Will the rest of you go along with that?"

"I'll agree with what you say if asked," Josh said, "but I couldn't bring myself to say that devil came to Baltimore to protect Molly and Trey!"

"We can lie if we have to," Sarah said. "But we aren't likely to be asked, being just a couple of old black servants."

"If they ask me, I'm sure I could burst into convincing tears," Molly said. "As long as I don't have to say what I'm crying about!"

That produced a laugh. "We can do that, though I hate to say he ever had a selfless impulse," Trey said.

"But I imagine they'd mostly talk to you since you're our guardian, Miss Callista?"

Peter pulled a piece of folded paper and a short pencil from his pocket. As he wrote, he said, "Here is a note and the address for a nearby physician my family uses. He's less likely to be with the militia than a surgeon would be. He can give you a certificate of death and help you arrange a burial."

Callie accepted the paper, murmuring, "This week just keeps getting better and better. But my thanks, Peter. You're making this much easier."

"I'm glad to help, ma'am." He got to his feet and let Molly help him into his uniform jacket, allowing it to lie open over the sling that supported his right arm. "I must return to my regiment now. I don't know if I'll be of much use, but the British are likely to attack our Hampstead Hill defenses tomorrow, and I must be there."

Looking unhappy but not arguing, Molly stood. "Come back safely!"

"I plan to," he said with a crooked smile as he reclaimed his rifle and ammunition. "Just as well I'm leaving now, in case you have other things to discuss that a lawyer shouldn't hear!"

A very clever lad, Gordon thought. *Good enough for Molly.*

The women all gave Peter farewell hugs and Molly walked him down to the street for a private good-bye. When they were out of earshot, Gordon said, "Josh, do you have any good ideas for the best way to dump Henry's associates into the harbor without being noticed?"

"It's going to rain soon," Josh said. "A bad storm, I think. We can put the bodies in the canvas sling behind the house and lower them to the ground with the hoist, then take 'em out in the Newell boat. If we row toward the fort, we can just slide them overboard and come home."

"That sounds wet but efficient," Gordon said. "If we're going to use the hoist, we can lower Henry as well and put him into the office. I doubt that anyone wants to sleep with his corpse here."

"You're right about that!" Callie said fervently. "Have you often had to dispose of unwanted bodies?"

"No, but it's a new skill to add to my list," he said with mock seriousness.

Callie laughed and got up from the table. "Someday I'd like to see that list. But now, it's time for all of us to get to work."

Chapter 25

Callie had always found Josh to be a reliable predictor of weather, and he was right once again. As heavy rain pounded down, Richard and Josh secured the three bodies in a canvas sling and lowered them to the ground with the hoist. Grim work, but they did it stoically. She gave thanks that their household contained two well-muscled men with strong stomachs.

In the darkness and rain, it was doubtful they were observed, but if there were questions, lowering Henry's body down to the warehouse office was legitimate reason for their behavior. Henry the hero, come to Baltimore to protect his family. The idea would have been laughable if she weren't still shaking inside from his threats.

As Richard and Josh stoically rowed out into the downpour, Callie concentrated on cleaning up the spilled blood. She forced herself to think of it as just another stain, like red wine or soup. After that, she helped Molly put away the food and wash the dishes. Luckily the hoist was also good for bringing up water for washing and cooking.

Callie was drying plates when Molly asked, "What do you think of Peter Carroll?"

Unsurprised by the question, Callie replied, "I think he's a fine young man."

"Do you think there could be anything . . . lasting between someone from one of Maryland's first families and a slave girl?"

"You're no longer a slave!" Callie said sharply. "You're a beautiful, well-educated young woman and an heiress. But as to whether there might be a lasting relationship—that's always a question. I'm sure that Peter doesn't care about your origins, but his family might. Even if they don't object, you're both very young, and first loves are often like summer storms. Intense but swiftly passing."

Molly gave her a sidelong glance. "Peter's nineteen. I'm sixteen. You were married at sixteen."

That was inarguable, and rather shocking. Molly was the same age Callie had been? She was so young! But Callie had been young, too. Far too young. "I didn't marry by choice. Though it didn't work out badly, I can't recommend it."

"Did you have a first love who consumed your mind and heart?" Molly asked intently. "Someone you desperately wanted to be with, though you were forced to marry my father?"

"Not really," Callie said, her voice apologetic as she stacked dry plates and set them on a kitchen shelf. "The girls I knew were always becoming infatuated with dancing masters and stable boys and handsome young curates, but that never happened to me. I guess I'm just not very passionate."

"I don't believe that!" Molly exclaimed. "Surely there was someone!"

Callie frowned as she thought about it, then shook her head. "I suppose because Richard was my best friend, I didn't notice the stable boys."

"Weren't you ever infatuated with him?" Molly asked in amazement. "He's so handsome!"

Callie shook her head. "We were best friends. We rode and swam and got into mischief together. That's different."

"Was it?" Molly asked skeptically.

"It was," Callie said firmly as she suppressed thoughts of several recent kisses that were very different from their childhood relationship. "And don't question your elders!"

Molly laughed and they finished up the cleaning in silence. Sarah had already gone to bed, tired from the day, and so had Trey.

Callie said, "You look asleep on your feet, but I won't rest until the men are home. Before you go to bed, will you help me move several of the tobacco barrels to make an alcove? I want to put my pallet there because I don't think I'll sleep well tonight and I don't want to wake Sarah."

"What about keeping me awake?" Molly said as she moved toward the tobacco barrels.

"Oh, I don't mind if I ruin your sleep!" They both laughed, and once more Callie thought about how Molly was more like a little sister than a daughter.

It was easy to arrange barrels to create a U-shaped alcove that faced the balcony and the bay. Callie spread out the blankets as wide as they could go because she knew she'd be tossing and turning all night. And if she wept from shattered nerves, no one would hear.

Callie packed Molly off to bed, then took a lemonade and brandy out onto the balcony. The city had told residents to turn off all lights so as not to present targets to the enemy, which meant all was rain and darkness outside. They had two shielded lanterns that cast only a narrow band of light. One hung in the stairwell, the other sat inside on a table to guide the men when they returned.

It was a relief to hear the splash of oars, then the rasp of wood on wood as the sturdy rowboat pulled up to the pier. A minute or two passed, then a key grated in the lock of the street door below the balcony. That door was undamaged, so Henry must have had a skeleton key.

She heard the sounds of slow footsteps as two tired men climbed up to the apartment. As they entered, Josh muttered, "First thing tomorrow, I get this door fixed and give the one downstairs a better lock!"

She set her drink aside, collected the two small shots of brandy that she'd poured earlier, and met them at the door. "You're both dripping like laundry just pulled from a tub," she observed as Richard followed Josh inside.

"Feels like that, too. I could give a fish swimming lessons." Josh covered a yawn. He'd brought up the lantern from the stairwell, carefully keeping the sliver of light turned away from the balcony.

Callie handed him a brandy. "Trey is asleep in your room. He wanted to give you the bed, but we bullied him into keeping it by pointing out that he'd been shot twice today so he might as well take advantage."

"That boy!" Josh said affectionately. "No matter. I'll be fine on the floor. Could sleep on rocks tonight." He tossed off the brandy in one gulp and handed the glass back to Callie. "It surely has been a long day."

"That it has." There were pegs on the wall by the door, so Richard hung up his saturated hat and coat before accepting his drink.

"There are towels and dry clothes in the kitchen area," she said. "Do you want to join me on the balcony to relax before you go to bed?"

"I'd like that." His smile in the dim light was tired but peaceful. He took the second lamp and headed toward the kitchen.

Callie felt her way back to the balcony and folded her tired body into one of the chairs. A few minutes later, Richard settled into the chair on her left, lantern in one hand and in the other a tall glass that was probably a lemonade and brandy mixture like hers.

Though the noise of the rain drowned out most sounds, it felt natural to speak softly. She asked, "Your task went well?"

"Yes, we rowed out into the harbor and gave them to the sea in two different places. I don't know how long until they're found. Their deaths may or may not be associated with the fighting. I don't think it matters." He raised his glass toward the harbor and the fort that lay at the end. "There are more important things to worry about."

"As Peter Carroll said, they deserved their fates. I don't mind about those two, yet . . ." She hesitated as she searched for the right words. "I'm sad about Henry, who was the worst of them all. I despised him, but Matthew loved him."

He reached out and took her hand. "Love can be very blind."

They sipped in silence as the rain went from wild downpour to steady but more normal. After a last swallow of her lemonade, she set her empty glass on the floor by her chair. "I gather you intend to forge that very useful codicil to Matthew's will?"

"Yes. Show me the old draft will and any other samples of his handwriting you have, and I should be able to create a document that will look convincing. It's not as if there are other heirs standing by to take this to court."

"True. And it really is what Matthew would have wanted. Justice, if not precisely the law. I like Peter's perspective on this."

"How are you feeling?" he asked. "I've had a long and tiring day, but all I did was travel to a battlefield to retrieve a friend, then dispose of a couple of dead villains. Your day was much worse."

She tried to come up with a light warrior woman comment, but instead she began to shake. Gripping his hand like a lifeline in storm-tossed seas, she said raggedly, "I think this has been the worst day of my life. Worse than when we eloped and wrecked both our lives, worse than when the British burned my house and almost lynched me. Today, everyone I care deeply about was threatened. Trey was wounded and you and Josh could have been killed going after him. Then Henry came and . . ." She broke down, unable to speak.

He rose and lifted her in his arms, then sat down again with her in his lap. He tucked her head under his chin and stroked her back. "Those you love were violently threatened, and you had to kill. You have every right to have strong hysterics. Feel free to break china or throw yourself on the floor and pound your fists and heels."

She wasn't sure if it was his intention to make her laugh, but she did. "If I'm going to do that, better to throw myself down and pound the floor before I start breaking the china."

"Very practical." His long fingers gently massaged her nape, spreading warmth and relaxation through her knotted body. "There's been enough blood today."

She exhaled with exhaustion. "I'm sorry to have become such a watering pot. You used to say admiringly that I was like another boy, not a weepy girl."

His laughter was soft and tender. "How times have changed. I've now noticed that you're a girl and I don't mind that at all. In fact, I quite like it. Breaking down after a horrible day is not the same as being a watering pot."

"I suppose not, but there isn't time to indulge myself for very long. Tomorrow Baltimore may be bombed to splinters, and I need to be ready for anything."

"The Royal Navy won't have it easy," he assured her. "They'll have to destroy the Star Fort and the artillery battery on Lazaretto Point on the opposite side of the channel. Then they'll have to get past the boom at the mouth of the inner harbor. The forts might hold out under the bombardment so long that the British will get bored and just head home."

"Let us hope so! This isn't Washington. Baltimoreans are digging in and fighting for their homes." She sighed. "Tomorrow I should be able to pretend I'm strong again, but tonight I don't want to sleep alone. I've made up a pallet among the tobacco barrels. Will you join me there?"

His body stiffened under hers. "Define what you mean by joining you."

"Sleeping. Holding each other. No more." She slid from his lap and offered her hand. "You must be at least as tired as I am, Mr. Bold Adventurer. Come rest."

He took her hand and rose from the chair. "Gladly, Catkin." He gave her his intimate, entrancing smile. "You can purr me to sleep."

Chapter 26

It had been a very long day. In fact, it was already the next day, Gordon suspected. Even with as stalwart a partner as Josh Adams, battling through storm waves in the harbor had been exhausting. Gordon was weary to the bone, which made Callie's invitation to her pallet very welcome. Fatigue should make it possible to behave like a gentleman, though it would be a challenge. She inspired dangerously intense feelings of tenderness and lust.

The alcove between the barrels was cozy, with a faint scent of tobacco and a view out the windows, not that there was much to see in a heavy rain over a blacked out city.

Callie flipped back the top blanket and crawled onto the pallet, which was wide enough for two. He stretched out beside her, asking, "Is the floor less hard than previous nights, or am I just so tired I'm not noticing?"

"The pallet is somewhat thicker. Earlier today Molly and I found empty burlap sacks in the warehouse so we brought up enough to provide better padding," she explained as she stretched out on the right side of the pallet. "It's not a real bed, but better than the floor."

True. But even the unpadded floor would have been fine with Callie beside him.

She rolled onto her side to face him and circled an arm over his waist as she exhaled softly against his neck. "Thank you for joining me."

"The pleasure is mine," he said, meaning it. "It's been an appalling day. Yet we're all here and alive and Trey isn't badly hurt. There is much to be grateful for." He stroked down her back and confirmed what he'd suspected when he held her in his lap. She wasn't wearing anything under her worn, often-washed linen shift. This felt almost as good as if she wasn't wearing anything at all.

"Molly is mad for Peter and apparently he is for her," Callie murmured. "Do you think anything will come of it?"

"I trust you mean marriage, not a by-blow."

"Of course!" she said indignantly. "I want her to find a kind, devoted husband who will care for her and any family they might have. Like Sarah and Josh."

"Peter seems like a thoroughly good fellow. Assuming he survives the British attack, yes, I think they might have a future. I suppose her inheritance will be decent?"

"With the slaves all freed it won't be a great fortune, but should be enough to let her live independently or take a good dowry into a marriage."

"Money always makes a potential mate more attractive," Gordon said. "But they're young. The attraction might be fleeting."

"I told Molly that, and she wanted to know if at her age I'd been so entranced by a young man that I wanted him above everything." She chuckled. "I had to admit that never happened to me."

"No?"

"I thought about it and decided that being friends with you absorbed all my energy where boys were concerned."

He considered. "The same was true for me. Maybe that made us slower to think about mating than others our age."

"I'd rather think I was just slow than that there was something wrong with me," she said wryly.

"There's nothing wrong with you," he said reassuringly. "You just lacked opportunity since you went directly from being my best friend into marriage with a man old enough to be your father. I assume that when you reached Jamaica, you were too honorable to take up with a man nearer your own age?"

"I never met anyone who tempted me enough for adultery," she replied. "What about you? Once you got out into the world, did you find yourself to have the normal amount of interest in the opposite sex?"

Trust Callie to ask such a direct question. He smiled into the night. "Oh, yes. Quite unremarkably normal." But though he'd met women he enjoyed in and out of bed, he'd never met one who held his mind and heart, or drove him to youthful madness.

"Ever since we met in Washington, I keep thinking how different our lives would have been if we hadn't been caught by our fathers when we eloped," she mused. "If we'd married in Scotland, would our lives have been better or worse? Would we have bored each other as we matured and developed roving eyes? Would friendship have been a strong enough foundation for a marriage even if we weren't mad for each other?"

"I've thought about that, too," he admitted. "I offered to marry you as a friend to save you from an unwanted marriage. But when you gave me a thank-you kiss—well, I realized you were a girl, and that elopement wasn't such a bad idea."

She laughed. "Really? I remember being enormously relieved and grateful and excited by the adventure, but not romantic about you. I guess I'm just not very passionate."

"I beg to differ." Remembering the way she'd responded to his good-bye kiss earlier in the day—or rather, yesterday—he rolled face to face and kissed her again. Slowly, thoroughly, and feeling quite passionate enough for both of them.

He caressed the subtle arc of her elegant back, sliding over the worn linen till he reached the sweet curve of her backside. His palm stilled there as he drew her tight against his groin.

She made a soft sound deep in her throat and pressed closer yet, her mouth hungry and responsive. She didn't shift her lower body away but instead slid her leg between his, bringing them into searing contact even through layers of fabric.

Fatigue vanished and he gasped, "If you don't want this to continue, the time to stop is now!"

Her reply was to slide her hands under his loose shirt, erotically cool against his heated skin. "Let us forget this day, together," she breathed.

Burying any last gentlemanly scruples, he moved his hand to her breast, feeling the warm fullness through the fabric of her shift. She sucked in her breath and arched into his hand when he thumbed her nipple. She captured his mouth again and her tongue danced against his, teasing and inviting.

He slipped one hand under the hem of her loose

shift, skimming his palm up her smooth, shapely leg. Higher, higher, over her hip. Then, delicately, between her thighs until he reached silken, intimate heat. She whimpered and moved her legs apart, the small sound drowned by the rain.

As he explored the sensitive folds, she began to writhe against his deft fingers, her hips rocking into his touch. He realized dizzily that he could take her now and she would welcome him, and his yearning for that mesmerizing fulfillment almost destroyed the last vestiges of his control.

But he had just enough sense left to realize that full intimacy would cross a line that would change everything between them, and perhaps destroy any chance for a future. So tonight there would be no ultimate joining, but he would, by God, prove that she had her share of a woman's passion!

He reclaimed her irresistible mouth while his fingers delved ever deeper into her most secret places. Heat and moisture and sensual scents, more intoxicating than the best of brandies.

When she shattered under his touch, his mouth captured her cry. She softened against him as her tension slowly dissolved.

He moved his lips to her throat and the delicate hollow of her shoulder, feeling the hot beat of her blood against his tongue. She was so desirable, so sweetly edible.

As her breathing slowed, she flowed bonelessly against him, molding herself so closely that it was hard to tell where she ended and he began. His blood pounded frantically through his veins, demanding satisfaction, but the intensity of her pleasure was almost enough to compensate.

He was halfway back to sane when he realized that

her hand was shyly sliding under the waist of his drawers. He'd barely registered that when she clasped him and his whole body went rigid.

She wasn't expert in her ministrations, but she didn't need to be. Callie's hand stroking him, Callie's body pressed against his, Callie's essence were enough to melt his brain into blazing oblivion. He crushed her close, groaning, "Callie . . . dear God, *Callie!*"

"My Richard," she whispered, her breath a caress against his throat. "My Lionheart."

Her hand tightened with experimental pressure and triggered a violent culmination that seemed to go on forever, yet was too swiftly done. Blissful oblivion.

He held her close as his mind and body slowly aligned again. When had he known such fierce satisfaction?

Never.

Such contentment?

Never.

"Sorry, Catkin," he murmured unsteadily. "I didn't mean this to happen."

"Nor did I. But it certainly was a fine distraction from a difficult day," she said with a hint of laughter.

"I'm glad you think so." He smiled ruefully. "I lied. I'm not the least bit sorry about this even if it was unplanned."

He gently kneaded her back and neck, not wanting to let her go, ever. Acting on that yearning, he said, "Callie, will you marry me? We're both rather damaged by life and have our share of limitations, but I think we're better together than apart."

She didn't reply for long, long moments. But she didn't try to pull away, either. Finally she said, "It's hard to see beyond the next few days. But if we're alive and intact after this battle, the subject is worth discussing."

He laughed exuberantly. "I'm finally beginning to wear you down!"

"I believe you are," she said with a smile in her voice. "But also, everything has changed since you swept back into my life three weeks ago."

"My world is different, too." He'd moved from constant restless seeking to peace. He'd literally traveled around the world to find his way home. Now he just needed to persuade his wary warrior woman to share her life with his.

He kissed the top of her head, then pulled the blankets over them. The rain was slowing, but the temperature had dropped so that the night air was cool. "I'd like to hold you like this forever."

"I'll settle for tonight since we don't know what tomorrow will bring." She wriggled delightfully as she found the most comfortable position against him. She fit so well into his embrace. "May dawn be slow in coming!"

His bone deep fatigue had dissolved, leaving relaxed contentment. When had he ever been happier? Never.

He drifted off to sleep with a smile on his lips.

The night shattered when the British began to bombard Fort McHenry at dawn. The most powerful navy in the world was knocking on Baltimore's door.

Chapter 27

Josh guided the physician and his assistant into the warehouse office, all three of them dripping with rain. A dignified man of middle years, the physician had responded immediately to the power of the Carroll name at the end of Peter's note. After waiting for the sound of a particularly noisy series of bombs to diminish, Josh announced, "Dr. Williams and his assistant, Miss Callista."

Callie moved around the counter to greet the doctor. "Thank you for coming so promptly, Dr. Williams. The . . . the body is on the worktable back here." She led the doctor back to where the long, tarpaulin-wrapped shape rested on the table where Molly had worked on her rag rugs.

When they were all gathered around the table, Callie gestured to Richard and Molly and introduced them with the names they'd decided were most appropriate. So many different names! Richard shouldn't be a lord, and there didn't need to be any mention that

Molly and Trey were illegitimate. Best if she and the young people were all Newells. "This is Mr. Audley and Miss Mary Newell. I assume Josh explained that the deceased is my stepson, Henry Newell, who just arrived from Jamaica in search of his family and became a victim of this dreadful violence?"

Williams nodded as he removed his streaming cloak and handed it to Josh without even glancing at him. Josh played the role of unnoticeable slave very well. "Yes, I gather the unfortunate gentleman was shot. What were the circumstances?"

"Peter Carroll had brought us news that Molly's brother, a militia sharpshooter, had been wounded during the fighting at North Point," Richard explained. He'd claimed the honor of telling the necessary lies because he would be best at it. "Josh and I took our cart out to retrieve Trey under Peter's guidance. We were bringing him home when we discovered Mr. Newell, who was mortally wounded on the road back to the city. Trey was unconscious, but Josh recognized Mr. Newell immediately. His horse had disappeared. Likely stolen by the British."

Williams made a note in a small notebook. He didn't seem to find anything suspicious in the account. "Do you know why he rode out into a battlefield?"

"Mr. Newell was still breathing and semiconscious. He said he was seeking his younger brother, whom he knew to be a fine marksman and with the courage to volunteer for the most dangerous position." Richard's voice lowered. "He was aware enough to understand that Trey was beside him and not critically wounded. We brought Mr. Newell back to the city in the hope we could get him to a surgeon in time."

"Alas, it was too late." Callie dabbed at her eyes with a fine muslin handkerchief. "He had already passed by the time he arrived here. To think that he came all this way because of his young brother and sister!"

"Admirable but foolish," Williams said gravely as he made another note. "I gather you're a friend of the family, Mr. Audley?"

"Mrs. Newell and I are betrothed," Richard said blandly, ignoring startled glances from Callie, Molly, and Josh. "We plan to wed when things have settled down."

"I was completely undone by Henry's death," Callie said, doing her best to sound helpless. "Mr. Audley has been invaluable in helping us through this trying time. He was the one who explained the importance of a certificate of death. Henry was a man of property, and with neither wife nor child of his own, his brother and sister are his heirs. The situation is complicated by the fact that he is from Jamaica, so all must be done properly here."

"I understand entirely." The doctor tucked his notebook away inside his coat. "I'm honored that Mr. Carroll suggested me to serve you in such an important matter."

An unusually violent set of concussions at the fort briefly shook the warehouse. Everyone flinched, but after hours of the bombardment, there were no stronger reactions.

Richard continued, "Henry Newell would have been my stepson. Though I never had the opportunity to truly know him before his tragic demise, I must do my best for him now." He solemnly pulled the tarpaulin down to reveal Henry's face. Even in death, lines of anger and brutality showed in his face.

"There is no question of the identity of the deceased?" Dr. Williams asked, which sounded like an official question required before he issued a death certificate.

"Yes, it is certainly my stepson. Here are the papers he carried." Callie produced the documents that Richard had taken from Henry's pockets. There had also been a substantial amount of money. They'd confiscated most of it on behalf of Molly and Trey.

"There was also this signet ring." She showed the gold ring with an elaborate initial *N* engraved on the flat top. "It belonged to my husband and went to Henry on his father's death. Now it must go to Matthew's younger son." Though she wasn't sure that Trey would want any part of something Henry had worn.

Williams nodded. "Can anyone else identify the body?"

Molly stepped forward. "Yes, it is certainly my older brother, Henry. If only he hadn't come to America!" She began to cry, her sobs echoing through the warehouse office. Callie put a comforting arm around her shoulders.

"Trey, the younger brother, can also swear to his identity," Richard said. "He can't manage the stairs because of his leg wound, but he saw Henry yesterday and was conscious enough to testify. I can take you up to him if you like."

"No, that isn't necessary." Williams pulled the canvas all the way down to Henry's waist, revealing the wound in the center of his chest, blood dried on the shirt around it. "Nor is there any question of the manner of death." The physician shook his head sadly. "Such a young man. A pity that Mr. Newell traveled so far to aid his family only to meet death so far from his home."

"A great loss for Jamaican society and for his family," Richard agreed piously. Callie had to admit that he lied very well. He continued, "Our last duty to Mr. Newell is to give him a proper Christian burial. He was

Church of England and that would be our choice if a church is convenient."

"St. Paul's, which I attend, is quite near." Williams smiled with a touch of humor as he pulled the tarpaulin over Henry's head again. "We Baltimoreans are proud of our city, but it's a modest size compared to London! Everything is nearby."

"Do you think the vicar would be able to help us?" Callie asked. No one mentioned that the hot weather made time a significant issue.

"The vicar, Reverend Harbow, is a friend of mine." Williams smiled soberly. "In the last fortnight, he told me he'd have the sexton dig extra graves in case they were needed after the battle. I'm sure he'd be willing to oblige you with a swift funeral. There's a coffin maker nearby who also made extras just in case."

How very practical. Callie drew a deep breath, realizing she couldn't wait to get Henry safely buried. "Richard, my dear, shall we call on the vicar?"

"Of course." Richard lifted one of the oilskin capes they'd brought down because of the pouring rain and draped it over her shoulders. "Dr. Williams, could you send your assistant to the coffin shop to order one brought here? We have a cart that can transport the coffin to the church if the Reverend Harbow can accommodate us."

"I'm happy to lend what aid I can." Williams beckoned the assistant closer and explained, after which Richard gave the man some of Henry's money for the coffin. The money was proving useful since even Richard didn't have unlimited resources.

It was decided that Molly and Josh would stay with the body till the coffin arrived. Callie and Richard would go to St. Paul's and try to persuade the vicar to bury a distinguished foreigner who was not of his parish. Callie silently prayed that the funeral could be held right away, preferably this afternoon.

Dr. Williams accompanied them out and gave directions to St. Paul's before taking his leave. Callie took a firm hold of Richard's arm as wind and rain buffeted them and cannons boomed in the distance. When they were out of earshot of the doctor, she asked with dangerous sweetness, "How did I miss the fact that we're betrothed?"

Richard grinned. "I thought if we were on the verge of marriage it would give me more standing to deal with doctors and vicars and the like."

She rolled her eyes. "Remind me to break our betrothal after we've buried Henry."

"Yes, Catkin," he said meekly, but his eyes were dancing. "It will be as if the betrothal never happened."

She ducked her head and concentrated on the sloppy footing. She'd never admit it, but she found it . . . interesting to test the idea of being betrothed to Richard. It no longer sounded impossible or undesirable.

She glanced at him askance. Blast the man! After the previous night and the discovery of a passionate side she hadn't realized she possessed, it was becoming harder and harder to imagine sending him away. Easier and easier to imagine them sharing a bed . . .

Later! She'd think about the future later. For now, she'd concentrate on burying her stepson, and on blocking out the constant boom of the guns.

The funeral of Henry Newell was swift and simple. Callie guessed that everyone in the city who wasn't on the front lines of battle was taut with nerves from the ongoing battle and grateful to have worthwhile work to do. Reverend Harbow had been very sympathetic and helpful. It surely didn't hurt that Richard had mentioned the name "Carroll" a time or two.

As the heavy rain persisted, her stepson was buried in the muddy graveyard of St. Paul's Church. Trey couldn't attend and Molly flatly refused to, so they stayed home while Callie, Richard, Josh, and Sarah attended.

Since Reverend Harbow knew nothing of the deceased, he asked if anyone wanted to say a few words. Callie had a sudden horrific urge to shout, "*My stepson was a bully and a brute and I'm glad I killed him!*"

She choked back the words and buried her face in her hands, hoping her reaction looked like grief. Richard smoothly rose to his feet. "I didn't know Henry Newell in life, and due to the sad circumstances, we will never be members of the same family. A sophisticated man of the world who had been educated in Britain, he was well known in his native Jamaican society and will be greatly missed by all his friends."

If he had any, Callie thought, not lifting her head. Though Jamaica certainly had other drunken brutes, so perhaps he did.

Richard continued, "His extraordinary journey to America in search of his brother, sister, and stepmother will never be forgotten by them. I know that he was beloved by his mother and father, and with the grace of God, he is surely with them now." Richard bowed his head. "May Henry Newell know peace."

Callie realized that last sentence sounded sincere. Perhaps it was.

Thus ended the mortal existence of Henry Newell. Richard gave generous fees to the church and to the vicar, and commissioned a very respectable tombstone that gave Henry's name, dates of birth and death, and another pious wish that he rest in peace.

As the four nominal mourners walked home through the saturated streets, Josh remarked, "I'm glad I went. I wanted to make sure that devil was dead!"

His comment made the others break out in tension-relieving laughter. The battle for Baltimore was still in progress, but at least the devil was dead.

They arrived back at the warehouse to find Molly and Trey sleeping. Richard and Josh took the spyglass out to the balcony to observe the continuing cannonade. They had an excellent view of the flashes from mortars and the rockets blazing through the skies.

Despite the rain, adjacent rooftops held numerous solemn observers of the battle. From this distance it was impossible to know how the battle was progressing, but the continuing bombardment was a good sign because it meant Fort McHenry had not yet surrendered.

Callie and Sarah headed to the kitchen to prepare supper. Callie sliced ham and cheese while Sarah made a batch of her lemonade, using the last of the lemons. With the city under siege, who knew when lemons might be available again? "A good thing you bought this Virginia ham. It's kept us fed for days."

"Lots of fine things you can do with a ham," Sarah agreed as she split biscuits in half and layered ham and cheese in the middle. "Soon that bone will end its days in a pot of bean soup. But it's a pity we don't have fancier food on hand. If ever a funeral deserved celebrating, it's this one!"

Callie laughed, then covered her mouth with one hand. "I keep thinking I should be more respectful, but I can't."

"Justice was done, and we got away with it," Sarah said with a glint of humor in her eyes. "I can tell you that a heavy, heavy load has been lifted from my soul."

"I'm starting to feel less dreadful about what I did." The griddle had been heating over the small fire, so Callie melted a knob of butter, then covered the cast iron surface with ham and cheese biscuits.

As the cheese gently melted and the biscuits browned, Callie wiped her hands on a small towel. Without looking at her friend, she said, "Richard has asked me to marry him for real, not just to fool the doctor and the vicar."

"Are you going to say yes?" Sarah asked with interest.

"I don't know," Callie said in a low voice. "When he first asked in Washington, the idea seemed out of the question. I had too many other responsibilities. But the more time that passes, the harder it is to imagine not having him around."

"Your Lord George, or Gordon or Richard or Audley or whatever he calls himself, is a fine man and he thinks the sun rises and sets on you." Sarah grinned. "And as handsome a fellow as I've ever seen. Why are you dragging your heels?"

"Because you're my family, and I can't bear the thought of leaving you!" she blurted out painfully. "And I'd have to leave because Richard wants to return to his home in England."

"Miss Callista, you look at me instead of that griddle," Sarah said firmly. When Callie raised her gaze, Sarah continued, "You are the beloved angel of my family. You carried us out of slavery like God's own chariot and you supported us when we hadn't a penny to bless ourselves with.

"Best of all, you gave us the chance to raise our heads and become free and independent. You gave us the lives we have now and the futures we can look forward to." Her voice softened. "Now it's time to move into your own life. If you love him, why not marry him?"

"I don't know that I love him the way you and Josh love each other, or the way Molly and Peter feel about each other. Richard and I were best friends. I think we still are. Is that a strong enough foundation for marriage?"

"Every marriage has its own story," Sarah mused. "They all start in different places and follow different paths. Josh and I fell in love when we were about the same age as Molly and young Peter, and we jumped over the broom together long before we were able to get officially married in a church. Did you know that Master Matthew bought me from another plantation so me and Josh could be together?"

"I didn't know that," Callie said, startled at her ignorance of another large piece of her friend's story. "That was incredibly kind of him."

"Josh asked him to buy me and he did because he valued Josh and I was cheap, just being a scullery maid at the time," Sarah said with a laugh. "He got a bargain since I turned into such a fine cook.

"But he didn't have to make it possible for us to be together, and I've never forgotten." Her voice turned nostalgic. "Josh and I loved each other then and we love each other now, but that love has grown and changed over the years. It's quieter, deeper, stronger. Beyond anything we could imagine when we were young and just wanted to get each other naked."

"I don't have to know that!" Callie exclaimed. "It's like thinking of my parents sharing a bed."

Sarah laughed. "I'm just saying that if you don't love your man now the way you think you should, I guarantee

you'll come to love him in ways you've never dreamed
of. You're a good woman and he's a good man, and together you'll find good ways of loving."

Callie drew a deep, slow breath. "So you're giving
me your blessing?"

Sarah crossed the small kitchen to draw Callie into
her arms. "I am. You've lived for us for so long. Now
it's time to live for yourself. Doesn't mean we won't
still love you or you don't love us. We'll write lots of letters. Maybe you'll come for a visit someday, or maybe
we'll visit you. I've a mind to see London before I die."

Callie hugged Sarah, wishing her own mother had
been so warm and wise. Then she smelled something
scorching and pulled away to swiftly flip the biscuits on
the griddle before they burned.

Sarah had given her much to think about. Her friends
didn't really need her anymore. The thought was
sad—but it was also liberating.

Chapter 28

The half dozen chairs on the balcony had been improved with padded burlap sacking and they made a fine gallery for viewing the bombardment of Baltimore. Callie and Sarah carried out platters of steaming ham and cheese biscuits, a pitcher of lemonade, and two small bowls of pickled onions.

Like the Pied Piper of Hamelin, they lured followers, in this case Molly and Trey, who had woken up hungry. Trey used an improvised cane Josh had fashioned for him.

Sarah asked, "How are you feeling? You look stronger."

"I'm fine," her grandson said cheerfully as he took a chair beside his grandfather. "I can go back to the battlefield tomorrow."

"No, you will *not!*" Sarah and Callie said in unison. Sarah continued, "This battle will be won or lost without you. You've done your part."

Callie chose the chair next to Gordon. Within patting distance, he was pleased to see as he bit through the crispy crust of a ham and cheese biscuit and washed it down with a swallow of lemonade. Lightly spiked with brandy, he noted. Sarah knew how to soothe a household in difficult times.

After swiftly demolishing a biscuit, Callie asked, "How goes the battle?"

"We don't know." He passed her the spyglass and reached for another ham and cheese biscuit. "Between the darkness and the rain, all we can see is the bombs and rockets blasting at the Star Fort and the battery across at Lazaretto Point."

She adjusted the spyglass. "When a rocket goes off over the fort, I can see the brick walls, but nothing more." She sighed and passed the spyglass on to Sarah. "What a very, very strange day this is."

"Someday the history books will describe this day as the Battle of Baltimore and this will all be seen as obvious and predictable because history books know who won," Gordon mused. "But tonight it's a mystery. For what it's worth, I'm beginning to feel optimistic for the city. The Royal Navy has been blasting away at the fort for hours to very little effect."

"Looks to me like the British ships have cannons with a greater range than the American guns," Josh said judiciously. "But keeping far enough away to stay safe maybe makes the cannons less accurate."

"I can't hear any firing from the east," Molly said. "Do you think the British troops have withdrawn?" she asked without much hope.

"More likely the two armies are staring at each other and shifting their troops around like a chess game," Gordon replied. "The American forces are much larger and they're dug in behind formidable earthworks. My guess is that the British troops are waiting for the naval attack to succeed. If that happens, the

British Army attacks and the city will be caught like a nut in a nutcracker." He demonstrated a pincer movement with thumb and forefinger.

Molly winced at a particularly ear-numbing blast. "They must be able to hear this in Washington!"

"Maybe even in Philadelphia," Trey said as he scooped up two more biscuits.

Callie sighed. "How long can the British keep this up? They've been blasting away for"—she paused to calculate—"fifteen hours now. Won't they run out of ammunition?"

"Eventually, but they haven't yet," Josh said grimly. "The fort isn't using as much since they know the British warships are out of range of their guns. I guess they're saving their ammunition to use if the British come closer."

They ate in silence until all the food and drink were gone. The spyglass had come to rest with Callie, who looked through it now and then. "Even though we can't see much of anything, there's a ghastly fascination to it all," she observed.

"Maybe so," Josh said as he got to his feet. "But I'm tired. Wake me if anything interesting happens."

Sarah also rose. "You can get used to anything, can't you? I'm pretty sure I can sleep through a few hundred more cannon shots. Molly, Trey, time for bed for you, too. These have been difficult days."

Proof of their fatigue was that the young people headed inside without protest. Josh slung his arm around Sarah's shoulders and they followed.

"It's just us now. Come sit on my lap," Gordon suggested. "I find it comforting."

"So do I." Callie rose from her chair and scooped up a blanket from their pallet, which was still made up between the tobacco barrels. When she settled into his welcoming lap, she tugged the blanket over them both and rested her head on his shoulder with a sight of relaxation. "I could become accustomed to this."

"I hope you do." Gordon toyed with her hair, pulling out the pins she'd used earlier to look like a respectable widow. Then he combed the heavy silken mass over her shoulders. "I love your hair. It shines red-gold in the glare of the Congreve rockets."

"I think we're a little too far away for that," she said with a laugh. "I hate those horrible rockets—they shoot around like mad things. I'll never forget when the British blasted two of them into my house." She sighed. "That seems a thousand years ago."

"I feel the same. So much has happened since then. We're living in a strange limbo." He frowned as he tried to define his feelings. "It's odd not doing anything. I'm not used to being a spectator. Generally when there's trouble, I'm either fighting or fleeing for my life."

She chuckled. "I expect you fight more often than you flee. Where are your loyalties now?"

"I admire this city. Boys like Trey and a handful of canny old veterans like Sam Smith are facing down the greatest military power on earth. Wellington's Invincibles defeated Napoleon himself, yet inexperienced American troops are holding the line against them." He let his hand rest on the nape of her neck, warm and protective. "I don't want to see Baltimore defeated."

"Neither do I." Callie yawned. "As Josh said, wake me if something interesting happens."

"I will. Sleep well, Catkin," he whispered. He loved having her sleeping in his arms. Their intimacies of the previous night had made this possible. How long until she was so used to having him around that she'd be willing to marry him? Not long, he hoped. He wanted to go home, and he wanted Callie by his side.

Despite the continuing cannonade, he also dozed. Then an abrupt change woke him up. Not more cannon blasts, but silence. Eerie silence. The bombardment had stopped.

He came sharply alert, staring out at the dark, rain-filled skies over Fort McHenry. In the distance, a clock struck four times.

Callie stirred, then snapped awake. "The guns have stopped firing! The battle for the fort must be over, but who won?"

"Impossible to tell," he said grimly. "But even if Fort McHenry has surrendered, the Royal Navy will still have to pass by the blockade of ships that were sunk in the channel. That won't be easy."

She stared into the darkness with frustration. "I *hate* not knowing!"

"So do I," he agreed as he tightened his arms around her. "There are so many things to hate about war, but lack of information about what is happening is one of the worst. We'll have to wait until dawn to see which flag is flying over the fort."

She slid from his lap and stretched. "You make a good mattress, but my muscles are stiff."

"So are mine." He rose creakily from the chair. Even burlap padding wasn't enough to make it comfortable for a night's sleep. "Shall we pace back and forth along the balcony?"

"I have an idea." She moved behind the chair and began kneading his neck and shoulders. It felt wonderful. More proof of the physical ease between them.

When she was done, he did the same for her, some of the massage moving into areas that made her swat his hand away. "Behave!" she ordered.

"Yes, ma'am," he said meekly.

When they were feeling more flexible, they walked back and forth on the balcony, holding hands while watching the darkness and rain. He thought about the troops out in the entrenchments on Hampstead Hill, who must be up to their eyeballs in mud. But he hadn't yet heard anything to suggest that they'd been attacked by British forces.

Eventually the eastern horizon began to lighten, but to their mutual frustration, the sky was still too heavy to see any detail of the fort. Gordon retrieved the spyglass for a closer study, then shook his head. "I can see the flagpole and there is a flag hanging on it, but it's impossible to see what flag it is."

They were joined by Josh and Sarah, then Molly and Trey. Sarah fried up some eggs and sandwiched them into the last of the biscuits and served them with hot tea. They ate, watched, and waited, saying very little.

The clouds began to thin and the sky lightened. With striking suddenness, the clouds shifted and sunshine illuminated the star-shaped fort and the flag unfurling over it in the wind. "Look!" Molly breathed. "Just look at that!"

The morning breeze caught the flag and the huge banner rolled out with lazy power. Red, white, and blue, stars and stripes.

Fort McHenry was undefeated.

Callie gasped. The most beautiful flag she'd ever seen flew over the fort, the stripes and stars clear as the breeze snapped the banner out to its full, magnificent size. "We won," she breathed. On the horizon she saw masts of British ships. They were sailing away, already disappearing into the morning mist.

As exhilaration blazed through her, she shouted it out. "We won! They're gone! The little brick Star Fort withstood the greatest navy in the world!"

As Trey whooped, Molly wept, and Sarah and Josh hugged, Callie grabbed Richard and spun him around. Laughing, he caught her close. "They could be planning an attack from a different direction," he warned, but he was also grinning like a fool.

"They won't. It's autumn and they're going to go off to some nice warm place like Bermuda or Barbados," she said firmly. "I have one of my feelings, Richard. Remember them? Baltimore is *safe.*"

"You're usually rather accurate with your feelings," he said as he tucked her under his arm and gazed across the harbor at the luxuriantly rippling flag as if he couldn't get enough of the sight of it.

As she gazed in the same direction, she realized with a shock that it had been years since she'd had one of her feelings of certainty. They'd been common in her youth, but they'd vanished—when?

When she'd married and moved to Jamaica. For fifteen years she had done what was necessary and moved forward one step at a time, but the vivid, rebellious spirit of her youthful self had been buried.

With sharp-edged clarity, she recognized how she had adopted her stepchildren and their grandparents as family not just because they needed her, but because she had desperately needed them.

But now she felt reborn, and she was ready for a new adventure. As more jubilant cries began to be heard from the streets and rooftops around them, she grabbed Richard's hand and drew him back inside, away from the rising clamor of victory.

Staring into his enigmatic gray eyes, she asked, "Lord

George Gordon Richard Augustus Audley, do you still want to marry me?"

He blinked at her use of his full string of names. "Yes."

"Then do you want to ask me again, or shall I ask you?"

He laughed exuberantly and embraced her with an energy that swept her from her feet as he swung her around in a circle. "Ask me, Catkin! I hadn't realized that I was dreaming of a day when a beautiful woman would ask me to marry her!"

He set her down, his smile bright enough to illuminate the dawn-lit living area of their attic home. Becoming serious, she caught both his hands and looked up into his dear, handsome face, more familiar than her own ever since they were introduced in the nursery of Rush Hall.

"As you said to me, we're both damaged in different ways, but we're better off together than apart. Outside on the balcony I realized that I haven't had any deep feelings of certainty since I lost you and had to marry against my will. Until today. I *know* that the British are withdrawing from this battle, and I *know* that I want to travel on the adventure of a lifetime with you. The same adventure that was cut off once before, but now it's our time." She drew a deep breath. "Will you marry me, my Lionheart?"

His expression changed and for the first time she saw vulnerability and need in his eyes. Ever since he'd galloped to her rescue in a ridiculously romantic fashion when Washington burned, he'd been endlessly competent and in control. But this was a glimpse of the deeper man, and it touched her heart.

"I don't know if I'll ever be able to give you as much

as you deserve, Callie," he said gravely. "But I swear and vow, I will marry you and give you all that I have."

Her hands tightened on his. "What more can a woman ask?"

"Well, a roof over her head, and I can give you that," he said with a grin. "It's in London, but if you like, we can find a different roof in a different place."

"Even here?" she asked, curious.

"Even here. I've developed a fondness for this city." He shrugged. "Anywhere will do as long as it's with you. But first—England!"

A shiver ran down her spine at hearing the words out loud. "I just had another one of my feelings."

"They're coming thick and fast this morning," he said with interest.

That's because she was reborn. "There are going to be great challenges when we return to England. Danger, even."

This time when he smiled, it was gentle. "We're going to be confronting our pasts, which will be challenging. As for danger—didn't we want adventure?"

"The adventure of a lifetime." She rose on her toes, wrapped her arms around his neck, and sank into a kiss that had no restrictions or doubts. She was marrying her best friend, and it was right.

Chapter 29

Scarcely able to believe his good luck, Gordon kissed his bride-to-be. Now that she had decided, Callie held nothing back. This was the fearless best friend of his childhood, the girl he'd yearned for in dark and despairing places ever since.

A very loud throat clearing sounded from the open doors to the balcony. He looked up to see all four Adamses regarding them with broad smiles. Sarah said, "Miss Callista, isn't it about time you made an honest man of this poor fellow?"

Callie blushed as only a fair-skinned female with red-gold hair could blush. "I intend to. I just proposed and he said yes."

Bright eyed, Molly asked, "When and where will the wedding be?"

"As soon as possible here in Baltimore," Gordon said promptly. He wrapped an arm around Callie's shoulders and locked her to his side. "I don't want her to get away this time. Josh, will you stand up with me?"

Grinning, Josh said, "Yes, my lord."

"If you call me lord again, I'm dropping you in favor of Trey," Gordon threatened.

"If you insist, Gordon," Josh said. "But I did like the idea of standing up with a real English lord."

"It's only a courtesy title, Josh," Callie explained. "Sarah, will you stand up with me? And, Molly, I want you as an attendant, too."

"Everyone's in the wedding but me?" Trey said, insulted.

"You'll be our guard," Gordon said. "If someone speaks up when the vicar asks if there is an impediment to our marrying, whack him with your cane."

"I have my sharpshooter rifle," Trey said hopefully. "Can I use that?"

His joke cast a moment of uneasy silence over them. Callie ended it by saying, "How about the four of you go for a nice walk along the waterfront? Share the celebrations, see what people are saying. My betrothed and I need two hours or so to . . . discuss our wedding arrangements."

"Come along, children," Sarah said. "We've been dismissed and I don't want you to stay around to be corrupted by these lovebirds."

Giggling, Molly went for a shawl since the rain had stopped and the air was cool. It took a few minutes for the Adamses to collect themselves and leave. Luckily Trey was walking very well this morning. Before they left, Gordon tossed a gold coin to Josh, who was bringing up the rear of the procession. "Have a celebratory luncheon on me."

Josh caught the coin expertly. "Given how early it is, more of a second breakfast. We'll toast you in good strong, hot coffee if we're lucky." He stepped into the stairwell and closed the door firmly behind him.

"Wedding arrangements," Gordon said. "St. Paul's or the Methodist church, where the minister sent us all off with the god of battles watching over us? He seems to give effective blessings."

"We can decide later." Laughing, she launched herself at him and started to rip off his coat. "I propose we anticipate our vows just to see if we're making a wise decision."

"We are," he said as he finished peeling off his coat and tugged her shawl from her shoulders. "But I'm a great believer in making sure." Her dress was designed to fasten at the front so he proceeded to unfasten it with ridiculously clumsy fingers. "Which bed should we use?"

"The beds already have owners, so let's use the pallet. It may be uncomfortable, but it's ours and no one can see in." She went at the buttons at the throat of his shirt, her fingers as clumsy as his.

When had he felt such insane lust? Never. But he'd never bedded Callie before. "We've been waiting a long time for this," he said huskily. "We should take it more slowly."

"I know you're right." She leaned in to kiss the bare skin at his throat with a teasing lick. "But when were we ever sensible?"

"That's a good point. But this . . . this matters, Callie," he said seriously. "This is our future. A woman once told me that marriage is like taking hold of another person's hand and jumping over a cliff together."

Callie laughed. "So the question is, do we soar, or do we crash at the bottom of the cliff?"

"As long as we do it together," he said softly as he peeled off her gown, leaving her in a translucent shift and a light set of stays. "Soar with me, Catkin!"

"Always." As she unbuttoned the fall of his trousers,

she realized that this was their true marriage, though they would make it official soon. These were their promises to each other, and they were about to make the ultimate physical commitment.

She tugged his shirt from his trousers and, in a fit of wickedness, ripped it down the front, revealing his broad chest. Well muscled, dusted with golden hair several shades darker than the sun-bleached hair on his head. She ran both hands over his bare skin, loving the warm pulse of muscled strength.

And scars. Several of them. "Did someone use you for shooting practice?" she asked as she touched a rough depression that looked like it had been made by a musket ball.

"The scars didn't all come in a day," he chuckled. "I have a carefully curated collection. I probably have scars I've forgotten about."

Not letting herself think of his perilous past, she said firmly, "Well, it's time to stop collecting them! That's an order." She pulled his shirt down over his shoulders and arms, wondering how many scars she'd find if she did a thorough inventory. She'd save that for another day.

"Yes, ma'am," he said with mock meekness. "Although if you want to add a bite mark . . ."

"That sounds like an idea worth exploring." She tossed his shirt aside and nipped his shoulder. Warm, salty skin under her tongue, an essence of Richardness.

His eyes blazed like a lion's in sunlight and he swiftly unlaced her stays, leaving her in only a thin shift. She shivered a little despite the heat in his eyes.

Feeling shy, she dragged his trousers down his legs, enjoying the strength and textures of thighs, knees, ankles. Then she knelt before him to hold the fabric of each leg so he could pull his foot out. He wore only his drawers now, and as she stood up she had a good view of his readiness to consummate their—betrothal.

Reading her mind, he asked gently, "Feeling a little shy?"

She blushed. "I was married for a dozen years and a widow for three, but no man has ever seen me unclothed."

"I look forward to being the lucky first, but full revelation can wait." He caught her hand and led her around the tobacco barrels to the nest that awaited them.

In the growing morning light, he was beautiful, fair skinned and golden haired. His mother had been Norwegian and he had that otherworldly Nordic beauty.

He flipped the top blanket aside. It was ragged around the edges. Sarah had bought the blankets used and cheap, then boiled them with lavender to make sure they were clean and sweet smelling. Not particularly soft since the fabric was coarse, but the roughness was erotic where it brushed bare skin. Callie suspected everything would feel erotic in her present state.

Richard pulled her down beside him so they lay face to face. Then he stroked her head and back while he kissed her with great tenderness. She could feel how he held himself back, not wanting to upset her. She felt like a nervous virgin, though she was no virgin. But nervous, yes. It had been a long time since she'd lain with a man, and that had been duty, not desire. She was entering unknown territory.

Her nerves faded as his caresses and kisses rekindled the desire that had set her aflame earlier. She buried her fingers in his hair. The pale strands fell silkily over her hand. "I hope you keep your hair rather longer than fashion dictates," she murmured. "It's so lovely."

He chuckled. "I believe that's what I'm supposed to say." He brushed her hair out with his fingers so he could spread it across her shoulder. "My fire cat, red and gold and brimming with vitality."

"I feel as if I've come to life after years of being a banked fire." She cupped his cheek, feeling the prickle of whiskers since he hadn't shaved this morning. They were almost invisible because of his fair coloring, but the feel was alluringly male. She ran her hand from his cheek to his jaw, his throat, continuing down his body in sheer delight.

Since she was the one who had needed to slow down, she must be the one to turn up the heat again. Her hand kept moving, lower and lower over smooth skin and taut muscles, fingertips brushing through coarser hair until she could clasp that tantalizing heat and hardness.

He sucked in his breath, becoming even harder. She loved that she could affect him like this.

Before she could test her power further, he said huskily, "It's time for me to withdraw from the boiling point by concentrating on you."

He rolled her onto her back and kissed her more deeply. She didn't realize that he'd tugged her shift up to her shoulders until she felt his warm, bare hand on her breast. She gasped and gave a shimmy of pleasure.

Obligingly he bent his head and kissed her breast, teasing with his tongue and lightly nipping until she was ready to shriek from cascading sensations. He transferred his mouth to her other breast while sliding his palm lower over waist and belly until he reached the most sensitive places of all.

"Please don't take too much time," she whispered,

and her hips churned around his questing fingers.
"*Please!*"

"Your wish is my pleasure, milady," he said in a grav-
elly voice. He moved between her legs, using his fingers to position himself. Braced above her, he was
beautiful, a tawny, powerful lion who took her breath
away.

Sweat glistened on his forehead as he entered slowly
out of care for her long celibacy, but despite her tight-
ness, her body welcomed him. Yearning for completion, she surged her hips upward until they were fully
joined.

She caught her breath with amazement and delight.
Matthew had been a thoughtful lover for an unenthu-
siastic bride, and she'd had no reason to complain of
him, but it had never been like this. *Never.*

As he began rocking into her, she surrendered to
flooding sensations, swiftly finding a rhythm with him
that made her blood dance. He thrust, she responded,
he thrust again and she mirrored that movement. Mutual fire rose higher and higher until it consumed her.
When he touched her just above where they were
joined, she shattered into pure passion, no body, only
emotion and intoxicating pleasure.

As she convulsed, she clutched his torso, needing
him to hold her so she didn't fly to pieces. Instinctively
understanding, he secured her in his embrace as he
thrust a last time and culminated with a deep groan,
burying his face in her hair.

She held him, shaken to her core. A dizzy interval
passed before she said unsteadily, "I think this means
we're compatible?"

He laughed, rolling onto his side and bringing her
with him so that they were face to face as he drew the
top blanket over them. She loved being skin to skin

with him. That was another kind of intimacy as powerful in its way as their mating had been.

"Very compatible indeed," he said. "I wonder if it would have been like this if we'd made it to Gretna Green and married then."

"I don't think so," she said. "We were young and much simpler then. I don't think we would have brought as much to our bed." She nipped his shoulder. "Mind you, I think we would have figured it all out quickly!"

He drew her closer. "As you said earlier, this is the right time for us. Though . . ." He paused, then continued in a more serious voice with echoes of pain, "Then I would have been able to come to you with a more open heart. More than I can manage now." He gently stroked her cheek with his knuckles. "But though I might not be able to love as well as you deserve, I would die for you."

"I hope you don't have to," she said with equal seriousness. "I will say in return that I would kill for you." She'd already proved that she could kill. As horrible as that had been, she'd do it without a moment's hesitation to protect Richard.

"What a bloodthirsty pair we are!" He slid his fingers into her hair, massaging her scalp and the nape of her neck. "I'm thinking we won't need such skills in England."

"I expect you're right." She hadn't realized how much he loved to touch, but she liked it very well. Especially since he was awakening a matching craving for touch in her.

She nuzzled against him, sure she would never get enough of this closeness. "I wonder how long we'll have until the Adamses return."

"Not long enough. I'd like to spend the next week

here with you." His fingers wandered to her breast and began doing delicious things.

With a sigh, she pushed his hand away. "We were lucky to get this much time alone, so we'd best marry quickly and make it legal."

"Very true." He rose and stretched, tawny and beautiful. "I shan't mind trying this in a real bed."

She laughed as she stood. She was ready to laugh at anything. "Isn't a first time supposed to be special? Burlap sacks in a warehouse attic will never be forgotten."

Feeling much less shy than she had earlier, she pulled her shift off over her head, leaving her as bare as he was since he seemed to have lost his drawers somewhere. "In case you're wondering what you're getting . . ."

He caught his breath, his eyes darkening. "You are so beautiful. You always were. You always will be. And you'd better cover yourself up before I forget that we won't be alone much longer!"

She tugged the shift on again, feeling agreeably naughty. "Once we're properly dressed, maybe we can take a nap till the others return? Neither of us got much sleep last night."

She looked outside and felt another thrill at the sight of that grand waving American flag. She wasn't exactly an American, but she knew what side she was on in this war.

"A nap would be lovely." He paused in his dressing to kiss her temple. "And after that, we can devote ourselves to our next job."

"Which will be?"

Looking like the mischievous seventeen-year-old boy she'd eloped with, he said, "Forgery!"

Chapter 30

∽ঐ∽

Callie was not the least bit surprised to discover that Richard was a meticulous forger. Such a multitalented husband she was acquiring!

After the long, sleepless night and the exuberant dawn victory celebration, she and Richard had dressed and lain down on the pallet together and slept until noon. Luckily they'd fallen asleep facing each other and holding hands, not doing anything that might embarrass their housemates.

When Callie woke and saw Richard, she had an intense desire to roll over and wrap herself around him to find out if she'd dreamed the passion of the previous hours. The same desire was in his eyes, but they controlled themselves, mostly because he'd gotten to his feet before she could pounce on him.

After a lunch of sausage rolls, Josh, Molly, and Trey went out again, and it was time for Callie and Richard to get to work. While she made alterations to the gown she would wear for her wedding, Richard started on his forgery.

He began by reading all the documents written in Matthew's own hand that Callie possessed. Fortunately she'd sent a box of important papers to Baltimore when the Adamses evacuated so she had a number of examples.

With samples in front of him, Richard started to practice writing in the same style, with particular attention to duplicating Matthew Newell's signature. Callie asked, "Is it more difficult to copy his handwriting because you're left-handed?"

"Yes, but I am a very good forger," he said, amusement in his gray eyes.

"Someday you'll have to explain how you became so skilled," she said. "Perhaps when we're sailing back to England and time lies heavy on our hands."

"Time will never hang heavy with you," he said, his gaze reminding her of the earlier hours. "But sadly, I must concentrate on this. How shall we word the codicil?"

Callie thought of the wording of the draft will she'd studied. "It should be short, just a few sentences specifying the disposition of Matthew's estate 'in the event my beloved son Henry Newell dies without spouse or issue.' Except for individual bequests as outlined in his full will and testament, everything to be divided between 'Mary Adams Newell, known as Molly, and Matthew Adams Newell, known as Trey.' And I'm to be the sole guardian."

"That makes sense. The simpler, the better." With content decided, Richard started work on a draft of the codicil. He'd already located writing paper of the type Matthew used, and the sheets waited for when he was ready to create the final version.

Callie returned to her alterations. Since both their enterprises required good lamplight, they sat on opposite sides of the same table. She sewed on trim, he refined his forgery. Very domestic.

When she needed a break, she set the gown aside and drifted into the kitchen area, where Sarah was making a large batch of biscuits in the simple oven Josh had built for her. Josh could build or improvise just about anything.

The first sheet of biscuits had already come out, so Callie confiscated one, split it, and spread on the apple butter Sarah had made. The biscuit crumbled deliciously in her mouth with the taste of spiced apple setting off the crunchy texture of the crust. "I'm going to miss your cooking!"

"I expect you'll have a fancy French chef, but he won't be able to match my biscuits," Sarah agreed as she formed a double handful of biscuit dough into a ball, then gently patted it into a broad, flat circle. "But I'll give you the recipe."

"Mine will never be as good." Callie swiped another biscuit and lavished apple butter on it. "Now that the battle is over, it's possible to think about the future again. I'm sure you and Josh have discussed what you want to do next. Will you stay in Baltimore?"

"Yes, we want to start our own businesses," Sarah said as she finished patting the dough to the right thickness on the floured board. "Josh will do carpentry and build things and I'll run a cook shop. We'll set up in a building large enough for both our businesses and we'll live above. Josh has been looking around for a good location."

"You have it well worked out." Callie felt a twinge that these plans had nothing to do with her, but they were going in different directions now. "What about visiting your son and his family?"

"It's not so far to Philadelphia. We'll visit him or he and his family can visit us." Sarah smiled and turned a glass upside down, using it to cut circles of biscuit dough. "Maybe we can lure him down here for good. We'll see. We have a whole world of possibilities, and we owe it all to you."

Callie blushed a little and finished the last bite of biscuit. She had benefited even more from her foster family's friendship. "Henry had quite a lot of money on him. Considering what he stole from you and his brother and sister, I think it should go to the Adams family to support this new phase of your life."

Sarah stopped cutting out biscuits, her eyes widening. "We figured that we'd be able to manage with what we've saved, but that money surely would make it easier for us. But what about your jointure? He stole from you, too."

"Eventually I'll get what I'm owed, when Matthew's will has gone through probate." Callie grinned. "Between then and now, I'm marrying a man who says he can support me decently."

"I'm sure he can!" Sarah returned to cutting out biscuits and laying the circles of dough on an iron baking sheet.

"What plans do Molly and Trey have?"

"Molly has been practicing writing 'Mrs. Peter Carroll,' " Sarah said dryly. "If that doesn't work out, after she's finished crying her eyes out there will be other young men. I'll keep her busy until she marries. You've trained her to be a fine seamstress. As for Trey, he's thinking of reading law."

"Really? Peter Carroll is really having an influence on your family!"

"He certainly is. Trey says that they discussed the law when their militia unit took breaks from drilling, and he found it very interesting. If he's serious, we should be able to find someone he can read law with."

"I imagine that the militia will be discharged to return home soon, so the warehouse manager should be back here in the next few days, but he's an amiable fellow. Since I'm more or less the owner of this warehouse, you can stay here until you find your new home."

"Before winter, I hope! This place would be like living in an ice house."

Callie was about to return to her alterations when the hanging bell clanged by the door that entered the loft. Josh had rigged a rope that ran from the street door to the top of the stairs so visitors could make their presence known. "I'll go down and see who it is."

"I'll go with you." Richard rose and stretched. "I need a break."

"In case I need to be defended in the stairwell?" Callie said with a smile. Not that she minded having him with her.

"Remember that a victory celebration is going on out there, which means some men will be drinking way too heavily," he said seriously. "If a couple of drunks have noticed that three beautiful women live up here, it is indeed possible that you might need protection in your own stairwell."

Sarah stuck her head out of the kitchen. "*Three* beautiful women? Thank you, Lord George!"

Her tone was laughing, but his was serious when he crossed to Sarah and kissed her cheek. "You *are* beautiful, Sarah. I hope Josh tells you that regularly."

Under her dark skin, Sarah blushed. "He does!"

As Callie and Richard headed down the steps, she said, "You'd best be careful, Richard. You're turning into a really nice man."

"Heaven forbid!" he said with mock horror. "I'll make a point of practicing my bad temper." He smiled down at her. "But that won't happen until memories of this morning fade. It could be quite a while."

This time it was Callie who blushed.

She opened the door to the street to find a young militiaman. He asked, "Are you Mrs. Newell?" When she nodded, he continued, "Peter Carroll sent me with a message. The British Army troops withdrew in the middle of the night without attacking the American fortifications, and they're being loaded onto Royal Navy ships to sail away. He wanted to assure Miss Molly Adams that he's well and will call on her as soon as he is released from duty."

"Wonderful news! Thank you," Callie said warmly. "Can I offer you refreshments?"

"Thank you, ma'am, but I live nearby and I have to show my mother that I'm safe and sound," he said with a grin. He tipped his hat and went on his way.

Richard closed the door. "Your feeling this morning was right. It's really over. Shall we visit the local churches tomorrow and see how quickly one can marry us? I'm reasonably confident we can find a vicar or minister who won't insist on reading the banns." He smiled wickedly. "I don't want to wait any longer than absolutely necessary."

"I couldn't agree more!" The light was better in the stairwell now, since Josh had installed a tall window above.

Richard was watching her, his gaze intent and his fingers ink stained. "There are other reasons for coming down with you apart from protection." He caught her hand and pulled her into his arms. "The opportunity to steal a kiss, for example."

She moved eagerly into his embrace, pressing her body full length against his. "Can you steal a kiss when it's given freely?"

"A philosophical point I shall ponder at some later time," he said huskily before his mouth closed over hers.

She hadn't known a simple kiss could be so intoxicating. Of course, this one wasn't simple. Their tongues touched, they breathed each other's air. His skilled hand kneaded her backside, pulling her more closely against him.

She was delighted to feel solid proof of his arousal. She slid her hand between them and squeezed. He caught his breath and she found herself with her back pressed to the wall and his hand moving up her thigh. Then between her legs . . .

She moaned as he lifted her and wrapped a leg around his hips. So swift a joining. So sudden and shattering a culmination. Their bodies clashed in ecstasy and once again she lost all sense of who and where she was as she spiraled into pure sensation with him. Better together than apart . . .

Awareness returned when Richard exhaled roughly and gently returned her feet to the ground, panting, "I really intended not to do this again until we're properly married and have a real bed!"

She gave a choke of laughter. "I now understand why marriage has such enduring popularity. How long does this honeymoon phase last?"

"Given that we aren't even married yet, I think we have much time to look forward to. Years." He kissed her ear. "Decades."

They stayed in each other's arms as they recovered.

With release came a startling new thought. "Since I wasn't interested in marrying again, it hadn't occurred to me that I might have children of my own," Callie whispered. "How would you feel about that?"

He lifted his head from hers and was quiet for so long that she became worried. "Richard? It might not happen. It didn't in my first marriage. If you hate the idea, there are things that can be done to prevent babies." Though it might already be too late for precautions.

He hugged her reassuringly. "I don't hate the idea. Even more than you, though, I never thought that I might have children. But . . . I like the idea. Having children with you." His eyes narrowed. "In fact, I like this idea very much. Only we would raise them better than we were raised."

"I would hope so!" she exclaimed. "We're intelligent people. We can work out how to be better parents than ours were."

"That's a low standard," he said with a breath of humor. "Let's aim to be as good as Josh and Sarah. I doubt we'll achieve that, but it's a good goal to aim for." He slung an arm around her shoulders and they started up the stairs. "Tomorrow we work on the details of getting married. A church, a vicar, and a jewelry shop to buy a ring."

"To buy two rings," she said firmly. "Why should women be the only ones marked as taken?"

He laughed. "That's a fair point. Two rings, then."

"How will we get back to England? Do you think Hawkins will come for us?"

"Yes, if he can. He's an honorable fellow. After the news that Baltimore has held out against the British reaches St. Michaels, he'll surely sail up here. His ship repairs should be done by now." Richard shrugged. "And if for some reason he can't return for us, we'll find another way home."

Home to England with her best friend beside her. How did she get so lucky?

Chapter 31

The next two days convinced Gordon that he was going to like being married. He'd always loved Callie's company, and having her beside him was like their childhood except that instead of catching frogs or riding hell-for-leather, they were organizing a wedding and occasionally stealing secret kisses.

Their first stop was a jeweler and goldsmith, Mr. Tate. When they entered his shop, he was setting trays containing jewelry on the counter. "Good day!" he said cheerfully. "As you can see, I'm just reopening after removing my business from the city for the last unfortunate fortnight."

"Battles are bad for business," Gordon agreed. Particularly for a business that dealt in small, valuable, easily looted items. "I hope you'll be able to give us swift service on a pair of matched wedding rings."

"Plain gold bands," Callie said, giving Gordon a mischievous glance. She was looking particularly ravishing this morning with her apricot hair set off by a simple but beautifully fitted dark blue morning gown. "Inside the man's ring that I'll give my husband, I'd like you to engrave 'My Lionheart.'"

Gordon grinned. "In that case, inside the ring for my lady, please engrave 'My Catkin.'"

Mr. Tate blinked but recovered quickly. "Please write out the spelling that you wish. Very forward thinking of you to exchange rings. I do believe that it may be a coming fashion." He smiled. "Naturally it's a trend I approve of. Let me show you a few versions of a plain gold band, and then I'll get your sizes. I can have the rings ready tomorrow, if you like."

"That would be excellent." Gordon was about to put a deposit on the rings when he noticed a tray of earrings on the counter. One pair was golden topazes dangling on delicate gold wires. He lifted one out and admired how the sunlight sparkled through the faceted gems. He glanced at Callie. "Do you like these? I haven't given you a proper engagement present."

"You don't have to give me anything. It's enough that you said yes when I proposed to you." Nonetheless, she picked up the other earring and held it by her ear as she looked into a small mirror on the counter. "But these are lovely."

For three years she'd been supporting a household of five people with never any money to spare. He had a sudden powerful urge to spoil her. "The gold matches your eyes. How much are the earrings, Mr. Tate?"

The negotiation was quick and satisfying for both parties. Callie slipped the gold wires in her ears, then rose on tiptoes to kiss Gordon's cheek. "No one has ever taken such good care of me," she whispered. "And sometimes even the most independent of women wants to be taken care of."

Feeling ridiculously pleased, he kissed back more thoroughly while Mr. Tate tactfully ignored them and wrote up an invoice.

Then, laughing, he and Callie left arm in arm. He hadn't laughed so much since their doomed elopement. Callie had always been able to make him laugh and feel good about life, and now that she was no longer tight with worry over war, her responsibilities to her foster family, or fear of being found by Henry Newell, she was her bright, happy self again—Callie, but enriched by fifteen more years of maturity and worldly wisdom.

Yes, he had his best friend back, and the prospect of sharing a bed with her for as long as they both should live was insanely appealing. But for now, he avoided being alone with her in any stairwells since they couldn't keep their hands off each other. She deserved a proper bed, and that was only a few days away.

The vicar of St. Paul's had agreed readily to a swift wedding. Harbow had lived many years in Maryland, but he was English born and still capable of being impressed by the fact that Gordon was the son of a marquess. He was also male enough to understand why a man would want to get Callie into his bed as soon as possible.

With church and wedding rings secured, the whole loft family went hunting for premises for the Adamses' new home and businesses. Even Trey joined in, since the bullet wound in his left leg was healing so well he barely needed a cane.

On the afternoon of the second day, they found the perfect place. A spacious building on Charles Street, in the center of the city, it was only a few blocks from the waterfront. The current owner was a barrel maker, so the large backyard already had a woodworking shed and storage space.

Sarah loved the long kitchen and immediately decided where to place the large oven she would need for her cook shop. The building was in sound condition and the living quarters above were roomy and comfortable. The present owner had decided he wanted to move out of the city, so he was willing to take a bargain price in return for a quick transaction. Henry's money would cover the purchase price handily.

After, Gordon bought everyone a celebration dinner at the grandest of the city's taverns. Before they began to eat, he offered a toast. "To future happiness and satisfaction for us all, and no more wars!"

Everyone laughed and drank to that. As he looked around the circle of faces, he realized how much he would miss the Adamses. In a mere fortnight, they'd become like family. No, rather better than his own family. The six of them had been bonded by the shared experiences of war, and it was a bond they would never forget.

He raised his glass for a second toast. "We will all meet again, I promise you!"

"I will happily drink to that!" Josh said as they raised their glasses once more.

No one drank to excess, but they were all merry as they left the tavern and made their way back to the warehouse, two blocks away. It was already dark, but the streets were full of muddy, happy militiamen who had been released from their positions on Hampstead Hill and were now celebrating.

The mood was bright and Gordon and Callie brought up the rear of their small group, holding hands. When they reached the warehouse, a figure was pulling at the door rope and looking up hopefully. Molly recognized him first. "Peter!"

She bolted toward him in a most unladylike fashion, and he caught her in his arms with a kiss. "Molly!"

Ending the kiss but keeping his arm around Molly, Peter turned and greeted the others. "I'm glad to see you all. I wanted to assure Molly of my safety, and I have some news for you, Mrs. Newell."

"Come upstairs and tell me there, Peter," she said as Josh unlocked the door, which now had a new and much more secure lock. "We've just come from dinner, but if you'd like something to eat, there is always fine food in Sarah's kitchen!"

"That would be splendid, ma'am." His gaze went to Molly again. The lad was seriously smitten, and so was the lass.

Josh lit a lantern in the short passage at the bottom of the stairs and guided them up. The door at the top had also been rebuilt more sturdily and with a new lock.

Inside, as lamps were lit, Peter said, "Mrs. Newell, I thought you'd want to know that your lawyer, Mr. Key, and the other Americans with him were just released by the British and arrived here in Baltimore this evening."

He paused to gratefully accept a tankard of ale from Sarah. "He and Mr. Skinner were able to obtain the release of the elderly doctor whose captivity sent them to the fleet to begin with, and they also have a list of all prisoners held by the British, which is a great relief to the families."

"Wonderful!" Callie exclaimed. "For the prisoners, and for me. I have several legal issues that need to be addressed and we were thinking of calling on your uncle, but talking to Mr. Key will be even better. Do you know where he's staying? It's too late to call on him this evening, but perhaps first thing in the morning."

"They're at the Indian Queen Hotel, not far from here. That big building on the corner of Baltimore and Hanover streets."

Peter's eyes lit up when he saw Molly approaching with a tray of hot food. "Thank you, Molly! It's wonderful to return to civilization after days in muddy ditches. Our big news is the lack of news because after a day of playing cat and mouse opposite our lines, the British troops withdrew in the middle of the night without offering battle. We wondered if they might attack elsewhere, but they boarded the naval ships and they're now well and truly gone. Is there any news here?"

"You may offer me congratulations," Gordon said with a ridiculously wide smile. "Callie has agreed to marry me. The wedding will be in three days in St. Paul's, and of course you're invited."

"How splendid!" Peter exclaimed. "I shall certainly attend. Has anything else interesting happened?"

That gave Josh the chance to talk about their new home and businesses. Peter knew the location on Charles Street and approved. If he was bothered by the idea of the girl he fancied living above a shop, there was no sign of it.

Nonetheless, Gordon found himself with a strange paternal desire to ask Peter's intentions with regard to Molly. Such inquiries should properly come from Josh, but realistically, former slaves might be reluctant to question a young white man from a distinguished and wealthy local family.

Gordon waited till the flurry of conversation had died down and Peter had finished eating before he invited the young man to join him on the balcony. Looking somewhat wary, Peter accompanied him outside.

Gordon closed the door behind them, then leaned on the railing, his hands clasped in front of him as he gazed out at the harbor. "I like your city."

Mirroring his pose, Peter replied, "So do I. Baltimore's defense is going to inspire the rest of the country and help our peace negotiators in Ghent, I think. This city is going to grow and prosper and I'm excited to be part of it."

"I had the impression that the Carroll family already owns a good bit of the city and the state."

Peter chuckled. "The family is a large one. My branch is well off but not the extremely wealthy Carrolls."

Glad to hear this, Gordon commented, "So it might be less of an issue if you marry a girl who isn't as wealthy and isn't from an old Maryland family." His voice became edged. "Assuming you're serious about Molly."

"If you're asking whether my intentions are honorable, sir, the answer is yes. Molly is beautiful, but even better, she's good and she's wise." Peter glanced at Gordon in the darkness. "And she makes *me* feel good. As a newly betrothed man, I should think you would understand that."

Peter had just given a fine summary of how Gordon felt about Callie. "Yes, I do understand. But Callie and I have known each other since the nursery."

"While Molly and I have known each other only days," Peter said quietly. "My feelings might change and so might hers. She's young and I'm not that much older. I will be unable to consider marriage until my legal training is complete. But for now, I want to court her honorably for as long as we both care for each other. My hope is that someday we'll be standing at that same altar where you and Mrs. Newell will take your vows. Does that address your concerns?"

"It does." Gordon chuckled. "I'll probably be in England and not well placed to observe your courtship, but Josh is quite capable of thrashing you should that be needed."

"It won't be."

The harbor water was dark, but lights were visible on the triumphant Star Fort and around the harbor. Gordon asked, "Do you know how Key and the others returned to the city? The ships sunk to block the entrance to the harbor haven't been raised yet, so there isn't normal traffic."

"Key and Skinner were in a small sloop that edged by the blockade ships. Nothing larger would have been able to get into the harbor."

"I'm glad small boats can make it in. Our transportation back to England should be along soon." If a small sloop could enter the harbor, a dinghy from the *Zephyr* wouldn't have any problem.

"Back to England?" Peter asked curiously.

"I'm English in my bones," Gordon replied. "But that doesn't mean I didn't celebrate when Baltimore withstood the British attack. If the city had been conquered and burned, it might have effectively destroyed your United States. The world is better off with another Anglo-Saxon nation to balance British arrogance."

Peter laughed. "You're very clear sighted about your homeland."

"I've seen a great deal of the world. The parts shaped by British notions of law and justice are better off, but too much power breeds arrogance and bullying. Better when power is shared between nations." He gazed over the harbor, thinking that within a week, he'd be sailing away with his bride by his side. But this city and these people were part of him now. He and Callie would be back.

Chapter 32

The Indian Queen Hotel was very grand, more like London than Baltimore, not that Callie had seen much of London before her exile to the Indies. She and Richard had deliberately dressed like people of consequence, so a harried desk clerk gave them the number of Mr. Key's hotel room without questioning the request.

As they climbed the stairs, Callie said, "Mr. Key and his wife have a lovely home in Georgetown, just north of Washington. Six children, a law office, right on the Potomac River. They love to entertain, so I've visited several times. Even though Frank looks like a rather dreamy poet, he's an extremely fine lawyer, and well connected to the Maryland establishment."

"Just what we need to start working on the probate of Matthew's will in Jamaica." Richard smiled at her. "I love watching your topaz earrings dance."

She laughed. "I love wearing them. I might never take them off." She was enjoying this brief betrothal period, but even more she looked forward to actually being married and waking up to Richard's arms around her and his lazy, intimate smile across the pillows.

Blushing, she reminded herself that they were here on business. They'd reached Key's room, so she knocked briskly, calling, "Mr. Key? It's Callista Audley with some rather important legal business, if this isn't a horridly bad time."

After a moment the door swung open, revealing Frank Key. His tangled dark curls and rumpled shirt made him look as if he hadn't slept in days. But his smile was welcoming. "Callista, how lovely to see you here and safe! Please, come in. I gather you and your family were able to make it out of Washington unscathed."

"Yes, though I believe my house had the sad distinction of being the only residence in Washington to be burned by the British."

"I'm so sorry to hear that!" he exclaimed. "It was beautiful and well located."

"I'm not going back, so I'm interested in selling the lot. Here are the addresses of my helpful neighbor, Mrs. Turner, and my future home in London." She gave Key the paper with the addresses, then drew Richard forward. "I'd like you to meet Gordon Audley. He and I are to be married on Monday."

Key and Richard exchanged an assessing handshake, then Key waved them to a pair of uncomfortable chairs. "Are you a relation of Mrs. Audley's first husband, sir?"

"It's far more complicated than that," Richard replied. "I'll let Callie tell the story."

"Which I will," Callie said. "I need help probating a will in Jamaica, but first, how are you? I'm told that you and Mr. Skinner, the prisoner of war agent, were held

captive by the Royal Navy, but you emerged triumphant with your freed doctor and a list of all the prisoners
of war."

"Yes, but it was terrifying to watch the bombardment
from miles away and not know how the battle was going!
I'd had doubts about this war, but they vanished when I
saw Baltimore under attack." His eyes were intense. "I've
never felt more an American."

Looking shy, he continued, "You know I'm prone to
scribbling bits of poetry. During the battle and after, I
was filled with powerful emotions such as I'd never
known. I jotted down my feelings on the back of an en-
velope and last night I expanded them into a poem.
Would . . . would you like to see it?"

"By all means yes!" Callie had read some of Key's
other poetry. He was very talented and this subject was
powerful.

He handed her a long sheet of writing paper well
filled with lines and some words scratched out. "It still
needs work," he said apologetically. "But I thought it
captured the fear and triumph of the event."

She began to read while Richard shamelessly
looked over her shoulder. The first stanza read:

> *"O! say can you see, by the dawn's early light . . .*
> *What so proudly we hailed at the twilight's last*
>   *gleaming,*
> *Whose broad stripes and bright stars through the*
>   *perilous fight,*
> *O'er the ramparts we watched, were so gallantly*
>   *streaming?*
> *And the rockets' red glare, the bombs bursting in*
>   *air,*
> *Gave proof through the night that our flag was still*
>   *there;*

O! say does that star-spangled banner yet wave
O'er the land of the free and the home of the
    brave?"

By the end of the stanza, she was crying. "Yes," she whispered. "It was exactly like that."

Richard rested his hand on her shoulder. "We watched the rockets and mortars, too. Seeing them was bad enough, but worse was wondering what it meant when the bombardment ended. When dawn came, at first it was impossible to see what flag flew over the fort. It was a stunning moment when the sun came out and showed those 'broad stripes and bright stars' of yours." He tapped a corner of the page. "This is a poem not just for Baltimore, but for a whole nation."

Key swallowed hard, his face flushed. "I'm glad my words conveyed that to you. They came in such a powerful rush that they could not be denied."

"It should be a song," Callie said when she finished the fourth and final stanza and handed the poem back to Key, the words soaring through her mind. "The whole city will gladly sing it."

"I have a melody in mind," Key admitted, "but for now, tell me about your legal questions."

Pulled from the power of poetry, Callie succinctly related the carefully edited version of why she and her stepfamily had been living under assumed names. Then she gave the official story of Henry Newell's death and how she had a draft copy of the will and a newly discovered codicil.

She'd considered claiming she'd found the codicil folded into her Bible, but since Key was a devout member of the Church of England, she thought it wiser to "find" the unexpected addition to Matthew's will in her cherished copy of *Robinson Crusoe*. Richard had given her the book on her twelfth birthday and it was the only one of her books that she'd sent to Baltimore with the Adamses. The others were now ash.

In focused lawyer mode, Key scanned Henry's death certificate, the will drafted in Matthew's own hand, and the codicil. He didn't question the codicil's authenticity, a tribute to Richard's skill as a forger. When he finished studying the papers, he said, "This all looks straightforward enough, though it will take time to prove the will."

"Can it be done from another country?" she asked. "None of us want to return to Jamaica."

Key considered, then gave a nod. "I know a young lawyer in Washington who is Jamaican by birth. He's a fine attorney and I think he'd be willing to take your documents to Jamaica and shepherd them through the probate process. A chance to visit family and be paid for it."

"That would be marvelous!" Callie said. "Since my new husband and I will be leaving for England very soon, I assume there are a large number of legalities that must be completed before I depart to ensure all has been done properly. I don't want to waste time having queries travel back and forth across the Atlantic."

He nodded. "As you say, a great deal of copying and notarizing will need to be done. I can do the notary work since I've known you for several years"—he smiled briefly—"albeit under two different names. I work regularly with a lawyer here in Baltimore, George Carroll, and he has people who can help with the copying and filing of papers. Since your stepfamily will be staying in Baltimore, it will be good for them to develop a relationship with him for possible future issues."

"We know George Carroll's nephew, Peter." Callie

smiled. "He and my stepdaughter, Molly, are showing great interest in each other."

"Excellent! Peter is a fine young man." Key neatly squared the stack of papers and slid them back in the portfolio. "Now I must render myself presentable and meet with my brother-in-law about another matter."

Callie stood and offered her hand. "Thank you so much for taking the time to help us during such a confused period!"

With a charming smile, Key shook her hand. "We poets are a nervous lot. It was worth being a lawyer before breakfast in order to hear enthusiasm for my latest work."

"Very genuine enthusiasm," Richard said as he shook Key's hand. "Good day, sir. I look forward to hearing 'The Defence of Fort McHenry' being sung on every street corner!"

Callie took Richard's arm and they left the hotel room together. And once again, the words "*the land of the free and the home of the brave*" rang in her mind.

Chapter 33

***

The next days were spent talking to lawyers and signing papers. Peter Carroll took a day off work after returning from the battlefield, and he spent it with Molly. Callie envied the innocent purity of their romance, uncomplicated by the scars and betrayals of life. She'd never had that, but now she had Richard, and that made up for the rest.

The next day Peter returned to his desk in his uncle's office and became one of the assistants copying the original documents. It was a huge job since copies were needed for Callie, the Adams family, Mr. Key, and the courts. Callie's hand was tired from signing, but she thought the process would go smoothly since the paperwork hadn't been questioned. Though it would take months to settle the probate, when it was done, Molly and Trey would be comfortably set for life.

The weather had cooled to a pleasant autumn. The night before their wedding, she and Richard decided to stroll along the waterfront, holding hands, saying little, simply absorbing the sights and sounds of Baltimore. As the sky darkened, they headed back to the warehouse, and saw a familiar dinghy gliding up to the nearby pier.

"The dinghy from the *Zephyr*!" Richard exclaimed as he recognized the two men aboard. "Hawkins has excellent timing."

"He certainly does!"

They quickened their pace and met him on the pier as his crewman secured the dinghy. "Hello there!" Hawkins called. "I'm glad to see that you survived the late excitement. Any interest in sailing away home?"

Richard reached a hand down and helped the other man up onto the pier. "Indeed, yes. But first, care to attend a wedding tomorrow morning?"

Hawkins's gaze moved from Richard to Callie. "I'd love to, and I'm glad to see that you two finally figured out what to do with each other!"

Callie laughed and offered her hand. "Was it that obvious?"

"Not to you, maybe, but to everyone else." Hawkins bowed formally over her hand. "I haven't a proper gift, but I'll give you the use of my cabin on the *Zephyr* for the return voyage."

Callie said uncertainly, "It seems wrong of us to drive you from your own bed, Captain Hawkins."

"We accept," Richard said, overriding Callie's qualms. "And thank you, Hawkins." He gave Callie a teasing glance. "I really do not want to spend my honeymoon in a bunk bed."

"Nor do I," Callie admitted. She kissed Hawkins's cheek. "Thank you, Captain."

He colored and quickly changed the subject. Callie

smiled as she invited him and his crewman up to the loft for dinner. This was going to be one fine honeymoon.

On the whole, Gordon decided, it was easier to face down a group of armed and drunken soldiers than it was to get married. As he waited at the altar of St. Paul's, he muttered, "I am never going to do this again!"

Josh, an experienced married man, gave his deep chuckle. "You'll only have to do it once. Miss Callista isn't the sort to give up on anyone, so you're going to be mated for life like a pair of geese."

"Interesting way to put it," Gordon said, but the thought of grooming Callie's feathers was sufficiently arresting to distract him. He didn't really think she'd change her mind, but he wanted this to be *over.*

The only guests were Peter Carroll and Hawkins, with Trey ready to wield a cane if needed. The church seemed very empty until the organ sounded. It filled the great space with celebration, and the ladies filed in.

Molly walked down the aisle first, a small bouquet in her hands and a wide smile on her face. She was dark and stunning in a garnet-colored gown and looked much more mature than when Gordon had first met her just weeks before. She had to be thinking about her own future marriage. From the way she and Peter exchanged glances, the subject was obviously on their minds.

Then Sarah, mature and magnificent in green satin. Lastly, his Callie, glowing in gold and cream, her bright hair like fire, and topazes dancing in her ears. Gordon's heart considered stopping at the sight of her gliding down the aisle.

He realized with sharp awareness that however he
and Callie defined the terms of their marriage, she
would give meaning to his life. For so many years his
life had been first about survival, and then later it was
about solving intriguing problems for people who
needed help. Some of those tasks counted as redemption for past sins, but it wasn't the same kind of meaning that Callie brought to this marriage.

How had he become so lucky?

She reached the altar and gave him a smile to re-
start the heart that had almost forgotten to beat. He
remembered the first time he'd met her, when she was
a happy, fearless toddler. Even then he'd sensed that
she was a girl in a million.

So many memories. Begging food from the kitchens
together. Heated discussions about books. Her scream-
ing at her father not to kill him. Now that they were
here at the altar, it all seemed somehow inevitable.

With shining eyes she took his hand, they turned to
Reverend Harbow, and became husband and wife.

Callie felt she should be more nervous given how
dramatically her life had changed, but she couldn't
summon any worry. This was Richard, after all. There
shouldn't be any great surprises in their marriage, and
that was *good*.

He'd hired a private parlor in the Indian Queen
Hotel for the wedding breakfast, which was more of a
wedding luncheon. The food was good, though perhaps not as good as Sarah's. But none of them should
have to cook or clean up after a wedding feast.

The talk and laughter went well into the afternoon,
until Richard stood and raised his glass. "A toast to
friends, and our thanks to you all for being here." He

looked each person in the eye, beginning and ending with Callie. Then he grinned. "Nothing but good times ahead!"

He drank the toast amid much laughter, then set the glass down and took Callie's arm, raising her to her feet. "I leave you to enjoy each other's company for as long as you wish, but I've booked the honeymoon suite in this hotel for Callie and me. As fond as I am of those tobacco barrels, I don't want to sleep with them tonight!"

More laughter while Callie blushed. She suspected that everyone had known what mischief they'd been up to among the barrels. Richard said, "We'll stop by the loft in the morning to say good-bye. And, Hawkins, we'll join you on your dinghy in time to catch the tide." Then he whisked Callie away.

She took his arm as they headed toward the stairs that led to the hotel's upper floors. "A genuine, proper bed? With no tobacco barrels? Such luxury, my lord!"

He chuckled. "I'm not sure we'll see such luxury again. Even though Hawkins is giving us his cabin, it's compact and I'm not sure how large the bed is. And while my house in London is comfortable, I wouldn't go so far as to call it luxurious."

"No matter." The honeymoon suite was on the top floor along with the other suites. As they stepped from the stairway onto the deep carpet, she saw that a sizable mirror had been mounted on the wall opposite the top steps.

She was startled by the image of a strikingly handsome couple before she recognized who it was. Of course Richard was handsome enough for any two people with his height, broad shoulders, and shining blond hair. The surprising part was that she looked his equal. Though not as beautiful as Richard, her image showed

a confident, elegantly dressed woman who seemed a
fit partner.

The reflection was brief because he swept her by the
mirror and unlocked the door to the honeymoon suite.
It was on a corner with a sitting room and a bedroom
visible through a door on the left, and it had many
windows. "This would have been a fine place to watch
the bombardment," he observed.

She entered the sitting room and crossed to a broad
window that framed a splendid view over the harbor.
"You're right, we're higher than the warehouse here
and the star shape of the fort is very clear." She turned
with her back to the window and said, "We've already
proved we're compatible, so we can pass the time in
other ways. A game of cards, perhaps?"

He laughed as he swept her from her feet, a tawny
lion in truth. "I've never found cards very interesting.
But you, my Catkin, are endlessly fascinating." He carried her into the bedroom and deposited her in the
middle of the wide bed, following her down and kissing her as soon as they were both horizontal.

When they came up for air, she gave a gurgle of
laughter. "What a very fine bed this is!"

"And I intend to make sure we don't waste a minute of
time with it." He caught her around the waist and rolled
onto his back with her on top. "Finally we're legal!"

She wriggled against him, finding the most comfortable place to lie. Their bodies fit together so well.
As his hand found one breast, she said breathlessly,
"Nothing that feels this good can be anything less than
sinful!"

"Sinful, maybe." He nibbled along her neck, to melting effect. "But *legally* sinful."

Clothing started melting away under impatient fingers. Though there was no reason to rush, the first

time they came together it was swift with the passion they'd repressed for the last days. Oh, yes, they were compatible . . . *yesss!*

After, they lay naked under a sheet as they recovered. She loved that she had the right to touch him wherever and whenever she liked. She loved sharing a pillow with his face turned to hers, his gray eyes as clear and light-filled as quartz.

"I think," she said slowly, "that this marriage will be relatively easy to adjust to because we trust each other completely. Isn't that a splendid foundation for marriage? When strangers marry, trust takes time to build."

"You speak from experience, I assume. I like that I don't have to spend a lot of time guessing what you feel or what you want. It helps that you're so admirably direct." He toyed with her hair where it spilled over her shoulder. Clearly he liked the "touching wherever and whenever" part as much as she did. "Have you thought about what kind of life you'd like us to live, Callie? You know about the London house, but if you don't like it, we can buy another."

"I expect I'll like it very well," she said immediately. "London is the beating heart of England, yet I know nothing of it. I shan't grow bored any time soon!"

"Would you like to have a country place as well? A manor not far from the city so we don't have to spend a great deal of time traveling to and fro."

"I'd like that, but can we afford it?" She reached out a hand and ran it down his side, then paused as she found a scar on his upper arm. "Someone shot you?"

"Only a little bit," he assured her. Before she could ask what *that* meant, he went on. "As for what we can afford, you may recall I was always good at saving my money."

She suspected that was because he'd never been able

to trust those around him, so he wanted to have his
own resources to fall back on. "Yes, you even had elopement money when we needed it. I hadn't had much
experience with money then, but I've become fairly
good at squeezing pennies till they squeak. Plus, eventually I'll have my jointure from Matthew's estate. That
should augment our finances nicely."

"Remind me to get marriage settlements drawn up
in London," he said. "I thought of it when we were up
to our ears in Baltimore lawyers, but settlements seemed
less important than the inheritance issues."

"I thought the same." Because she trusted him, mar-
riage settlements really hadn't seemed important.
Though if they had children, it would matter then.
The thought tingled all the way through her.

"At any rate, I can afford a modest country manor. It
will be fun looking for one." He grinned. "I can become a country squire. Do you think I could be a magistrate, or would the authorities shrink back in horror?"

"I think you'd make a good magistrate because you're
practical, not a rigid moralist," she said thoughtfully.
"Have you thought of standing for Parliament? You'd
make a splendid MP since you've seen so much of the
world."

He gave a shout of laughter. "You think I could join
the handful of other rebels in the House of Commons
and drive the traditionalists mad? It could be amusing,
but no sensible constituency would adopt me as a can-
didate."

"Do you have any old school friends who control
rotten boroughs?" she asked half seriously. "Maybe
one of them would send you to Parliament if you're interested."

He hesitated. "It's an interesting thought for the future, perhaps, though given my reformist tendencies, I want to eliminate rotten boroughs. It's not right for powerful men to put their own MPs into Parliament. But it's true that I no longer have much interest in doing dubious missions for people willing to pay me well for fixing their problems. My investments have been successful enough that I needn't do that sort of work anymore."

"Dubious missions like rescuing widows in war zones?" She smiled at him fondly. "I'm glad you didn't give up that work sooner!"

He caught her hand and held it. "So am I. But one thing I must do is balance the scales with people I've wronged in the past. I told you about sharing a cellar with other condemned men and all of us drunkenly considering ways to redeem ourselves if we survived. It's time to make amends."

"Make peace with the past before moving into the future? That's a fine idea." She paused. "Does that include making peace with your father if he's still alive?"

"No." It was said without hesitation. "Maybe with some of my brothers, but when I was young, I did nothing to deserve my father's ill treatment. My bad behavior was a result of his. There's nothing to redeem. But there were people who deserved better from me. Schoolmates. A headmistress." He studied her face. "What about you? Do you have any issues from the past you feel the need to address?"

"Apart from wringing the neck of the sister who betrayed our elopement to my father? I probably shouldn't do that. Otherwise . . ." She sighed. "It's been so many years. I have very few connections left."

"Then we'll just have to build newer, better connections." He leaned over and kissed her. Knowing that one thing would lead to another, she rolled so that her breasts were pressed to his chest. If this was pillow talk, she liked it very well indeed.

Farewells the next morning were every bit as emotional and soggy as Gordon expected. He wasn't overly concerned about female tears as long as he hadn't caused them, and he didn't blame Callie and her adopted family for feeling profoundly emotional. This was the end of a significant time in all their lives. No matter how bright everyone's future looked, this ending was also a profound loss.

Hawkins and his crewman waited stoically in the dinghy. Gordon and Callie's modest luggage had already been stowed aboard, and it was just a matter of waiting for Callie to be ready to leave.

Being a wise woman, she didn't drag the farewells out for very long. More tears wouldn't make the good-byes less painful. He was glad when she wiped her eyes and said, "It's time, Richard."

"Yes. Just remember, we will return for a visit someday." He did a swift round of handshakes with Josh and Trey and hugs with Sarah and Molly. Then he handed Callie down into the dinghy and Hawkins pushed the boat away from the pier.

After one last wave, Callie resolutely faced forward, perched beside Gordon on one of the bench seats. "In true female fashion," she said wryly, "I'm now thinking that with a red nose and eyes, I must look dreadful."

Gordon laughed. "You look adorable and about ten years old."

"I'm not sure that's an improvement on dreadful." She took hold of his hand. "How long do you think before we might return? It's such a long journey."

"The day isn't far off when steamships will be crossing the Atlantic," he said. "They'll be faster and safer than sailing ships."

Hawkins snorted, not interrupting his smooth rowing. "Ugly and smelly. Beastly things, steamships."

"I don't entirely disagree with you," Gordon admitted. "But having spent some time captaining a steamship, I think they are the way of the future."

Callie stared at him. "You were captain of a steamship? When did that happen?"

"A year or two ago," he replied. "I'm not a true blue water sailor like Hawkins here, but I know something of sailing and something about steam engines, so I helped out a friend who needed a captain while his steamship was doing trials in the Thames River."

"I am *definitely* starting a list of all the many things you've done!" she said. "I want to hear all about your steamship days while we're sailing back to London. It will give us something to talk about."

He gave her a lazy, suggestive smile. "I don't think we'll get bored."

She returned a sultry, provocative smile that guaranteed there would be no boredom. And there wasn't.

Chapter 34

The white cliffs of Dover, October 1814

Callie clutched the railing of the *Zephyr* and gazed raptly at the broad swath of chalk cliffs ahead, a lump in her throat. "I've never seen the white cliffs before, but they're so much a part of English lore that they say home to me. Did you ask Hawkins to return by this route so I could see the cliffs?"

"The white cliffs were one reason for coming this way," her husband—husband!—said. "I like seeing them, too. But the Westerfield Academy is just off the Dover road, and it's a good place to start making amends."

Richard looped his arm around her shoulders, so she slid her arm around his waist with a happy sigh. They'd had the best honeymoon imaginable on this smooth, lovely voyage. Each day had been a little cooler as they headed north and east, but the notoriously chancy Atlantic had sent no storms. Though Hawkins's bed wasn't as large as the one at the Indian Queen Hotel, it had been *entirely* satisfactory.

"That was your last school, wasn't it? You were still a student there when we eloped, and of course you never went back." She glanced at him askance and saw his nod. She was briefly distracted by how lovely his blond hair looked in a brisk sea breeze.

Telling herself not to lose the thread of this discussion, she asked, "How badly did you behave at this particular school?"

He shifted uneasily. "Well, I didn't try to burn the place down, but I was angry and uncooperative and often skipped classes. I was rude and sometimes a bully, though luckily such behavior was always stopped very quickly. I'm told by one of my London acquaintances that I'm considered Lady Agnes Westerfield's one failure."

She blinked. "That's a distinction, but how could you be called that when you're so lovely and reasonable?"

He chuckled and tightened his arm on her shoulders. "A lot of years have passed. Not only have I changed, but you bring out the best in me, Catkin. I'm still quite capable of being an appalling person."

She thought of how terrifying he'd looked when he'd thundered up to her burning house, and decided she'd allow his point. "I look forward to meeting Lady Agnes. If she tries to beat you, I'll fend her off."

"I don't expect she will. She was a remarkably patient woman." After a long pause, he said, "I'm not looking forward to seeing her again. But it seems the right thing to do." He gave her a rueful smile. "Doing the right thing seems so boringly mature."

"Don't you want to try everything at least once?" she

said teasingly. He laughed, but she was glad that she'd be at his side when he faced this piece of his past.

The Westerfield Academy was a vast, rambling country house suitable to the daughter of a duke. As Gordon helped Callie from the coach he'd hired, he explained, "The house was part of Lady Agnes's personal inheritance. She traveled all over the world when she was young. When she returned to England, she started the school to keep herself busy. I expect you know it's for boys of good birth and bad behavior."

"I laugh whenever I hear that." Callie took his arm and they headed toward the entrance to the right wing. "But what does it mean in practice?"

"Her rather subversive goal is to help boys who don't fit in learn to play the games of society without losing our souls." He thought of his fellow students and how many of them had blossomed under her wise care. "She's rather good at it, too."

"It sounds like the perfect place for you." Callie cocked an ear. "I presume the screams coming from behind the house are playing fields rather than a massacre?"

He knew she was trying to alleviate his nerves, but he couldn't manage a smile. "Lady Agnes and her two partners are great believers in sport as a way of burning off youthful energy." He rang the bell by the wide entrance door. "This wing is her personal living quarters. The rest of the house is the classrooms, and now there are living quarters behind for the boys. They were just starting to build them when I left."

It was only a couple of minutes before an elderly butler with an imperturbable expression opened the door. He looked familiar, but Gordon couldn't put a name to him. "Sir. Madam." He gave the slight bow due expensively dressed strangers. "How may I assist you?"

"I'd like to see Lady Agnes if she's available," Gordon replied. "Tell her that the bad penny has returned."

Not batting an eyelash, the butler ushered them inside to a small salon on the right. "I shall see if her ladyship is available."

Callie settled calmly into a wing chair, but Gordon paced. He hoped Lady Agnes's curiosity was piqued enough for her to see who was calling. She had treated him well, and he had not reciprocated. One would think he would be more comfortable with being in the wrong since he'd spent much of his youth in that state, but Lady Agnes was different. Her, he respected.

After about five minutes, a firm step could be heard and Lady Agnes swept into the salon. Tall and authoritative, she was not a woman who would be overlooked anywhere. There was more silver in her hair than when he'd been in school, but she looked otherwise ageless. "I wonder which bad penny might this be."

Gordon moved into her line of sight and bowed, feeling the schoolboy fear of authority he'd always been good at concealing. "Lady Agnes."

She stopped in the doorway, staring. "Lord George Audley! This is an unexpected pleasure." Her gaze moved to Callie. "And this would be?"

Callie rose and smiled cheerfully. "Good day, Lady Agnes. I'm Mrs. Bad Penny. Or perhaps that should be Lady George Bad Penny."

Lady Agnes laughed and called over her shoulder, "Refreshments, please. I foresee a long and interesting visit with the Bad Pennies."

She waved them to be seated, but Gordon remained standing. "Perhaps your memory is deficient, Lady

Agnes. I'm told I'm considered your one failure, and I've come rather belatedly to apologize."

"There is nothing wrong with my memory." The headmistress subsided on the sofa in a flurry of skirts. "Sit down, my boy. Where did you hear that you were allegedly my one failure? *I* never said such a thing."

Reluctantly smiling at her calling him a boy, he chose a chair where he could see both women clearly. "I heard as much from some old schoolmates I met in London recently. None of them seemed inclined to dispute the description."

Lady Agnes sighed. "You were certainly one of the more challenging students I've taken on. When you arrived here, you were like a puppy that has been beaten so often that he trusts no one. All you knew how to do was bite. Yet you seemed to be gradually improving while you were here. Was I wrong?"

"No," he admitted. "But I was far from being really right when I left."

She studied his face. "I've always believed that if you'd had another year here, you would have been decently sorted out and ready to face the world on your terms."

He thought back to the boy he'd been then and the way he was reluctantly coming to respect the school and his classmates. "It's possible. I was beginning to realize that I needed to change and stop bashing angrily into brick walls."

"I thought as much." Lady Agnes spread her hands in frustration. "But you left for the summer holidays and never returned. I received a terse note from your father's secretary saying you were being withdrawn because you had ruined a young lady of good birth and were being dealt with." She gave a wintry smile. "And I was expected to refund the money paid for your next term's tuition by return post."

Callie had been watching the conversation with quiet fascination, but at that point she slid to the front edge of her chair, her eyes snapping. "Outrageous! I'm the 'young lady of good birth' that Richard was alleged to have ruined. He did that by offering honorable matrimony to save me from being married off to a stranger three times my age. A man who would allow my father to get rid of me for a profit."

Lady Agnes studied Callie, her expression arrested. "I was sure there was more to the story. If you're willing to tell me, it will go no further."

Callie glanced at Gordon and he gave her a nod of permission. Lady Agnes had deflected his apology, but she deserved the truth.

"Richard suggested Gretna Green to save me from the unwanted marriage," Callie said. "Society might consider that ruination, but to me, he was salvation."

"So you two were childhood sweethearts?"

"No, we were best friends. There was nothing romantic between us." Callie gave Gordon an intimate glance. "At least, not then. But I was frantic, and when he suggested eloping as the only escape, I accepted gratefully."

She took a shuddering breath. "But our fathers, Lord Stanfield and Lord Kingston, caught up with us almost immediately. The only way to stop my father from beating Richard to death was to swear that I'd marry his rich Jamaican planter if he promised not to hurt Richard anymore."

"Stanfield kept his word," Gordon said dryly. "Instead of finishing me off with his horsewhip, he had me convicted of theft and kidnapping and transported to Botany Bay."

It took a great deal to shock Lady Agnes, but those words caused her jaw to drop. She was given time to recover by the arrival of the butler and a maid with a rolling cart of small sandwiches, cakes, and pots of coffee and tea.

When the servants had withdrawn, Lady Agnes said, "After telling me that, perhaps you both need something stronger?"

Gordon chuckled. "Thank you, but sobriety is my usual state. It's a rather horrible story, but it was a long time ago." He accepted a steaming cup of coffee from Lady Agnes, then filled a small plate with sandwiches. Her ladyship had always kept good cooks.

Lady Agnes poured tea for Callie. "If you're Stanfield's daughter, you'd be Catherine, if I recall correctly. How did the marriage turn out?"

"I used to be called Catherine, but now I generally go by my middle name, Callista." Callie took an appreciative sip of the tea, then collected sandwiches for herself. "I had an easier time of it than Richard. My husband was much older, but a kind man. His oldest son by his first wife was—difficult. But I became very fond of my two younger stepchildren."

Gordon noticed that Callie was leaving the impression that the younger ones shared a mother with Henry. Well, there was no need to go into more detail.

Callie continued, "After my husband's death, there was reason to doubt his heir's goodwill, so I collected the two youngest and their grandparents and we escaped to Washington and lived quite comfortably there under the name of Audley." She smiled at Gordon. "That was in memory of my childhood friend, whom I was told had died. Then Richard was sent by someone in London to rescue the Widow Audley, which he did. After several weeks in Baltimore, here we are, now properly married."

"I'm sure that explanation covers many fascinating events. Were you in Washington when it was burned? A disgraceful business!" Lady Agnes said indignantly. "What about Baltimore? The Americans did an admirable job of standing their ground."

"One can't say the British didn't have provocation for burning the American capital, though I wish they hadn't." Callie finished off a potted ham sandwich. "In Baltimore, we had a splendid view of the bombardment. It was all very educational and will enliven my eventual memoirs if I ever write any. Which I don't suppose I will."

Lady Agnes chuckled. "Lord George, you've chosen the perfect wife, though you don't need me to tell you that."

"No, I don't," he said fondly.

"I have a question about names." Lady Agnes studied him again while pushing the much depleted plate of sandwiches in his direction. "When you were a student here, you were correctly called Lord George. Recently Westerfield old boys have referred to you as Gordon when discussing various hair-raising adventures. I know that you're entitled to all those names, but which do you prefer?"

Now that he was settling in to respectable marriage in England, he realized that it was time to decide how he wanted to present himself to the world. He considered the question while taking more sandwiches.

"Lord George was a very annoying fellow and I never liked the name. Consider him dead. Richard belongs to Callie. Gordon suits me as I am now. So I choose to be Mr. Gordon Audley. You may call me Gordon if you like." He glanced at Callie. "Are you willing to sacrifice being Lady George?"

"I shan't miss it. I don't like the name George, either." She glanced at Lady Agnes. "Is that treason? But your title is merely a courtesy one. As long as I'm Mrs. Audley, not the Widow Audley, I'm satisfied."

"Gordon, then," Lady Agnes said with a nod. "It suits you."

Callie said, "I want to hear more about the hair-raising adventures! Lady Agnes, will you tell me some? I'm sure Richard won't."

The headmistress chuckled. "Well, he was instrumental in helping Lord Kirkland rescue his kidnapped wife and her maid."

When Callie turned to him, eyebrows raised, Gordon shrugged. "Mere chance that I happened to be in London and captain of Ashton's latest steamboat. I just drove the boat. It was Kirkland and his friends who risked their lives boarding the kidnappers' vessel, and it was Ashton in the engine room who got so much speed out of his ship. That man is wasted as a duke. He's a really first-class engineer."

"You are definitely telling me more about this or *else*!" Callie said threateningly, her eyes like wide golden coins.

Gordon smiled wickedly. "I look forward to finding out what your 'or else' will look like."

Callie laughed. "So do I. Lady Agnes, what other tales do you have to tell of my husband's adventures?"

Lady Agnes considered. "The only really dramatic one I know is that he used his most excellent marksmanship to save the lives of another of my boys and his wife. And there's a story about a cellar in Portugal."

"I've heard about the cellar," Callie said as her thoughtful gaze returned to Gordon. "I'm not going to write my memoirs; I'm going to have to write yours. *Terrifying Tales of an English Gentleman*!"

He rolled his eyes in schoolboy fashion. "Such a book would never sell. As I've told you, I'm always an accidental and cowardly adventurer." Wanting to change the subject, he asked, "Lady Agnes, you always are in touch with the *ton*. Neither of us have had news of our families in some years. To begin with, are our fathers still alive?"

The headmistress shook her head. "No, Lord Stanfield died about two years ago. Callista's brother Marcus is now Lord Stanfield and he seems to be quite a pleasant young man."

"My father's passing is no loss to humanity. I'm glad to know my brother hasn't turned out like him," Callie said tartly. "What about Richard's father?"

"Lord Kingston died about a year ago. His heart failed, I believe."

Gordon regretfully let go of his fantasy of confronting his father and telling him what an appalling specimen he was. But that anger was old and easily released.

"So my oldest brother, Welham, is now Marquess of Kingston. I'm sure that's making him very happy." Gordon made a mental note not to go near the family seat, Kingston Court. He had no desire ever to see Welham again. Welham and Julian, the sons of the first Marchioness of Kingston, had both been coarse and difficult, though Welham had been worse, having the arrogance of an heir.

"From what I've heard, the newest Lord Kingston annoys everyone." Lady Agnes thought a moment. "I don't recall hearing anything about your younger brothers, which presumably means they're alive and well."

There was a better chance of developing a decent relationship with his younger brothers. Their mother had been generally pleasant to her three older step-sons, and with luck her boys would have inherited their mother's temperament, not their father's.

The next brother in line after Gordon was Eldon, the youngest was Francis. Gordon could barely remember their faces, but they'd be young men in their twenties now, so he probably wouldn't recognize them. Maybe someday he'd look them up.

Lady Agnes said, "It's late in the day to continue on to London, so why not spend the night here? I've plenty of guest rooms and they're used regularly by my old boys. Emily and General Rawlings will be here for dinner, and I know they'd like to see you." She glanced at Callie. "They are my partners in running the school."

"Would they be as agreeable as you've been?" Gordon asked warily.

"I expect so. You've come up as a topic of conversation now and then over the years. They'll be glad to see that you've not only survived but are flourishing."

Callie looked a question at Gordon. "Unless you wish to get back to London right away, I'd be happy to spend the night here. With luck, I'll learn more alarming stories about your wild youth."

He chuckled. "How could I deny you such a treat? Thank you, Lady Agnes. We're happy to accept your hospitality."

She'd been the challenge he'd feared most. Instead, she'd made his apologies easy. He wondered if that meant other attempts at redemption would be more difficult than expected.

He hoped not. He was growing fond of doing things the easy way. Callie made everything easy, and he liked this new turn his life had taken.

Chapter 35

"Look at the way the leaves are changing color. Green and beautiful and also golden." Callie stared out the carriage window, entranced by everything she saw. It had been fifteen years, after all. "I didn't know that I liked having four seasons until I didn't."

"Washington had four seasons," Richard pointed out.

"Yes, but they weren't English seasons. They were too extreme, and Jamaica was mostly very hot."

He chuckled and caught her hand to draw her back onto the seat beside him. "You're leaving nose prints on the window. You might feel a little less fond of having four English seasons when icy gales are blasting down from the North Sea."

She batted her lashes at him. "Why do you think I got married? It's your job to keep me warm all winter."

He laughed and tucked her against his side. "I'll do my best."

She rested her head against his shoulder. "We can be very silly. You might have noticed."

"Yes, and I like it." He stroked her arm. "Why not try to get a bit of rest so you'll have new exclamations available when we reach London? You must be tired since we were up half the night talking over the dinner table."

"Yes, and it was lovely." She covered a yawn. "You're right about being tired though. Wake me when we reach London."

She dozed off, and didn't wake until Richard said, "We're entering Mayfair and will be home soon."

She shot up in the seat. "You let me miss most of London!" she said indignantly.

"It will still be there tomorrow, and you'll be less tired."

"I look forward to spending years exploring London." She returned to pressing her nose on the carriage window. "I was brought here once or twice as a child, but I don't remember much of anything."

He looked out the opposite window. "We're almost there. The house is on Mount Row, which is kind of a pocket Berkeley Square. The private garden in the center of the square is much smaller and has no Gunter's for ices, but it's pleasant to look out and see a bit of greenery."

"It looks lovely!"

The carriage rumbled to a stop by a house on a corner. Richard climbed out, flipped down the step, and offered his hand. "Welcome to your new castle, my princess!"

She was almost bouncing with excitement. The square was surrounded by neat terraced houses, all of them well kept. She realized that the front doors were each painted a different color, subdued enough not to be distracting, but quietly enriching the square. Richard's house—*their* house—was distinguished by a very dark red door. "I think you said the couple who take care of your house are named Bolton?"

"Yes. They're both very capable, with the magical ability to appear when needed and remain invisible the rest of the time." He led Callie up the half dozen steps to the front door and rapped briskly with the shining brass knocker. Callie smiled to see that it was a lion's head.

Having given warning that they were there, Richard opened the door with a key and ushered her into a small vestibule. It was shiny clean and brightly lit by the afternoon sun, with a vase of autumn flowers set on a long table against the wall. Next to the vase were three baskets overflowing with letters and invitations.

"Go away for a few months and the post gets quite out of hand," Richard remarked as he helped Callie with her cloak. By the time he had it off her shoulders, a man who must be Bolton had appeared. He was burly and had a ragged scar down the left side of his face.

"Lord George!" He bowed, seeming genuinely pleased. "How good to see you home again."

"My wife and I have decided to dispense with being Lord and Lady George," Richard said. "We'll be Mr. and Mrs. Gordon Audley. I'm sorry if that diminishes the respect that your positions inspire with other servants."

"We shall endure, sir." Bolton's expression was sober, but his eyes were amused. "Welcome to London, Mrs. Audley. And may I offer my congratulations to you both?"

"You may." Callie smiled at him warmly. "I'm anxious for a tour of the house."

"It will be my pleasure to show you around, Catkin, though it won't take long." As Richard offered her his arm, he said to Bolton, "Will you see to the luggage and driver, please? When we're downstairs, I'll ask Mrs. Bolton to have dinner ready in an hour and a half. Nothing elaborate, if that suits you, Callie?"

"That will be perfect." Under her breath, she said, "I assume the last stop on this tour will be the master bedroom?"

He gave her a devilish smile that required no words.

Mrs. Bolton proved to be a sturdy woman with shrewd eyes and quiet confidence. Callie thought the two of them would get on very well.

They moved from the kitchen level to the public rooms a flight up. The house was attractive, with most rooms warmed by richly colored Persian carpets, though it could use some small decorating touches.

Richard said apologetically, "The place needs more work. I haven't owned it long and I've been away a good bit of the time. Feel free to make what changes you wish."

"I enjoy home decoration." She suppressed a pang at the thought of her beautiful vanished home in Washington. "I love this house, Richard. It's so much warmer and more welcoming than the houses we grew up in."

"That was rather the point," he said wryly.

As he led her up to the bedrooms, she trailed her fingers along the silken oak of the railing. "The Boltons must love this house, too. They take such good care of it even though you haven't been here for months."

"They do love the place," he agreed. "Bolton was a sergeant in the army and this is the first lasting home they've had." He guided her toward the back of the house. "There are two bedrooms overlooking the back garden, and they have a connecting door. I use the one on the right as a sitting room and study, but it can be turned into a bedroom for the lady of the house if you like."

She chuckled. "I am nowhere near tired of our marital bed, my Lionheart!"

"I am very glad to hear that," he said solemnly as he led her into the bedroom. She caught a pleasing glimpse of the back garden before their attention turned to the bed. It was almost as large as the one at the Indian Queen Hotel.

And even more comfortable.

Having tested the bed, which passed with flying colors, they had a relaxed evening meal, then adjourned to the sitting room next to the bedroom. October had arrived and the evening was cool, but a neat little fire kept the room cozy. Callie found it deliciously domestic and didn't miss the tobacco barrels and Congreve rockets at all. Best of all, very little effort would be required to reach the bedroom.

She glanced up to admire Richard's thoughtful profile as he systematically worked his way through the baskets of correspondence that had accumulated in his absence. Most of the letters went into a waste bin. A few he set aside for later attention.

He glanced up with a smile and took a sip of the claret he'd brought up from dinner. "Comfortable?"

"Very. I'm writing letters to Baltimore and Washington to let our friends know that we've arrived safely." She arched her back and stretched. "I'll need to develop some kind of routine here, which is complicated by the fact that you're the only person I know in London."

"You'll remedy that soon. You attract people and make friends of them easily."

She had never thought of that, but realized he was right. "I suppose if I'm feeling brave I can call at Stanfield House and see if any family members are in residence. If not, the servants will probably know where they are."

"You don't sound enthusiastic about that."

"You and I have been living in an enchanted cloud, not having to deal with the outside world. With both my parents gone, I'm now the eldest of my family. I've been gone so long, I'll feel like a stranger among them." She smiled ruefully. "I must look them up soon, but to be honest, I'd rather visit the famous Hatchards bookshop than go to Stanfield House."

"Then let's do some touring of London tomorrow," he said. "I'll rent a carriage from the local livery stable and take you to see some of the sights. Hatchards is always a pleasure, and it's the post box for the Rogues Redeemed."

"A post box?"

"We all send messages there and Mr. Hatchard holds them for whatever cellar rat might come by. There may be some new messages, and I need to write an update to leave there also." He scribbled a note to himself. "Will it sound too boastful if I say that I've married the most beautiful woman in the world?"

"Yes, it will sound boastful, and they won't believe you because they may have beautiful ladies of their own. I appreciate the sentiment, though." A thought struck her. "I presume you must report to your employer that you found me. I'd like to learn more about the mysterious Sir Andrew Harding, who sponsored your mission."

"Here's an easy way to do that. Lord Kirkland is the one who sent me off, and he and his wife are both superb musicians. Before I left, Lady Kirkland mentioned that they sometimes have informal musical evenings for friends. I said I'd like to attend one if I was in London, and I've just found an invitation to a private musicale to be held tomorrow night. I will reveal you with a flourish to Kirkland to prove my mission was successful, and you will get a chance to meet people. I think you'll like Lady Kirkland."

Callie blinked. "Lord Kirkland—the fellow whose wife you rescued as well as the wife herself?"

"As I said, I just drove the boat. But yes, that's him."

"Then I most certainly want to attend!" She considered her wardrobe. "I'll need more clothes. Wearing remade, used garments doesn't seem right if I'm going to be on visiting terms with lords and ladies."

"You grew up with lords and ladies just as I did, so you shouldn't be overly impressed," he said dryly. "Since you're such a fine seamstress, one of your remade gowns will do very well for tomorrow evening. Lady Kirkland always looks well turned out, so you can ask her the name of her modiste for adding to your wardrobe."

"That's a good plan. I love sewing and designing new gowns, but I'm willing to let someone else do the routine bits." She hesitated, then decided to ask the question hovering in the back of her mind. "Do you think you'll tire of the quiet life and go back to adventuring?"

"No," he said immediately. "As I've said, I've always been a reluctant adventurer. Now that I have you, there's no reason to keep moving."

She smiled, thinking he was much more romantic than he gave himself credit for. "Will we ever tire of making wild, passionate love?"

He shook his head. "In the nature of things, we'll surely slow down, but I can't imagine ever not wanting to lie with you. You'll be eighty years old and dead-heading roses in the garden and I'll be sneaking up behind you and trying to coax you into making mischief in the garden shed."

She laughed. "I like that thought! I can imagine it, too." She returned once more to her letter writing. It was good to be back in safe, green England.

Yet she had a swift memory of the feeling she'd had in Maryland. Their way would not be as clear and safe as it appeared now.

She reminded herself that all lives had troubles. Surely together they could face anything.

Chapter 36

❧

The next morning was cool and sunny, a fine day for Gordon to show London to his bride. He ordered a curricle from his local livery, along with a boy to ride on the back and look after the horses when they got out. Now that he was going to be in London more, he must get a carriage of his own.

He started by giving Callie a tour of the parks and palaces of the West End, then a stop at Westminster Abbey to see the grandeur within. She loved the sights, and it delighted him to make her as happy as she deserved to be.

Their stop at Hatchards bookstore ran longer than expected because both of them became entranced with the bonanza of books. After Gordon added her to his personal account, he asked if there were any Rogues Redeemed messages.

Curious, Callie accompanied him to the Hatchards office. There were two new messages in the Rogues Redeemed file. Gordon opened the first. "This is from

Duval, a French Royalist. Very sound fellow. With Napoleon gone, he's back in France, not surprisingly. He says someday he'll make it to London again, but he has no idea when."

He folded the first message up and opened the other. "Ah, this one is from Will Masterson. He's another Westerfield old boy, but the well-behaved sort, not like me. He's the man who figured out how to get us out of that cellar alive." He skimmed the note and his brows rose. "Interesting."

"Interesting good or interesting bad?" Callie asked.

"Interesting good. He spent years as an officer fighting the French in Portugal and Spain, but after the emperor abdicated, he sold out and acquired a wife on his way home to England. He may be in London now, in fact. I shall have to see if I can find him. Kirkland will know. Kirkland always knows."

"I look forward to meeting the omniscient Kirkland," Callie murmured.

Gordon grinned. "Think of him as a sinister spymaster, but charming. And musical." He folded Masterson's letter and put it back in the file. "Even though it's a little cool, would you like to stop at Gunter's for one of their famous ices?"

"Oh, yes! It's one of those things that I intended to do when I had a London Season." She made a face. "Which I never got, of course."

"This will be better than a Season," he promised. "Since you're stuck with me, you don't have to worry about looking for an acceptable husband among the dreary hordes of nervous young men in search of a wife." He gave a mock leer. "And the sleeping arrangements are so much better than if you were on the Marriage Mart."

She laughed and tucked her hand around his arm. "That last is certainly true!"

A Hatchards employee carried two sizable boxes of books out to their curricle and stored them behind the seat under the interested eye of Skip, the boy who had come with the curricle. Gordon helped Callie into the carriage and took the reins for the drive to Berkeley Square, location of Gunter's, the most famous confectioner's shop in the city.

When they reached the shop, he ordered three dishes of the day's special, bitter orange, including one for Skip, the carriage boy, who was wide eyed with pleasure at the unexpected treat. As was the custom, Gordon ate his while standing next to the carriage, where Callie was attacking her ice with ladylike gluttony.

"This is *heaven!*" she exclaimed. "I sometimes made ices in Washington, but these are in a whole different class! Imagine how wonderful such good ices would taste in the blaze of a Chesapeake summer."

"We would have wanted to drown ourselves in a barrel of this in order to escape the heat." He took another small bite, enjoying the delicious bittersweet taste as the ice melted, filling his mouth with flavor. "Maybe you should suggest to Sarah that she sell ices in her bake shop."

"That's a very good idea. I'll come back another day to talk to the Gunter's owner to find out how he makes his ices so superb, if he's willing to tell me."

"Bribe him," Gordon suggested. "Sarah is far enough away so as not to be competition for Gunter's."

"That's a rather good idea. We can discuss a bribery budget later." With regret, she finished her ice and Gordon returned the three empty dishes to a waiter. Skip had apparently licked his dish. If Gordon had been younger, he might have done the same.

As he returned to the carriage and climbed inside, he said, "Kirkland House, where the musicale is to-night, is just over there on the other side of Berkeley Square. Perhaps there will be ices among the refreshments."

"An incentive to attend even if I didn't like music," Callie said with a smile.

They had left Berkeley Square and were heading home toward Mount Row when Callie caught hold of his arm. "That's South Street!"

"Yes?" he asked, wondering at the significance.

"Stanfield House is on South Street. Number twenty-two. Let's stop and see if any of my family is there." She drew a deep breath. "I should probably get this first meeting over with. If none of the Brookes are in residence, even better. I can say that I tried and forget them for a while longer."

Understanding the impulse to get it over with, he turned into South Street. Number twenty-two was about halfway down on the right. The knocker was up, so some of the family were in residence.

Callie gazed up at the house. It was large, anonymous, and expensive looking. "Though I stayed here as a child, I don't remember it at all."

Richard climbed from the carriage and gave the reins to Skip, then helped Callie down and took her arm as they walked to the house. "If I recall correctly, you got on reasonably well with your sisters and brother when you lived at home. Whom in your family are you most reluctant to meet again?"

His question steadied her by making her analyze her anxiety. "Jane," she said. "The next oldest after me. She was always such a prig. She'd lecture me on my wild behavior and tattle to my parents. I'm sure she was the one who told my father we were running away. I don't think I can ever forgive her for that because of the ghastly consequences. You came so close to being killed that night!"

"But I wasn't." His voice was calm as they climbed the steps. "She couldn't have known how disastrous it would be, and she was very young. Fifteen or so? Perhaps she's learned some tolerance with the years."

And perhaps Callie would scratch her sister's eyes out. She slammed the knocker hard into the door. She didn't think she'd actually do any eye scratching, but she was less charitable about Jane's youthful betrayal than Richard was.

The door was opened by an impeccable butler who made her think of a stuffed owl. She'd met three butlers in two days, and she liked Richard's the best, but she smiled at this one pleasantly. "Good day. Are any of the family in residence?"

The butler frowned. "And who would you be?"

"A long lost relative. I hope to surprise my family."

He didn't stop frowning, but there was a general resemblance among the Brookes, and apparently she passed the appearance test. "Sir Andrew and Lady Harding are currently staying here since their own residence is being remodeled, but Sir Andrew is out. Lady Harding is taking tea in the morning room. I'll see if she's receiving guests."

Lady Harding! Surely she was the one who had persuaded her husband to send a man all the way to America to find Callie. As act of expiation, perhaps.

The butler admitted them to the foyer, but didn't invite them to sit. Rather than waiting in the front hall, Richard quietly followed the butler, taking Callie by the hand to draw her with him.

The butler opened the morning room door and announced, "A person claiming to be a long lost relative is here and says she wishes to surprise you, my lady."

The elegantly dressed young woman on the sofa looked up, her fair hair pulled back primly. The very image of a proper young matron, just as Callie would have expected of Jane.

Lady Harding saw her visitor and leaped to her feet. "Catherine, you're here!"

Callie blinked. Not Jane, but Elinor, the next youngest sister. Most of the Brookes had the same shade of blond hair. Only Callie had inherited the red-gold color that her father had claimed was the mark of the devil. Though Jane and Elinor had similar coloring and features, Ellie was shorter and slighter than Jane. Sweet and shy. She'd been Callie's shadow, following her around adoringly, sometimes to the point of being a nuisance. She was the sister who would have missed Callie most.

"Yes, it's me, home from the wilds of the New World," Callie said lightly. "You're the one who sent a rescuer to save me from the war?"

As Elinor nodded, Callie stepped into the salon and drew Richard forward. "I imagine you'll recognize my husband since he was our neighbor."

"Dear God, Lord George!" Elinor stopped in her tracks, her face going dead white. Then she folded onto the sofa and buried her face in her hands, her shoulders shaking as she began to sob uncontrollably.

Shocked, Callie plumped down on the sofa beside her sister and put a comforting hand on her back. "Darling, what's wrong? Since you went to such efforts to bring me home, I'd have thought you'd be glad to see me."

She patted her sister gently when the tears didn't

abate. "I thought Lady Harding would turn out to be Jane, trying to make amends for past sins."

Richard said coolly, "Do you think if I slapped her she might snap out of her crying fit?"

Callie scowled, surprised by his lack of sympathy. "You will not slap my sister!"

But the words must have reached Elinor. She lifted her face and produced a handkerchief, blotting her eyes and blowing her nose before crumpling it in one hand. "I . . . I'm sorry." She gulped. "I was so glad that Andrew was willing to try to find you, but I didn't really think the search would be successful. And I . . . I thought Lord George was dead."

"Alive and well and happily married to your sister." He was leaning against the door, his arms crossed on his chest and his narrow-eyed gaze assessing. "But given your reaction, I'm wondering if you might have something to feel guilty about."

Elinor's face twisted and she began crying again. She'd always been a watering pot, Callie remembered. A little impatiently, she said, "Why not tell us what's wrong? Clearing the air is generally a good start."

Elinor gazed at her with pale, watery blue eyes. She still had her delicate porcelain prettiness, but she looked twenty years older than her actual age.

"I . . . I was the one who told Papa that you were running away with Lord George," she said starkly. "I peeked out of my room when you were leaving and guessed what you were doing. But I never, never expected the results to be so ghastly!" Her gaze moved to Richard. "I thought you had died, and it was all my fault!"

Callie drew away from Elinor, horrified. "I thought you liked me! Why did you do something so hateful?"

Elinor began crying again. Richard said in a conversational tone, "Are you sure you won't allow me to slap her, my dear? Not too hard, just enough to get her attention."

This time Callie was tempted to let him, but she really couldn't. Maybe if it had been Jane, but not Elinor. Still, she did want answers. She stood and gazed down at her sister. "Why, Ellie? Just explain *why*. Or I might slap you myself!"

Elinor swallowed hard. "I loved you, but I also envied you dreadfully. You were so beautiful, so brave. So confident. You never backed down, no matter how horribly Papa treated you. You were everything I wanted to be. I wanted to *be* you."

Her agonized gaze shifted to Richard. "And . . . and I fancied myself in love with Lord George. I desperately wanted him to look at me the way he looked at you. When I guessed that you were running off with him, I impulsively told Papa. I never imagined the consequences." She gazed down at her knotted handkerchief. In a whisper, she finished, "I've never forgiven myself."

His voice surprisingly gentle, Richard said, "You couldn't have been above thirteen or fourteen. Very young, and many would say that what you did was right and proper. But you've earned your guilt because you acted from spite. Your actions did very nearly get me killed and forced your sister into exile and a marriage to a stranger old enough to be her father. You came close to destroying us both."

"That's more than sufficient reason for you to be racked with guilt," Callie agreed with barely suppressed fury. The image of Richard crouched in the hay with his arms wrapped over his head to protect himself against her father's killing rage made her want to vomit. The *blood*! Her father's bellowing insults and threats, the certainty that her best friend was going to be killed right before her eyes . . .

And all because her favorite sister was suffering from calf love. Feeling kicked in the stomach, Callie crossed the room to Richard. He put a comforting arm around her. "Yet we both survived and we've found each other again, Catkin."

His gaze moved to Elinor. "Obviously I didn't die as reported on the voyage to New South Wales. There's profound irony in the fact that it was your desire to rescue your sister from the war that brought us together again. I was the man sent to find her and bring her home. That's some compensation, though accidental."

"Perhaps God has an appalling sense of humor." Callie turned back to Elinor, feeling weary. Her sister looked as if she was expecting their father's horse-whip, though he never used that on his daughters. He preferred the traditional method of punishing his old-est daughter with his bare hands. Very powerful hands driven by rage . . .

She swallowed hard and reached for her better self. "I accept that you never meant to cause the harm you did. But it will take time for me to get over being angry."

Elinor nodded bleakly. "I understand. Perhaps . . . perhaps someday we can be friends again?"

"Perhaps. But not today." Callie took hold of Richard's arm, desperately needing his support, and they left the small salon.

Outside, Richard called to the horse boy, "Skip, we're going to walk around the block and will join you back here."

Grateful for an interlude to collect herself, Callie remained silent for the rest of the long block. After

they turned right into the cross street, she said haltingly, "I wronged Jane. All these years I've blamed her
for what happened that night."

"She might have done the same thing if she'd known
your plans, but her motives would have been different.
Though not necessarily better." Richard steered her
around a hound that was flopped in the middle of the
sidewalk. "Strange to think that the whole chain of
events was triggered by a schoolgirl's infatuation. I had
no idea she thought of me that way. I scarcely noticed
her, other than the fact that she was shy and often followed you around."

"I didn't guess, either. But though you might not remember it, you were always very nice to my little sisters. When they spoke, you listened, and of course you
were the best-looking young man in the neighbor-
hood." She gave an unsteady laugh. "Disaster fell on Lady
Agnes's one failure because you were too nice! Now,
there's an irony."

"Laughter is better than rage." He took her hand,
their interlaced fingers more intimate than her grip
on his coat sleeve. "I don't know that I'd ever have
chosen such a path in life, but I learned much on my
strange journey, met many interesting people, not all
of them trying to kill me, and became much more the
man I wanted to be than if I'd stayed my father's son in
England."

She gave a twisted smile. "What percentage of those
interesting people *did* want to kill you?"

"Hardly any; less than five percent, I believe." His
voice became more serious. "We've both changed over
those years. At seventeen, I thought I ought to marry
you because you were my friend and marriage to me
would save you from a fate you loathed. But when we
met again in Washington, I realized that I wanted to

marry you for *you*. Because it was the right time and you were the right woman. Not because you needed rescuing."

She thought of her years in Jamaica: the friendships, the fears, the frustrations. Would she wish them away if she could? "It's not possible to imagine the life we might have had, is it? Not when that would mean losing all we've learned." She tightened her clasp on his hand. "I'm just glad we found each other when we did."

They continued around the block and were approaching the hired curricle from the back when she said, "What does it say about me that I was sure I'd never forgive Jane for betraying us, but I think I will be able to forgive Elinor eventually?"

"It means that you and Jane never got along well, so there's less of a foundation for forgiveness. You always liked Ellie, so there are more good things to remember."

"That makes sense. And it's easier to forgive a mistake made from love, no matter how misguided." As she remembered her little sister's face, she realized how much Elinor had already suffered. Yes, perhaps someday they could be friends again.

Someday.

Chapter 37

❧

"It's a good night for music," Callie said as she inserted the wires of her topaz earrings. "Soothing, one would hope."

Gordon arranged his cravat while watching Callie dress. He never tired of observing her. Though her dark green gown with gold trim was used and restyled, Callie's careful tailoring made her and the gown look superb. "I believe these musical evenings are small and informal, perhaps fifteen or twenty people. Not a great, stressful crowd. A good introduction to London."

She turned and smiled at him. "I wonder if there will be ices."

"I'd be surprised if the Kirklands don't have a standing arrangement with Gunter's involving portable chests of ice and prompt service. Doable since they live so close."

"Then I shall hope." She grinned. "And if there are no ices, I'll nibble on you later." They headed downstairs together and he helped her with her cloak. Not that she needed help, but he liked having an excuse to touch her. As she'd said, they were sometimes silly. And they both liked it.

Since the evening was mild and there was a moon, they walked to Kirkland House. Callie was a little quiet this evening, but she no longer looked upset. He guessed that she was coming to terms with what Elinor had done.

Kirkland House was well lit when they arrived and the ethereal music of a harp floated down the stairs when they were admitted. Lady Kirkland herself greeted them when the butler had taken Gordon's hat and Callie's cloak.

Smiling warmly, she said, "Gordon! I was so glad when I received your note that you could come this evening. Will you introduce me to your guest?" She turned expectantly to Callie.

"Lady Kirkland, I'm pleased to present my wife, Callista Audley."

Lady Kirkland's eyes widened with delight. Taking Callie's hand, she said, "What a pleasure to meet you! I gather this is rather sudden? When Gordon was last here at the beginning of the summer, he didn't seem at all married."

Callie smiled back, responding to the countess's warmth. "Marriage wasn't even a gleam on the horizon then, but it wasn't as sudden as it seems."

Before she could say more, Kirkland joined them. "Did I hear something about a recent marriage?"

Gordon put his hand on the small of Callie's back. "Meet the successful results of my mission to America. The unknown Widow Audley is now my wife. As it turned out, we were childhood friends and it was a delight to find each other again."

"Well done!" Kirkland's shrewd gaze suggested that

he knew the story was more complicated than Gordon's simple comment. "I'll send word to Sir Andrew Harding that you succeeded in finding the lost lady and bringing her home to England."

"No need," Callie said with a touch of dryness. "This afternoon I learned that Lady Harding is my sister Elinor. Her husband was out, but I'm sure she must have given him the news."

"I want to hear more about how you came to marry," Lady Kirkland said. "I'm sure it's a romantic story! But now I must greet some new arrivals."

"So you're one of the Brooke sisters," Kirkland said as he offered Callie his hand, his eyes thoughtful. "Knowing that makes your husband's mysterious and alarming past rather clearer."

"And rather less alarming," Callie remarked as she shook his hand. "He and I got into mischief together with great regularity. We thought we'd lost each other forever, so I must thank you for sending him off to rescue the widow."

"The Lord works in mysterious ways," Kirkland said with a private smile. "I've experienced that myself. But I regret that I'll lose your particular talents for future missions, Gordon. Marriage does tend to make a man want to stay closer to home."

"It has already had that effect on me," Gordon agreed. "Why would I want to go someplace where Callie isn't?"

"True, not to mention that you're going to be too busy to wander off to far places." Kirkland's expression was wry. "I just heard the news. I'm not sure whether to offer congratulation or commiseration."

"If you mean my marriage, definitely congratulation," Gordon said, puzzled.

Kirkland's brows drew together. "You haven't heard? You've just become the seventh Marquess of Kingston."

Gordon gasped, feeling as if a swinging spar had slammed into his midriff, stopping his breath and leaving him too numb to feel the pain. Callie grabbed his left hand hard, anchoring him to reality. "Richard!" she whispered urgently. "*Richard!*"

Her warm hand was a lifeline, but he was still so shaken he could barely speak. "I've spent half my life getting as far from Kingston Court as I could," he said unevenly. "Now . . . *this.*"

"Come in here," Kirkland said as he took hold of Gordon's other arm and steered him from the reception room across the front hall to his private study.

Callie maintained her grip on his left hand. When they were safely inside Kirkland's study, she guided him to a sofa set at right angles to the massive desk. There she knelt before him and caught both hands. "Talk to me? Please?"

He saw that she was terrified and trying to conceal it, so he made a huge effort to pull himself together. He squeezed her hands, not letting go, and looked up at Kirkland, who had poured brandy and was offering it to him. "Take this," his friend said quietly.

He took one hand back from Callie and sipped the brandy. The burn helped clear his wits a little. "How can I have inherited the title? Lady Agnes said that my father had died a year or so ago and my oldest brother, Welham, inherited. Even if he died unexpectedly, there's my second brother, Julian."

Kirkland had poured two more brandies. He gave one to Callie and indicated the sofa. "You sit, too. You can still hold his hand."

She gave a crooked smile as she settled beside Gordon. "You have the air of a man used to dealing with shocking news."

"For my sins, yes." Kirkland took a nearby chair. "To

answer your question, your brother Julian died in a riding accident not long after your father's death. Taking fences while drunk, I think.

"Welham . . ." Kirkland hesitated. "He died just a few days ago, perhaps by his own hand. The official explanation is an accident while cleaning his guns. He loved guns and had a lot of them, so no one who knows him found that improbable."

"Did he leave a note to suggest it was suicide?" Gordon asked, impressed as always by Kirkland's sources of information.

"Not that I know of, but if there was one, the family wouldn't want it made public." Kirkland glanced at Callie before continuing. "There have been recent rumors that he wasn't fond of females. That his tastes ran in a different, illegal direction."

"You needn't mince words around me, Lord Kirkland," Callie said. "I know what you mean, and I must say it surprises me. Growing up, every girl in our part of Lancashire learned not to get caught alone by Welham. He was known for being a groping brute. He tried to do things to me, but luckily I'm better at standing up for myself than many girls."

Kirkland's gaze sharpened. "Interesting. Perhaps his bad behavior with females was to conceal his true preferences. Or he might like both genders."

Gordon frowned. "If he liked both, he shouldn't have to kill himself over it."

"Perhaps he had become a drunk and it made him so unbalanced that in a moment of misery, he decided to end it all," Callie suggested.

"That's a possibility," Kirkland agreed. "Another is that he was rumored to be on the verge of betrothing himself to a well-born and very wealthy young lady. Perhaps she changed her mind and that upset him badly.

We may never know why or how he died. But like it or not, and it seems you don't, the title and estate come to you."

Gordon exhaled roughly. "I should have stayed in America and pretended I was dead. I'm sure my next younger brother, Eldon, would enjoy being Lord Kingston a great deal more than I will."

The faint sound of a piano playing floated into the office and Kirkland cocked his head. "I need to go upstairs to the music room. Laurel and I planned to play several duets together. Did you bring a carriage? If not, would you like one of my people to drive you home now?"

"Thank you, but I'll be fine. My brain is starting to work again." Gordon sighed. "I suppose that the first step is to visit the family lawyer and tell him I'm alive. I don't imagine I can just stay invisible and hope that no one notices me."

"By this time, too many people know you're alive. If you like, I can go with you to the lawyer's office tomorrow morning to vouch for your identity in case there's any question. Lady Kingston, I assume you'll go with him?"

Callie looked blank. "Lady Kingston? My mind hasn't moved that far!"

Gordon smiled a little. "I outrank you, Kirkland, since you're a mere earl."

Kirkland laughed. "I can endure that. Since you don't have a carriage in town, shall I pick you up in the morning?"

Callie answered for them both. "Thank you, that would be very convenient. Ten in the morning?"

After Gordon and Kirkland agreed, the earl left and Callie moved so that she was pressed against Gordon's side. "Have you figured out why the idea of inheriting the Audley wealth and honors is so upsetting?"

"I hated being part of that family," Gordon said slowly as he sorted through the tumult of his emotions. His father's voice echoed in his mind. *"Feel free to kill him. I have better sons."* "I despised most of my relatives because they were so beastly, and I hate Kingston Court, which is surely the ugliest, most mildewed great house in Britain. Sitting on the lake makes it damp and musty and it's downwind from a coal seam fire. The house made me ill whenever I stayed there very long."

"All good reasons to loathe the idea of becoming lord and master at Kingston Court. It is a dismal place," Callie observed. "But the worst of your relatives are dead, and you've moved far beyond your miserable childhood."

He squeezed her hand, never wanting to let go. "You were the best part of my childhood, Callie. Because of you, I managed to grow up at least somewhat sane and happy. But I have no desire to return there." He grimaced. "Among other things, this inheritance will make it impossible to return to America if you decide you don't want to live in England permanently."

"Where you go, I go," she said calmly. "Your sense of responsibility is too great to walk away from the land and tenants and businesses that are part of the Kingston estate. Since that responsibility has fallen on you, I'll be right there by your side."

He studied her lovely, delicate features, complete with stubborn chin, and wondered how he had become so lucky. With Callie beside him, he could face anything. "I was better friends with the Kingston tenants than with my family," he said, remembering. "I can't let them down. My father was a competent lord, but not a likable one, and Welham would have been worse in all ways."

"A selfish brute," Callie agreed. "If he had proposed to a young woman, she might have decided that living at Kingston Court with him was too high a price to pay, even to be a marchioness."

"No sane person would want to live at the Court," he said dourly.

"Fortunately we don't have to live there," Callie pointed out. "Though you can't walk away from your responsibilities, there's no requirement that we live at the family seat. We can build a pleasant, modern house elsewhere on the property, far enough from the lake and the smoldering coal seam to be healthy. I assume the entail includes a London house, but there's no need to live there, either. I like your house on Mount Row. *Our* house on Mount Row. We can jolly well stay there."

"Thank God for you, Catkin." He released her hand and put an arm around her to draw her even closer. "I'm realizing that I took the news of my inheritance so badly because it brought up everything I hated about my childhood. I thought I'd recovered from it, but I haven't. All the pain and anger were simmering deep inside, waiting to erupt like a volcano."

Callie frowned. "One can move beyond a difficult childhood, but I don't think it's possible to really forget. The scars are always there and the pain will flare up again if struck unexpectedly, as you just were."

"Exactly. And these scars have just been bludgeoned by English inheritance laws. If I could leave the whole mess to my next younger brother, I would." His mouth tightened. "I'm happier now than I've ever been in my life. I don't want to lose that."

"You won't." She rested her cheek on his shoulder. "We'll both have more responsibilities, especially you, but we'll also have great power to shape our lives as we want. You can build a new house and hire good people to run the estates while you become the resident rebel in the House of Lords."

He smiled a little. "That part I might like."

"You will," she predicted with an answering smile. "Are there any modest Kingston estates near London? If so, we can have our convenient country manor without having to look for one."

"There is such a manor in Hertfordshire, if I recall correctly. I visited once and the place was quite pleasant. I'll have to ask the lawyer about it when I see him tomorrow." He kissed her with deep gratitude. "You're a miracle, Callie."

The kiss deepened and hands began to move. He was shocked when he realized she was unbuttoning the fall of his trousers. Almost paralyzed when her fingers touched bare, heated flesh, he gasped, "What the devil are you doing?"

She chuckled. "Isn't it obvious? I just hope that everyone in the house is upstairs listening to the music."

Then she bent and put her mouth on him and he lost whatever awareness he had left. The pleasure lasted and lasted, deliberately prolonged as the cascading brilliance of a Vivaldi piano concerto twined through the voluptuous sensations.

When he reached the point where he thought he would incinerate into ashes, she brought him to a swift, annihilating culmination. As the madness faded into peace, he held her close, her cheek resting on his chest as he stroked her head and neck.

When he was coherent again, he said in a rusty voice, "If your intent was to distract me, it certainly worked. But what about you?" He caressed the provocative curves of her waist and hip, thinking how wondrous a woman's body was.

She tried to brush him away. "We can discuss that once we're home and in our very fine bed."

"No. Now." Despite her willingness to wait, he sensed her arousal in her quickened breath and flushed cheeks. He needed to give her the intimate pleasure she'd given him. Doing that would bind them even closer, and he needed that closeness desperately if he was to survive having his world turned upside down again.

His hand slid under the hem of her gown, then glided up her stockinged calf. Silken seduction. She gasped and rolled back a little, her legs separating to his touch. His own breath quickened as he touched intimate heat and moisture. They knew each other's bodies well by now, and it was so easy, so satisfying, to bring her to the kind of shattering completion she'd given him.

He caught her cry in his mouth as he kissed her, inhaling her passion and returning it to her with his own. If he was a marquess, she was his marchioness, his match, his mate.

Most of all, she was his savior.

As her silent convulsions ended, he drew her against him, her head on his shoulder again. Wise man, Kirkland, to have a sofa in his study. It made misbehaving so much easier.

As he brushed back her shining apricot hair, he said softly, "Were you ever told the whole story of my mother and father? It was a great scandal."

"I heard that she was very beautiful, of Scandinavian blood, and that you look very like her," Callie said with equal softness. "That she was an actress and that she died when you were very young, about four. When I was a child, I simply accepted those facts and didn't think to wonder more."

"My father fell insanely in lust for her and they married in a matter of weeks, or so I'm told." It was hard to imagine his father feeling such passion, but Gordon's birth was proof. "The lust burned out quickly and, being the man he was, he blamed *her* for the fact that he'd married an actress. He began taking mistresses, which enraged her. She might have looked like a cool northern blonde, but apparently she blazed with fire and temper. She left my father and took a lover of her own. My father was outraged and planning to divorce her when she and her lover died in a carriage accident."

Callie winced. "Surely you didn't know all that when you were so young!"

"I knew my father despised me, but not why." He smiled humorlessly. "A boy at my first school told me the stories about my mother. You can imagine what he called her. I was expelled for half killing him. Insults about her were the cause of several of my expulsions. I scarcely remembered her, but I couldn't bear to hear her slandered."

"I knew none of this," Callie whispered, appalled.

"I couldn't speak of it. Not even to you," he said simply.

"My family's domestic tragedies were much quieter than yours." Her fingers moved restlessly at his waist. "My mother endured endless pregnancies trying to give my father his male heir, but he was cursed with healthy daughters and sickly sons. It was such a relief when my brother Marcus was born and he was a healthy, jolly little boy." Callie sighed. "But my father wasn't content with his heir. He needed a spare. That next pregnancy killed my mother."

Gordon swore under his breath. "How can a man do that to his wife? Your life is infinitely more important than having a male heir. Though I'd like to have a daughter or two that look like you."

"You wouldn't mind if she had red-blond hair that has been touched by the devil?" Callie asked.

"Never." He smiled briefly before shaking his head. "No wonder neither of us wants to return to our childhood homes. We both had reason to escape."

"Going back won't be so bad since we'll be together. I'm certainly not letting you go to Kingston Court alone!" She reluctantly pulled away from his embrace and rose from the sofa. "By tomorrow, we'll be more accustomed to the thought. For now, let's go upstairs and listen to fine music. It will soothe us both."

"It's either that or fall asleep on this rather undersized sofa, which would be rude." He stood also and began straightening his appearance.

Callie smoothed back her hair with both hands, using some magic that allowed her to look as if she hadn't just been doing what she'd done. Then she smiled and took his arm, and they headed upstairs into a healing river of great music.

Callie found herself relaxing during the concert. As Richard had told her, Kirkland and his wife were superb pianists, especially when they played together on the same instrument. Though Callie was no musician, she could tell that their playing was love expressed as music.

There were indeed ices.

She and Richard left after the refreshments, pleading fatigue, which was true, though it was more emotional than physical. Arms around each other's waists like young lovers, they walked the blocks to Mount Row in silence.

When they reached home and bed, they made love again, this time with slow tenderness. Richard fell asleep swiftly afterward, his arm around her, but Callie lay awake. He'd come back into her life with an easy confidence and a mastery of life's challenges that she had desperately needed then.

But tonight he'd been vulnerable in a way she'd never seen before in all the years they'd known each other. For the first time she realized that he needed her as much as she needed him.

At what point did friendship become what the world defined as love?

Chapter 38

❦

The clerk opened the door to the inner office and announced, "Mr. Roberts, Lord Kirkland and Lord and Lady George Audley are here to see you."

The gray-haired solicitor looked up, surprised, but he recovered swiftly. Rising, he said, "This is an unexpected pleasure. Lord George, I assume you're my missing Kingston heir?"

"I am." Gordon offered his hand. "Lord Kirkland and my wife are here to testify to my identity."

"It's true that you don't resemble any of your family, but I believe your mother was of Norwegian blood?"

If the lawyer had shown any hint of disdain, Gordon would have been tempted to hit him, but Roberts's expression was neutral. "She was, and I inherited her coloring."

"Very distinctive, and it matches the descriptions I've had of you." Roberts gestured to the chairs. "Please, sit down. I'm sure this discussion will be a lengthy one."

He glanced at the clerk. "Tea, coffee, and refreshments, please."

After Kirkland and Callie testified that they'd known Gordon for many years and there was no question of his identity, the lawyer apologetically asked for a handwriting sample. That matched the occasional letters Gordon had sent over the years, and the issue of his identity was settled. The family lawyer accepted him as the new Marquess of Kingston and would start on the paperwork needed to affirm his inheritance.

After that, Roberts gave him a swift overview of the family properties and income. Gordon hadn't realized how much of the Kingston revenue came from the Lancashire coal mines. He was pleased to see that there was indeed a manor in Hertfordshire that would be a convenient retreat from London.

After glancing through the long list of properties, Gordon asked, "Do my younger brothers know I'm alive, or does Eldon think he's inherited?"

"I'm not sure," Roberts admitted. "I always reported your occasional messages to your father, but he forbade me to mention them to others in your family."

"Probably hoping I'd die somewhere far away," Gordon said acerbically.

"Perhaps," the lawyer said uncomfortably. "I hadn't received any of your letters since your father died, and I don't know if he'd ever informed his heir of your continued existence. I did send my son up to Kingston Court to attend your oldest brother's funeral and to explain the legal situation to your younger brothers." He gave a swift smile. "I'm glad you presented yourself here since I wasn't sure how to go about looking for you."

"Kirkland gets the credit for making your life easier. I was quite accustomed to ignoring all family news." Resigning himself to the inevitable, he continued. "I'd best travel up to Lancashire before Eldon gets too attached to the possibility of being the new Lord Kingston."

"Is he apt to make trouble?" Kirkland asked.

Gordon shrugged. "I really don't know. I barely remember him. But he and his younger brother, Francis, always seemed more reasonable than my older brothers."

"Given the length of time you've been absent, it may be difficult for Lord Eldon to believe you're alive," Roberts admitted. "So traveling up there soon is advisable."

Wishing he could just give the damned title and inheritance to Eldon, Gordon said, "I'll make sure that he and Francis are well taken care of." The estate certainly had enough wealth to ensure that his brothers could live very comfortably.

As the three of them left Roberts's office, Gordon thanked Kirkland for his aid. "Not a problem," Kirkland said. "Let me know if there is anything else I can help with. I have a fair amount of experience navigating the shoals of London officialdom."

"I may take you up on that," Gordon said. Looking down at Callie, he added, "For now, we go to Lancashire."

Callie took his hand. "To get it over with!"

"Please keep me posted on your progress." Kirkland tipped his hat. "You'll get used to this soon, Lord Kingston. You might even find you enjoy the challenges of your new position."

That was probably true, but Gordon still wished he wouldn't have to.

Chapter 39

It had been fifteen years since Gordon had traveled this road, but he remembered it well. When they approached the top of the hill that overlooked the valley containing Long Lake and Kingston Court, he signaled the postilion to stop the chaise. As he opened the door, he said to Callie, "Time for a brief survey of our future."

She stretched, then climbed out after him. "I'll join you. After three days of rattling around in a coach, I welcome all opportunities to stretch my legs."

Knowing they'd reach Kingston Court today, they'd both taken pains with their clothing. If there was one thing Gordon had learned in his checkered career, it was that dressing for the part was halfway to convincing people that he belonged in the role. If he was to be a marquess, he'd damn well look the part, and he did.

But he paled next to Callie, whose expert remodeling of a forest green gown with gold embroidered trim made her look like a queen. A glorious one, like Elizabeth, who had also had red in her hair. "One of these days there will be time enough for you to visit a modiste for a new wardrobe," he said wryly.

She laughed, tightening her Kashmiri shawl around her shoulders against the autumn wind. "I hope so, but in the meantime, think how much money I'm saving you!"

"Since we don't need to be frugal, I'll have to spend any wardrobe savings on jewels to adorn you, not that you need jewels to look beautiful."

"I'd rather have a really good riding horse."

"That's my girl," he said fondly. "You can have both."

He draped an arm around Callie's shoulders and they strolled to the crest of the hill. The day had been overcast, but in late afternoon the sun had come out and the lake below gleamed like a mirror.

Callie said, "Rush Hall is just over that hill. Maybe tomorrow we can ride over and see if some members of my family are in residence. I left Elinor so quickly that I didn't ask about anyone else."

"We'll do that. I wonder if the path we followed between our houses is still well worn, or if it's grown over." He fell silent, thinking of the easy joy of their friendship, and the difficulties of every other part of his childhood.

"We Brookes always took a different road into our valley, so I don't think I've ever seen this view of your house before," Callie said. "It looks really Gothic! Will there be bats and rattling chains?"

He smiled at the way she countered his tension. The rambling family seat did look rather Gothic, particularly the oldest section, which was a tower left over from a medieval castle. The stubby but suitably threatening tower stood on a steep hill overlooking the unimaginatively named Long Lake. The master's quarters were in the tower, with a view of the water.

Later additions to the structure rambled down from the tower. That side of the hill was less steep, but it lacked the dramatic views of the lake. "I'm glad my room was in the newer section of the Court," he said. "It was still damp and musty, but at least there were no bats, and any rattling chains were probably the sounds I made when I slipped out illegally at night."

She said warningly, "Having a strong sense of the order of things, the servants will make us sleep in the master's rooms in the old tower. Grand furniture and smoking fireplaces, I suspect. I never visited the tower."

"I never saw much of the master's rooms, but I did explore the lower tower. The stone walls are so thick that there's a secret staircase hidden inside."

"Really? I wish I'd known!" she exclaimed.

"You wouldn't like it. The passage is very small, built for our shorter ancestors. The staircase runs all the way down to the cellar level. It was either an escape route in the event of siege, or a way for lecherous Audleys to descend and seduce the housemaids."

"Would there be spiders?" she asked with mock anxiety.

"Almost certainly. Along with other small creatures that rustle around in the darkness." His hand tightened on hers. "But we won't stay in the tower long. You can look for a location for our new house while I visit the tenant farms and mines and have meetings with the managers of the family businesses."

"I already know where we should build. Remember that protected dell between our family estates? It's on Kingston land, it's lovely, and it doesn't get hit by the worst of the winds from the Irish Sea." She looked thoughtful. "Building will take time, so I'll look for a property we can live in until the new house is finished."

"A cottage will do as long as it's away from the Court." It was time to return to the coach, but Gordon hesitated, his gaze moving over the valley. "It's strange. I don't want to live in Kingston Court—I have far too many difficult memories of my childhood here. And yet, this valley feels like home as nowhere else does."

Callie bit her lower lip. "I know what you mean. The light, the hills, everything about Lancashire shaped our growing years. I'm happy to be back in England, delighted to have a home in London, and I'm oddly pleased that we'll have a home here as well."

"It will be a beautiful, modern, comfortable home," he promised. "A good use for some of the Kingston wealth."

"Bathing chambers with hot water and deep tubs?" she asked hopefully.

"Absolutely." He grinned at her. "Tubs big enough for two. If there is one thing I remember from my childhood, it's that managing an extravagant fortune is a lot of work. But since there's no help for it, we might as well at least have decadent bathtubs."

Laughing, she took his arm and they returned to the chaise. As they drove down into the valley and toward the Court, Gordon observed, "The coal seam fire has spread."

He gestured to where a thin plume of white smoke trickled from the ground. "There are several places smoking now. That one ahead is quite close to the house."

"How long has the fire been burning?" Callie asked. "It's been smoldering for as long as I can remember."

"Almost forty years, I think." He thought back to his childhood again. "Mining can be ugly, but I loved going

down into the coal tunnels and learning about the
steam engines that pumped the water out. Didn't I
take you down a time or two?"

"Once. I did not share your enjoyment of filthy, suf-
focating spaces."

"That's right. You couldn't wait to get out, so I never
invited you to come with me again. I was the mine
engineer's pet because I was so interested in his equip-
ment, and it served me well later." He smiled, remi-
niscing. "My experience in the mines got me the job as
captain of the Duke of Ashton's experimental steam
packet. By that time, I'd done quite a bit of sailing, and
I knew steam engines, so I was well qualified."

"So that's how you ended up driving the ship that
rescued Lady Kirkland," Callie said with interest. "How
did Ashton come to hire you?"

"That's a long story for another day since we've
reached our destination." He gazed out the window as
their chaise drove under the ancient stone arch into
the central courtyard. The tower loomed over one side
while the newer sections and outbuildings ran down
the hill to the left.

The carriage rattled to a stop and they descended
to the cobblestones. With Callie on his arm, Gordon
walked to the door of his ancestral home and rang the
great bell. The deep gong echoed like the voice of doom.
Though he didn't like the house any better than he
ever had, entering with Callie beside him was an improvement on the past.

The footman who admitted them was young and
dressed very traditionally in knee breeches and pow-
dered wig. Gordon hadn't had time to have cards
printed, so before the footman could ask who he was,
he said, "I am the new Lord Kingston. In the past I've

been known as Lord George Audley. Are my younger brothers in residence?"

The footman was young and he'd never met Gordon, but he wasn't stupid. He probably knew there was a long absent middle brother who would be the heir if he was alive. Eyes widening, the footman bowed deeply. "They are taking predinner sherry, my lord. I shall escort you to them."

Ugly house, ugly furnishings, drafty passageways. It was as bad as Gordon remembered, but at least he didn't have to worry about running into his father. *"Feel free to kill him. I have better sons."*

Callie must be remembering those words, too, because her hand was locked tight on his arm. She looked very beautiful and every inch an aristocrat. But even if she'd been wearing flour sacks, she would look like a marchioness. He didn't think he could have tolerated being here without her beside him.

The small salon where family and guests gathered for predinner drinks was at least warmed by a fire, albeit a smoky one. He'd not been old enough for the drinks ritual when he was last in this house.

But if he'd been the most worthless of the old lord's sons then, he made up for it now. The footman ushered them in, saying, "The Marquess of Kingston."

The words paralyzed the two young men chatting in the salon. That would be Eldon with the brown hair and the air of ironic detachment. He looked very much like an Audley. Francis, the youngest of the five sons, strongly resembled his mother, with fair hair, freckles, and a cheerful face. Neither of them looked at all like Gordon. As always, he was the odd man out.

Francis spoke first. "George, is that really you?" he asked, incredulous. "You've been presumed dead for almost fifteen years! But I remember that blond hair."

He came forward and offered his hand, looking genuinely pleased.

"I've been going by my middle name, Gordon, for years now." Gordon shook his brother's hand, glad someone seemed happy to see him. "I didn't die as reported and I sent occasional notes to the family lawyers to rub in the fact that I was still alive. I imagine our father kept the information to himself in the hope that eventually I would remedy my failure to die while being transported to Botany Bay."

Eldon rallied and also offered his hand. "You should have warned us, George! Or rather, Gordon. We could have killed the fatted calf for you. Instead, you'll have to settle for lamb collops tonight."

"The fatted calf can continue to graze in peace," Gordon said as he drew Callie forward. "Let me introduce you to my wife."

Before he could say Callie's name, Eldon exclaimed, "Catherine Brooke! Surely that's you all grown up. I've never known anyone else with that shade of red-gold hair."

"Indeed it is I, Eldon." She offered a smile and her hand. "I go by my middle name, Callista, these days, but you can call me Catherine if you prefer."

Eldon took her hand, his eyes gleaming with curiosity. "Maybe now we can learn what happened to you two! Gordon, you just vanished while Francis and I were away at school, and we learned later that Catherine was married off in a suspiciously swift way. Speculation was rampant."

Thinking his brothers deserved to know, Gordon said, "If you're asking whether I seduced Callie and got her with child, the answer is no."

"My father wanted me to marry a much older Jamaican planter and I hated the idea." Callie took up the story. "Since your brother and I were friends, he gallantly offered to marry me in Gretna Green to protect me from an unwanted husband. But our fathers found out almost immediately and caught up with us. So I married the planter and Gordon was convicted of various crimes and transported, which was horridly unfair."

"So that's the story, much less scandalous than it might have been," Gordon finished. He accepted a glass of sherry from Francis, who'd poured for the two newcomers. "What have you two been up to?"

"Let's discuss the last fifteen years of history over dinner," Eldon suggested. "The servants have had time to add two more place settings by now, and I'm sure our discussion will be a long one, so we might as well eat!"

They moved into the adjoining family dining room, which gave Gordon the chance to abandon his sherry, of which he was not overly fond, though he'd appreciated Francis's courtesy. He'd been a nice little boy, and now he seemed a nice young man.

Gordon was briefly disconcerted when he was automatically seated at the head of the table. How could he be head of a family when he'd never felt he was part of it in the first place? But that might be changing, which was a warming thought.

After the four of them took seats around one end of the long table, Gordon said bluntly, "Eldon, for the last fortnight or so, you've been thinking you're likely the next marquess. How do you feel about my unexpected reappearance?"

"The younger Mr. Roberts explained that there was reason to believe you were alive, so I wasn't totally surprised at your return." Eldon looked thoughtful. "I had mixed feelings about inheriting. As a fourth son, I never expected it, but yes, I was becoming accustomed to the idea of the title and wealth. Yet here you are." He smiled mischievously. "To make up for my blasted hopes, you can increase my allowance!"

They all laughed. Gordon was glad that his brother didn't seem resentful. "I will review the allowances," he promised. "Do you have any goals in mind? Have you busied yourself with any particular pursuits over the years?"

"I've mostly lived in London enjoying the life of a young English gentleman, but lately I've been thinking it's time for a change," Eldon said seriously. "I'm considering politics. The Kingston estate controls several parliamentary seats, and I'd like the next one that becomes available. It's time to establish myself as a man of substance."

Gordon was glad to hear that Eldon had goals beyond frivolity. "You've always had a quick mind and a quick tongue. I think you'd make a good MP."

Eldon nodded, looking pleased. Gordon turned his attention to his youngest brother, bemused to find himself acting so much like the head of the family. "Francis, how do you spend your time? Have you also been enjoying the life of a gentleman of leisure in London?"

"Not at all! After attending Cambridge, I've become the assistant estate manager," Francis said. "The current manager, Martin—you must remember him—is getting along in years. The plan is for me to replace him when he's ready to step down."

"Do you enjoy the work?" Callie asked with interest.

"I do!" Francis said enthusiastically. "There are so many new developments in both agriculture and mining. For example . . ."

Eldon cut his brother off with a drawled, "As interesting as breeding programs are, that's more detail than we need on a night when we're catching up with each other's news."

Francis smiled apologetically. "Sorry, I tend to be more of a farmer than the son of a marquess should be! But if you're interested, I'll be happy to talk your ears off later." His expression turned wary. "I have an understanding with a young lady who lives nearby. I hope you'll approve of our marriage."

Gordon's brows arched. "Why wouldn't I? You're the one who will be living with her, so the choice should be yours."

"Neither Father nor Welham approved." Francis looked defensive. "Julie's parents are yeoman farmers, not aristocrats, but they're generous, hardworking people. I've learned a great deal about practical farming from Mr. Frane."

From the tone of his brother's voice, Gordon guessed that the Franes had been a warmer and more welcoming family than the Audleys. Perhaps hearing the same thing, Callie said warmly, "I'd love to meet your Julie. We can call on her family, or perhaps she and her mother can join us here for tea soon."

Francis's eyes widened. "She . . . we would both like that very much!"

As the first course of the meal was removed and the second course served, Gordon sipped at his wine and commented, "When we drove into the valley, I saw that the coal seam fires have expanded. The smell of them is all through the house."

"It's not always this bad," Francis said apologetically. "Only when the wind is from the west."

Which it usually was if Gordon remembered correctly. "Are the fires undermining the house? Maybe it's time to abandon Kingston Court for a healthier site."

Francis looked appalled. "But the history, Gordon! The oldest section is over six hundred years old!"

"And every day of that is felt in the lack of comforts," Gordon said dryly. "I'll let you have the master's rooms, which I recall as cold and drafty."

"But very grand." Eldon chuckled. "I think you're stuck there since the servants are surely preparing those rooms now for the new lord and lady."

Callie asked, "Are any reasonable houses on the estate currently vacant? Preferably ones that aren't six hundred years old."

Francis thought a moment. "The dower house is empty. It's basically sound, though it would take a day or two to prepare it for occupancy."

"As long as badgers haven't taken up residence in the drawing room, that should do nicely," Gordon said. "Callie, what do you think?"

"I remember the dower house as a fine, well placed residence. It will be perfect." She smiled. "We'll appreciate it all the more if we must spend several nights in the Gothic tower."

That occasioned more laughter. The meal turned out to be surprisingly enjoyable. Maybe being Lord Kingston wouldn't be so bad.

Gordon's opinion changed when he and Callie bade his brothers good night and they retired to the tower. Callie studied the vast bedchamber with dismay. "If Welham lived in here, I don't blame him if he committed suicide!"

"You don't like priceless tapestries showing saints dying in various horrible ways and animals being torn to pieces by hounds and huntsman?" Gordon asked dryly.

"No, I do *not*!" She began pacing around the room, frowning at the tapestries and the heavy carved wardrobe that matched the bed. The massive four-poster was fit for royalty, with carved mahogany pillars at the corners to support the velvet canopy. The brocade coverlet was turned down, revealing fine sheets and extravagant pillows. He thought of his father in that bed, rutting with wives and maids and mistresses and conceiving multiple sons, and his stomach knotted. "I cannot sleep in that bed."

Callie's gaze moved swiftly to his face. Understanding, she said lightly, "I'd rather not sleep there, either. Beds are too personal to make good family heirlooms. Let's find an alternative."

She opened a door on the left. "This dressing room is much better. We can make up a pallet on the very handsome carpet. I'll rumple the blankets on the bed so in the morning the servants won't realize we didn't appreciate their efforts."

Gordon joined her and drew her against his side with one arm. "You don't mind sleeping on the floor in here?"

"It will be more comfortable than a warehouse floor surrounded by tobacco barrels, and we found that quite pleasing." She leaned into him like a cat. "We can manage here for a couple of nights until we move into the dower house."

"Thank you for understanding," he said quietly.

"The fact that your younger brothers are amiable doesn't take away years of misery," she said softly. "Now, let's make up that pallet and get some rest."

She was right. The pallet was comfortable, and Callie's sweet welcome made all the dark clouds of Kingston Court melt away.

Chapter 40

Callie smothered a yawn as they entered the master bedroom for their second night. "I look forward to moving into the dower house tomorrow, but before we abandon the tower, I want to see the secret stairway. Last night we were too tired to bother."

"Since I never want to set foot in this room again, tonight is the time," Richard replied. "It's hidden behind the mahogany wardrobe. I came up from the cellar level to see where the stairs went. When I opened the door at the top, I was horrified to find myself in my father's bedchamber."

"That hasn't changed," she said wryly.

"Let's see if I can remember how it opens from this side." He studied the wardrobe, then ran his fingers behind one of the mahogany columns that matched the bedposts. When that didn't work, he twisted the whole column. Moving smoothly but with a Gothic groan, the wardrobe pivoted from the wall like a great door.

Callie carried a lamp to the opening, her nose wrinkling at the dank smell. The stone steps were narrow and descended in sharp turns. "I'd get dizzy going up or down that, and the ceiling is so low I'd probably have to duck. You certainly would have to."

"We can go down if you like," Richard said obligingly.

"No, it's less romantic than I thought." She shoved the wardrobe back into place. "After that, I want to get some fresh air and admire the view from the balcony."

"That's a better choice," he agreed as he pulled back the draperies that covered the double doors to the balcony, which were cut through the six-foot-thick stone walls.

Callie opened the door and stepped out onto the wide wooden platform. A brisk wind was blowing and clouds scudded over the moon, creating dramatic contrasts of light and shadow. She drew in a deep, exhilarated breath. "A storm is coming. I love storms as long as I'm inside and safe."

She peered over the railing. "Goodness, this is built right over the cliff that drops to the lake, and it's a very long way down. Was the castle ever attacked?"

"Not that I've heard, but if someone did try to capture it, it wouldn't have been from the lake side." Richard joined her at the railing and looked down at the lethal drop.

The night was cold so he brought a blanket out. He moved behind Callie and wrapped it around them both so that her back was tucked against his chest. "Now, this is romantic," she murmured.

"Much better than creeping down a stone staircase," he agreed. "It's been a good day, hasn't it? Particularly the visit to Rush Hall and your family."

"It was lovely to see my little brother Marcus all grown

up," she said. "He's become a fine young lord. Not at all like my father."

"He'll be a good neighbor to us," Richard said thoughtfully. "Your littlest sister, Annie, is delightful, and your sister Jane was a pleasant surprise."

"That was the real shock," Callie said with a grin. "She seems to have done a good job of running Marcus's household these last few years. As she said, marrying the local vicar will give her plenty of opportunities to boss people around as well as keeping an eye on Rush Hall to ensure that it continues to run smoothly."

"And she laughed when she said it! A sense of humor is not something I ever associated with Jane."

"She's improved with the years." Callie chuckled. "She'd probably say the same of me. I like that I can be friends with my sisters and brother. For so long, I didn't believe I'd ever see them again."

"Yet here we are." Richard tightened his embrace, rocking her a little. "That location you chose is perfect for building a better version of Kingston Court. Since the dell faces south, the new house will be warm and bright all year round and the hills will protect us from the winds."

"It will be a happy house," Callie said with a flash of intuition that felt very true. "We'll have three children, and they'll all be hellions like we were!"

He chuckled. "But we'll be much better at handling them than our parents were with us."

That also felt like truth. "I'm thinking about the floor plan for the new house, but I have some ideas for the dower house, too. We'll probably be living there for a couple of years and it can use some improvements."

"Whatever you like, Catkin. I'm just glad that we'll be able to move in tomorrow. I'd settle for a dovecote in order to get away from Kingston Court."

She slanted a glance. "The floor of the dressing room wasn't that bad, was it?"

"Entirely acceptable for a night or two, but winter is coming. I want a warm bed with a warm wife." He grinned. "Fortunately, I've already got the warm wife."

"All I need is the warm husband," she said provocatively. "Having a real bed is optional."

"You realize that if you keep rubbing your delectable backside against me, we won't be getting any sleep for a while?"

"My wicked plan has succeeded!" Laughing, she turned in his arms and raised her face for a kiss. His hair was silvery pale in the moonlight and he was so handsome she could barely breathe. But it was the tenderness in his eyes that melted her heart. "My Lionheart . . ." she whispered.

The world shattered into flame, pain, and darkness.

The explosion in the bedroom behind them threw Gordon and Callie hard against the balcony railing. They teetered precariously on the verge of pitching over into the lake. Instinctively he locked her in his arms and wrenched them to the left. His head banged hard into the railing before he came down on top of her as burning debris blasted through the open door.

Dazed, he rolled away from Callie after the rain of shattered wood and stone ended. She lay limp and bleeding in the angle between the balcony floor and railings. Terrified, he checked her throat for a pulse and found one. Her breathing was regular, but she was unconscious and blood trickled down her temple.

When he scrambled to his feet, the balcony lurched underneath him and he realized that it was about to tear loose from the tower and plunge down the cliff.

He had to get them off before that happened, but where could they go? The grandest bedchamber in Lancashire had become a flaming holocaust. Though the walls were stone, the floor and furnishings were wood and fabric and they were being consumed by hungry flames. The bed and its hangings were ablaze, and as he watched, the left front corner of the heavy bed sank into the floor as the floorboards beneath burned away.

Towering flames completely blocked the entrance to the room, and the drop below the balcony onto the stony cliff would surely kill them both. *The stairway within the walls.* Stone was much more resistant to burning and the old stairs were within reach.

Grimly aware of the acrid scent of gunpowder, he turned back to Callie. She was still unconscious so he savagely ripped the blanket that had been protecting them from the cold in half. Hands shaking, he fashioned a sling large enough to hold her limp body and arranged her across his chest.

He had to enter the bedroom to reach the staircase, and the heat was vicious. Behind him, he heard the balcony tearing away and crashing noisily down the cliff until it splashed into the lake. He protected Callie's face with one arm while he dashed the half dozen steps to the wardrobe.

Gasping from the lack of air, he wrenched the column that controlled the wardrobe and swung the heavy piece of furniture toward him. He had to duck his head when he stepped onto the small landing at the top of the stairwell. The stale air smelled damp and unwholesome, but it was blessedly cool.

He dragged the wardrobe back into place behind him. He was immediately in Stygian darkness, but it felt safer to have something between them and the fire.

He banged his head and swore when he took the

first step down, so he forced himself to stop and take a deep, slow breath. He must focus on descending this cramped, slimy set of stairs while keeping his head low to avoid bashing his wits away. It was frightening to move at what felt like a snail's pace, but to go faster would only court disaster.

The narrow staircase turned to the left, so he used his left arm to keep Callie close and skimmed his right hand along the rough, damp stone wall. He estimated they were perhaps halfway down when Callie stirred in his arms.

"Richard?" She pressed a hand flat against his chest. "What happened?"

"The bedroom exploded," he said tersely. "If we'd been inside, we'd be ashes by now. You were knocked unconscious. Do you have other injuries?"

There was a pause while she took inventory. "My head is aching, my wits are scrambled, I have rather a lot of bruises, and my left ankle hurts. But nothing significant, I think." She drew a ragged breath. "Did the coal seam fire cause the explosion?"

"No, but that might have been how it was intended to look." He paused to rest and draw breath. "I smelled gunpowder. Someone was trying to kill us."

Callie gasped. "Who? One of your brothers? They have the most to gain."

"That would be my best guess." The knowledge was sour. He'd thought he finally had some real family, and now one or both of them were trying to kill him.

He'd worry about that when they were safely outside. He began descending again. Callie said, "I think I can walk on my own," but she didn't sound very sure.

"You can try when we get to level ground." He repressed an oath when he accidentally lifted his head too high and banged it again. Carrying a not insubstantial weight while bending over was damnably tiring. But not too much farther now.

Finally he reached the dirt floor of the cellar, stumbling when there was no longer a step below him. The cellar was far too hot and smoke was swirling around them. Above they could hear the roar of flames and the sound of burned timbers collapsing.

When Callie wriggled out of the sling, she wavered beside him so he offered his arm for support. "How do we get out of here?"

"This part of the cellar is above ground level because of the way the hill slants. If we follow the wall around to the right, we'll come to a doorway that opens onto the hill. We need to get outside before all the floors above us collapse."

He could hear Callie swallow. "Then let's get moving. I can walk if I hold onto your arm. Is there anything else I can do?"

"Hold your free hand out so we won't walk into anything disastrous. Watch your footing, the floor is slippery." He found the wall with his right hand and began moving along it, Callie in tow. From her tight breathing, he knew that she was hurting, but this was faster than carrying her and time was running out.

Behind them a section of flooring collapsed in flames. It was terrifyingly close, but did give them enough light for Gordon to see the door. "There, just ahead!"

He slid his left arm around her waist and half carried her the last dozen feet. He was panting with exhaustion by the time he reached the door. A massive wooden bar held it closed. With the strength of desperation, he wrenched it away. The door moved with great difficulty, but when he applied his full strength, it screeched open.

As soon as the way was clear, he caught Callie's waist and pulled her through beside him. "We have to get away from the building as fast as we can!"

Even though Callie was limping badly, she moved with surprising speed. The fresh air on the hillside was a huge relief. He kept them moving away from the tower. Any moment now, any moment . . .

The interior floors collapsed behind them with a deafening roar, throwing blazing wreckage in all directions. At the first crash, Gordon pulled Callie down and covered her with his body, panting in great gulps as his lungs fought for breath.

Burning brands were falling around them, but the ground was cold and damp and nothing caught fire. Wearily he pushed himself to a sitting position. Callie sat up also and he pulled her close. In the distance, he heard shouts as people fought the fire.

As they gazed at the fountain of flames erupting from the tower, Callie said wryly, "You're going to have to buy me a new wardrobe now. You'll need one, too."

He laughed a little, giddy with relief that they'd survived. "At least those horrible tapestries are gone."

"They're no loss, but I'm glad I'm wearing my topaz earrings." She winced as another burst of flame spouted skyward. "This end of Kingston Court is definitely gone."

Gordon shrugged. "As long as everyone got out safely, I don't care. May it burn and be damned!"

"You didn't deserve Kingston Court!" a voice snarled from nearby. "It's your fault it's burning, and you must have made a deal with the devil to have survived!"

He turned and saw his brother Eldon holding a pistol aimed directly at his heart.

Chapter 41

❦

Gordon had known one of his brothers must have caused the explosion, but confirmation made him want to vomit. Forcing his voice to steadiness, he said, "I'm not the one who set that explosion, Eldon."

He whispered to Callie, "Stay down and look limp and helpless, Catkin."

"Not difficult!" she murmured with black humor.

Gordon stood slowly so as not to startle his brother into shooting. "Were you hoping that explosion would seem to be a result of burning coal seams? Surely someone besides me must have noticed the smell of gunpowder."

"No one would have cared," Eldon said with lethal coolness. He looked shockingly like their father. A crack of thunder added to the threatening Gothic atmosphere. "No one cared when I shot Welham and made it look like a suicide."

Not suicide, not an accident, but murder. Given the events of this night, that all made sense now. Matching

Eldon in coolness, Gordon said, "Well done! He was a nasty piece of work." He put a note of admiration in his voice as he tried to buy time. The three of them were in a pocket of isolation here, but there were other people not far away.

Eldon was close enough that he didn't need to be a good shot, unfortunately. Callie looked suitably dazed and helpless, but Gordon noticed that her left hand was exploring the damp earth as she stealthily felt around for a possible weapon.

Hoping she found something, Gordon edged away from her to keep Eldon's attention on him. "Did you arrange Julius's death as well? If he was riding drunk, it wouldn't have been difficult to cause a fatal accident."

"He killed himself without any help from me." Eldon smiled. "That's what gave me the idea. With Julius gone, only Welham stood between me and the Kingston inheritance. And he was so easy to kill. No one liked him. No one cared. Everyone assumed I was the new Lord Kingston. Then *you* showed up!"

"I'm sorry to have disrupted your plans," Gordon said apologetically. "I don't even want the title. If I'd known how much it meant to you, I could have stayed in some distant country. I could have even supplied proof of death for you. But since I returned to London to live a couple of years ago, too many people have learned about my continued existence."

"Yes, you should have stayed away," Eldon said in icy agreement. "I really don't want to kill you and Catherine, but you've left me no choice."

Playing on that reluctance, Gordon said, "No? It's not too late for me to return to America and seem to be dead. I can't mourn your sending Welham off this mortal coil prematurely, and I've always hated Kingston Court, so I don't mind your burning it down as long as no one has been killed in the fire. Or do you enjoy killing?"

"No, dammit, I don't!" Eldon flinched as thunder roared again, and the barrel of his pistol shook. He might want people dead, but he didn't like killing them himself. Vile little coward.

"Do you accept my proposal?" Gordon asked. "Callie and I can quietly disappear tonight and it will be assumed we died in the fire. You become Lord Kingston and you can build a new and better house."

Eldon looked tempted, but after a long moment, he shook his head. "I can't trust you to stay dead unless I make sure of it myself. Sorry, Gordon." He took a step closer. "You're more amusing than my other brothers, but you should have stayed away."

He cocked the pistol and prepared to fire at point blank range. Gordon dove to his left and at the same instant, Callie rose on her knees and hurled a stone that smashed into the middle of Eldon's face. "Take that, you vicious little swine!" she spat out furiously.

Swearing, Eldon fell back, clawing at his nose. "*What the devil?*"

Gordon leaped forward and tackled his brother. The pistol went flying as the two men grappled. Eldon fought frantically but with little skill. He'd never battled for his life in deadly distant lands.

As they rolled across the ground, Gordon locked his hands around his brother's neck. Lord Eldon Audley, who had killed one brother and done his damnedest to murder Gordon and Callie.

The thought of Callie in danger ignited Gordon's rage. He caught his brother's gaze, watching as anger turned first to fear, then to terror.

He waited as terror built. Then in one lethal movement, Gordon broke his brother's neck.

One learned many useful things at the Westerfield Academy.

Sudden silence except for the sounds of the fire, distant firefighters, and approaching thunder. Callie crawled over the rough ground and snatched up the fallen pistol. "He's dead?"

"Yes." Gordon pushed himself up and stared at the lifeless body of his brother. Unlike Eldon, Gordon was experienced at killing. But he did it only when necessary, and he'd never killed a brother before. He wished to God it hadn't been necessary.

Callie bridged the short distance between them and took his hand, raising it to her cheek. "I'm sorry, Richard," she said softly.

"So am I." He squeezed her hand, grateful for her touch. "My thanks for your very fine stone throwing. You always did have a good arm."

"Dear God!" The new voice came from Francis, who was racing toward them. The light from the fire illuminated them clearly, but he seemed unable to grasp the scene before him. "I saw Eldon heading in this direction and wondered if you might have escaped the tower this way. But Eldon is dead?"

"Yes," Gordon said flatly. "I killed him."

"How could you?" Francis looked like a horrified child, not a capable young man. "*Why?*"

"Because Eldon set the explosion that blew up the tower!" Callie snapped. "Unfortunately for him, he failed to kill us. Were you in on his murderous plans?"

Francis shook his head as he struggled to grasp what he was hearing. "Eldon had no murderous plans! Why would he want to kill you?"

"Isn't it obvious?" Gordon said, feeling numb. "He killed Welham, too. He expected to inherit the title until I had the bad manners to show up alive."

Francis fell silent for long moments, his face strained. "I didn't think Welham would kill himself," he said haltingly. "I thought his death must be a drunken accident, but it did seem odd. What makes you think Eldon killed him?"

"Because he proudly admitted it!" Callie rose unsteadily to her feet, her eyes flashing. "Richard is the only decent brother you had! Welham and Julius were brutes and Eldon was a murderer. They all took after your abominable father."

"You shouldn't say such things!" Francis said, appalled. "Father was stern with us, but he was a good and honorable man."

"That 'good and honorable man' gave my father permission to beat Richard to death when we were caught in our attempt to elope!" Callie said fiercely. "Richard was already half dead when your father told mine, *Feel free to kill him. I have better sons.*'"

"No," Francis said, his face paling. "No, he couldn't have been that cruel!"

"No? I was *there*, Francis!" she spat out. "To save your brother's life, I swore to my father that I'd marry his planter. So instead of killing Richard outright, my father trumped up false criminal charges and got him condemned to transportation. Our fathers were *vile* men, both of them. And if you want to punish Richard for what he's endured, I swear before God that I'll kill you myself!" She raised the pistol.

"Callie, don't." Gordon lurched to his feet and took the weapon from her. "Killing brothers is a bad habit to cultivate."

She let him have the pistol without protest. She was shaking from shock and pain. "Are you sure Francis wasn't in on the plot to kill you?"

Gordon studied his youngest brother. In the flickering firelight, his face was so pale the freckles showed. "I'm sure. He is like his mother as I am like mine. The fatal flaw in Audley men is to be like our late and unlamented father."

"You . . . may be right," Francis whispered. "Eldon was clever and could be very amusing, and he seldom sharpened his tongue on me. But he had a cold, ruthless streak. I just didn't know . . . how ruthless. Did he cause Julius's death, too?"

"He said he didn't, but that accidental death gave him the idea of clearing the way to the title for himself," Gordon said dryly. "So annoying to rid himself of Welham and then have me get in the way."

"I never knew how much he wanted to inherit. But he used to mock me for my simple rural ambitions." Francis swallowed hard. "Perhaps I should have guessed from that."

"Are you going to turn me over to a magistrate because I killed Eldon? As a peer of the realm, I would be tried in the House of Lords and would surely be acquitted." Gordon sighed, exhausted at the thought. "But it would be a long, drawn out affair."

"You've convinced me that justice was done tonight." Francis stared at Eldon, then took a deep breath. "I suggest that we throw his body into the fire. It will be assumed that was how he died."

Gordon gazed at the devastated tower. The flames were dying down, but they would suffice. "That would certainly simplify matters."

"I have a request," Francis said uncertainly. "Will you not make it public that Eldon killed Welham and tried to kill you? He doesn't deserve to have his reputation preserved, but I'd rather avoid a horrible scandal."

Young Francis was showing himself to be pragmatic and able to deal with harsh reality, traits he shared with

Gordon. "If you want to put it about that he died hero-
ically trying to rescue me and Callie, I won't argue the
point. He's gone. We're alive."

Gordon turned to Callie, who had slumped to the
ground again. "Will you be all right for a few minutes
while we do what's necessary?"

"Yes," she said in a raw whisper. "And then, please,
let's go to the dower house. I don't care if they haven't
finished cleaning it properly."

"Neither do I." She was obviously at the end of her
tether, with drying blood in her hair and pain in her
face. He touched her cheek. "Yes, Catkin. The dower
house."

He and Francis each took one of Eldon's arms and
dragged him back to the burning tower. The flames
were diminishing now that most of the flammable interior had been burned through, but the blackened
stone walls remained.

"We need to toss him through the door into the cellar," Gordon said.

Francis gave a grim-faced nod and between them,
they swung the limp, heavy body into the fire. It swiftly
vanished in the flames. Francis said heavily, "I wish that
he'd been a better man."

"So do I," Gordon said bitterly. "I was looking forward to having a brother who could be a friend as Welham and Julius never had been."

After a long silence, Francis said, "You still have one
brother left."

Danger and loss forged unexpected bonds, and
Gordon realized that he and Francis had similarities
that he'd never shared with his other brothers. "I do,
and I hope we can be friends in the future." He offered
a hesitant hand.

Francis took it in a hard clasp and they met each

other's gazes. Yes, in the future they could become true brothers.

Releasing the clasp, Gordon asked, "Are there any other casualties of the fire?"

"No, everyone else was in the lower house. You and Callista were the only ones thought to be dead." As Francis spoke, the threatening rain finally burst from the sky in a downpour. Francis smiled wryly. "That should help put out the fire. I think the lower house is largely undamaged."

Gordon shrugged, not caring. What mattered was Callie. He splashed through the rain and gently lifted her in his arms. "Francis, can you arrange a carriage to the dower house for us?"

"Of course."

As Francis headed off at a fast jog, Callie protested weakly, "You don't have to carry me. You've done enough of that tonight."

"Never." He kissed her forehead. "I'd carry you to the ends of the earth, Catkin."

Releasing her breath in a tired sigh, she burrowed into his arms. "About now, that sounds very good." The rain was washing soot from her face, leaving it pale but peaceful.

In the distance, Francis's voice could be heard calling, "Lord and Lady Kingston are safe! They escaped the tower! They're safe!"

There were shouts and people began running toward Gordon. He tensed, but the faces and voices were relieved and glad.

"Lord Kingston, thank God!" The words came from Martin, the estate steward whom Gordon had met with that afternoon.

Similar sentiments came from the housekeeper, the butler, the tenants of the nearest farms. The chief groom said, "You look right knackered, Lord Kingston. I can take your lady wife."

He reached for Callie, but Gordon shook his head and said firmly, "No. *Mine!*"

That produced relieved laughter. Callie rallied enough for a warm smile at their well wishers. "Thank you all. Really, I'm all right except for my ankle."

A gruff voice asked, "How did you survive, sir?"

"We were on the balcony when the tower exploded," Gordon said succinctly. "It was a damned near thing, but I remembered an ancient staircase inside the stone wall and we got out just before the inside of the tower collapsed."

A covered cart driven by Francis approached. When it stopped, Gordon set Callie inside, then climbed in after her. She was more unconscious than not. He pulled his battered coat off and held it over her to block the rain.

As Francis drove them toward the dower house, Gordon saw that the fire had been largely confined to the old tower and the rain was now extinguishing the remaining flames. The lower section of Kingston Court would need some rebuilding at the upper end, but it was fairly undamaged. Fine. Francis could have it.

He had Callie. He needed no more.

Chapter 42

Callie slept the sleep of exhaustion, not waking until dawn. It took her a moment to recognize that she was in the quietly elegant master bedroom of the dower house and Richard was sleeping beside her. The storm had blown over, leaving a sky that was clear and pale blue.

The previous night seemed like a mad dream, but she had vague memories of having her head and ankle bandaged, then being undressed by Richard and put in a dry shift. She'd have to borrow clothing. It occurred to her that she should start a dressmaking business using local women who needed work. She'd design, they'd sew, and ready-made garments could be sold at modest prices in the local markets. Perhaps a shop later. Yes, such a business would be good for all concerned.

With that settled in her mind, Callie wiggled her foot cautiously. Her ankle hurt, but not as much as a broken bone would. Good, just a bad sprain.

Her memories after she'd banged her head during

the explosion were clouded, but she remembered what had happened. She shuddered as she recalled how they'd almost died twice over.

But, by God, they had survived! Richard lay with his arm over her waist. There was soot in his blond hair and he needed a shave, but he looked undamaged, so there was no good reason for her to roll over and grab him as if she was drowning and he was her lifeline.

He woke up immediately and his arm tightened around her. "You're shaking, Catkin. Delayed reaction from last night?"

She nodded and hid her face against his chest. He knew her so well. "I can't help thinking dower houses are built for the widows of dead lords." She took a gulp of air. "And I'm so glad that I'm not your widow!"

He gently stroked her hair, which was an appallingly tangled mess. "Is it any comfort that Eldon intended to kill both of us so you wouldn't have had to survive into widowhood again?"

The thought was so absurd that she had to laugh. "Not much comfort, no. But I like this house and I'm glad we're here." Her amusement faded as she wondered how to ask the vital question. "Are you going to be haunted by what you had to do last night?"

He sighed and rolled onto his back. "I wish I hadn't had to kill my brother. But in my years as a cowardly adventurer, I learned to kill when necessary and without regrets. Eldon needed killing."

"That he did." Though Callie wished she'd been the one to do the killing to spare Richard from it. Her mouth twisted. "We talked about returning to the peace and safety of England, but I had a nagging suspicion that it wouldn't be that simple. I wish I hadn't been right. Do you think our murderous adventures are over now?"

"My intuition isn't as good as yours, but I think so. Francis was genuinely horrified by Eldon's actions and isn't going to try to murder us. You won his heart by wanting to meet his Julie." Richard hesitated, then continued almost shyly, "I saw last night that the people of the Kingston estate seem to welcome the fact that I'm now Lord Kingston and that lovely Catherine Brooke is my lady. I'm not surprised that you're remembered fondly, but I am rather surprised that I am, too."

"You shouldn't be. Your two older brothers were arrogant bullies. You actually traveled about the estate and talked to people, and listened as if they mattered. They haven't forgotten." She chuckled. "Am I imagining it, or when you were carrying me to the carriage did an older woman say that she'd always known we should get married?"

"You're not imagining it." There was a smile in Richard's voice. "It was Mrs. Moore, who runs the shop in the village. She liked wayward children like us."

"Mrs. Moore, of course! I loved her ginger biscuits. I'll call on her soon." Callie was lying on her side so she rested her hand on his chest, feeling the beat of his heart and the soft texture of dark gold hair. He was beautiful and kind and *hers*. She could not imagine anywhere in the world she would rather be.

"Callie?"

His voice had changed. She lifted her head, wincing a little as the previous night's injury made itself known. Ignoring the twinge, she said, "Yes, my Lionheart?"

He met her gaze, his gray eyes deadly serious. "When I thought we were going to die last night, I belatedly realized how much I love you. Not just as a best friend and companion in mischief, but in every way a man can love a woman."

He bent his head and brushed her lips with a kiss of exquisite tenderness. "During all of those years of traveling and surviving, I believed I was no longer capable of feeling deeply about anyone. Now I realize that I couldn't give my heart because it already belonged to you. You were my sanity and my salvation."

"As you were mine." She felt a sting of tears forming in her eyes and blinked them back. "After my father wrote that you were dead, I realized you were the love of my life. I couldn't stop living, and I've loved other people in different ways over the years. But I could never love anyone the way I love you."

He lifted her hand, interlacing their fingers. "I've never said this to anyone else, and I never will," he said with no trace of his habitual humor. "I love you, my dearest girl, now and forever, amen. You bring me peace."

"And you bring me joy," she whispered. "We've always loved each other, but saying the words makes a difference, doesn't it?"

"It does." He gave her a slow, wicked smile. "I believe you said something about our having three children. Since we are both here more or less naked in a very fine bed, isn't it about time we got to work on that?"

She laughed joyously. "Indeed it is. I'm ready. Are you?"

He was. He absolutely *was*!

Historical Notes

In the study of American history, the War of 1812 is usually more of a footnote than a major event. Thirty years after the Revolution, the young United States fought Britain again, the results were pretty much a stalemate, and the only noteworthy event was the bombardment of Fort McHenry, which inspired Francis Scott Key's "The Star-Spangled Banner." I'm not sure that the average Briton has any awareness of the war at all. But in the US and Canada, the war mattered.

In my hometown of Baltimore, the war is very, very personal. When I first moved here, I was surprised to find a Maryland State holiday called Defenders Day, on September 12. Say what?

It turned out that September 12 was the land part of the Battle of Baltimore, when the militia stopped the advance of British troops at the Battle of North Point, allowing time for the Americans to prepare for the naval part of the battle, which was the defense of the city at Fort McHenry.

The reasons for the war are murky. On the American side, there was a feeling that Britain was dissing our new little republic. The British blockade of the Continent was interfering with our trade with France, and the Royal Navy was impressing sailors from American ships to serve on British vessels. If we fought, we could teach them respect and maybe collect Canada and add it to the United States.

I suspect that in Britain, the fighting was seen as a bloomin' nuisance—just get those colonials out of the way, please, so Britain could take care of Napoleon. I do know that the issue of impressing American sailors to serve on British ships was taught in my school as a huge infringement of our sovereign rights, but it looked very different after I read *Life in Nelson's Navy*, by Dudley Pope. It was a lesson in different points of view.

A good part of the war was fought grimly along the Niagara Frontier between Canada and the United States. The war in the Chesapeake Bay was right on my doorstep and it's well documented. In my research, I was able to find weather conditions, troop movements, the blowing up of bridges and ammunition dumps, not to mention ministers' benedictions and idiotic mistakes to weave into my own story.

With Napoleon defeated and exiled to Elba in 1814, battle-seasoned British troops were freed up to sail to North America and administer the spanking those Americans so richly deserved. When the British walked into Washington with no opposition after some American troops had disgraced themselves at the Battle of Bladensburg, they primarily burned government buildings, but one house was used by snipers and burned down, an incident I was able to borrow for my own characters.

The easy occupation of America's capital was a national humiliation and could have had dire effects on the peace negotiations that were being held in Ghent. After that victory, the Royal Navy, the most powerful in the world, sailed up the Chesapeake Bay, determined to destroy Baltimore. The city was one of the largest and richest in America, and had quite justly earned the label "a nest of pirates," though Americans preferred the term "privateers."

The British troops were led by Major General Robert Ross, a distinguished veteran of the Peninsular War. With the might of the empire bearing down on the city, the local citizens, white and black, rich and poor, dug in grimly, because that's what you do when enemies threaten your home. The territorial instinct is powerful. Earthworks were dug, twenty-two merchant ships were sunk in the mouth of the harbor to prevent the British from entering, and both regular troops and militia took positions and prepared for whatever might come.

The British land invasion retreated after General Ross was shot, the Royal Navy began bombarding Fort McHenry, and the rest of the story is well known. The United States regained its pride by standing firm against the might of the British Empire and the peace negotiations in Europe were concluded with no changes of territory.

It could be called a stalemate, but that doesn't mean the war had no lasting effects. Both the United States and Canada developed much stronger senses of their national identity, to the extent that the War of 1812 is sometimes called the "second American Revolution." Having declined to join America, Canada has been a steadfast, invaluable member of the British Empire ever since, and a very good neighbor to the United States.

If you'd like to learn more about the war in the Chesapeake, the classic history is Walter Lord's excellent *The Dawn's Early Light: The Climactic Shaping of "the*

Land of the Free" During the Hazardous Events of 1814 in Washington, Baltimore, and London. Another fine book is Steve Vogel's *Through the Perilous Fight: From the Burning of Washington to the Star-Spangled Banner: The Six Weeks That Saved the Nation.*

One last note: coal seam fires are real and can burn for decades or even centuries. The fire in Centralia, Pennsylvania, has been burning since the 1960s and caused the entire town to be evacuated.

Please read on for an excerpt from
Mary Jo Putney's next Rogues Redeemed novel,
Once a Pirate.

London, Autumn, 1814

Lord and Lady Lawrence were enjoying a pleasant afternoon in the library when the letter arrived. The butler himself delivered it to the earl. Sylvia Lawrence glanced up and saw that the missive was wrapped in stained oilcloth and must have traveled a long way. "Is that a letter from Rory?" she asked eagerly. "We haven't heard from her in such a long time! Is she coming home?"

Her husband unwrapped the letter and read it with a deepening frown. Then he swore with the vibrant profanity that only one person ever invoked. "Your daughter, Lady Aurora Octavia Lawrence, has gone and done it this time!"

"She's your daughter, too," Sylvia pointed out as she began to worry. "What's wrong?"

The earl snarled, "The letter is from the British consul in Algiers. Your damned daughter was captured by

Barbary pirates and they're demanding an outrageous ransom to return her!"

Sylvia gasped as levity was replaced by horror. "How is that possible? I thought the Barbary pirates had given up their thieving ways after the Americans blasted their cities to pieces."

"The pirates of Barbary are not great believers in treaties," her husband said bitterly. "The consul says she's unhurt, but she's locked in a harem and will be sold into slavery unless she's ransomed." His voice rose. "Twenty thousand pounds! *Twenty thousand pounds!*"

He slapped the letter onto the desk, sending a fine goose quill pen flying. "Well, they can damned well keep her! I'm not paying a ha'penny to get the girl back."

"Geoffrey, you can't possibly mean that!" Sylvia gasped. "Our youngest daughter! Rory was the delight of your life."

"Until she grew up—she's been nothing but trouble ever since." He scowled at Sylvia. "She won't make a proper marriage and she's spent most of the money intended for her portion on her travels. She's a clever minx. Let her get out of this scrape on her own. I can't afford her anymore."

"She's our *daughter*!"

"You think I don't know that?" His initial rage was cooling to even more dangerous icy anger, but there was pain in his eyes. "We may be aristocrats, but we don't have unlimited funds, Sylvia. I'm still paying off debts left over from my father's time. And you had to have eight children, all of whom have had to be established."

"You had something to do with that!" she snapped. "We've been blessed with eight healthy, charming, intelligent offspring. Which of them would you give up?"

His eyes narrowed. "None. But should we rob their futures to pay for the foolish behavior of the youngest?"

Sylvia bit her lip because that was a hard argument to counter. "But slavery in Barbary, Geoffrey! That's not a scrape, it's disaster! Just think of the atrocities she might suffer."

His expression was unyielding. "She's pretty enough to avoid the worst atrocities. She'll probably end up as chief wife of the Dey of Algiers. That's my last word, Sylvia. Rory has made her bed, and now she must lie in it with whatever man is willing to pay her price."

The countess cringed at the words. Geoffrey was generally quite reasonable—for a man—but when he made up his mind, he was unyielding. He wouldn't lift a finger to help Rory.

But the same was not true of Rory's mother. She closed her eyes, shuddering as images of her youngest filled her mind. She loved all her children deeply, but Rory had been such a golden, happy baby. That was why Sylvia had insisted on the name Aurora, for the dawn.

Aurora had quickly become Rory as her daughter grew into laughter and mischief. Yes, she sometimes got into trouble, but that was because of her appetite for life. There was no malice in her.

Geoffrey might leave her to rot in Barbary, but that didn't mean Sylvia would do the same. She'd heard of a man who was good at dealing with difficult situations. An aristocrat with connections to people in all walks of life. She'd call on him in the morning. Perhaps—pray God!—he knew someone who could bring her daughter home.

Connect with Us

Visit us online at
KensingtonBooks.com
to read more from your favorite authors, see books
by series, view reading group guides, and more.

Join us on social media

for sneak peeks, chances to win books and prize packs,
and to share your thoughts with other readers.

facebook.com/kensingtonpublishing
twitter.com/kensingtonbooks

Tell us what you think!

To share your thoughts, submit a review,
or sign up for our eNewsletters, please visit:
KensingtonBooks.com/TellUs.